The Gas Man Cometh

By

John Avanzato

KCM PUBLISHING

A DIVISION OF KCM DIGITAL MEDIA, LLC

CREDITS

Published by KCM Publishing
A Division of KCM Digital Media, LLC

The Gas Man Cometh by John Avanzato

ISBN-13: 978-1-939961-55-6
ISBN-10: 1-939961-55-6

First Edition
Publisher: Michael Fabiano
KCM Publishing

Books in the John Cesari series by

John Avanzato

Hostile Hospital

Prescription for Disaster

Temperature Rising

Claim Denied

Dedication

To my wife, Cheryl, the love of my life and the apple of my eye. We met almost accidentally at a dinner party three decades past and here we are still going strong. Through three children and challenging medical careers, our love has never wavered nor has my confidence in you. We've made it through five books together despite all of our other responsibilities. Wow! Did I really say five books? Quite a ride so far and I know I could not have done it without you.

You are without doubt the strongest woman I have ever known and have managed effortlessly to keep me and the boys in line these many years. No easy task to make sure four spirited men are always spit-shined and pointing in the same direction at the same time. I applaud you, madam. You run a tight ship and we are all thankful for it.

And now as we both transition into the next phase of life, I am even more impressed by the way you have adapted on the fly to our changing life's circumstances. Not least of all has been your participation in my new writing career. Countless hours of reading and re-reading my work and non-stop plot and dialogue discussions over dinner and on long drives wasn't something you counted on when you said, I do. How many bad jokes have I run by you and then discarded only to start over? You are my copy and creative editor extraordinaire, but most importantly you challenge me to be better than I believe I am.

These books are for fun and I love the way you humor me about my dubious talent. Thank you. The joy for me is in the process. I have always wanted to place pen to paper and it is not a stretch to say that I am fulfilling a lifelong dream. I feel a rush when I am writing and discussing the stories with you. Publishing the finished product is anticlimactic to say the least.

When I reflect on these last few years, I realize that I cannot conceive of any of this without having you by my side to act as a voice of reason to keep me grounded. You are as much a part of these novels as you are a part of my life, inextricably blended in, enhancing and flavoring each page with your unique perspective. You may not realize this but I don't think of these as my books but rather they are our books. So, here is to sweet success and many new adventures together.

John

Acknowledgements

Thank you to all my friends and family for your time and effort on my behalf. With each new labor I become increasingly humbled at how difficult it is to construct a gratifying story without the help of others.

Don Alford

Denise Lathey

Peter Lutz

Michele Keith Atty.

Bonnie Curbeau

Kelley Stout RN

Amy Secor FNP

Kimberly Yerkes RN

Kayleigh Difranco

Natalie Kanellis Atty.

Mary O'Neill RN

A special thanks to Terry McNulty, a new friend in an unexpected place. Thank you for participating in this, my fifth novel. You have a keen eye for detail and it was greatly appreciated.

Contents

Credits ii
Dedication iv
Acknowledgements vi
Chapter 1 1
Chapter 2 5
Chapter 3 9
Chapter 4 17
Chapter 5 24
Chapter 6 28
Chapter 7 36
Chapter 8 45
Chapter 9 49
Chapter 10 56
Chapter 11 60
Chapter 12 68
Chapter 13 83
Chapter 14 92
Chapter 15 101
Chapter 16 105

Chapter 17 117
Chapter 18 125
Chapter 19 132
Chapter 20 134
Chapter 21 142
Chapter 22 150
Chapter 23 158
Chapter 24 160
Chapter 25 181
Chapter 26 185
Chapter 27 192
Chapter 28 195
Chapter 29 205
Chapter 30 209
Chapter 31 219
Chapter 32 222
Chapter 33 232
Chapter 34 242
Chapter 35 248
Chapter 36 259
Chapter 37 272
Chapter 38 279
Chapter 39 291
Chapter 40 300
Chapter 41 316
Chapter 42 325
Chapter 43 331

Chapter 44 341
Chapter 45 347
Chapter 46 353
Chapter 47 362
Chapter 48 366
Chapter 49 371
Chapter 50 377
About the Author 385
Author's Note. 386
Hostile Hospital 387
Prescription for Disaster 388
Temperature Rising 390
Claim Denied 391

The Gas Man Cometh

John Avanzato

Chapter 1

When he was young his mother called him chunky, her chunky monkey. As a teen, when they would go clothes shopping she would discreetly ask the salesperson where they kept the husky sizes. By the time he was in college, there was no euphemism available to hide the obvious fact that he was fat. In medical school, he was morbidly obese and now the only word that could adequately describe him was—ginormous. Five feet ten inches tall and easily pushing 450 pounds, his chin had chins. He literally shook the room when he entered and the OR had to order special chairs to support his corpulence. He had long since stopped caring what people thought of him or what the adverse health consequences might be of his great size. He was a two-fisted Manhattan drinking son of a bitch and everybody else could shove it you know where. In his mind, he was Clint Eastwood on steroids.

He liked girls. Oh yeah, did he ever like girls, but that was a problem. Constantly and profusely sweating, his personal hygiene was atrocious. This in combination with his flatulent nature caused few people to dare enter his personal space, and those unfortunates who did so accidentally, held their breath for as long as they could. Several OR nurses had actually passed out as a consequence but blamed it on sudden hypoglycemia or the heat rather than confront him either directly or through an intermediary. This phenomenon earned him the nickname 'lady killer' in the nurse's locker room.

That's why he liked Vegas so much. The girls on the strip didn't judge you. As long as you had the right amount of cash and maybe a couple of lines of coke, you could get any itch scratched. There were the professionals, the weekend party-goers, the dance club girls and the endless supply of vixens roaming the casinos. You didn't have to look very hard. They were everywhere in every size, shape, and color. There were boys too. That was fun once in a while for a change of pace, and the best part was that if every now and then one just disappeared, no one even cared. In fact the Vegas P.D. and the gaming commission did their best to suppress any unpleasantness that might be bad for business. You could be found hanging by a rope from a chandelier over one of the craps tables with your hands tied behind your back and a twelve inch butcher's knife sticking out of your chest and it would be months before anyone would officially admit that it was a homicide. It was almost as if they were on his side. Yes, life was good.

"Hey, Seymour, stop dreaming about jelly doughnuts and take care of my patient. Her oxygen level's dropping."

The harsh rebuke jolted him from his preoccupation and he turned toward the machine by his side that was beeping loudly. He reached down and adjusted the nasal cannula in the woman's nose and tilted her jaw upward. Soon the machine settled down. He said, "She's fine, Cesari. How much longer is this going to take?" He hated doing colonoscopies with this prick, Cesari. He had a big mouth. He'd like to put something in that mouth.

Stop, stop thinking like that.

Save it for Vegas. Besides, Cesari was big; six feet, well over 220 pounds and, more importantly, he looked dangerous. A lot of people thought he was mob-connected.

"I'll be done when I'm done, Seymour. You just make sure she keeps breathing."

"Sure thing." He seethed internally. Who the hell did this guy think he was talking to him like that? Who was he anyway? One minute he's nobody and the next he's practically in charge of everything. Nobody in the rank and file knew the particulars but apparently someone had donated a boat load of money to the hospital in his name, and just like that everyone was kissing his ass. Thank God this was the last case he had to do with him today.

Later, as he sat in the recovery room charting the case and monitoring the patient, Seymour unabashedly eyed a young volunteer at the nursing station. She couldn't have been older than sixteen but so what. She had to grow up sometime. It might as well be with him. Several nurses were performing their duties nearby when Cesari entered the room. Muscular and darkly handsome with a full head of dark brown hair, he cut quite a figure in his blue surgical scrubs. It was obvious that the women in the room noticed, giving him yet another reason to dislike the guy. The way he swaggered they should just tattoo 'alpha male' on him.

Cesari said, "Seymour, can I have a word with you in private?"

"Look, Cesari, the woman is fine. Don't make a federal case out of it."

"That's not what I want to talk to you about."

"What is it then? I got a lot of shit to do."

"Okay, if you want to be like that. You're a board certified anesthesiologist, right?"

Seymour nodded, unsure of where this was going. "Yeah."

"That gives you the right to pass gas in the OR, not wind. Are you getting my drift? You're making six figures. For God's sake, buy some Gas-X or something. It's not fair to everyone else to have to work under these conditions. The other thing you might consider is a prescription strength antiperspirant."

One of the nurses heard and started chuckling quietly. Seymour glared at her and then back at Cesari. The great Dr. John Cesari, gastroenterologist extraordinaire, Chairman of the Department of Ethics, permanent member of the board of trustees at Saint Matthew's Hospital, king-maker and dragon-slayer, he was—a legend in his own mind. All of Manhattan was his oyster it seemed.

He replied unfazed by the affront, "Thanks for the advice, Cesari. I'll do my best to improve myself."

"Great. Then I'll be on my way. Maybe there's someone else into whose life I can bring some sunshine."

What an asshole. He was furious as he watched Cesari walk away although he had to admit, the guy did have a rather nice butt.

Stop, stop, stop...Save it for Vegas.

Chapter 2

I left the recovery room and meandered over to the radiology department. One of my patients was getting an abdominal CT scan so I figured I might as well see it hot off the press. The entire department had just recently undergone a massive year-long, makeover and upgrade including the purchase of a brand new CT scanner, MRI, and interventional suite. Everything looked and smelled brand new from the hardwood floors to the plush leather waiting room chairs.

As I entered the department, I stood in front of a large, gold-framed portrait of the Boston heiress who had left the bulk of her considerable wealth to St. Matthews. She had passed away six months ago while we were still under construction and the portrait had been placed in her memory. I studied her face for a moment. Her clear blue eyes were just as kindly as they were in life. She was a good woman. I headed for the Keurig coffee machine placed strategically for family members and brewed myself a cup of French roast.

The CT room was antiseptic white and I entered standing behind the protective glass with the technologist who was giving instructions to my patient lying in the machine.

Speaking into a microphone he said, "Breathe in—now hold it."

He signaled hello and continued. "Okay, breathe out. We're just about done, Mr. O'Mara."

I sipped my coffee and looked at the image on the computer screen sitting on the desk nearby. I asked, "Is this him, Gary?"

"Yes, Dr. Cesari, just scroll up and down with the mouse wheel. Dr. Campbell is in his office. He'll get the images momentarily."

You didn't have to be a radiologist to see there was something wrong with his liver. There were multiple space-occupying lesions almost completely replacing the normal hepatic parenchyma consistent with metastatic carcinoma. He was seventy and in reasonably good health until about three months ago when he started losing weight without clear explanation. Two weeks ago he became deeply jaundiced and now here we are. All that was left was the crying. There were some palliative options but the reality was that his life expectancy was on the order of weeks to a few months at best. I hoped that he had a good attitude. Not everyone did.

"Do you want to talk to him, Dr. Cesari?"

"Not right now, Gary. I'll see him in his room later. I want to go over the study with the radiologist first."

"Got it."

I walked through the department to the doctor's offices and politely knocked on one of the doors.

"Come on in. It's open."

"Hey Troy, how are you?" Troy Campbell, forty years old, black, and bald as a cue ball, was chief of radiology at St. Matt's. He wore a button-down blue shirt and a knit tie.

"Really good, Cesari, really good, and you?"

"Same here. Nice office, Troy. Guess I haven't been here in a while." It had been recently renovated along with the rest of the department. It was a twenty by twenty square with wall to wall book cases and a large mahogany desk supporting no less than eight computer monitors. It was quite impressive. Maybe not for the CEO of Goldman Sachs but for a physician it was downright palatial. Most doctors these days worked in cubby holes or shared office space to keep overhead down.

"No, you haven't. You really should drop by more often. I miss our broad ranging philosophical discussions. There's nothing quite like trying to save the world with Dr. John Cesari. Do you play chess, Cesari?" He pointed to an ornate chess board he had set up on a small table off to one side of the office. The board was made of alternating white and black squares with a highly lacquered surface. The pieces were lined up in orderly rows facing each other like two armies on a battlefield just waiting for someone to give the order to advance. I walked over and picked up the black king. It was heavy and obviously high quality.

"I dabble in it a little, Troy." I placed the piece back on the board. I had been an avid chess player during my childhood and had belonged to the Manhattan Chess Club back in the day but life had intervened and I rarely had the opportunity to play anymore. Bobby Fischer was and will always be one of my personal heroes. Back in the 1970's when chess was a surrogate battlefield of the cold war with the Soviet Union, Bobby Fischer was our David versus their Goliath, Boris Spassky, and just as in the biblical story he took them down hard. Even people who knew nothing about chess stood in awe and admiration as one gawky kid from Brooklyn took on the entire might of the Soviet's chess empire and completely trashed them. As a teenager, I had read his biography and was overwhelmed by his story. It was before my time but my heart used to pound watching the old videos of that famous match. Hushed voices and analysis. Sweating brows, clocks ticking, hand wringing, and suddenly, too late to avoid the intricate trap set, the abrupt capitulation. I had never felt such joy.

He said, "We'll have to play some time. So, what can I do for you?"

I nodded. “I’d like to go over Mr. O’Mara’s CT scan with you. He just had it done a few minutes ago.”

He turned around to one of the monitors, typed in my patient’s name and pulled up his images to review. “Give me a second.”

I sipped my coffee and winced at the bitterness, “Take your time.”

“What can you tell me about him?”

“He’s seventy, three months of weight loss, mild epigastric discomfort, and now jaundice.”

He studied the images in front of him. “Not good, Cesari, not good at all. Diffusely metastatic disease to the liver with a mass in the head of the pancreas which is probably the primary. There’s mild biliary dilatation, a small amount of ascites tracking up the paracolic gutters and enlarged lymph nodes everywhere. Game over. Sorry.”

“Yeah, I was afraid of that. The oncologists are going to want tissue. Think you can stick a needle in it?”

“Child’s play. I’ll put him on the schedule for this afternoon if you want.”

“Thanks, Troy. I’ll go tell him and his family what his options are and let you know what he wants to do.”

“Will you be at the staff meeting later today?”

Shit, I’d forgotten. “When is it again?”

“Five p.m. Conference Room C in the basement. There’ll be chocolate chip cookies for us.”

I smiled. “Yeah, I’ll be there.”

Chapter 3

In Mr. O'Mara's room I shook hands with his wife and son and took a chair next to them. Family conferences of this nature were never easy. Everyone knew that sooner or later they were going to die but no one ever expected to hear it spoken out loud. The art I found was not so much what you said but how you said it.

"Mr. O'Mara."

"Call me Tim, please."

"Call me John, Tim."

"Okay, John."

"Well, Tim, there's no way of sugar-coating this. The CT scan you just had revealed a tumor in the pancreas and that it has spread to the liver. That's the reason you are jaundiced and haven't been feeling well these last few weeks."

His wife, Maureen, looking very apprehensive asked, "What does that mean? Is there anything we can do?"

"We are going to explore all possible options of course, but pancreatic cancer that has already metastasized is one of the more frustrating tumors to treat."

The son was a well-dressed thirty year old who carried himself with an air of importance. "Doctor, I wish to reassure you that money is no object."

I turned to him and with as much compassion and sympathy as I could muster replied, "And I wish to assure you that as long as I'm breathing that will never be an issue with one of my patients."

He nodded his head, "I didn't mean to imply…"

"I understand. I just thought I would clear the air on that as long as you brought it up. Your dad is going to get the best care we can provide, and I just want us all to be on the same page."

He nodded and I turned back to Tim, who was lying in bed, and held his hand. "This is the plan right now. First, we need to have a tissue sample to make an exact diagnosis if we're going to plan appropriate treatment options. So, in that regard I would like to schedule you for a liver biopsy this afternoon to be performed in the radiology department. Once we have tissue, I will call an oncologist, a cancer doctor, and a surgeon to consult and render an opinion. In the meanwhile, we will continue to monitor your blood work and try to support your nutritional status with a dietary consult and intravenous fluids. At some point, we may want to alleviate your jaundice with a stent in the bile ducts that I can place through a specialized endoscopic procedure called ERCP. If and when it comes to that I will explain in greater detail what that will mean for you. If you start having pain, I need you to let me know right away. We can take care of that. Okay?"

He sighed. "That's a lot to chew on, Doc."

"I know and it's just starting, unfortunately." I turned to his wife and son, took out a pen and wrote my cellphone number on a piece of paper. "There's going to be a lot of confusion in the coming days and weeks. Please feel free to call me for any questions or concerns."

The son took the number saying, "Thank you."

His mother had anxiety written all over her face. Tim was quiet, deep in thought. I looked around the room and thought that hospitals were tough places for sick people. Cold, sparsely decorated, with institutional lighting, and little sunlight; if you weren't depressed before you got here, you certainly would be after a few days.

I asked softly, "What are you thinking about Tim?"

"What if I don't want anything done?"

I smiled. "Then we will still be friends and I will still do whatever I can to help you."

"Thanks, Doc."

Mrs. O'Mara chided him, "Don't talk like that, Tim. Doctor, I don't mean to be rude but would there be any benefit to transferring him to another hospital like Sloan Kettering that specializes in cancer?"

"That's not a rude question. In fact, it's very reasonable one, but that's a personal decision only you can make. If I thought that you would get better care there, I would transfer you in a heartbeat. Medically, however, they do not have any more to offer than we do here. This kind of cancer at this stage has few treatment options available even at a cancer center like Sloan. However, if you do decide to transfer him I will help you in any way I can. Rest assured that neither I nor anyone else here will be offended in the slightest."

Tim clutched my hand. "I like you, Doc. You're a straight shooter. I'm not going anywhere and we're going to fight this thing to the bitter end. I fought every day of my life for everything I have and I ain't gonna give up now, but I gotta know something…" He paused for a moment before continuing. "Is there something I could've done differently? I mean I spent twenty years in the service and used to smoke and drink like a son of a bitch and I ain't exactly been a model citizen since."

I shook my head. "You didn't cause this, Mr. O'Mara. You're right that smoking and drinking too much isn't good for you but I've met many people much younger than yourself, very healthy people with no bad habits, who have cancer and other serious diseases. It's not their fault either. Stuff happens. It's just part of life so don't knock yourself out. It's just the way it is. It's also our nature as human beings to want to know why these things happen but sometimes there is no why."

He squeezed my hand tightly and then released it. Maureen became tearful. "Thank you, doctor. I guess we have a lot to talk over."

"Yes, I know you do. One more thing and then I'll be on my way. We have a variety of counselors and social workers available for you to speak with. They are very caring and compassionate people and I urge you to strongly consider it. I will leave word with the nurses and all you have to do is let them know what you want to do."

They nodded glumly. Tim said, "Thanks, Doc. We'll think about it."

"Okay, then I'll see you in the morning."

****

The meeting started in the usual fashion with Arnie Goldstein, the chief of staff, presiding. The medical secretary read the minutes from the last meeting. We finished up old business and began new business. I nibbled on a chocolate chip cookie and sipped yet another cup of coffee from a Styrofoam cup as I scanned around the room observing all the usual suspects listening attentively to Arnie pontificate. Thirty minutes late, Seymour Kraken, abruptly entered the room, briskly swinging the wood door open so it banged loudly into the wall behind. All eyes turned toward him and Arnie stopped talking. Seymour waddled in unapologetically, grabbed a pile of cookies from the tray set up on a credenza nearby, and sat down opposite me at the long table. I caught Arnie rolling his eyes as he began speaking again.

Seymour was perhaps the most abrasive human being I had ever met and that was saying something because I had met a lot. I grew up in the Bronx which was ground zero for assholes, but this guy rivaled even the worst of them. You would have thought that someone with his obvious shortcomings would at least try to be nice to people. Not Seymour. I stared across the table at him but he could care less as he sat there shoveling cookies into his mouth two and three at a time.

Suddenly, he pushed his chair backward, scraping it loudly along the tiled floor. He stood up, walked back to the credenza, poured himself a cup of coffee, and returned to his seat. I thought Arnie was going to have a stroke. How Seymour ever got to be chief of anesthesia I will never understand. Usually, to run a department required having some interpersonal skills and polish. Personal hygiene aside he was a decent anesthesiologist. I had to give him that. He couldn't stand me but that couldn't be helped. I tell it like it is and wasn't big on political correctness.

When I first met him, I kind of felt sorry for him and offered to join a gym with him figuring that might give him the confidence and motivation to lose weight. Before I had even finished my proposal he told me in no uncertain terms to shove it up my ass. I didn't take it too personally though. People have been talking to me like that my whole life.

I did get upset, however, when I invited him out for a beer after work a while back and was again advised to perform the previously recommended anal maneuver. It was after that episode, I decided to take the gloves off with my friend Seymour. If he thought he was Cesari tough and wanted to go head to head with me then I would be happy to oblige him. Our relationship has been spiraling downward ever since.

Arnie said, "Okay, now to the last order of business. The National Yearly Meeting of Private Hospitals, known as NYMPH, will be devoting the entirety of this year's conference to discuss the impact of the new government regulations and financial cut-backs on the delivery of healthcare. Needless to say, we are all very concerned about what is just on the horizon and it is not pleasant. Despite the Orwellian double-speak coming out of Washington these days, things continue to go from bad to worse economically. Healthcare costs continue to spiral out of control and the payers continue to slash and burn reimbursements." He paused to take a sip of water.

I loved the way Arnie dramatized things. According to him we'll all soon be waiting hours in line for the last slice of baloney. I told him once that if I heard 'the sky is falling story' one more time I was going to prescribe him a tranquilizer.

He dabbed his lip with a napkin and continued. "Almost every hospital in the country will be sending representatives to the meeting this year to share ideas, brainstorm with their peers, form alliances and hopefully come up with a plan on how to deal with the coming mayhem. Because of limited seating, NYMPH has requested that all hospitals limit their representation to no more than four delegates. Last year's meeting at the mid-town Hilton was a zoo because of the overcrowding. Okay, as the chief of staff, I will be going to attend. That means I will need three volunteers."

Seymour hadn't noticed a piece of cookie had fallen onto one of his chins. I signaled him with my hand to clean his face and he discreetly flipped me the bird with his right hand resting on the table in front of him.

Arnie misinterpreted my hand gesture and said, "Thank you for volunteering, Dr. Cesari. Now we only need two more."

I turned toward him to correct the misunderstanding but was too late. Troy Campbell had stepped up to the plate saying, "If Cesari's going then you can count me in."

Smiling ear to ear, Arnie said, "Thanks Troy. Okay everybody, I think we're off to a great start. C'mon, one more volunteer. That's all we need." I felt bad that Troy had stepped in it on my behalf so I kept quiet.

The room was dead silent for the next few minutes. Finally, he said. "All right, let's all think it over. If anybody changes their mind and wants to come just give me a buzz. Just for the record, Troy, Cesari, you're on your own for conference fees, meals, hotel, and airline expenses. The hospital is broke enough."

I said, "Hold on there, Arnie. Airlines and hotels? Isn't the meeting here in Manhattan? I thought you said something about the mid-town Hilton."

"Clean the wax out of your ears, Cesari. I said last year's meeting was at the mid-town Hilton.

"So, where is it this year?"

"The Venetian Hotel in Las Vegas."

My jaw dropped. "C'mon, Arnie. That's not fair. You're supposed to say that before you ask for volunteers." Troy rolled his eyes and I guessed he was under the same impression about the conference being in New York. I had nothing against Vegas but I had a 250 pound English Mastiff, named Cleopatra, as a roommate that I couldn't just leave unattended. Not to mention, a three day meeting in Sin City with a guy as stiff as Arnie was going to be brutal.

"I don't know why you're upset, Cesari. I would've thought you'd be thrilled by that revelation."

"And why is that?"

"It just seems like your kind of town. Lots of showgirls, lots of paesans."

I was hoping he was joking but I knew Arnie a long time and cultural sensitivity wasn't his strong suit. I took a breath and glanced around the room. Maybe I imagined it but I thought I saw Seymour's eyes light up at the exchange, and just as I was about to give Arnie some serious grief, he raised his pudgy hand slowly as if in school. He said, "I'd like to volunteer, Arnie."

Arnie was elated. I was stunned and put Arnie's crack on the back-burner. Arnie said, "Great job, Seymour. Thank you. Well, that completes the delegation. If there is no other business then this meeting is adjourned. My secretary will have all the details and registration information."

Chapter 4

After the meeting, I caught up with Arnie and walked with him to his office. He was a hematologist by trade and although he received a stipend to be chief of staff it certainly wasn't enough to cover all the aggravation he had to put up with. Nearing sixty, with grandchildren and his own budding health issues, he could almost taste retirement. The last two years as chief of staff had turned his hair white.

"Look Arnie, I didn't want to rock the boat in there but there isn't any way in hell I'm going to a conference with Seymour."

He took a seat behind his desk. "Maybe you should try giving him a chance, Cesari, instead of picking on him all the time."

"Picking on him? What the hell is that supposed to mean?"

He gave me a harsh look. "True or false, Cesari? The OR nurses tell me you've renamed him Seymour 'Eatmore' Kraken." I hesitated and he said, "That's what I thought. Isn't that a bit childish even for you?"

"Who ratted me out on that one?"

"It's irrelevant."

"Well, you should hear what the nurses say about him."

"This isn't high school, Cesari. Grow up. Besides, I already know what they say about him and I told them to knock it off too. So everybody just knock it off before we all get slapped with a weight discrimination suit. Now sit down."

Jesus.

"Seriously Arnie?" I asked sitting in the chair opposite him.

He turned and tugged on a rope cord, raising the window blinds. It was 6:30 p.m. in early February and quite dark out. The city lights looked pretty from our vantage point on the tenth floor. He sat down behind his desk. "Very serious. This is no laughing matter."

I took a deep breath. "But I've tried to be nice to the guy. He's a total jerk."

"Well try harder, and if it doesn't work then just stay away from him. There's no rule that says you have to be friends."

"Fine, but this conference is really going to be difficult. You know I have a dog and I hate leaving her in kennels."

"It's only for three days, Cesari. Can't you have somebody dog-sit for the weekend. What about that girl, Cocoa? Are you two still dating?"

He was referring to Myrtle Rosenblatt, aka Cocoa, an exotic dancer now full time student at Juilliard. "We're giving it a break for a while, but we're still friends and she might agree to watch Cleo." Yeah, the more I thought about it I knew she would. She was very fond of Cleo in fact and vice versa.

"Well, that settles it then."

"That settles nothing, Arnie. I'll back off on Seymour but you better promise me that you're sitting next to him on the plane."

"You're a piece of work, Cesari…" Before he could finish that thought there was a knock on the door. He said "Come in."

It was Troy, and he didn't look happy. "Arnie, I just got off the phone with my wife and she's pissed."

Uh oh.

Arnie asked, "What happened?'

"What happened? Her husband just volunteered to go to Las Vegas the weekend of his oldest child's violin recital. That's what happened."

"Well, didn't you tell her how important this meeting is we're going to?"

Troy rolled his eyes. "Seriously? I don't think you understand women too well, Arnie. Nothing is more important than an eight year old's violin recital."

Arnie shook his head. "Take a seat and calm down, Troy. You two guys are killing me. Seymour's starting to look like the most reasonable guy I got on staff."

Troy laughed. "Are you kidding? He just wants to go to Vegas for the all you can eat buffets."

I snorted and Arnie fumed saying, "Not you too, Troy. What am I going to do with you guys? That's enough with the weight jokes. Being weight challenged is a serious problem in this country."

Weight challenged?

Not quite finished venting his spleen, Troy added, "Well, I'm not sitting next to him on the plane."

I chuckled. "Well, that settles that, Arnie. You're elected."

"For Christ's sake, fine."

I always found it amusing when Jewish guys used that expression. You'd think they would say for Moses' sake or for Abraham's sake.

Arnie wasn't quite done. "You know Troy, being black, I would have thought you'd be just a little more sensitive to Seymour's condition."

Oh boy. Nice one Arnie.

Troy bristled and then unloaded, "So let me get this straight, Arnie. You consider being black a condition like being morbidly obese?"

Back peddling Arnie groped for the right words, "That's not what I meant."

"Let me give you a news flash Arnie. Being black is not a disability despite what liberals would have you believe. I don't need or desire a special parking space. All anybody, black, yellow, green or white, wants is to be treated fairly and judged by the content of their character."

Arnie stammered and I sat quietly suppressing my desire to burst out laughing. Man, it was fun watching from the outside for a change. My sides were starting to ache though.

Arnie said, "That's all I was trying to say, Troy. Let's give Seymour a break."

"No, what you were trying to say is that because I'm black I shouldn't be able to render my honest opinion. Telling people how they're supposed to think and talk based on the color of their skin, my dear chief of staff, is the definition of racial stereotyping."

This was great. The thought crossed my mind that if I didn't already work here, I'd pay to get in. Arnie glanced at me for support and I shook my head. It was time to shed clarity on the situation. I said, "Sorry Arnie, but I'm on the black guy's side. Besides, who's kidding who? Eatmore's a total asshole."

"Shut up Cesari," Arnie snapped.

Troy said, "But that is the whole point, Arnie. Seymour is an asshole. He's an obnoxious son of a bitch and that's why no one likes him, not because of his weight."

"All right already. I surrender. I stand corrected."

"Good, because I have to go calm my wife down. If you think you just got a beat down you haven't seen anything. I'll be lucky if she doesn't greet me at the door holding one of my golf clubs."

He said good night and left the room, closing the door behind him. Much to Arnie's annoyance I burst out laughing.

He said, "Forgive me if I don't see the humor in what just happened, Cesari."

"Arnie, you are such a dinosaur. That was classic. I'm just glad you didn't ask him why his kid was learning to play violin instead of banjo."

"Will you shut up already?" He sighed deeply and continued. "There's something else I've been meaning to talk to you about."

He hesitated and I asked, "Spit it out Arnie. It's late and I'm hungry."

"Well, it's about ERCP's…"

ERCP was the eponym for Endoscopic Retrograde Cholangiopancreatography. It was a specialized procedure performed to diagnose and treat problems of the gallbladder, pancreas, liver and bile ducts.

"What about them?"

"Well, you're the only one here at St. Matt's that does them."

"So."

"Well, you're not always around and we've had to transfer quite a few patients out to other hospitals for the procedure because of your lack of availability. There's the obvious loss of income to the hospital but then there's the poor public relations aspect to it as well. Case in point, a month ago the wife of a board member came into the ER with a common bile duct stone and cholangitis. You were out of town and we had to transfer her to Lenox Hill for her ERCP. That went over like a lead balloon. You see where I'm going with this?"

"No, not really. None of the other guys on staff want to do ERCP's and you can't expect me to be available 24/7."

"No, we can't expect that, which is why we've decided to get you some help."

"Help? If you mean you want to recruit another gastroenterologist to do ERCP's be my guest. We've been through this before. They're almost impossible to find. They all want to go to the prestigious academic centers."

"That's true, but as luck would have it, the resume of someone who's available came across my desk a few weeks ago and I jumped on it. He seems like a nice guy and I'm sure you'll get along with him."

"A resume came across your desk in the middle of winter and you didn't find that strange?" In general, the medical world revolved around the academic calendar. Jobs and contracts usually began in July. A mid-winter availability suggested something had gone precipitously awry at his previous gig.

"Apparently, he was working across town at Cabrini Medical Center and things didn't work out. Since we have a need…"

I interrupted him. "Since we have a need you don't really care what he did to get his ass fired in the middle of winter."

"Take it easy Cesari. No need to make accusations. We'll find out soon enough what happened, but in the meanwhile I want you to be nice to him and smooth his transition here."

"You've already hired the guy? Without talking to me?"

"I had to make a quick decision. He was interviewing at several of the other hospitals and I didn't want to lose him." Arnie fidgeted uncomfortably with the disclosure.

"Fine. So he does ERCP's?"

"Well, he's done a few and he's willing to learn. I can't think of a better teacher than you."

I stood up outraged. "You've got to be joking?! He doesn't know how to do ERCP's and I'm supposed to wet-nurse him? This is total bullshit."

He stood up too. "Be reasonable, Cesari. Lancelot seems like a nice guy."

"Lancelot?! Are you fucking kidding me?"

"No, I'm not. He goes by Lance, but that's his real name—Lancelot Facheux."

"That's sounds dangerously close to being French, Arnie."

I had raised my voice and he said, "Calm down, he's Canadian and he starts next week. So be nice to your new partner."

Chapter 5

Seymour trudged slowly and laboriously up the ten steps leading to the entrance of his brownstone on W. 11th Street just off Fifth Avenue. At the top he took a breather before letting himself in. The frigid night air and exertion had triggered his asthma and he pulled out an inhaler from his coat pocket, taking a couple of puffs. Allowing the medicine to take effect, he glanced up and down the street which was lightly dusted with snow. He liked the cold. In fact, the colder the better he thought. His great weight generated a tremendous amount of heat and if he didn't have to take care of his mother, he would have moved some place even further north a long time ago. It was a moot point because she refused to move under any circumstances. She had lived her entire life in Manhattan and intended on dying here. On the other hand he didn't like shoveling snow so maybe things had worked out for the best.

He opened the door and called out to her. "Mother, I'm home." There was no response and he called to her again. He looked at his watch. It was after 8 p.m. She had probably gone to bed.

The brownstone was three stories and he lived in the basement. The main floor had been renovated so that it was completely handicap accessible. Although she could get around with a walker she didn't care to go out much these days. A mild form of dementia had been slowly creeping up on her and she was content to just sit by a window. All her friends had long since passed on or checked into nursing homes but Seymour would never allow that. It was just the two of them now. The third floor was unoccupied and rarely used. It too was fully furnished and once in a while he would rent it out to tourists for weekend getaways when he felt the need for companionship.

He went down the stairs to his living quarters in the basement. It was a spacious apartment with a large central living area, two bedrooms with full baths, and a reasonably sized kitchen and dining area. A few years ago he had extensively renovated the brownstone to accommodate his needs.

Taking all his clothes off, he donned a flannel robe and slippers. From the refrigerator, he retrieved a thirty-two ounce porterhouse steak and started working on dinner. While the meat sizzled in the pan, he busied himself making a tossed salad and garlic bread. What shall we drink tonight, he thought, perusing his efficient wine rack ultimately selecting a seven year old Châteauneuf-du-Pape. Yes, that will do nicely.

There was a large sofa in the living room opposite a ninety-six inch flat screen TV mounted on the wall. He placed his dinner tray on the coffee table and clicked on his preferred porn channel. This was generally his favorite time of day; a good meal, good wine, erotica, but tonight he just couldn't seem to enjoy himself. Even watching two women use a variety of toys on themselves couldn't take his mind off it. He was pissed off. Cesari had managed to get under his skin and now he couldn't get him out. At work, he did his best to ignore the guy and pretend his barbs and insults didn't bother him, but they did. Today's latest round of verbal abuse almost prompted a response which would not have been good. He had lasted as long as he had by flying under the radar and not making waves. Usually, guys like Cesari just tired and went away but not this asshole. Well, if he wouldn't go away on his own, perhaps he could help him. That's why he had volunteered to go to that stupid conference.

He picked up his cellphone and dialed. Three rings later.

"What?" asked a rough, deep voice with a western drawl.

"It's Seymour, Luther."

"I know who it is, Seymour. That's how cellphones work."

"Yes, of course. Well, I'll be making a return trip to Vegas in two weeks, Luther. I was hoping that would be enough time for you to make the necessary arrangements."

"Two weeks? Yeah, that should be enough time. How old and what color?"

"You pick for me this time. I trust you… Um, Luther, I had sort of a special thing I was hoping you could help me with. It's a little different than what we've done in the past. Naturally, I'd be willing to pay whatever you think is fair."

"I'm listening."

After he concluded his conversation, he hung up in a decidedly better mood, settled back to finish his dinner and switched to a different porn station.

Much better.

After an hour passed, the bottle down to the last drop, the steak just a fond memory, the movie stimulating, he was now sated and thoroughly randy. He turned the TV and living room lights off and went to his bed room. Opening the door he clicked on the nearby floor lamp, illuminating the room. The shape on the bed wiggled in response. Naked, her wrists and ankles were secured to the bed posts with handcuffs and her mouth duct taped. Her eyes were puffy from crying and she had peed on the bed. He shook his head in disgust. He had warned her about that.

Two weeks ago she had answered an ad he had placed on Craigslist for someone to sit with his mother during the day. They fell for that one every time and now she was his. Twenty-five years old and quite attractive, she had just moved to the city six months ago from Wichita. Her job opportunity at a production company on Broadway had fallen through and now, like everyone else, she was having trouble making ends meet. He sat on the bed next to her and watched the terror fill her eyes.

"Didn't I tell you not to mess up my bed?" He asked with an edge in his voice. She was starting to irritate him and thankfully this would be her last night. He would place another ad in Craigslist so that when he returned from Vegas, he could hit the ground running with the next one.

Through the duct tape she begged for mercy, trying to explain that she couldn't help herself. He reached for a pair of plyers he kept on the night table next to her causing her to frantically struggle to get away. She knew what was coming.

"Now, now, don't be like that. When one does something wrong then one must suffer the consequences."

Beads of sweat dripped down his forehead and his breathing came in short rapid bursts as his excitement grew. He studied her beauty as he gently traced the metal tip of the plyers down from her neck through her cleavage across her belly finishing its journey at the delicate shaved mound between her spread legs. She shuddered and braced herself.

Opening his robe, he revealed himself to her, layer upon layer upon layer causing her to shrink away in horror as much as she could. Suddenly, with explosive sexual energy, he rolled his massive body on top of her grabbing one of her nipples with the plyers.

Sweat dripped off his face onto hers as he leered lustfully into her puffy red eyes. She couldn't even scream because of his extreme weight on her chest. It was all she could do just to breathe. He squeezed the plyers tightly and said, "I've missed you so much, Mommy."

Chapter 6

It was a chilly morning and I shivered as I entered the coffee shop on Third Avenue across the street from St. Matt's. I kicked snow off my shoes and scanned the room looking for Arnie who I found sitting in a booth. He had already ordered coffee and was playing with his cellphone. Taking off my winter coat as I approached, I greeted him and slipped into the opposite side of the booth.

"Good morning, Dr. Goldstein."

He put his cellphone down, looked at me suspiciously and grumbled. "Yeah, right. So what do you want, Cesari, that necessitated the need of a clandestine meeting outside of the hospital before working hours?"

I signaled the waitress for coffee and a menu. It was 7:30 a.m. and I was ravenous. "C'mon Arnie. Can't two friends break bread once in a while. Geez." I ordered black coffee, corned beef hash, and three sunny side up eggs with rye toast. As the waitress turned to Arnie, I added, "And lots of strawberry jam."

Arnie's eyes grew wide. "For Christ's sake Cesari, are you trying to commit suicide? No one eats like that anymore."

"Relax. If I'm going to die prematurely, I'm quite certain it won't be from a heart attack. C'mon order something healthy." So he did; an egg white omelet with spinach, whole grain toast, and a cup of cubed cantaloupe. I shook my head.

He said, "Well…?"

"This new guy—Assalot…"

"Lancelot, and I told you to stop saying that."

"Okay, have it your way. This new guy Lancelot is a pompous asshole, with almost no clinical skills and even less dexterity. When it comes to ERCP's, he has two left thumbs and most of the time one of them is stuck up his own ass."

"Oh please, Cesari, give me a break. He's only been here two weeks. How bad can he be?"

"Look, Arnie, I have a moral responsibility to tell it like it is. This guy is awful. He doesn't just need remedial training. He needs to go back to square one. He barely knows which end of the scope is supposed to go into which end of the patient. I mean he's that bad. I don't know what they're teaching these guys in France these days but they ain't teaching them endoscopy."

"Stop it. He's Canadian not French."

"Bullshit. Just ask him. 'I'm Frahnch—from Keebeck. My peoples were deezplaced generations ago. We yearn to return to our rightful home one day.'" I spoke with a comically exaggerated faux French accent.

Arnie cracked a smile—a very small one. "Very funny Cesari. Well look, all his paper work's in order and there have been no complaints registered against him either in New York State or the province of Quebec. I checked, so be patient. Maybe he's just a little nervous. It's not like you're the least intimidating human being on the planet."

The waitress served us our breakfast and we dug in. The hash was delicious and much to Arnie's disgust I poured ketchup all over it and then proceeded to slather my toast with butter and gobs of jam.

"Well, I did a little checking myself too."

"And what's that supposed to mean, Cesari?"

"It means I called a friend in the GI department at Cabrini where this guy was practicing and asked him why Assalot left so precipitously. You know what he said?"

"I'm listening."

"He said he didn't know. In fact he said no one knew. One day he was there and the next he was gone and no one from administration was talking. He left so fast that they didn't have time to cancel his OR schedule. He just didn't show up one day with fifteen patients waiting for their colonoscopy."

Arnie stopped eating and thought about that. "That really doesn't prove anything, Cesari."

"A guy just out of training with a green card from Canada doesn't just quit a six figure job in the middle of the night, Arnie. He was told to get out or else."

"Hmm."

I responded triumphantly, "Damn right, hmm. I know you've been eager to get another ERCP guy here for a while but you should have done this research yourself."

"I did call over to the chief of GI there and all he would say was that he left for personal reasons. Wouldn't or couldn't give me any other reason. Once again, other than fanning the flames of your paranoia, you've got nothing but innuendo. Unless you got some hard facts, I suggest you cut the guy some slack. How hard can it be to train a guy to do ERCP's anyway? He should be out of your hair in a couple of weeks."

I almost choked on my toast. "How hard can it be? A couple of weeks? Are you kidding? ERCP is one of the most technically difficult procedures ever devised and more importantly, one of the most dangerous. The risk of complications approaches ten percent in the best of hands, which is astronomical compared to other surgical procedures. It takes months just to gain the bare minimum of proficiency and years before you can claim technical competency. I don't know what this guy told you on his interview but he ain't even close to being capable of doing

ERCP's. The real problem for me is that he's practicing on my patients. I'm lending him my seal of approval and I don't like it. I didn't ask for a protégé, and if I did it wouldn't have been him. I'm seriously afraid he's going to hurt someone and everyone is going to blame me."

Arnie took a sip of coffee and pushed back from the table frustrated. He let out a deep sigh. "All right, how about we shelve any final decision for a week until we get back from the conference. Maybe we can send him for some type of remedial training? That's a thought. He could work part-time during the day here to earn his keep and maybe go uptown to Columbia or Mount Sinai to train with the fellows the rest of the time. They do thousands of ERCP's every year and they're used to training inexperienced people. I'll give a call up there to talk to the head guy."

"Would they do that, Arnie? I mean the Mount Sinai GI department is a pretty prestigious place. They may not just take in some guy off the street like this."

"Are you kidding? For the right price the GI whores there would lick your balls in front of a camera, Cesari. Okay, we'll work on this when we get back. I'll tell Lancelot not to do any ERCP's while we're away. Right now, I need to focus on the meeting. Are you all set for the trip?"

"Yeah, the limo's going to pick us all up in front of the hospital tomorrow morning. As far as I know Troy and Seymour are all set too." I looked at my watch. "Shit, I have to go. I'm supposed meet Robespierre in the radiology department for what I hope will be his last ERCP. I'll give him the happy news about you wanting to further his education at Mount Sinai."

"Just take it easy with him all right. He's a young guy. There's no need to crush his spirit."

"Sure there is. He's French." I wiped my face and looked at Arnie who had resumed eating.

"What?" he asked with a mouthful of cantaloupe.

"This is on you, right?"

"Get out of my sight, please."

I donned my coat and headed for the door. Crossing the street dodging slush puddles, I entered the main lobby of St. Matt's, waved at the security guard, and made a beeline towards the radiology department. One of the techs informed me that my patient was in Room 4 so I hung my coat and put on a lead apron and thyroid collar to protect me from radiation. Minimal as it was per procedure, the cumulative effect over many years of exposure had been associated with the increased risk of a variety of cancers.

I was alarmed when I reached the door and saw a sign overhead saying *Procedure in Progress.* I entered the dark room quietly. Lance had started the procedure and was passing a cannula into the ampulla of Vater, the opening from the duodenum into the pancreatic and common bile duct. There were two nurses assisting him, a radiology tech and Troy, who was studying the fluoroscopy images intently. I remained quiet so as not to disturb Lancelot while he worked but I seethed internally. Having recognized on day one that he was completely inept, I had told him not to start any ERCP's unless I was present in the room to back him up. I wasn't his boss per se, but I was ten years his senior and I had been charged with supervising him. Not to mention, this was my patient after all. Now I was pissed at his disrespect.

I nodded at Troy who nodded back. Whispering, he said, "Hey Cesari."

"Hi Troy. Where are we?"

"He's injected the pancreatic duct a couple of times but hasn't quite found the bile duct yet."

That was the tricky part of this procedure, finding the bile duct. Some guys spent years trying and never found it. I looked at my watch. I was only five minutes late. "When did he start the procedure, Troy?"

He looked at the wall clock. "About forty minutes ago." He said he needed to start early because he had some meeting he had to go to and couldn't be late."

I nodded, "That's what he said, huh?"

Troy nodded but picked up on my tone. "I gather you didn't know?"

I shook my head and walked past Troy until I stood just behind Lancelot. "Morning, Lance."

He turned his head around to see me better and said with a smile, "Johneee, how are you?" He was maybe an inch taller, 200 pounds, clean shaven with wavy, light brown hair and blue eyes. For the most part, he was a good looking guy.

Ignoring his greeting I asked. "How many times have you injected the pancreatic duct?"

"Three maybe four times. No more than five."

I turned to the nurse holding the syringe. "How many cc's of contrast have you used, Mary?"

She replied, "Six cc's." That wasn't too bad, I thought. Just as I breathed a sigh of relief she added. "From this syringe but we already went through a twenty cc syringe so a total of twenty six cc's."

I bit my lip and choked back my fear. I turned back to Troy. "Could you fluoro please?"

"What's the matter Johneee?" Lance asked.

I didn't answer him. Troy and I studied the screen. The pancreatic duct lit up like a Christmas tree from all the contrast material in it. Every tiny little branch and sub-branch could be seen from the sheer volume of contrast and force of the repeated injections resulting in a radiologic phenomenon known as acinarization of the pancreas. This was a common novice mistake and could only lead to a bad outcome such as pancreatitis due to irritation to the pancreas from the chemical agent used. Chemical pancreatitis could be quite severe and even potentially fatal. It would be a miracle if this woman didn't spend the next two months in our ICU writhing in agonizing pain.

I let out a slow deep breath and Troy said, "I don't think I like the look of this."

I turned to Lancelot, "Give me the scope. You're done."

"But why, Johneee? I'm almost in the bile duct."

I hissed at him angrily. "Because that's my patient lying on the table and I said you're done. Now give me the Goddamn scope and we'll talk over the nuances of what's going on here later."

He handed me the instrument and stepped away from the patient suddenly realizing he might be in over his head. I found the bile duct, removed a small stone and finished the procedure in total silence only occasionally whispering instructions to my nurses.

Withdrawing the scope from the patient, I turned to the nurse and said, "Mary, I want her admitted overnight for observation. Keep her N.P.O. and the IV in for hydration. I'll write more orders later after I talk to the family and explain what's going on."

Troy instinctively knew this wasn't going to end well. "If you don't need me Cesari, I have to get back to work."

"Thanks Troy, I'll talk to you later." I pointed at Lancelot who had drifted slowly toward the back of the room. "You, come with me."

We walked in silence to the medical staff lounge. Once I determined we were alone, I locked the door and turned to him, sizing him up. He looked at me with wide open blue eyes. He opened his mouth to say something and I punched him hard in the solar plexus. He gasped and doubled over, clutching his chest. I shoved him roughly backward and he tripped over a small table coffee and landed on the floor.

I sat on the edge of the coffee table and studied him. He was too short of breath for me to begin so I waited patiently as his breathing returned to normal. When it did, I stood over him and grabbed him by the hair, slapping him hard until both his cheeks were nice and rosy. Then I sat back down as he started to cry.

"You better save your crying. If that woman wakes up screaming in pain from pancreatitis then I'm going to really give you something to cry about. Let's get something straight, mon ami. I don't know what your story is—yet, but I will. Have no doubt about that. In the meanwhile, the gloves are now off between you and me. In case you haven't noticed, I take patient care very seriously. Therefore, I don't want to see you near that ERCP room again. Dr. Goldstein is going to talk to you about going for some remedial training. It's your decision, but in the meanwhile you had better stay out of my way. I want you to check on this woman every hour beginning now until tomorrow morning and I mean through the entire night. I don't care if you have to sleep in a chair outside her room. If she so much as clears her throat I expect a call from you. For the next twenty four hours you're her personal nurse and my total bitch. Nod if you understand."

He nodded.

"Good, I'm going to a conference tomorrow with Dr. Goldstein. We'll talk more when I get back. If the lady does well overnight you can discharge her to home and have her follow up with me in two weeks. If she develops pancreatitis, I won't fault you for handing in your resignation and hopping a flight back to Quebec."

"But Johneee," he sniveled.

I left him there.

Chapter 7

Lance called me first thing in the morning as I waited to check in at JFK. Fortunately for him, things went well and my patient had a good night. She went home uneventfully but I had to listen to his whining apology for near on thirty minutes.

During the flight to Vegas, Troy and I played a couple of games of chess on a small six inch magnetic chess board with accompanying tiny pieces that he purchased in the airport. I won one game and I let him think he won one. Seymour was in remarkably good spirits chatting away with Arnie three rows away. I wondered if maybe I was wrong about him and the thought crossed my mind to give him another chance.

Our connecting flight in Detroit was delayed several hours due to weather but we eventually made it out of there and touched down in Vegas without incident, checking into our rooms at the Venetian shortly after 8:00 p.m. west coast time. It was a long day. I phoned Arnie and Troy to go hit the casinos but they were exhausted and all they wanted to do was lie in bed and call their wives so I bit the bullet and asked Seymour if he wanted to catch dinner somewhere. To my surprise he enthusiastically said yes and we met down in the lobby.

"You're looking sharp, Seymour." He had cleaned up, shaved, and wore a fresh white shirt and an ill-fitting massive beige sport coat that hung over him like a sack. Nonetheless, next to me he looked like he had stepped off the cover of GQ magazine. I wore blue jeans, loafers, and a red Tommy Bahama beach shirt. If we were going to a Jimmy Buffett concert I was doing fine.

"Thanks, Cesari. So where do you want to eat?"

"I don't know. I haven't been in Vegas in years. It looks like there are tons of great restaurants in every direction. Do you have any preferences?"

"Well, I came here last year for an anesthesia conference and remember eating at a great place down the strip a bit by the Golden Nugget. We'd have to take a cab if that's okay. You like Italian food, don't you?"

I smiled. "Never touch the stuff."

It was Thursday night in Vegas and seventy-seven degrees out on the strip, not a cloud in the sky. Registration for the conference was at 8:00 a.m. sharp in one of the Venetian's many large meeting halls. I was actually looking forward to getting to know Seymour better. Maybe this is what we needed to re-set our relationship. I made a mental note to pick up the tab.

The restaurant was a short cab ride down the strip, maybe five miles from the Venetian. The driver let us off in front of an ornate palazzo-like structure with tall, white marble columns, statues of Roman gods and historical figures, and fountains lit up by multi-colored lights.

"Whoa. Not bad Seymour, not bad at all. Are you sure this is a restaurant?" I asked noting two muscular guys dressed as Roman legionnaires standing at attention on either side of the entrance holding what I hoped were fake spears.

"The best. It's called *The Fall of Rome*."

The legionnaires nodded to us as we passed through the main entrance entering a large vestibule with a beautiful mosaic tiled floor, potted palm trees, and wall murals depicting scenes from the golden age of the Roman Empire. A curvaceous young woman, scantily clad in a loose fitting toga and sandals greeted us pleasantly. She wore multiple gold bangle bracelets on both arms. Apparently, wearing a bra was not a requirement here.

"Hello citizens of Rome. Have you dined with us before?"

I smiled and Seymour nodded, taking charge. "Yes, I have. Is there any chance we could have dinner in the bath house?"

Bath house?

Before I could start worrying about what Seymour had in mind she replied, "I'm sorry. The bath house is closed for renovations but we have room in Nero's gardens. Will that be to your satisfaction?"

Seymour looked slightly disappointed but nodded. "That will be fine."

"Then please follow me."

Walking behind her, I couldn't help noticing that not only wasn't she wearing a bra but she had left her panties at home too. I whispered to Seymour. "Bath house?"

"Relax, Cesari. You're going to love this place."

I said, "I already do."

She stopped in front of a large wood door with a brass handle. "The attendant inside will give you a key to your locker. The entrance to the dining hall is on the other side."

Locker?

Inside was a pristine locker-room with marble benches and tiled floors. A young, slender man with long hair in a red toga, makeup and gold earrings handed us two keys and pointed out lockers for us to use. There was a long rack of togas in various colors and sizes for us to choose from. The attendant pointed out that the only color not available was purple as that was reserved for the emperor. I chose a light blue toga and Seymour, a green one.

I chuckled as I changed. "Seymour, I can't believe we're doing this."

He managed a smile too and I had to admire the sudden turn-around in his demeanor toward me. He practically glowed as he spoke, “I ate here twice last year when I attended the gas convention. What a hoot. Too bad about the bath house though. That would have been a riot. I’ll explain over dinner.”

I put my clothes and personal effects in the locker and secured it. The key fit nicely into a zippered pocket on the inside fold of my toga which was big enough to accommodate my wallet and cellphone as well. Seymour took his underwear and socks off but I hesitated. This was getting weird.

He saw my reluctance and said, “Don’t be a sissy, Cesari.”

I thought it over briefly. What the hell. As I took my underwear off I said, “What happens in Vegas, right?”

“Of course.”

He put his wallet in the locker. “You’re not going to hold on to your wallet?” I asked.

“Why? You’re in Vegas, Cesari. No one robs you in Vegas unless the Nevada gaming commission approves it.”

“Well, I’ll hang onto mine. That’s a little too much trust if you ask me.”

“Whatever floats your boat, Cesari.”

We closed the lockers and dropped the attendant a ten as a tip, proceeding to the dining area. The room was a large glass-enclosed botanical garden, lit by massive gas torches positioned strategically around the perimeter. It was a moonless night and many stars shone brightly in the sky above. A quartet of classical musicians in period costumes played gentle, relaxing background music while the toga clad patrons dined in ancient opulence. Palm trees, rose bushes in bloom, and a variety of other horticultural delights dotted the room separating the guests from each other. We were escorted toward the center where there was a large, round pool stocked with Koi and a central fountain spraying water far overhead.

Instead of the usual table and chairs we were invited to recline on two cushioned divans with a low lying ornately sculpted marble table between us. I looked at Seymour and said, "Fuck, Seymour, you know how to live."

"Glad you like it. The food's even better."

"What kind of menu is it? I'm guessing no chicken parm."

"You're guessing right. In fact, there is no menu. They serve you whatever they think is appropriate and you can take it or leave it and don't bother mentioning any food allergies you might have. They don't give a shit, but trust me you won't be disappointed."

And I wasn't.

It was ten o'clock. Beautiful girls with their breasts falling out of their togas served us house wine in crystal decanters. Marinated olives, fresh sardines, and figs stuffed with goat cheese drizzled with aged balsamic vinegar started us on our culinary journey. In between courses, small bowls of mint flavored sorbet helped cleanse our palates. The main course was whole roasted piglet served to us on gold plated dishes with accompanying winter vegetables.

"So Seymour, is it safe to assume this is going to cost a lot?"

He chuckled, "Oh yeah."

It was a little strange eating lying on my side like that but I got used to it. At one point I spilled wine on my toga and a waitress brought me a brand new one to change into. I looked at her and Seymour confused.

Seymour laughed. "Go ahead, Cesari. Don't be shy."

I stood up and several waitresses surrounded me with arms outstretched holding a sheet for my privacy. I changed into the clean toga while they watched, giggling.

"Damn, Seymour, this place is unbelievable. We going to stick around for dessert? I'm stuffed."

"We can skip desert but we can't leave without an after dinner aperitif."

Make that three, no four, glasses of grappa from Sienna, apparently the most expensive money can buy, and I was barely seeing straight. I looked at my watch and saw that it was almost 1:30 a.m. Shit, I was surprised at how fast the time had flown by and said, "Say, Seymour, this has been a great night, but I think we should start thinking about leaving before I get double vision."

He smiled. "I give you credit Cesari, you should have been seeing double about an hour ago."

I chuckled but there was something about the look in his eyes that didn't seem very friendly. Just about then, I noticed that I really was seeing double and seeing two of Seymour was no laughing matter. Okay, we had at least two bottles of wine, maybe three, judging from the size of the decanter and three, no four or was it five, shots of grappa. That was a lot but nothing I wasn't used to.

Lying down fully, I closed my eyes to stop the room from spinning and when I opened them again I saw Seymour talking to a big guy in a ten gallon hat, blue jeans, and cowboy boots. The guy looked at me and said in a low raspy voice, "Is that him, Seymour?"

Seymour had stood up. "Yes, thanks for your help, Luther."

The one called Luther said, "Okay, let's bring him over to the room."

They both came over to me and helped me up because I really wasn't able to stand on my own. Looking around, I couldn't tell how many other patrons were still present but guessed there couldn't be many left at this hour. The plants and statues really made for a private dining experience. Everything was swirling around me now and I felt like I was at the bottom of a funnel.

"Where are we going Seymour?" I asked with slurred almost incomprehensible speech.

"Some place nice, Cesari. Don't worry."

"Who is this guy?"

"A friend, Cesari. Just a friend. C'mon, keep walking. You can do it. Don't pass out on me now."

I turned to Luther. "Hi pal."

"Yeah," he replied gruffly.

We eventually came to a dimly lit, red-carpeted hallway lined on either side by ordinary looking doors. It looked like a gauche motel. We arrived at our destination and the one called Luther knocked and then entered. The room was dominated by a king-sized bed in its center, a couple of armchairs, and a TV. A voluptuous blonde wearing nothing but high heels and a see through robe greeted us with a southwestern drawl. "Hi boys, what do we have here?"

Luther said, "This is the guy I told you about, Jenny. Make it look good, okay? You remember Seymour?"

"Of course I remember Seymour. Hi Seymour."

"Hi Jenny."

She said, "Well, throw him on the bed, Luther. He looks heavy. So how bad do you want me to make this?

Seymour jumped in. "Real bad."

They threw me roughly on the bed as Luther agreed. "Seymour wants him to suffer so rather than just bury him in the desert we thought the next best thing would be ten to fifteen years in the Nevada State Prison for aggravated sexual assault. I checked him out. He's got a record back in New York so I'm confident they'll throw the book at him. Are you sure you're okay with this, Jenny? I don't want you to do anything you're not comfortable with. I could always get one of the other girls if you want."

I stared blankly at the ceiling, half in, half out. What did he mean *bury him in the desert?*

Jenny said, "Luther, darling, for twenty-five thousand dollars I'd tell the judge my own father raped me. Besides, he's kind of cute. This might be fun. I'm just curious though, I've never done anything quite like this. Given my questionable lifestyle do you think anyone will buy it?"

"That's not my problem who wants to believe you or not. Besides, I don't see why not. Everyone knows it's not okay to rape hookers especially in Vegas where for business reasons it's *really* frowned upon, and no one out here is going to give a shit about some rich asshole doctor from New York."

"You have a point, Luther. Letting a guy get away with assaulting one of the girls could be bad for business. Okay, you guys leave and I'll get to work. It shouldn't take me more than an hour tops, to make this look good. Then I'll call the police."

Semiconscious and trying to sort things out, I tried hard not to pass out. My mind was more than just a little fuzzy, and I could move, but was very uncoordinated. It was unclear what was happening or why. Who exactly was about to be raped? I tried to say something but couldn't get my lips to move.

The blonde leaned over studying me and I watched her through half closed eyes. She seemed nice. Luther said, "I hope you'll be able to get some DNA from him, Jenny. That will make it a lot easier to sell to the law."

She laughed, "You don't worry about that. I could get DNA from a rock. How much Viagra did you give him, anyway? Look, he's already starting to get hard and I haven't even touched him." She pulled aside my toga to look at me better.

"How much? A whole bottle with God knows how many roofies. I had the girls slipping them into his drinks all night. By all rights the guy should be in a coma right now. Just remember, I want his DNA everywhere, all right?"

Jenny chuckled. "I understood you the first time, Luther, and it will be. Now take Seymour and go have a smoke or something. I'll take care of Tony the tiger here. By the way, Seymour, keep me in mind for future jobs like this. I can retire early at this rate. Okay, now out you two and let me get to work. From the way that banana is swelling up this may not take all that long."

Chapter 8

Disoriented and nauseated, the sounds of approaching police sirens permeated my subconscious, rousing me from my stupor. I willed myself to get up and swung my legs over the side of the bed. The room was pitch black so I turned on a light and looked around. Where was I? It was 3:00 a.m. and my head was pounding, I didn't recognize the room and where were my clothes? There, in a pile on the floor off to one side, I saw them. As I dressed, my head cleared a little and things gradually came into focus. I had dinner with Seymour at some exotic place off the strip and drank too much. There had to be more than that. This wasn't the Venetian, was it?

I stretched and yawned, shaking myself. It helped. I had to pee real bad and staggered over to the bathroom. Opening the door, I turned on the light and stepped back in horror. There was a dead blonde in the bath tub. Her eyes were wide open with fright and she was a ghastly shade of white. She was lying in a pool of her own blood and had been horribly mutilated by a ten inch chef's knife lying on the floor next to the tub. There were multiple stab wounds in her upper chest and a long slash down her abdomen exposing her intestines which now lay on top of her.

Holy shit!

Overwhelmed with shock and revulsion, my brain muddled with drugs and alcohol, I suddenly lurched over vomiting up my dinner. Panting, I cleaned myself at the sink and splashed cold water on my face. Who would do such a thing? On top of the toilet tank sat a familiar brown wallet. My wallet. I picked it up and my driver's license was missing. Looking in the tub, I saw it floating by her feet. I picked it up, wiped it dry and processed the scene as rapidly as my befuddled brain would allow. I had a strange feeling in my groin. Oh my God. I was getting hard. Jesus Christ almighty. What was happening? Did I do this? Who was this girl?

Vaguely, I remembered a blonde but only vaguely. The sirens were getting closer. Shit. Were they coming here? I looked at the knife. If I did this my prints would be all over the handle. If I didn't I could be exonerated if somebody else's prints were on it. I grabbed a nearby towel and wiped the knife clean and then dumped it into the tub. I wasn't into taking chances like that.

The adrenaline surge cleared my head and helped me focus. It was time to get out of here. My heart pounding, I bolted for the door and once in the hallway ran towards the nearest exit. The sirens had pulled up outside the building and the voices of large, angry men could be heard. Room doors started opening and one by one half naked men and women started coming out to see what was going on. At the far end of the hall several uniformed officers approached blocking my escape. I turned around and searched frantically for another way out.

An attractive girl with long dark hair and pouty lips wearing a camisole saw me anxiously scanning for an escape route. The look on my face gave away my secret and she took two steps toward me, grabbing my hand. "This way," she urged.

She led me into her room and closed the door, locking it. "What did you do?" she asked. I was close to her. She smelled nice.

"Possibly something really bad. Possibly not. I don't know."

She thought about that for a second or two as she sized me up trying to decide whether she was making the right decision. I got the feeling I was in a place where people lived on the fringe all the time and right or wrong was simply a suggestion.

She said, "There's a small escape hatch at the top of the linen closet in the bathroom. You should be able to fit through it. It leads to the roof. All the rooms have them. They're emergency exits for the girls if a date doesn't go right or for when the shooting starts. The bathroom doors are made of metal and have deadbolts to give us a head start. Ladders leading down the side of the building will bring you into the parking lot. Do you have a way to get out of here? Like a car?"

"I don't even know where I am."

She took a deep breath obviously conflicted about what she was doing. "I should have my head examined. Are you strung out?"

"No—I don't know. I honestly have no idea what's going on."

She grabbed my arms checking for track marks but found none. "Maybe they're not after you?"

I took a deep breath. "Trust me. They're after me."

Having made her decision, she walked over to the night table and took out a set of car keys. She said, "They're going to search all the rooms. They always do when something happens. You're at The Fall of Rome Gentlemen's Club on the strip across from the Golden Nugget. I have an old, yellow Volkswagen Beetle parked in space 29. You can't miss it. What's your name and where are you staying?"

"John Cesari and I'm staying at the Venetian."

She smiled. "A nice Italian boy."

"Yeah."

"Well, I know a lot of the guys at the Venetian. Leave my car in the hotel lot and give the claim ticket to Marco. If it's not there tomorrow I'll call it in stolen along with your description and I'll hate you forever. Well, it was nice to meet you Mr. John Cesari. You better not have killed anyone."

"Thank you. What's your name?"

"That's none of your business."

"I could just check the registration in the glove compartment."

"And I could start screaming."

Good point.

"Understood. I just wish there was some way I could thank you."

She looked with curiosity at the growing bulge in my pants and chuckled. "You can't be serious. I think you'd better go now."

I turned to leave and as I entered the bathroom she said, "Wait."

I hesitated, looking at her. "Yes?"

"My name is Francesca—Francesca Di Benedetto."

I smiled. "A nice Italian girl."

To my surprise, she blushed.

"Yeah."

Chapter 9

Pulling the Beetle into the Venetian's main entrance, I spotted several police cars with flashing lights out front and decided to keep on moving. There could literally be a thousand reasons why the police were here but I didn't like the feel of it so I drove down South Las Vegas Boulevard for a short distance, eventually finding an all-night White Castle with a mostly empty parking lot.

It was 4:00 a.m. and I called Arnie on my cellphone hoping he was a light sleeper. I was surprised at how fast he answered.

"Cesari, where are you?"

"Never mind that, Arnie. Something's happened."

"You're telling me? The Las Vegas police are swarming the place looking for you. They've got me, Seymour, and Troy in one of the conference rooms. We're waiting for a detective to come and interview us."

"Seymour's there?"

"Yeah, why?"

I didn't know why. If I went to dinner with him and wound up in a whorehouse, I just assumed he would have been there too. I said, "Nothing. Can you put him on?"

"You going to tell me what happened?"

"It's complicated Arnie. Put Seymour on."

"Since when did he become your best friend?"

"Arnie, please."

A second or two later Seymour said, "Cesari, what happened?"

"You tell me Seymour. I can't remember anything after having dinner with you at that fancy roman place."

"Really? You didn't seem that drunk. I mean we were both a little tipsy but not that bad."

"And…?"

"And we met a couple of girls who work there. You went off with some blonde named Jenny."

"And you?"

"I wanted to do the same but I was really tired so I took a raincheck with mine and cabbed it back to my room. So what happened? The police haven't told us anything yet other than they want you."

Shit.

"I don't know what happened. I woke up in a room in that cathouse. You didn't tell me that it was whorehouse, Seymour. Did you know that?"

"What difference would it have made? The food was great."

He had a point. The food was great.

"Yeah, I suppose."

"So where are you, Cesari?"

"It's not important. I assume they've been to my room?"

"Oh yeah, and don't waste your time looking for your luggage. They got it. Look, I'd better go. There's a hard-boiled looking guy in a suit coming. It's probably not a good idea if he catches me on the phone talking to you."

"Yeah, you're probably right about that. I'll stay in touch."

"What are you going to do?"

"I don't know. Bye." I clicked off and threw my cellphone down on the passenger seat in frustration. The police already knew who I was and where to find me. How? I took out my wallet and perused the contents; credit cards, driver's license,

New York State Physician's Photo ID, and two hundred dollars in cash. Nothing was missing. Why was my driver's license floating in the tub with that girl? Good question. I couldn't go back to the Venetian now, and if I didn't, Francesca would report the vehicle stolen although grand theft auto was the least of my problems at the moment. Then there was the vexing issue of this erection I kept getting. I looked down as I felt it happening again. Damn. This is the most ridiculous thing that's ever happened to me.

Staring ahead contemplating my options, I was short on ideas, mostly because all the evidence was pointing to the fact that I picked up a hooker after dinner and she took me to her room. Did we do drugs together? That wasn't my nature but how else to explain why I couldn't remember anything? Even in death, the girl was striking. If all I had was alcohol, I should have remembered her. On the other hand, if I was drunk and my judgment was impaired I may I taken something that made me crazy. Angel dust, crack, heroin, LSD, meth, any number of drugs could have produced temporary insanity, psychosis, paranoia.

Great.

After about thirty minutes of batting my options around, I shifted the car into gear and drove back to *The Fall of Rome*. I might as well leave the car where I found it. A yellow Beetle stuck out like a sore thumb and I didn't see any point in having Francesca file yet another felony charge against me. I'd try to pick up a rental car somewhere and drive to LA or Phoenix and sort things out from there. The club was still an active crime scene when I arrived with police cars, news vans, an ambulance and crowds of people milling about with curiosity. I couldn't get into the parking lot because of the commotion. Now what?

I pulled into the Golden Nugget and parked the car, telling the attendant that I was checking in. He gave me the ticket but now I had to let Francesca know somehow. Plus, I had to get new clothes in a hurry. The red Tommy Bahama shirt was too easily identifiable, but at this hour there wouldn't be any hotel shops open to purchase a new one. First things first anyway. Francesca was nice to me so I wanted to do the right thing and make sure she knew where her car was. The thought crossed my mind to give somebody a twenty to walk over there with the claim ticket but I wasn't sure if I could trust anyone here or if that in itself would raise suspicions. No, I'd be better off taking a chance and going over there myself. No one would expect that, and the red shirt wasn't that bad. There were a lot of guys wearing beach shirts walking around.

I grabbed a cup of coffee at a Starbucks inside the Golden Nugget and passed some time letting the hullabaloo across the street die down. By 5 a. m., I felt my eyes closing from fatigue and shook it off downing the last drop of my brew as I walked across the street. There were still a couple of cop cars parked out front near the entrance to the parking lot and I assumed they were still taking statements. The news vans and ambulance were gone and the crowd had dissipated. I strolled casually over to the back of the building, retracing my hasty exit earlier but taking a circuitous route to avoid the police cars. I found the ladder and climbed up on to the roof. It was pretty easy to find the escape hatch I had come out of and I gently lifted it open. The light was off and I listened for sound. Not hearing any, I quietly descended into the bathroom. The door was closed and I wondered what Francesca was up to. I didn't want to frighten her but there was no easy way of doing this. Even a hardened woman of the night would be surprised by a guy popping out of her bathroom at five in the morning. Fortunately, with all that had happened I doubted that she would be with anyone. I was sure all the Johns had cleared out once they were questioned.

I smelled an odd, acrid, and unpleasant odor sifting through from the other room and I immediately became alarmed. I opened the door slowly and peered into the darkness, listening and watching. The disagreeable scent grew as the door opened and the sound of hushed breathing, no—whimpering became readily apparent. I stepped into the room quietly allowing my eyes to adjust. There was a shape on the bed but only one small form.

Good.

I tapped gently on the door and whispered, "Francesca."

A muffled weeping voice cried softly and unintelligibly so I stepped toward the bed, turning on the night table lamp and held my breath. Francesca lay naked, curled up in a ball on the bed. She had been severely beaten and had one black eye and a swollen lip through which she could barely speak. There were multiple other fresh bruises decorating her torso and legs. On her back were strap marks from a belt. I sat down next to her and wrapped my arms around her, suddenly realizing what the stench was. She and the bed were covered in her own vomit.

I asked gently, "What happened?"

Her eyes grew wide when she recognized me. "You're what happened." She sobbed leaning into my chest and I realized that her tongue was very swollen. She must have bitten it while they were smacking her around.

"But why?"

"One of the other girls saw you come into my room and knew I helped you get away. When she realized you must have been the one that killed Jenny she ratted me out to Luther."

Luther?

Now that was familiar. The image of a tall, lanky cowboy came to mind. I had met him, but where?

"Who's Luther, Francesca?"

"Why'd you kill Jenny? She was nice."

"Francesca, I'm not going to lie. I don't know what happened because I can't remember anything but I'm not a murderer. I'm a doctor. I had dinner in the restaurant part of the club with a friend, had one too many drinks and woke up in Jenny's room. I can't swear what happened but I think I was drugged."

She thought about that and from the look on her face I could tell that wasn't the first time she'd heard a story like that. Through tears she said, "I want to believe you but everybody says you did it. When Luther heard I helped you escape, he became furious. He beat me right in front of the other girls and with the cops standing around in the hallway."

I was incredulous. "The cops knew what was happening?"

"Sure, they could care less. They were just as pissed at me. Luther pays them all off so they wouldn't lift a finger for anyone of us."

I felt my blood pressure rising and I think my right eye started to twitch from anger. "So who is this Luther? Is it safe to assume he's some sort of pimp?"

"Manager. That's his title. He's the manager here at *The Fall of Rome.* Why did you come back?"

I told her what happened at the Venetian and she tried to smile. "You're kidding? You're returning my car? Are you retarded? Half the police in Vegas are looking for you."

"Well, if you put it that way..."

She just looked at me, trying to understand the logic behind a cold-blooded killer returning to the scene of the crime with the police still there to return a beat up, ten year old Volkswagen Beetle. Finally, she said, "You're crazy."

"Or innocent. Is Luther a western type of guy? You know, boots, jeans, cowboy hat, rough looking with a deep voice?"

"Yeah, that's him. Have you met him?"

"I may have." I took the claim ticket out of my pocket and placed it on the night table. "Look, Francesca, I can't even begin to tell you how sorry I am that this happened to you on my account. In fact, I'm pretty pissed off right now at this guy Luther for doing this. I'm not sure what happened last night but I don't believe that I killed your friend. I just don't know how I can prove that to you or anybody. When I came here just now it was my intention to simply drop off the claim ticket and disappear but I'm having a hard time with that plan right now. I think I'd like to speak to Luther."

She looked horrified. "Oh no, not because of me, please. That will only make things worse, guaranteed. Look, I know a lot of people might look down on what I do but it's not that bad here. I got a good deal and it's a whole lot better than being on the street."

"Come with me for a second. I want to show you something."

I helped her off the bed and she limped into the bathroom holding on to me. Inside, I turned on the light and made her face the mirror. I said, "Does that seem like a good deal to you?"

She stared at her bruised and battered, vomit-caked face and broke down crying. Just two hours ago she was one of the prettiest girls I had ever seen. I said very gently with great sympathy, "Francesca, I'm not trying to save you, okay? I'm not some sort of religious fanatic who doesn't understand some of the forces that brought you to where you are right now. I've had my own ups and downs and lumps and bumps but I'm sure you can do better than this. You just have to make up your mind that you want to. It's still dark out and we can get out under cover of night. We can take the Beetle or I can rent a car but we need to get you some place safe because whether you want me to or not I'm going to find Luther and beat the living shit out of him for doing this. "

She looked at me, her good eye wide open. "Who are you?"

"Just a nice Italian boy."

Chapter 10

Francesca took a five-minute shower to clean off and I rinsed off in the sink. My shirt was too gross for words at this point so I just rolled it into a ball and tossed it away. We couldn't leave through the main entrance because among other things, Luther had locked Francesca in from the outside. As I helped her climb up to the roof all I could think about was how much I was going to hurt him.

Outside we skirted the police vehicles and headed over to the Golden Nugget. We were both too exhausted to go even a step further so I got us a room there and around 6:00 a.m. we crashed and burned on the king bed, waking up at eleven. I felt awful, hungover, starving, and had a massive headache. I also felt slimy. That had to be one of the worst nights of my life, but at least the erections seemed to have slowed down. I jumped into a steaming hot shower and just stood there eyes closed letting the water cleanse me. I was in deep shit and needed help. I couldn't just go back to New York and pretend nothing happened. I was now a fugitive wanted for murder with a wounded hooker on my hands. What the hell was I going to do with her? We hadn't talked too much but I would rectify that when she woke up. There had to be some place she could go.

I heard the glass door slide open and turned my head to see Francesca step into the shower stall behind me. She said, "Good morning."

Her eye and lips were only slightly better than a few hours ago. "Hi there Francesca."

She slipped her arms around my waist and leaned her face against my back. "My friends call me Frankie."

"Are we friends now?"

"I think so."

"How's your eye, Frankie?" It was almost completely swollen shut.

"I'll live. Did I say thank you?"

"I think so."

"I don't remember so I'll say it now. Thank you."

"You're very welcome."

She reached for the bar of soap on the shower shelf and began washing my back for me. I said, "Frankie, you don't have to do this."

"I want to."

She reached around with the bar of soap and began scrubbing my chest and abdomen. I felt tingly and looked down and sighed deeply. She sensed my arousal and asked softly, "You like?"

Whispering hoarsely I replied, "Yeah."

I turned around slowly, facing her. She stood there staring at me with her good eye. Her lip was terribly swollen and I looked at the bruises all over her. I took a deep breath and felt anger sweep over me again. She read my mind and shook her head, "Not now. Now, it's just you and me."

I leaned down and gently kissed her as the water rained down from above. She stepped in close and held me tightly, becoming tearful. "I didn't know there were men like you."

Holding her just as tightly. "Trust me, I'm not such a bargain."

That made her chuckle.

Afterward, we lay on the bed gazing at each other. "Are you okay?" she asked.

I nodded, "Hm hmm. What about you?"

"I hurt all over."

"I'm sorry. We'll get some ibuprofen, but first we have to eat."

She smiled. "So this is it. Just like that. You rescue some strange girl, make love to her in the shower, and now we eat like it's just another day."

I laughed. "Do you want me to order fireworks?"

That made her laugh too. "I don't even know you and you just rocked my whole world."

"I've been told that I'm pretty potent in that department."

She snorted. "I didn't mean the sex, silly, although that was pretty good for an amateur."

"Thanks. You're killing me."

I ordered room service and soon we were devouring omelets, english muffins with strawberry jam, and thick-sliced bacon. I looked at my watch and it was half-past twelve. My phone had died and I needed to get a charger quick to find out what was going on with Arnie and the guys. I wondered if they still went to the conference. I needed to get some clothes too. Checking into the hotel without a shirt had raised more than a few eyebrows. Even for Vegas, that was a little odd.

"So tell me Frankie. Where are we going to take you?"

She looked puzzled. "Who said you're going to take me anywhere?"

I hesitated and tried a different tack. "Where are you from?"

"Don't change the subject. I come and go as I please and it's my car, remember?" Last night was a great adventure and I'm very appreciative, Mister—Dr. Cesari, but this is my life after all."

I nodded. Okay. Not quite what I expected, but she had a point. "Of course. Let me rephrase that. So where do we go from here? Because my next stop is to interrogate your former boss with extreme prejudice and nothing you say or do is going to stop me so I need to know you'll be in safe place."

She took a bite of her omelet and washed it down with coffee as she thought it over. "I have a girlfriend in Henderson I can stay with for a while. Would that make you happy?"

"Exceedingly."

We finished our meal and went down to get the car. Before she went to Henderson, she had graciously offered to drive me to several stores where I picked up a new shirt, sneakers, a wind breaker, phone charger, and a shiny new crowbar.

She shook her head, looking at the weapon. "I don't know about this. He's got a gun you know."

"Too bad for him. Okay, you can let me off here." She had just pulled in front of the Golden Nugget.

"Not so fast cowboy." She leaned over the center console and kissed me. "Thank you, Dr. Cesari. I know this is going to sound ridiculous but—am I ever going to see you again?"

I smiled. "Professionally?"

She chuckled, "I'll take it."

"Go—now, and stay away from me. I'm bad luck." I gave her one more quick kiss and got out of the car. I stood there for a minute and watched her drive away.

I liked her.

Chapter 11

I went up to my room and plugged my phone charger into the wall outlet and rested on the bed thinking things over. Who was Luther and why did I remember him? We will soon find out.

Once my phone charged sufficiently, I turned it on and saw many missed calls and texts from Arnie, Troy and Seymour. In addition, there was a call from Cocoa, who was watching Cleopatra for me back in New York. I called Troy. "Hey big guy. What's the word?"

"Cesari, where the hell have you been? Do you have any idea what they're accusing you of?" He was very upset.

"Go ahead and tell me."

"Murder! They claim that you butchered some prostitute in her room. Even worse, Seymour confirmed that he saw you leave the restaurant with her. Poor guy. He didn't mean to blow you in but they had him by the nuts. They really did. I can't believe any of it." He spoke very fast and was clearly rattled.

I sighed loudly into the phone. So everybody knew. Great. And Seymour was their star witness. My, oh my, how that worm had turned. I said, "Okay, take a deep breath. Look, Troy I know it looks bad but don't judge this book by its cover, all right?"

"All right. I'll keep an open mind. So what really happened?"

"That's the million dollar question. I don't know, but as soon as I figure it out I'll fill you in. In the meanwhile, I could use a little help."

"What kind of help?"

"Just keep your phone on and promise not to tell anyone if and when I call. Okay?"

"Sure. I guess I can do that. They can't put me in jail for that, can they? I mean I can't help it if a murderer calls me."

"No, they can't put you in jail for that. They can put you in jail for being black but not for that."

He chuckled, "Thanks for reminding me."

"One more thing. Are you guys still going to the conference?"

"Hell yeah. That's where I am right now."

I guess that made sense. Whether I'm Jack the Ripper or not wouldn't change our purpose for coming here in the first place. "Okay, I'll stay in touch."

I hung up and let my phone finish charging. I watched the news on TV and saw that they were calling me a person of interest, not necessarily a murderer. That was good. They weren't making that big a deal about it just yet and one station even hinted that it may have been a drug deal gone bad. Another station elaborated on the girl's long history of prostitution and arrest records. Clearly the town wasn't in an uproar over the killing. Right now it seemed that they might just be looking at her as another unfortunate casualty of the sex trade. It was a dark and dangerous business and everyone knew and accepted that fact. Plus, this was Vegas. We wouldn't want to overly frighten the tourists.

I waited for it to get dark before checking out of my room and heading over to *The Fall of Rome* to say hi to Luther. I decided that despite the low key approach to the crime, it wouldn't be smart to stay in any one place for very long. Depending on the level of priority they assigned the case, they could be tracking my credit cards or the FBI may just be waiting for me to show up at my job in Manhattan. Just before leaving, I went to relieve myself in the bathroom. When I flipped on the light, I saw in big red lipstick letters on the mirror *Call Me 702 460 6305*. Maybe. I smiled and sent her a quick text message so she would have my number in case something came up.

I tucked the crowbar up the sleeve of my wind breaker and walked over to the gentlemen's club where it appeared that normalcy had returned. Cars were pulling into the valet parking lot and the legionnaires were back in their positions guarding the front door with their spears. It didn't take them long to get over the tragedy. Money had a way of doing that.

I walked around back and found the ladder to the rooftop. The only risk now was if Frankie's room was occupied. There was only one way to find out so I opened the latch quietly and descended into the dark bathroom. I didn't hear any sounds from the bedroom and opened the door a crack to look. It was dark and I stealthily crept toward the bed. No one there, I turned on the overhead light noting that room service had cleaned the room up pretty well.

It was eight and the place would soon be in full swing. Certainly by ten, all the rooms would be occupied Frankie had told me. The brothel side of the club didn't start slowing down until 2 a.m. or thereabouts. At this hour, Luther may be walking the floor checking on the girls or doing some last minute preparatory work in the restaurant but more than likely would be in his office at the far end of the hall crunching numbers. This was a business and like any other required strict accounting and solid business practices.

The building was really just a long one story motel attached to the restaurant. Lined on either side were the girl's apartments, the hallway dead ended in Luther's headquarters. I had asked about security and Frankie didn't know of any. There were the steroid enhanced legionnaires at the front door and a couple more like them who patrolled around the place. They may or may not be armed, she wasn't sure. Luther carried a pistol of some type but that was it. I was surprised. Four, maybe five gorillas and a cowboy. I didn't think it was going to be that easy.

I stepped into the empty corridor and looked left and then right. A few people to the left where the restaurant was and no one to the right. I made a beeline for Luther's office with the crowbar up my sleeve. Just before reaching it one of the rooms opened and a sexy, scantily clad, Mexican girl came into the hallway directly in front of me. She had long, dark hair and a seductive smile. She spoke with a distinct Texas drawl, "Hey there, pardner. You're a little early for the festivities, aren't ya?"

Shit. She made no attempt to keep her voice down but why would she?

I said, "I came to see Luther about a business proposition."

"You did? Well you're plum out of luck. Luther's down at the Venetian with some of the girls. There's a convention of horny doctors in town and he's hoping to clean up."

I smiled inwardly, thinking about Arnie but outwardly I was disappointed. "I didn't know that."

"Didn't know what; that doctors are horny or that there's a convention in town?"

I liked her. She was kind of funny.

It was just then that her eyes drifted downward, noticing the crowbar sticking out of the windbreaker. She chuckled. "Exactly what kind of business proposition did you have in mind there, Mr. Poncho Villa?"

"It's personal."

She sized me up and my brain raced. She stepped in real close, maybe an inch away, and I could smell her scent and practically feel her nipples. She batted her eyes and said, "He'll be back in about four or five hours. You could wait in my room if you want. The name's Valentina."

Not a bad offer. “Thanks. If you don’t mind I’ll take a raincheck.”

“And what if I do mind?”

“I’m still going to take a raincheck. I have a lot to do.”

She pouted. “You’re no fun at all.”

“Do you think he would mind if I waited for him in his office?”

She smiled even more broadly showing off her full lips and perfect white teeth. “Now why on earth would Luther mind if some dangerous looking gringo with a crowbar waited for him in his office?”

She was killing me. “That wasn’t an answer.”

“And that wasn’t a real question. What you meant to say was would I object to you snooping around Luther’s office? No, I couldn’t care less but you should know that we girl’s don’t take rejection well so keep that in mind the next time you ask one of us for a favor. Go ahead in. He doesn’t keep it locked. I’ll give you ten minutes before I sound the alarm. It would seem too odd if I didn’t notice something amiss with my room right next door.”

“Thanks.” I stepped toward the office.

She said, “If he asks, who shall I say was calling?”

“Just tell him it’s an old friend.”

“Yeah, right. Okay, old friend. You got ten minutes starting now.”

“Thanks.”

“Bye y’all.” She turned and went back into her room.

I stepped into his office and closed the door behind me. It was a nice sized, sparsely adorned, nondescript room with a desk, a couple of chairs and a large file cabinet. A computer monitor sat on the desk with several legal pads, penholder, and a calculator. There was a bathroom and out of curiosity I checked it to see if there was a similar escape route to the roof for him. I remembered Frankie saying something about when the shooting starts. What did that mean? Opening the linen closet, I saw the same metal ladder leading up to the roof. I went back and sat at the desk, turned on the pc, and while it booted up, I went through the drawers but didn't find anything particularly enlightening. The file cabinets were stuffed with papers concerning the business; balance sheets, bills, ledgers, payroll. The usual stuff.

The computer finished booting and I was relieved that there was no password to log on. On the other hand, that probably meant that there wasn't going to be anything interesting to discover. There was an everyday accounting program, some music files, and sticky note memos to himself about appointments and phone calls he needed to make or return. One little yellow sticky note stood out from the rest. It read simply—*Seymour's coming in two weeks.*

Was that my Seymour? Did they know each other? I thought that one over. Seymour did tell me that he had been here before so he might have met Luther. That would make sense, but why the sticky note? Putting that to the side for a moment, I clicked on his web browser and searched his email account but that was a dead end because it was password protected. His web browser history, however, was a gold mine of information.

He had done multiple searches of my name and background history. He was curious about who I was and whether I had a criminal record or not. There were several hits concerning accusations of assault when I was a young adult running with the wrong crowd but those charges were dropped. A few years ago I was mentioned as a possible co-conspirator in a drug ring but again no charges were made. There was no doubt that I had a questionable lifestyle and nefarious associations prior to straightening myself out and going to medical school. In fact, he wasn't able to google this but I had narrowly missed being a casualty of several turf wars in the Bronx, and my best friend, Vito Gianelli, was a local capo in lower Manhattan. We had fought our way out of the streets together, each in his own way, and were now highly successful. Well, this was all very interesting. Luther wanted to know all about me. Unfortunately for him, he was now scheduled to find out.

The next set of threads was followed by queries about Nevada state law concerning rape, in particular, sexual assault of prostitutes. He wanted to know if those cases were taken as seriously as others. In point of fact, it turns out, they were taken even more seriously because in Vegas the sex industry was not only legal but a huge source of tax revenue for local and state government. Even highly questionable cases were dealt with very harshly by the courts. Many civilians felt put out by this.

There was an article about a school teacher who was assaulted on her way home from work, and she was pissed off at what she felt was too light a sentence for her assailant. He got one year in the Nevada state prison and five years' probation. She was quoted in the news as saying that the next time she gets raped she would tell the judge she was a hooker and then maybe she would get justice.

The next series of searches involved the sexual assault of men by women. Did it happen and how? Apparently, it was more common than you might think. The door opened and I looked up. It was Valentina. She had used the time to put on makeup and high heels. Wow!

"Your ten minutes are up, cowboy."

I turned off the computer. "Thanks, let me leave him a quick note."

I grabbed one of the legal pads on his desk and with a sharpie I found in a cup holder wrote, *I'm coming for you, asshole.*

She came over to the desk, looked at the note and rolled her eyes. "Are you *trying* to get me in trouble?"

"You know, when I was growing up if a girl said that, it usually meant you were in too much of a rush to put on a condom."

She chuckled. "Who are you anyway? I mean really."

"Just a wop from the Bronx."

Chapter 12

I took a cab over to the Venetian and arrived shortly before nine, discreetly hiding the crowbar behind some shrubbery off to one side of the entrance. Nevada was an open carry state and I doubted there would be metal detectors inside but that didn't mean you could walk around with a 6 pound metal object without attracting all sorts of unwanted attention. People weren't that stupid—or trusting.

The casino floor was dark, crowded, and noisy. The tables were jammed with men and women happily throwing away their money while they were being plied with free drinks from half-naked cocktail waitresses. The professional girls were everywhere. You just had to recognize them for who they were; clothes just a little too suggestive, heels just a little too high, and they had roving eyes always scanning for fresh meat. They never drank. They sipped. The same glass of wine could last them all night. They were hard at work like anybody else and couldn't afford to lose track of time or money. The waitresses knew who they were as well. You could tell by the way they politely ignored them or gave them simple head nods.

So where was Luther?

The girls needed to have a male presence nearby to make sure guys paid up or didn't get out of control. I went up to the centrally located roulette table, ordered a whiskey from a waitress walking by, and waited to see what would happen as I scanned the room. My cellphone buzzed in my pocket. It was Cocoa.

"Hi Cocoa."

"John, what's going on? It was all over TV."

Shit. Of course it was. I didn't think the incident would make national news but apparently I had underestimated the thirst for gore by twenty-four hour cable stations.

"There's been a misunderstanding, Cocoa. I didn't kill anybody."

"That's not what it looks like."

"I know what it looks like Cocoa. How's Cleo?"

"She's fine. What's going to happen? Police have already been to the apartment and told me in no uncertain terms that I had better let them know when you show up."

"Great. Well, I'm working on it. I don't have time to explain it all right now. I may have to spend a few extra days out here if that's okay with you." As we spoke the waitress returned with my drink, handing it to me. I tipped her and she wandered off.

"Don't worry about Cleo, just take care of yourself. I didn't believe it anyway."

"Thanks."

"Is there anything I can do to help?"

"Just keep your phone charged, all right?"

"I will."

"Bye."

I clicked off just as an attractive girl in a skimpy top and bare midriff holding an unlit cigarette, caught my attention. A piece of glitter dangled from her belly button. She smiled seductively and said, "Hi. Got a light?"

They were like sharks circling in the water. This one was nineteen, maybe twenty years old with sandy brown shoulder length hair, a leather mini skirt, and four inch spikes. I wouldn't risk going to jail for her but she was cute. I gave her my best *okay I'm game* look and smiled back. "I heard smoking is bad for your health."

She chuckled. "So is masturbating in your room alone."

Right to the point and funny, I liked that. Sipping my whiskey, I suppressed the urge to laugh. Some of these girls were a riot. I offered her my hand. "John."

She took it. "Samantha—Samantha Lovecock."

That did it! The whiskey came shooting out my nostrils before I could stop it. Laughing, I said, "I'm sorry."

She smiled graciously and cleared her throat. "Don't do this much I gather?"

"No, almost never. In fact, this could possibly be my first time."

"Then I'm honored. Why don't we grab a seat at the bar and chat things over."

"You mean discuss the terms of engagement?"

"You really don't get out much, do you? Yeah, that's what I mean."

There was a large semi-circular bar off to one side of the room and we sat. I ordered her a white wine and asked, "So what happens now?"

"What happens is that you tell me that you're not an undercover cop and that you're not wearing a wire."

I looked puzzled. "Why?"

"Because prostitution is illegal in Clark County and if you are a cop it's equally against the law to withhold that information."

I didn't know that. "I'm not a cop but I thought prostitution was legal here at least that's the impression one gets."

"All the tourists think that but prostitution is only legal in several of Nevada's counties, not this one. That doesn't mean it doesn't happen. It does big time because most everybody looks the other way or gets paid off. Are you staying here at the Venetian?"

I nodded. Technically, I never checked out. "Yeah."

"Okay, then here's the deal. First off, I'm an escort, not a prostitute, so let's get that straight just in case you are wired. I get paid in cash, not personal check or credit card. It's one hundred dollars up front to *escort* you to your room and another two hundred dollars as soon as I enter. Once we're in if I want to be nice to you that's my decision. You don't touch me unless I say it's okay and you'd better stop when I say so. Don't expect any hugging. I'm not your mother. Okay, let's go over the list of in-room services I provide."

"Hold on a second. Can I ask a question?" I raised my hand like I was in school.

She found this amusing and humored me. "Sure, go ahead."

"A friend of mine came here last year and went to some gentlemen's club down the strip across from the Golden Nugget. From the way he described it, it sounded like a brothel to me. He said it was all legal. What was that all about?"

"Oh, he went to *The Fall of Rome.* We call places like that "dinner and a movie". They're very expensive whorehouses and very difficult to get in to work there. I've been on a waiting list for over a year. It's a cute way of skirting the law. You go there, have an overpriced dinner, and afterward they ask you if you'd like to go to one of the rooms and watch a movie to unwind and digest. They bring you a menu of movies to choose from and next to each movie is a picture of one of the girls that you can choose to keep you company wink wink. Technically, you're not paying for sex but for dinner, and if you want companionship afterward that's your choice. What goes on in the room is strictly between the two of you and no money ever changes hands because it's already included in the price of the meal."

I smiled. "Unbelievable. Why doesn't the law crack down on places like that?"

"I'm not J. Edgar Hoover. How should I know? No one really cares any way. It's all bullshit and it's all good for business. Everybody's getting rich. Besides, who's getting hurt? The girls aren't prisoners. It's the other way around. Every girl I know would love to get a job there. Yeah, except for that asshole Luther who runs the place, it's actually a pretty decent gig. Most guys who can afford to drop a thousand on a meal generally treat you all right. Big tips too. Okay, so let's go through this so there's no misunderstanding."

"One more thing if you don't mind. Do you know that guy Luther? My friend mentioned him to me."

"What is this? Twenty questions? I don't have all night."

I took a fifty dollar bill out of my wallet and slipped it over to her. "I appreciate your time."

She smiled and took it. "Sorry for being cranky. It's just that there are a lot of geeky doctors running around here. It's like shooting fish in a barrel for us."

I chuckled. "I bet. So tell me about Luther."

She looked at me as if a light just went off and her eyes narrowed. "You're not looking for a date are you?"

Busted. So I took a chance. "No, I'm not. I'm looking for Luther."

"Too bad about the date. What did he do?"

"You just said that he's an asshole. Do I need another reason?"

"No, but you may need another fifty."

I reached back into my wallet, fished out another bill, and gave it to her. I needed to get to an ATM machine in a hurry.

She said, "Thanks. Most of the *managers* hang out in the sports area next to the high end poker room. You can't miss it. There's a twenty foot high by hundred foot long TV in the middle of the room."

Managers?

Even the sex industry was politically correct. "What does Luther look like?"

"Well, I only met him once and that was a year ago when I applied to work at the club. I remember him being tall and sunburnt, kind of rough looking. I guess he's not hard on the eyes. He wore a cowboy hat and boots. I'm sure you know the look, but around here that doesn't mean too much. Lots of guys dress like that. He's from the south west and has a drawl. Look, that's all I have. I got to go before the herd starts to thin out. You know what I mean?"

I chuckled. "Fine. No identifying marks, tattoos, or features?"

She stood up to leave. "Not that I know of. Look, it was nice talking to you John. Thanks for the drink and the cash."

"Okay, thanks and good luck."

Hesitating she said, "Well, now that I think about it there might be something. He had a gold tooth if I'm remembering correctly. Not in front but not in back either. Sort of off to one side. But like I said I only met him the one time so I could be wrong."

I watched her slink off into the crowd, took my last five dollars out and tossed it on the counter as a tip. Wading through the room filled to overflowing with revelers, I was jostled, offered free drinks and propositioned at least two more times before I reached the sports area defined by the massive TV she had described. It was after ten and the place was rocking. I noted an ATM by the cashier's counter and withdrew five hundred bucks. By morning everyone would know I was there but I needed the cash. As I turned around, another friendly girl asked me if I had a light. I smiled and apologized but couldn't help wondering how many girls lay in wait by the cash machines like that. Was smoking even allowed on the casino floor? I didn't know.

It was called the Venetian Race and Sports Book and there were a couple of hundred chairs with desks that had laptops facing the massive flat-screen, wall-mounted TV. In addition to the seated patrons, countless others stood milling about, drinking and talking. Here, you could bet on anything and everything related to any sport from curling to competitive eating, but the big four were horse-racing, boxing, football, and basketball. You could even bet on guys betting. There was a madness to all of this that I found inexplicably intoxicating.

The place was packed and smoke-filled. Dozens of sunburnt guys with cowboy hats and boots milled about placing bets, drinking, and shouting at the screen. I casually meandered through the room trying to avoid making too much eye contact. There was some east coast game on that everyone was going nuts over; the Knicks were playing the Heat and not doing too well.

I ordered a Manhattan and took up a positon toward the far end of the room that gave me a clear view of the patrons while attempting to mingle in with the crowd. All eyes focused on the screen and gameplay and I too cheered in rhythm as I scanned for a gold toothed cowboy. Patiently biding my time, I was startled by the sight of Seymour walking into the room. I hadn't expected that and didn't really want to run into him, Arnie, or Troy tonight. I had too much to do and couldn't be sure that the Las Vegas police weren't keeping an eye on them to see if I made contact so I turned away looking at the TV but kept one eye on him. Because of his great size, he wasn't that hard to follow. Oddly enough, he too seemed to be searching for something or someone. There was an open chair here and there and he walked right by them causing me to wonder why he would pass up on the opportunity to settle his bulk down.

There, in a shadowy, secluded corner of the room he arrived at his destination. He leaned over to shake hands with a seated blonde haired guy with sun and wind burnt brawny features and broad muscular shoulders. He sported a braided pony tail. There was a guy sitting next to him who politely got up allowing Seymour to settle in next to his friend deep in conversation. I slowly made my way over two and three steps at a time, stopping to cheer, raising my Manhattan in the air with everyone else, all the time watching Seymour with great curiosity. Was Seymour a gambling man? Was the guy a fellow physician he had met at the conference? Then I remembered the sticky note on Luther's pc screen about Seymour.

I furrowed my brow in thought. Okay, so let's say Seymour met Luther last year when he was out here at the anesthesia conference. Even if he said hi to the guy when we had dinner there, big deal. But why would he be meeting him personally and fairly clandestinely in the Venetian sporting lounge? I was now maybe ten feet away and slightly in front and to the side of them. C'mon , smile asshole. Smile. Suddenly, the room erupted from some action on the screen. The guy next to Seymour jumped out of his seat, beer in hand, hoopin' and hollerin' with the rest. Broadly grinning, a gold tooth gleamed at me and now I knew I had another mystery on my hands. Why was Seymour palling around with a somewhat notorious pimp who has been trying to figure out who I am?

Seymour stood up, shook hands, and left the lounge for places unknown. Several minutes later, Luther picked up his brown cowboy hat placed it on his head, adjusted his lapels, and also strolled out to the casino floor with me following a discreet distance behind. He stopped several times to talk to one of his girls, giving them instructions, and gradually made his way to the exit. Outside, he took a deep breath, lit a cigarette and made a call on his cellphone. He was a solid twenty feet away and I slipped behind him as he strolled back and forth in animated conversation with whomever. I gathered up the crowbar from behind the bush, tucking it back up my windbreaker sleeve.

The front entrance of the Venetian was a madhouse of activity with dozens of cars waiting to be parked and many guests arriving with their luggage or waiting for taxis to take them to their destination of choice. Busy bellmen and parking attendants hustled back and forth earning their keep as I thought through my options. When he was done with his call and cigarette, he would probably return to the casino. This was my best opportunity even if there were a few dozen witnesses. Nevada had fairly lax gun laws and I already knew from Frankie he was packing heat. The real problem was that there might be more than one person armed out here who might want to intervene. What were the chances of pulling off a kidnapping of a large, armed, cowboy in the middle of the crowded Venetian main entrance? Probably not very good. What advantage did I have? It was dark, I had the element of surprise on my side and I had a crowbar. I couldn't count on my good looks, could I? Then I saw my opportunity.

A red convertible Ferrari with the top down came zipping up in front of Luther just as he hung up his phone and tossed the cigarette butt away. His path placed him directly in line with the passenger side of the shiny new car and he stepped close to admire it. The driver was a swarthy looking guy who exuded wealth and confidence. He wore a white turtle neck, sun glasses, and a thick gold chain. He got out of his car leaving the engine running and the keys inside while he waited impatiently for one of the busy attendants. I quickly marched up behind Luther and shoved the crowbar into his back.

"If you want to live, don't move or turn around. I'll put a hole in you the size of a melon. Nod, if you understand."

He stiffened and nodded. "Take it easy friend. I got plenty of money. Let's be reasonable. This is not the smartest stickup if you get my drift." He was referring to all the witnesses, none of whom were paying the slightest attention to us.

I patted him down quickly and in the small of his back under his two-toned suede jacket found a holstered .45 caliber Heckler and Koch semiautomatic with a ten round clip which I relieved him of. The HK45 was an expensive handgun and probably cost more than a thousand dollars new. Not a bad piece for a pimp. We were just a few feet from the Ferrari and I shoved him roughly toward it. I growled, "Get in now, asshole."

The owner registered surprise then outrage as Luther opened the passenger door and sat down. I slammed the door closed and brought the butt of the HK down hard on the top of his head, mashing his cowboy hat. He slumped forward unconscious. The guy in the turtleneck froze at the unexpected violence and gaped at me slack-jawed waiting for my next move. I ran around quickly to the driver's side .45 in full view and waved him away with it. He took two steps back but was otherwise paralyzed with fear and confusion. I let myself in, shifted into drive, and let the engine roar while peeling out of the driveway. The whole thing took less than a minute.

I let her rip down Las Vegas Boulevard eventually picking up Interstate 15 heading out to the north side of town and eventually the desert. After an hour, I was safely away from the city and approaching the Utah border. At this point, I pulled off the road and drove about a mile into the desert. It was a moonless night and about sixty-five degrees. Once I cut the engine, it became pitch black and suddenly the sounds of the desert pulsed ominously close. In the dark I could barely even see Luther slumped over next to me. I decided I couldn't work like this so I started the car and turned the head-lights on. Luther's face was pressing against the dash in what had to be a very uncomfortable position. I shook him vigorously but he didn't rouse. He was breathing and had a strong pulse. He needed more time or more stimulation.

I got out of the car, went over to his side, and dragged him out onto the desert floor ten feet in front of the Ferrari. He groaned when he hit the ground but still didn't wake. The car lights were blinding and I covered my eyes as I went to retrieve the crowbar. When I returned, I stood in front of the vehicle, legs spread, arms down, crowbar gripped firmly in my right hand, and waited, but not for long. In a minute or so, he started to rouse. Lying in front of me on his back several feet away, he began coughing weakly and eventually lifted his head to look around, shielding his eyes from the car lights.

I called out, “Luther, wake up.”

He responded in a confused voice, “What the fuck is going on?”

“That’s what I want to know, Luther.”

His sensorium was clearing and he raised himself to a sitting position as he grew stronger. He leaned back facing me supported by his hands. From his vantage point I must have seemed like a ghostly apparition silhouetted by the bright lights of the Ferrari. He must have seen the crowbar and said apprehensively, “Look, pardner, I don’t know what’s ailing you, but I’m sure we can work it out.”

“Maybe, but we need to clarify a few things first. Okay pardner?”

“Sho’ thing. It’s pretty plain I ain’t going nowhere.”

I walked over to his right side and looked down at him. He watched me with curiosity and suddenly I lifted my foot and stomped down hard on his hand snapping several bones. He clutched his hand and screamed in pain. “What the fuck, cowboy? That was uncalled for.”

“Yeah, I know, but now you’re completely awake and I just wanted to make sure that we had a clear understanding of my view on your pain situation. So do we have a clear understanding?”

He hissed, “Yes.”

“Okay, let’s start with Jenny. Remember her? She was murdered last night at your club, *The Fall of Rome*. Tell me everything you know.”

“There’s not much to tell. Some maniac doctor from New York was in town for a convention, comes to the club, meets Jenny, and they have a party in her room. The next thing is she’s dead and he’s gone. That’s all anybody knows.”

"So you think he murdered her?"

"What else am I supposed to think? The guy's loco."

I placed the curved end of the crowbar under his chin and tilted his head back a little daring him to grab it with his good hand. He knew better. Guys like him were survivors, not fighters. Slapping girls around in their under garments was more his speed. I said angrily, "You expect me to believe that pile of horse shit? Try again."

"Why don't you believe it? Everybody else does."

"Not everybody, asshole."

All of a sudden, his head clearing and eyes adjusting he looked at me carefully and recognition crept into his features. "Aw fuck. You're him, ain't ya?"

"Aw fuck is right Luther. I'm him and I'm not happy."

"Are you gonna kill me cowboy? Because if you are you need to know something first."

"Oh yeah, and what would that be?"

"The people I work for ain't never gonna let you get away with killing Jenny. I know you're upset but the reality is that you really did kill Jenny."

Without warning, I kicked him in the side. After he stopped groaning I said. "Why would I kill Jenny? I didn't even know her."

"Hombre, you were all liquored and drugged up. How the fuck do you know what you may or may not have done? The coroner already said that there's a high probability you had sex with her and he's thinking from the look of things it may not have been entirely consensual."

"If she was a hooker, how could it not have been consensual?"

"Too much trauma, dude. That's what the forensics guys are saying. It may have started out consensual but looks like it ended bad. Maybe you got out of hand and she said enough is enough. It don't matter what you think anyway. They're just waiting for the DNA report. When it comes back, boy you gonna be fucked every which way and you haven't even heard the best part."

I didn't like this logic. It was too close to being possible. "Why did you do a google search of my name two weeks before I even came to town?"

He was quiet. That one took him by surprise but he knew better than to lie. "Your pal Seymour called ahead. Said he had a VIP friend he was bringing to town, and wanted to arrange a special night for him. I was curious because I thought maybe you were a senator or somebody real important."

Fuck if that didn't make sense too, but why would Seymour do that? I took a deep breath and let it out. "Guess you were disappointed?"

"I didn't care one way or the other. Seymour always pays well. I had no idea you were a homicidal maniac."

"Say that again and I'll break the other hand."

"What do you want me to tell you, amigo? You went to the room with her and an hour later she's as dead as Santa Anna and you're gone with the wind."

"How do I know you didn't kill her just to set me up?"

"Why the fuck would I want to set you up? Until that night I didn't know you from a hole in the wall. Besides, if you knew who Jenny was you would know for a fact I wouldn't harm a hair on her head."

This piqued my curiosity. "That's twice you said something mysterious about her. Maybe you haven't figured it out yet but I'm not a patient man. So who was she?"

"Her full name was Jennifer Martens. Does that ring a bell, Mandingo?"

"No, it does not. Why should it?"

"She's Carmine Buonarroti's girlfriend. Please tell me you know who he is."

"Afraid not, Luther. Am I supposed to be scared?"

"If you had any brains you would. He's the head man on the strip for the guineas back east and Jenny was his favorite whore."

"Seems to me like you're the one who ought to be worried, Luther."

"Believe me I am. The DNA test will be back in a day or two and if it matches yours and they catch you then I'll definitely be off the hook—maybe."

"How can they match my DNA if they haven't caught me?"

"You're in the data base, asshole. Don't you even know that?"

Fuck, I'd forgotten. I was picked up for questioning in a homicide several years ago and they took samples from me. I was cleared but they don't just throw out DNA once they got it.

"So what is it with you and Seymour anyway? I saw you and him together tonight at the Venetian."

"He just wanted to know what was going on or if there was a chance anyone else could have done it. He was just concerned, is all."

"He was concerned? I thought he was the one who ID'd me to the cops?"

"He did but what choice did he have? You didn't expect him to commit perjury, did you?"

Fair enough. "You said Seymour always pays well. That sounds like you know him pretty well. I didn't get that impression talking to Seymour."

"C'mon you don't expect him to brag about knowing someone like me."

Touché.

I took a few steps toward the Ferrari and turned to face him same as before, legs apart, arms and crowbar at my side.

I said, "Stand up."

He stood slowly, facing me. We were just a few feet apart. He was about six feet two inches tall, 230 pounds, and looked to be in decent shape. A little taller and heavier than I was but he had a broken hand and I was pissed. He covered his eyes from the car lights and squinted in my direction.

He said, “So now what, hombre? We gonna dance?”

“So now we talk about what you did to Francesca.”

He looked surprised. “Francesca? Oh c’mon. She’s just a whore…” He didn’t have a chance to finish. His eyes went wide and he raised his arms too late to ward off the incoming blow from the crowbar.

Chapter 13

Luther was in pretty bad shape when I rolled him out of the car onto the street in front of a veterinary clinic at 4:00 a.m. in the town of Mesquite as I headed back to Vegas. He was never going to beat anyone ever again and would be lucky if he didn't spend the rest of his life sipping his meals through a straw. I was still pretty mad about what he did to Francesca and frustrated about what was going on. I was hoping that he would confess to killing Jenny but he swore right until he lost consciousness that he didn't and for some reason I believed him. He also swore that as far as he knew I was the last person in the room with her. So if I wasn't set up then who called the police in the first place? This is the part that made me the most upset. He said that Jenny had called the police and told them I was out of control and getting violent.

This wasn't looking good for team Cesari. Thinking things over, I stopped at an all-night Walmart Supercenter and purchased a duffel bag, throw away razor, and other personal effects before abandoning the Ferrari somewhere on the strip. I left the keys in plain view and figured it wouldn't be long before the car disappeared again. There was a big dent on the passenger side door from an errant blow with the crowbar but I doubted that would deter any would be car thief. I felt a little bad for the owner but you know what—fuck him and the one percenter horse he rode into town on.

Storing the crowbar and Luther's .45 in the duffel bag, I checked into an inexpensive motel to get some sleep. I was still a wanted man with even more questions now than before. More pressing at the moment, however, is that I was in danger of passing out from exhaustion. I counted my cash, stripped, and passed out before my head even hit the pillow.

At noon I woke ravenous and sore from the night's extracurricular activities. I showered, shaved, and spent an unusually long time brushing, flossing, and gargling as I considered the possibility that I may have actually murdered Jenny and couldn't remember it. No matter how many permutations of that night's events replayed in my mind none of them ended with me slicing up a hooker. I simply couldn't accept that. There had to be some other explanation. Could I be violent? Yes, obviously, but never gratuitously and never could I hurt a girl except maybe in self-defense. I was old-fashioned like that. Nothing made the hairs on the back of my neck stand up more than when I heard about girls getting hurt by guys. I could practically feel my blood pressure rise when I watched the news about such things and always figured it was some sort of primitive instinct of mine which I couldn't control.

As I dressed, Arnie called. "Cesari, how are you holding up?"

"Hanging in there Arnie. How's the conference?"

"So far so good. A lot of windbags but every now and then somebody says something useful. I'm sitting next to Troy. He says hi."

"Say hi back."

"I will. So what's the plan? Are you going to turn yourself in or just be a fugitive for the rest of your life?"

"I'm working on it Arnie. I don't have a lot to go on. Where's Seymour?"

"He's around. He didn't sit with us today. Why?"

"I just wanted to ask him something. No biggie. I have his number."

"I don't suppose you're going to tell me where you are."

"Can't do that, Arnie."

"I figured."

"What am I going to tell people?"

"Tell them the truth."

"Which is…?"

"That you don't know anything. Got to go now, I'm starving."

There was a Golden Corral restaurant across the street from my motel and I went there to eat. The bored waitress sat me in a booth and I ordered pancakes with extra maple syrup and a side of sausage. An old couple sat next to me at a table. They were in their eighties, silver haired, and arthritic. She used a cane. Her name was Harriet and he was Saul. Unfortunately, we were too close for comfort and apparently their hearing aids weren't properly fitted or the batteries had died. The waitress was trying to take their order.

Harriet asked, "How's the pastrami?"

The waitress replied. "It's very good."

Saul said, "Harriet, you hate salami."

Harriet said, "Be quiet, Saul, I can't hear the girl. Is the pastrami lean? I won't eat it if it's not lean."

Saul said, "She's not mean. Look at her. She's an angel."

"Saul, be quiet and let her speak."

The waitress was fifty, overweight, and missing a tooth. She replied, "Oh, it's lean, honey. I promise."

"Then I'll take it."

The waitress jotted down the order on a pad and turned to Saul. "And what would you like?"

"To be young again, sweetheart."

Harriet said, "Saul, stop it. She's out of your league. Now order your lunch."

He said, "I'll have the tuna salad but I don't like kale. Take the kale out or I won't eat it."

Harriet said, "Saul, stop it. They don't serve the tail with tuna salad. I know you can't hear but can't you read either?"

He shouted across the table. "What?"

Harriet turned to the waitress exasperated. "Honestly, I don't know what I'm going to do with him."

My food came and I wolfed it down. I needed to have a sit down with Seymour. I wanted a blow by blow, minute by minute account of that night. I could go to the conference and try to find him but then I would have to register and wear my ID badge in a plain sight in front of ten thousand physicians and hospital personnel who may or may not have been following the story. Not good. I also needed some wheels and made it my high priority to find a car rental place. But I would have to submit all sorts of ID which might trigger all sorts of alarms even more so than the use of my credit cards. I couldn't just walk in with a sack of cash and demand a car or could I? On the other hand, right now I was a just a person of interest. There was no proof of anything yet, so maybe there wouldn't be any of those automatic triggers I was worried about.

I paid my bill and left a nice tip. Outside I hailed a taxi to the Venetian and called Seymour as we drove. "Hey Seymour."

"Cesari, where are you?"

"Looking for you, Seymour. I need to go over a few things from the other night. Let's meet somewhere and talk."

"I can't right now. I'm in a small group break-out session on hospital reimbursement strategies. Arnie told me to take notes."

"Fine. When's it end?"

"Not 'til five."

I looked at my watch. It was just after two. "Fine. Meet me in the bar at Caesar's when you're done. Be there at six and wait for me if I'm late. Don't tell anybody, okay?"

"Caesars at six. Got it."

****

Seymour hung up his phone and his eyes narrowed. Fucking Cesari. How he got out of that motel room was beyond his ability to understand. He had been given enough roofies to knock out a horse. The Viagra alone should have sent him running to an emergency room from side effects.

He now stood at the main entrance to the Mesa View Regional Hospital in Mesquite. Apparently, Luther had been in some type of accident and was in the intensive care unit. No one knew what happened as he had been left on the street unconscious a few miles from here, possibly the victim of a hit and run. The doctors rummaged through his stuff and called everyone on his cellphone's contact list. Everyone they called denied knowing him and had no idea why their names were in his phone book. Everyone but Seymour. He was suspicious. This was too coincidental for him to ignore. Something had happened and it had to be bad. He felt it deep inside. A hospital employee gave him directions to the ICU on the second floor and the nurse there pointed him toward Luther's room where he found a middle-aged physician in a white lab coat caring for him.

God, Luther looked awful, like he had been hit by a truck. His head and hands were bandaged and both eyes were purple and swollen shut. A tube ran out of his nose draining green liquid into a nearby canister and an oxygen mask covered his face. Multiple intravenous lines poured antibiotics and pain medication into him and a bag collecting his urine hung off the side of the bed. The bag had blood in it. He was unconscious.

The doctor turned to him extending his hand. "Hello, I'm Dr. Willower, the staff intensivist."

"Hello, Dr. Willower. I'm Seymour. Luther's friend. We spoke on the phone."

"Ah, yes. Thank you for coming. He doesn't seem to have any family and out of the hundred or so contacts in his phone only you and one other even admitted to knowing him. The other one is also on the way."

"No problem, Doctor. So what happened?"

"We don't know. He's got multiple broken bones and quite a few internal injuries as well. The CT scan demonstrated a small laceration of his liver, a splenic hematoma, and moderate contusions of both kidneys. We're guessing he was hit by a car or truck. The only thing that isn't making sense are his hand injuries."

"And why is that?"

"Here, let me show you." There was a computer monitor in the room and he pulled up the x-rays of Luther's hands. Seymour approached closer and held his breath at the sight. He hadn't let on that he was a physician and never gave the doctor his last name. It didn't matter; you didn't have to be a trained physician to recognize the severity of the injury.

Dr. Willower said, "Well, what we're looking at is extremely unusual for a motor vehicle accident. One or two broken bones maybe, but every finger and every bone from his wrist down has been systematically broken almost as if someone had held his arm and smashed him repeatedly with a hammer. It's peculiar enough to have happened in one hand but extraordinary that it happened in identical fashion in both."

This wasn't good, Seymour thought, but maybe it had nothing to do with him or the Cesari fiasco as he was now calling it in his mind. Luther was an unmitigated asshole. Maybe it had finally caught up with him. "I see what you're saying Dr. Willower. So have the police been notified?"

"Of course and they'll probably want to speak to you."

"But I don't know anything. I only met Luther on one or two occasions at the restaurant he manages. We exchanged numbers. That's it."

"Well, that's already more than anyone else knows. I gave your number to the sheriff's office. I'm sure they'll appreciate your cooperation. If there's anything else you can tell us we'd also be very grateful. He'll be going to surgery in a couple of hours to repair his hands and legs."

"Legs?"

"Broken, both of them. Well, I have other patients to tend to. Sorry about your friend, Seymour."

Seymour nodded as the doctor walked away. He studied Luther carefully. Who could have done this and what was Luther doing way out here in nowhere anyway? When he spoke to him last night in the casino everything seemed under control. It's true Cesari was still on the loose, but he didn't know anything. How could he? Half the police in the state were looking for him anyway. Besides, would he be capable of something like this? For God's sake, Luther was a tough guy. He suddenly remembered the rumors about Cesari's mob connections that ran rampant around St. Matt's.

He was beginning to get a really bad feeling in the pit of his stomach. What if Cesari was the one who beat Luther and Luther squealed like a rat? Was that why Cesari wanted to meet him later? Perhaps to do this to him too? But if Luther talked then why would Cesari have let him live? That wouldn't make sense unless this was a warning; a warning to him, Seymour, that much worse was coming his way. Don't overreact, he told himself. Luther may have simply stepped in front of a bus or an old enemy which begged the question: If Luther hadn't already talked, might he do so at a later date?

Seymour looked around the room and spotted a video camera in one of the corners of the ceiling. Damn. All modern ICU's had live video feeds to the nursing stations. Too bad. It would have been easy to tidy up the Luther issue. He'd have to think it through a little bit more, but that was okay because Luther wasn't going anywhere for a long time from the look of him.

Lost in thought Seymour hadn't noticed the three men who had entered the room behind him. When he did, he almost jumped from surprise as he found them staring at him. One was average height and build with dark clean shaven features and jet black hair. He looked mean and was obviously the boss. The other two were gargantuan in stature, easily six foot five inches tall and three hundred or more pounds each. They stood slightly behind the mean looking one. They all wore dark suits and ties. The room felt very crowded now and extremely uncomfortable as the newcomers continued to stare at him.

Seymour said, "Hi."

The one in charge spoke slowly in a deep, guttural, and menacing voice. "Who are you, fat man?"

Seymour felt his cheeks flush and he gulped. He knew danger when he saw it and this was it. "I'm Seymour."

"I'm going to say it one more time, tubby. Who are you and what are you doing here?"

"I'm—I'm a friend of Luther's, sort of. My name was in his phone book and the doctor called me. I knew Luther from the club. We're not really pals or anything and I don't know what happened here. They didn't know who to call and I just thought I'd help out if could." Seymour thought about asking him who *he* was but wisely kept his mouth shut.

After an uncomfortable silence Seymour cleared his throat. "Well, I was just on my way out so if you'll excuse me."

The man hissed. "Sit down and shut up, friend of Luther."

He then turned to one of his men. “Curly, close the door. I want to talk to Jabba the Hut in private.”

“Sure thing, Carmine.”

Chapter 14

I bought a pair of cheap sunglasses and a black cap and sat in the lounge at Caesar's palace about a hundred feet from the dimly lit bar sipping club soda. For effect, I puffed on a Tiparillo and paged through a *USA Today* waiting for Seymour who was now officially late and not answering his phone. I figured I'd let him settle down at the bar and get a drink while I scanned for a police tail. They usually stuck out like beacons in the night. Most law enforcement were not very good at clandestine surveillance and I suspected it was mostly because they didn't have anything on the line. It's not like their lives were in danger if they were spotted.

A full thirty minutes late, Seymour waddled into the bar and wiggled his way onto a leather swivel stool facing away from me. He ordered a drink and I waited patiently. I had told him not to look around for me and to simply sip his drink. I would show up before he finished his first round. After ten minutes, I decided the coast was clear and stood up to approach the bar. There were mirrors everywhere in the lounge, wall mirrors, ceiling mirrors, a mirror behind the bar, and as I approached Seymour directly from behind I noticed in the mirror his eyes darting furtively right and left.

I paused, still about thirty feet away, leaned against a pole and unfolded the newspaper, taking a puff from the Tiparillo.

Rather than look with him, I simply watched through the triangulation of the mirrors. There, on either end of the room and away from the bar were two very large men in suits just standing and watching Seymour. Who were they? They didn't look like cops and they certainly were not trying very hard to stay out of sight although you couldn't really see them from the lounge area without the help of the mirrors. I didn't like it and walked quickly towards an exit and out of sight but with a clear view of the bar and at least one of the guys in the mirror.

I called Seymour who answered this time. "Cesari, where are you?"

"Sorry Seymour, but I'm running a little late. Everything okay?"

"Yeah, when are you going to get here?"

"Hang in there, Seymour, I need at least another half hour to tidy up what I'm doing."

"What exactly are you doing?"

"Can't tell you, Seymour. Just be patient and don't go anywhere. Thirty minutes tops, all right?"

I hung up the phone and watched carefully. The place was pretty crowded and it was easy to get lost in the shuffle but Seymour's large size gave me a distinct advantage in this regard. So when he stood up from the bar stool and navigated his way towards the guy visible to me in the mirror it was easy to follow. In the mirror I watched as he explained to the guy that I was going to be late. Fuck, so this was a trap, but who were these guys? I'd swear on a stack of bibles they weren't law enforcement.

I let Seymour reseat himself at the bar before I took off into the night unnoticed. I needed to lay low for a while or maybe even get out of town until things blew over but that meant I couldn't return to work either. I paid cash for the motel room so I should be okay there for at least another night. I had kept on the move so even if the police were tracking my card or cellphone all they could tell was that I was somewhere in Clark County, Nevada, which they already knew. They weren't splashing my face all over the news anymore so that was good. This was Vegas, a very seedy city in a very dangerous country. Shit happened all over the place and people didn't have the patience or the time to dwell on a murdered hooker. Most average people would of course be horrified by the crime but deep down would feel it was her own fault because of the life she led. There were already three other murders since hers to distract them.

I took a cab back to the motel and lying on the bed called Frankie. "Hey there."

"John, you called."

Why did women always say that? Of course I called. We were on the phone weren't we? I didn't understand women sometimes in this regard. They tended to use a lot of unnecessary or seemingly redundant words. "I was thinking about you. How are you feeling?"

"Much better. The swelling in my eye has gone way down and I can see out of it again. The Motrin and ice packs are helping but I'm still quite sore all over."

"I'll bet."

"And how are you? I haven't seen anything new on the news."

"No news is good news, I suppose. I haven't really figured it out yet. I did run into Luther by the way. He told me to tell you he was sorry."

"Yeah, I bet. Did you really talk to him?"

I thought about that. Talk to him, talk at him, interrogate him, hit him with a crowbar. "Yeah, we had a chat."

"Do I want to know details?"

"No. How's Henderson?"

"It's nice. My friend said I could stay as long as I like. She used to be in the business and knows how it is sometimes. Her home is a two bedroom ranch in a pleasant development. She's into modeling now and just left for a shoot in L.A. She'll be back in a couple of days. You could come and visit if you want. I know she wouldn't mind."

I thought about that. Maybe not such a bad idea and might be better than motel hopping. "You're alone?"

"Yes." I didn't like that. Luther was gone but she was still vulnerable. There might be someone else at *The Fall of Rome* who might not have taken kindly to her just running off especially since everyone there knew she had helped me. Would they know how to find her?

I asked, "How far is Henderson?"

"Half an hour, forty minutes tops. There's a pool." I smiled and could sense the excitement growing in her voice.

"What's the address? I'll be there in an hour."

I checked out of the motel and caught a cab, giving the driver the directions. I didn't have much; a duffel bag with a crowbar, Luther's .45, a tooth brush, couple of pairs of socks, and some clean underwear. You couldn't travel lighter than that.

By 10 p.m., I was knocking on the front door hoping I had the right house. She answered wearing shorts, sandals, and a light colored top. Her eye and lips were definitely looking better. Now it just looked like she went through a windshield.

"Hi."

She opened the door wide saying, "Come on in."

It was a nice home, neatly decorated and immaculately clean. I got right to it. "I get the sofa. It looks very comfortable." It did too. Large and oversized with big soft looking cushions, it was very inviting. Plus there was a large flat screen TV opposite it.

She smiled coyly and shrugged. "We can sleep there if you want. I think we can both fit."

I chuckled getting the message. "Thanks, but that's not why I came here."

"No, then why'd you come?"

"I needed a place to lay low for a couple of days. There are just too many people looking for me."

She nodded her head. "Well, at least you're honest."

I hesitated. "Not completely. I—I also didn't think you should be alone right now." I don't know why but I felt a little embarrassed saying that. For God's sake Cesari, get a grip. She works in a brothel. There's nothing you can say to her that could possibly surprise her.

That brought a huge smile to her face and she stepped in a little closer. "I know. I could tell in your voice when you called. You were worried about me."

We stood there looking at each other. I didn't know what to say. She said, "So?"

"So—what?"

"So, aren't you going to kiss me?"

Unbelievably, at that very moment in my mind's eye I conjured up the image of that scene from *The Little Mermaid* when Ariel was in the boat with the prince and Sebastian the crab sang *Kiss the Girl* in the background. I smiled and leaned down gently kissing her on her puffy, bruised lips. I was too gentle and she wrapped her arms around my neck pulling me down and holding me tightly, pressing her lips into mine.

When she came up for air she said, "Now that was a proper kiss. Are you hungry?"

"Hmm, is that a trick question?'

"No, there's wine and cheese. I'll bring it in here and we can talk or watch TV or whatever."

"That would be fine."

She went into the kitchen and as I sat on the couch my cellphone went off again. It was getting quite the workout lately. It was Seymour. I powered it off and took the battery out. It was time to stop taking chances on being traced. I'd call him and Arnie later from Frankie's phone and maybe tomorrow go to a drugstore or Walmart to pick up a throw away phone with pre-paid minutes. Frankie came back into the room with a cheese board, a bottle of inexpensive Chianti and a couple of glasses, placing them on top of the glass coffee table in front of us. On the board were an imported brie and some crackers. I uncorked the bottle and filled our glasses. Frankie snuggled up next to me on the sofa tucking her legs underneath, sipping her wine.

She said, "Thanks."

I spread some brie on a cracker. "For what?"

"For caring."

I looked at her for a few seconds. "So where are you from, originally?"

"A small town in Connecticut called Ridgefield. It's just over the New York border. What about you?"

"I'm from the Bronx."

"Do you have family?" I thought that was a reasonable question.

"Are you going to give me the third degree? You know—how'd a nice girl like you get into this business? I don't know why so many guys are obsessed with that."

"No, I wasn't unless you want me to. I was just talking. It's none of my business. I get that. Besides, statistics show that it's usually one of three things anyway."

She found this very amusing. "Please go on."

"C'mon. Really?"

"Sure."

"Okay, so the first reason is simple economics. You came out west to get into show business. You're beautiful and talented, maybe took dance lessons, but when you went looking for work you found yourself in line behind a thousand other beautiful and talented girls. You took what you thought was going to be a temporary job as a waitress but it was boring and didn't pay much. The weeks rolled into months. You met some guy at a party who told you that with your looks you could be doing much better at least for a short time until something opened up at one of the casinos. Am I getting warm?"

"I'm listening."

"You start dancing, then maybe stripping but even these jobs are fiercely competitive and then someone asks why are you wasting your talents making peanuts. Your rent's high and you're frustrated, so you figure why not? The second reason is drugs. It happens all the time. You come to Vegas with high expectations. You're pretty and get invited to all sorts of fun parties with all sorts of fun guys. You get hooked and have no way to support what has now become an expensive lifestyle. You've given up on the dream of becoming a star and all you care about is your next fix. How am I doing?"

She got very serious all of a sudden and when I didn't continue she said, "That's only two reasons. You said there were three."

I shrugged and shoved a cracker in my mouth. "We don't need to do the last one. Two's good enough."

She held her wine in one hand and pushed me with the other. "I want to hear it."

"It's just psycho-babble."

"So psycho-babble me."

"Okay, the third reason is that you're from a broken home, with a dysfunctional, probably abusive relationship with some male figure that led to a loss of self-esteem. With each sexual encounter, you hope to restore your trust in men that was lost at an early age but ultimately the encounters only serve to further convince you what scumbags men really are and how worthless you really feel deep inside."

She didn't look very happy and said sarcastically, "Wow, you're a regular Sigmund Freud. Maybe I just like sex?"

"I'm sure you do but that's not why you sell your body. Girls your age do what you're doing because they need food, drugs, or psychological rehabilitation. Those are the choices."

She stared at me silently and I regretted my candor. After a few seconds, she placed her wine glass down on the table top and stood up. Her lips quivered as she said, "I'm going to bed. I'll see you in the morning."

She turned around and walked toward one of the bedrooms. I said, "Frankie….?"

She ran the last few feet and closed the door behind her. Fucking Cesari, couldn't just keep your mouth shut. Always got to prove how smart you are. Less is more, asshole. Now what? This was classic. Do I follow, trying to smooth things over, or do I let her stew in her own juices? She's probably crying.

I took a deep breath and let it out. I never met a girl or woman, of any age, color, or religion that wanted to be left alone to stew in her own juices. Great, I was going to spend the rest of the night apologizing to a hooker because I was well read. I put my wine glass down and went to the bedroom. Without knocking I let myself in and saw her lying on her side facing away curled in a ball hugging a pillow. It was a nice room with a queen-sized bed, pretty curtains on the windows and a small TV on a credenza at the foot. I spotted the remote on the night table, picked it up, clicked on the set and lay down next to her.

Having been in these situations before, I knew that I needed to proceed with great care. I approached all crying women the way I approached cats—very cautiously as if they might lash out at you suddenly with their claws. She turned toward me puzzled by the sound of the television. Her eyes were red and tearful.

She asked, "What are you doing?"

"Watching TV."

"Watching TV?"

"Yes, watching TV."

"I wanted to be left alone."

"Then you should have locked the door."

"Go away."

"I can't. I'm in the middle of this show."

She sat up now, trying to decide whether anger was the appropriate response or not. "That wasn't very nice what you said back there."

I turned the TV off. Okay, now we were ready to rumble. "I know and I'm sorry. I didn't mean to be so insensitive."

Using a tissue from a box on the night table, she blew her nose and sniffled. "Well you were."

"Please forgive me," I said softly.

She hesitated. "I do."

Very sincerely I added. "That makes me very happy. How about we go back and finish the wine and maybe watch a movie?"

"Fine, but we're sleeping in here, not on the couch."

Chapter 15

Seymour's eyes darted furtively around the room, his brain racing for a way out. He had been playing it cool but this guy, Carmine, was a like a dog with a bone. It was a stroke of colossal bad luck to have run into him at Luther's bedside and now he couldn't get rid of him despite having put him on Cesari's scent. Why didn't Cesari show up at Caesar's? Did he get suspicious? Anyway, after Cesari's no show, Carmine made them regroup at *The Fall of Rome* and now here they were sitting in Luther's office at fucking midnight interviewing hookers.

How on earth was he supposed to know that Jenny was Carmine's girlfriend? Carmine wanted blood and wasn't going to settle for anything less than the scalps of everyone involved and right now Seymour was involved with only one possible escape route; to cough up Cesari.

Carmine had taken Luther's cellphone and after dialing Cesari for the third time with no answer, he threw it into the trash can nearby. In a low rumbling voice he said, "Your friend's not answering his phone."

Seymour said, "I don't have an explanation for that. He said he was tied up with something but he didn't say what."

"Unless maybe you tipped him off?"

"Why would I do that, Mr. Carmine? He's obviously a deranged murderer. I want him caught as much as you do and like I already told you we're not really friends. We work together and we're here at a medical conference. I hardly know him."

"You keep saying that; that you hardly know him. That's like the third or fourth time. It makes me wonder why. I'm also wondering why a doctor like you would be friends enough with that piece of garbage, Luther, that you would go visit him in the hospital."

"I already explained that."

"Yeah, so you did. You just wanted to be helpful. That was nice of you."

Seymour didn't take the bait and remained quiet as Carmine studied him. Carmine finally said, "You sweat a lot. Are you nervous?"

"I have hyperhidrosis. It's a medical condition. There's not much I can do for it. I've tried various medications and no, I'm not nervous at all."

"You're not nervous?"

"No, I'm not."

Carmine smiled and looked at one of his goons standing off to one side and then back at Seymour. "Well, that's funny because you don't look stupid. Are you stupid?"

"I didn't do anything wrong, Mr. Carmine, and I want to help you."

"Hmm, I beg to differ about whether you did anything wrong. You brought this asshole to my club. I'd say that qualifies as doing something wrong."

Seymour gulped. "And I'm sorry about that but I had no way of knowing that he was homicidal. I'm truly sorry."

Carmine said, "Curly bring the next girl in. It's getting late."

Curly stepped past Seymour and opened the door, signaling for someone to come into the room. On cue, a petite, gorgeous, Mexican girl with long dark hair entered and took a seat next to Seymour.

"Hi Valentina, how are you?" Carmine asked politely in a non-threatening tone.

She wasn't buying it and looked around the room at the cast of players, pretending not to be alarmed but she was. "I'm fine, Carmine."

He nodded. "I'm a little upset Valentina. I'm not going to pretend otherwise. I want you to tell me again about this guy, Cesari, and why you didn't tell anybody you saw him here."

"I'm sorry Carmine. I wasn't here the night Jenny was murdered. I heard about it of course but didn't see the news so I didn't recognize him when he came back. He said he was a friend of Luther's and I took it at face value. He certainly didn't act like he had just murdered someone. I told him Luther wasn't here and I thought he left. I was busy getting ready for the night and didn't pay too much attention. Later, I saw his face on TV, and well, you know the rest. I'm sorry."

Carmine rubbed his chin. He had strong masculine features and a broad nose. He looked as if he had taken a few punches in his day. Maybe thirty years old, muscular and clean shaven, he acted with an air of authority. "So, you didn't know he had come into this office even though your room is only ten feet away?" He held up the legal pad where Cesari had written *I'm coming for you, asshole* for her to see.

"No, I swear it, Carmine. When I told him Luther wasn't here, he turned around and walked away and I never saw him again."

Carmine thought that over trying to decide if that sounded reasonable. "Fine, but what about Francesca? Why would she help this guy? They got something going on?"

"I don't know. She never mentioned him if they did. As far as I know she wasn't seeing anyone right now."

Carmine strummed his fingers on Luther's desk staring her down. Calmly he asked, "So, where might she be now? She's not answering her phone and she's not in her apartment."

"I don't know. Luther hurt her pretty bad."

"Yeah, that's what everyone says, but she deserved it for helping that prick get away. You know what else everyone says?"

Valentina shook her head and was clearly becoming uneasy. "No, Carmine. What?"

"That you and Francesca are really good friends. The kind of friends that might call each other when they were in trouble or upset."

"I swear it Carmine; I haven't heard from her and I don't know where she is."

"That's what we're going to find out, Valentina. That's what we're going to find out."

Chapter 16

Rays of morning light splashing through a window woke us up early. I pushed away tangles of Francesca's long brown hair in my face and gently kissed her. She lay on top of me on the sofa and we were both fully clothed. On the coffee table sat three empty bottles of wine and a marijuana bowl, the scent of weed still strong in the air eclipsed only by the nearness of her raw sexuality. Apparently, we had quite the night. We talked, got buzzed, and watched *Casablanca* with Humphrey Bogart and Ingrid Bergman. She was a whole lot of fun and, despite the headache I was now experiencing, it was undoubtedly one of the best nights of my life. I felt completely relaxed with her and wound up telling her all about myself and my slightly complicated past. I told her way more about me than she did about herself which was fine. Obviously, I had touched a raw nerve last night and let it rest.

I thought about my checkered life and my dangerous friend, Vito, the mobbed up greaseball I grew up with in the Bronx. He ran Little Italy and its neighboring environs in Manhattan for one of the families. We had been on and off again associates despite my medical degree. The bond that had formed in the streets trumped all other loyalties and we were destined to sink or swim together down the river of life. It was time to give him a buzz. I had just under five hundred in cash but had no car and couldn't use my credit cards. I'd be fine for a few days but couldn't really impose on Francesca more than that. I didn't know what her economic status was and was sure her friend wouldn't want me here once she returned. I couldn't really blame her for that. Besides, I wanted to clear out before she set eyes on me. I needed to stay on the move so I gently disengaged myself from Francesca's arms and legs and slid her off of me onto the sofa.

With eyes closed she whispered hoarsely. "Where are you going? Come back."

I smiled and kissed her again. "I need to go into town and get a few things. Is it all right if I borrow your car? I won't be long."

"No, you can't go anywhere. You're my prisoner," she murmured. "The keys are in my bag in the kitchen. Don't speed."

She rolled over and fell asleep again and I went into the bathroom to brush my teeth and splash water on my face. I would shower when I returned. It was nine when I left the house and started the Beetle parked in the driveway. Henderson was a suburb of Vegas and not a particularly large place. I soon found yet another Walmart and picked up a prepaid phone and blonde hair color. I thought about shaving my head but people tended to remember that look. There was a Starbucks just a block away and I stopped for a cup of coffee and a croissant, sitting at a table off to one side.

While I ate, I called Vito. "Yeah, who is it?" he answered gruffly, not recognizing the number.

"It's me, Cesari."

"You got a new phone?"

"It's complicated. Have you been watching the news?"

"Why would I do that?"

I spent almost thirty minutes filling him in on the facts as I knew them. He interrupted me multiple times to expand on or clarify some point as I casually looked around to make sure no one was within earshot.

When I was done Vito said, "You're fucked Cesari. I don't see how I can help you. Besides, it's not entirely clear from what you told me that you didn't kill that girl."

"Oh c'mon Vito. Does that sound like something I would do?"

"No, but that don't mean anything especially if you were drunk or high."

"Shut up. So what can you tell me about this guy Carmine Buonarotti? The guy Luther told me about. He said the dead hooker was his girlfriend."

"I don't know him but I've heard of him. His mother is Brunella, a Staten Island boss. They say Carmine's not a bad guy but that's not saying much in this business. No one's ever a bad guy until you do something to piss them off, like kill their girlfriend. Supposedly, he takes care of his mom's business interests in Vegas. I don't know if he actually owns that particular club you mentioned or just skims off it."

"His mother is a boss?"

"Yeah, she was married to Luigi Buonarotti an old-school guinea from Palermo. He took one in the forehead eating lasagna on Easter Sunday in some restaurant in Staten Island five years ago. I can't remember the guy's name who was behind it but, apparently he thought it was time for a promotion. Boy, was he wrong. He sends two guys into the back of the restaurant dressed as waiters. They approach Luigi's table whipping out .45's and wale away on the guy emptying their clips into him while she's screaming and crying. Carmine himself took a stray bullet in the abdomen but obviously survived. She jumps onto her husband's body hugging him while the two hit men stare at her deciding whether to take her out too. In that moment of indecision guess what she does?"

"I have no idea."

"Well, it turns out that she didn't jump on the floor because she likes to be covered in blood. She reaches into her Gucci handbag lying under the table and pulls out an Uzi with a thirty round magazine and sprays the two fuckers while they're loading their .45's. So much for the gentler sex. And she wasn't done."

"No?"

"No."

"Rumor has it that when the hit went bad, all the lieutenants were so impressed with her actions, that they rallied behind her as the new boss. When she finally caught up with the guy behind the shooting she had him skinned alive and hung by his ankles in her basement like a prosciutto. They say it took him days to die and that she would go down there every morning, sip her espresso, and read the morning paper while he begged for mercy, and that's not the best part."

"No? So what's the best part?"

"She didn't do all that for her husband, Luigi. She hated him. She did all that because they touched her baby boy, Carmine. I hope you're listening Cesari. Stay away from the guy."

Great.

"I'll try to but he's bound to be looking for me. Everyone else is. Look, can you wire me some cash, maybe a couple of thousand? I don't want to use my credit cards or ATM card right now."

"I'll send you the cash, but what are you going to do, big picture, I mean?"

"I'll spend a few days here and there and I guess I'll take a train or bus back to New York eventually."

"I understand you have to lay low, Cesari, but you're wanted for murder and they know who you are. You just can't show up for work like nothing happened."

He was right. "I can't just walk in the front door and surrender either, Vito. It's not my nature. Besides, I don't believe I killed that girl. Maybe something will turn up exonerating me while I'm moving around."

"I suppose that's a plan. Not a great plan but a plan. Okay, so what else do you need?"

"Cocoa is staying at my apartment with Cleopatra. Could you swing by there with a couple of grand for expenses and see if she needs anything?"

"Cocoa, I thought you and her had moved on."

"We have. She's doing me a favor. We're still friends."

"That's interesting."

"What is?"

"Most girls you date usually wind up hating you when it's over, like Kelly."

"Kelly doesn't hate me and thanks for bringing that up." Kelly was an African-American nurse I used to date. I loved her and was devastated when she broke up with me. When she got married, I took it very hard and still had difficulty dealing with it. Vito knew that and enjoyed rubbing salt in the wound every now and then.

He chuckled, "Relax, Cesari. I'm just trying to help you get over her."

I ignored the barb. "I'll stay in touch."

"Sure but one more thing. If you do come back to New York would you mind staying away from my place. I don't need any headaches with Brunella."

"Understood."

I hung up and looked at my watch. It was after ten. I left the Starbucks and drove back to the house. I noticed her tank was almost on empty so I stopped at a station and gassed up. I needed a better plan, but I didn't know anything. If I didn't kill Jenny then someone else did, but who? Someone came into the room with a hooker and her client, me, and then killed the hooker. Who would do that? A jealous boyfriend? Carmine? But he knew what she did for a living so that wouldn't make sense.

Did she have another boyfriend? Maybe one who was unaware of her lifestyle?

And why kill the hooker and leave me alive? Okay, well that part was easy at least. If for some reason this was personal against Jenny, then I'd be the obvious suspect and with my DNA all over her I'd be on death's row in a heartbeat. The killer gets away scot free. But was my DNA all over her? I couldn't remember having sex with her but that didn't mean much right now because I couldn't remember too much of anything. Well that wasn't true. I did sort of vaguely remember Luther. I needed to check out the DNA angle.

Wait a minute, if this was personal and the killer was known to Jenny did she just let him in the room unsuspecting of his intentions or did he climb in through the rooftop escape hatch in the bathroom like I did? Possibly. There were no signs of a struggle from what I remembered so she must have been taken by surprise. I was closing in. I felt it.

As I pulled onto the block where the house was, I noticed something amiss. There was a shiny new black Suburban parked out front. I was distracted when I left earlier but was sure I would have remembered a monster like that. Francesca's friend wasn't due home for at least another couple of days but I suppose she could have cut her trip short. Nonetheless, prudence dictated a cautious approach.

I parked the Beetle a block away and walked the remaining distance. I didn't have any weapons because I had left the duffel bag with Luther's .45 and the crowbar in the living room by the sofa. I was getting careless. Hopefully, this was no big deal. My imagination had been known to run away on occasion. It certainly didn't look like a police vehicle which was reassuring. As I casually walked toward the house, I thought of how best to avoid the SUV but then realized that maybe that wasn't the right approach so I made a beeline right to the driver's side door. I would know immediately what I was up against anyway. I could recognize an asshole a mile away.

Approaching slowly but deliberately, I took Frankie's car and house keys and curled them up in my right hand letting the largest key jut out forward through the closed knuckles of my fist. It wasn't a gun but it would hurt for sure especially if I got lucky and caught him in the eye. The driver's window was heavily tinted and I couldn't see inside so I took a deep breath and tapped on the glass. No one answered and I paused thinking it over before testing the latch handle. The door was unlocked and I let myself in to look around, finding nothing unusual in the front and back seats or in the center console. In the glove compartment I found the driver's registration and insurance card. This was Carmine Buonarotti's Suburban.

Shit.

Of course he would come looking for Francesca. How stupid of me to be so complacent. Jenny was his girl. He thinks I killed her and Frankie helped me escape. Naturally, he'd want to talk to Francesca himself and by talk I meant smack her around some more. I'd better do something quick. I looked around the car and underneath the seats but found nothing.

Think, think, think!

They didn't know that Luther's gun was in the duffel bag. When I entered the house last night I placed it on the floor not too far from the door and behind the sofa. Unless I was extremely unlucky it might still be there. I had a key to the front door and could gain access without difficulty. The real question was how many were there and where would they feel most comfortable interrogating Francesca? I had to assume that she would tell them about me but would that be enough to save her?

I left the Suburban and checked out the house from the curb. All the shades and blinds had been closed and I presumed that Carmine did that to give him privacy from prying eyes. Probably, they would take her away from the living room and kitchen which had lots of windows albeit shaded. Someone could always peer around the sides which I was about to do. That would leave the bedrooms or the basement. I took a deep breath and went up the front steps and looked through the edge of the living room's bay window. From my limited view, I didn't see or hear anything, like a girl screaming in pain. That was good.

I tested the front door and it was locked. Using the key, I opened the door quietly a crack and peaked inside. Observing nothing, I tip-toed stealthily, making a beeline to the duffel bag still in its resting spot. I retrieved the .45, chambered a round as quietly as possible, and took a deep breath feeling much better now that I was armed. I then proceeded to search the house. The kitchen, bedrooms, living and dining rooms were vacant which left the basement. The door to the basement was just off the kitchen and closed. Pressing my ear against it, I could hear muffled sobbing and an occasional slapping sound.

Gently and slowly, I opened the door hoping it was well oiled. It was, and slid open silently. The next dilemma was the stairs. They were carpeted but I never went down a set of basement stairs that didn't make some noise so I took my shoes off and gingerly began my descent as the noise coming from the basement grew louder.

I could hear a rough male voice now. An angry voice. "I'm going to ask you one more time Francesca. How the fuck do you know this guy?"

"I swear Carmine. I never met him before that night. I swear it." He slapped her again and she started whimpering.

"How can I possibly believe that you would help some guy you never met escape from the club after he had just killed Jenny?"

Crying she replied, "I didn't know anything about that, Carmine, really I didn't. I never would have helped him if I'd known."

I crept slowly down the stairs and could now see them. Two male silver-backs and an average sized guy. The gorillas leaned back against a wall watching Carmine who stood in front of Francesca. His back was to me and she sat on a stool her face with fresh red slap marks. Her eye and lips had swollen up again.

He raised his hand to slap her again and I leapt down the last two steps and shouted. “Touch her one more time, asshole, and I’ll send you back to mommy in a box.”

The two goons instinctively jumped to attention. They were the same guys I spotted at Caesar’s Palace with Seymour. One of them went for his gun and I shot him in the thigh. The report was deafening in the small room and everyone flinched. The goon fell down moaning and clutching his leg as the other one wavered indecisively. I pointed the gun at him and said, “Down on your belly now.” He got down to his knees and then onto his stomach. I quickly turned my attention to Carmine and Francesca who were frozen in place by the gunfire.

I walked right up to him and smashed him hard in the face with the barrel of the .45. He spit out a tooth and fell to the floor dazed. I quickly frisked him as I carefully kept an eye on the other two. Carmine was unarmed and I went over to his friends and relieved them of their 9mm’s tucked away in the small of their backs. I placed the weapons on the steps going up to the kitchen. The wounded guy’s groaning annoyed me so I brought the butt of the gun down on the back of his head and he went out.

Carmine was coming to so I grabbed him by the scruff of the neck and dragged him over to his friends, tossing him forcefully. He tripped over one of them and fell backwards on top of the other. Francesca finally regained her composure and jumped off the chair throwing her arms around me, clutching me tightly.

I said, “Look, go upstairs, clean up and throw some clothes in a bag. We’re leaving. I’m sorry I’ve done this to you.”

She pressed her head into my chest and nodded. She knew there was no point in arguing. "What are you going to do?"

"Not one hundred percent certain yet."

She went up the stairs and Carmine started to speak so I walked up to him and kicked him hard in the face, breaking his nose this time and possibly loosening another tooth. Blood dribbled down his face and he kept quiet. The big guy on the floor was a problem.

"What's your name?"

"Curly."

"Are you going to be a problem, Curly?"

"No, sir."

"So I won't have to shoot you?"

"No, sir."

"Good. You tell Brunella when she asks you what happened that Carmine was beating up on a girl and got what he deserved. Can you remember that, Curly?"

"Yes, sir."

"Repeat it for me please."

"Carmine was beating up on a girl and got what he deserved."

"Good." I smashed him on top of the head with the butt of the gun and he lost consciousness. I then placed the .45 on the steps with the other two pistols. Returning to Carmine, I grabbed him off the floor and flung him into the opposite wall. He was a hair shorter and lighter than me but muscular and fit. Dazed and confused, he offered little resistance, but that didn't stop me from using him as a punching bag for the next ten minutes.

When I got tired, I let him slump into a corner and caught my breath. I searched all three, took their wallets, cellphones and the Suburban's ignition keys. I then collected all three weapons and went upstairs to find Francesca. Locking the basement door, I wedged a chair at an angle under the doorknob. All together they had seven hundred dollars in cash, when combined with mine, gave me a war chest of about twelve hundred dollars with more on the way from Vito. I kept one of their credit cards and tossed the wallets and cellphones into the kitchen trash can. By the time I stored the weapons in the duffel bag, Francesca was ready to go. She too had a small travel bag.

She said, “I don’t have much. I never had a chance to go to my apartment.”

“We’ll stop somewhere and get you some new stuff. It’s on Carmine.” I smiled and waved his American Express in the air.

We went out to the Suburban and drove off.

She said, “Do you know who he is?”

“The little guy?”

She smiled. “He wasn’t that little, but yeah.”

“Somebody important?”

She nodded. “Yup.”

“Should I have gotten his autograph?”

She shook her head. “I don’t know about you.”

“Don’t worry. He’ll get over it. You’d better call your friend the model and let her know there was situation at her house. She might want to stay out there in L.A. a few extra days if she can.”

She sighed. “I will, but what about my car?”

“Forget about it. We’d never make it far in that thing.”

“But this is stolen.”

“Yeah, I know, but I’m betting he’ll be so angry he won’t bother reporting it in at least not for a while. His pride won’t let him. Besides, with any luck, he won’t even know his own name for a couple of days at least.”

“Now what am I going to do? I’ll never be able to work in this town again.”

I chuckled. “Well, I was looking for a housekeeper. Can you dust?”

She snorted and laughed. “I don’t know about you, Mr. John Cesari.”

“That’s doctor to you.”

Chapter 17

We gassed up the Suburban, purchased food, clothes, and other supplies using Carmine's credit card and hit the road by noon. My plan was to drive to Chicago, dump the Suburban and take a train to New York. The GPS in the vehicle said the trip to Chicago should take twenty four hours. At this point it was cash only to remain under the radar so I tossed Carmine's credit card out the window on Highway 15. I'd save mine and Frankie's for emergencies.

Several hours into the drive, I called Arnie on the throw-away phone.

"Hi Arnie."

"Cesari?"

"Yeah, anything new going on?"

"Yes, there is."

"What now, Arnie?"

"Seymour took off. He didn't show up for the conference this morning and when I called him he said he had already checked out of his room and was catching an early flight back to New York. He said he wasn't feeling well."

I bet.

"Well, you never know what Seymour's going to do. Look Arnie, I need a favor."

"And what's that?"

"You know what I'm being accused of, right?"

He lowered his voice in sympathy. "Yeah, I know. Sorry."

"Yeah, well, the problem is that I don't really remember anything from that night. I suspect I was drugged but I can't figure out how or more importantly why. The results of the DNA tests and autopsy results might be ready tomorrow. The official reports won't be out for a few days or even a week, but as a fellow physician and my chief of staff back in New York they might tell you. I'd really like to know just how well I knew this girl if you get my drift."

I heard him sigh into the phone. "I get your drift. I'll see what I can do."

"Thanks, how's Troy?"

"Concerned, what do you think? His pal, Cesari, is wanted for murder and now Seymour's acting squirrelly."

"Understandable, I'll call him later to cheer him up."

Arnie chuckled. "Yeah, that should do it. Are you going to join us on the return flight to New York tomorrow night?"

"Probably not a good idea for me Arnie. I'll figure something out. Just make sure people hold off judging me until all the facts are in, all right?"

"I'll do my best."

I hung up the phone and looked at Francesca who had been watching me.

She said, "For what it's worth, I believe you."

"Is that so?"

"That you didn't kill Jenny."

"Thanks, I appreciate that."

"Other than drive to Chicago and take a train to New York, do you have a plan?"

"That's about it right now."

I needed to talk to Seymour. He was up to his eyeballs in something. I just didn't know what. Why were Carmine's men with him at Caesar's last night? He knew Luther so did that mean he knew Carmine too? Did Carmine muscle him into cooperating the way he was trying to muscle Francesca? I guess that was a possibility. Maybe that was why Seymour had expedited his way out of here; to get away from Carmine. I couldn't fault him for that. I nodded to myself because that did kind of make sense.

We passed Denver in the early evening and a couple of hours later decided to crash for the night just inside the Nebraska state line. Pulling into the parking lot of a small roadside motel, I got us a cheap room and a couple of odd looks when people saw Frankie's battered appearance. Road weary and stressed, we passed out from exhaustion.

Waking early the next day, we hit the road again, grabbing coffee, donuts and a few other supplies at a convenience store. I hadn't decided yet what to do with Francesca or where to bring her. She hadn't offered me any options other than to hang out with me while she healed up. I had hinted several times on the drive if there was any place in particular she wanted to go, and she had nimbly side-stepped the issue every time. We had time so I didn't see any point in pressing her. Besides, I liked her company. It turns out that she was very funny and liked to tell off-color jokes and do card tricks.

She asked, "So, how are linoleum and a man the same?"

I thought it over. "I give up."

"If you lay them right the first time you can walk all over them the rest of your life."

I chuckled. "Okay, good one. Try this. How are women and hurricanes alike?"

She said, "I'm listening."

"They make a lot of noise when they come, and take the house when they leave."

We both laughed at that, but then she got serious and asked, "So, if you could be anybody you wanted, who would you be?"

"Interesting question. I'm not sure." I paused for a second or two thinking about it. "James Bond maybe. I always thought he was kind of cool. What about you?"

"Matilda. You know—the little girl with the awful parents. She has telekinetic powers. It was my favorite book growing up. I read it over and over. They made it into a movie and it's a play on Broadway now. I've always wanted to go see it."

I smiled. "Well, maybe someday you will."

Somewhere in the middle of Iowa, it started snowing hard with vicious squalls rocking the Suburban. The temperature and visibility plummeted to zero and I was forced to pull the SUV over to the side of the road and wait it out. We had three quarters of a tank of gas, bottled water, and a bag of Cheetos. We'd be okay as long as we didn't get buried in snow. I hadn't thought to buy a shovel, but then again I'd never driven through the midwest in late February.

"Tell me again why you chose a northern route rather than maybe drive to Phoenix or Albuquerque?" she asked.

"Well, I thought that if someone were looking for us they would guess we would take the more southern route because it would be a faster and a more pleasant ride. Sorry."

Before long the windshield and windows were covered in snow and I turned on the back and front wipers so I could keep an eye on things. Francesca took out a pack of playing cards she bought at a gas station and shuffled them like a pro.

I was impressed. "That was pretty good."

"Thanks, I wanted to be a dealer at one point. Here, pick a card, any card." She splayed the deck out in front of me and I picked one from the center. It was the jack of diamonds. "Okay, look at it carefully and then place it back in the deck without letting me see."

I did what she instructed and then she handed me the cards and said. "Shuffle them."

I shuffled the cards clumsily like most amateurs and handed the deck back to her. She shuffled them a few more times and asked, "What month were you born in?"

"August."

"Good, hold out your hand. August is the eight month, right?"

"Yes."

"You're sure?"

I smiled. "Yes, I'm sure." She had the beginnings of a good act.

She counted out the first seven cards onto my outstretched hand. Before turning over the eighth card she looked at me very seriously and asked, "You're sure August is the eight month and that is the month you were born in?"

I nodded, trying not to laugh at her shtick. "Yeah, I'm sure."

She turned over the eighth card and it was the seven of clubs. My heart sank for her and she looked surprised saying, "That doesn't make sense. I've done this trick a thousand times. Did you cheat?"

I raised my eyebrows. "Cheat? Of course not. How could I cheat anyway?"

"I don't believe you put the card back in the deck. Empty your coat pockets."

I couldn't believe this. She was dead serious so I put my right hand in my coat pocket and was shocked by what I felt. I pulled out the jack of diamonds and grinned from ear to ear. "How on earth did you do that?" I was totally amazed and she started giggling uncontrollably.

Laughing she said. "Not bad, huh?"

"Not bad at all. You have many talents."

She put the cards away, unbuckled herself, kneeled on her seat, and leaned over the center console placing her arms around my neck, kissing me. She said very slowly and drawn out. "You—have no idea—how many talents I have."

"I bet."

"We could find out a few of them right now. There's plenty of room in the back seat."

Just as suddenly as the storm came upon us it settled back down to a light snowfall. I looked at her, then back at the road, and said, "Tonight, I promise."

She squinted her eyes, made a pouty face, returned to her seat, and buckled up. I shifted the Suburban into four-wheel drive and plunged my way out of the snowbank created by the squall. Reducing our speed because of the inclement weather conditions added about another hour to the trip and we arrived in Chicago at 7:00 p.m. where it was twenty degrees with cloudy skies and no precipitation. It had been a rough winter in the windy city and there were large mounds of sooty snow on every corner with slushy streets and sidewalks. I had called ahead to the Drake Hotel, just off of N. Michigan Avenue in a swanky part of town, and explained that I had lost my credit cards. As long as I had a driver's license they would accept cash. They wanted five hundred for the night which was steep but I didn't care because I needed to live it up a little. I was starting to get a little discouraged.

We checked into our room on the fourth floor uneventfully. It was large with a king-sized four poster bed, several Queen Anne sitting chairs, full bath with a Jacuzzi tub, and an antique armoire. Francesca was very happy. "Wow, this is very nice."

Thoroughly exhausted, I didn't answer her and threw myself on the bed face down, hugging a pillow. I had just driven the last seven hours of the trip without a break and most of that through snow. She jumped on top of me resting her head on my back.

She lay there quietly, rising up and down with my breathing. Not very heavy, she didn't really bother me and I was so tired that I thought I might fall asleep despite her presence. But she had other ideas.

"Why don't we take a bath together and then go out to eat?"

"A bath?"

"Yeah, a bath. Why not? C'mon, it'll be fun."

I had no doubt about that. Just the thought of being in the tub with her made me start to wake up. Springing to life I said, "Sure."

We went to the bathroom, took our clothes off staring at each other hungrily while the hot water poured out of the faucet. She was five feet five inches tall with long dark hair, brown eyes, and otherwise perfect proportions. She put her arms around my waist and hugged me. My hands ran down her back to her bottom and lingered there adoringly. I could feel the welt marks from Luther's belt and I felt myself getting angry again. I should have killed the bastard. She read my mind and hugged me tighter saying, "Stop. Put it out of your mind."

"I'm trying."

We got into the tub and Francesca poured in some bubble bath that she found on the sink. I turned on the Jacuzzi jets and she turned around to snuggle up against me in between my legs. I put my arms around her and we let the jets caress our weary muscles as she leaned back against me. She had a small tattoo of a yellow butterfly on her right shoulder and I studied it. It was discreet and very tasteful.

She tilted her head to one side exposing her neck and I took the bait, kissing it gently over and over as my hands explored her body. She loved what I was doing and purred softly while reaching up behind her with one hand to hold my head.

I whispered into her ear. "So how much is this going to cost me exactly?"

She laughed. "You're lucky. I'm running a sale tonight. Guineas are half-price. So are you going to use that thing or just beat me up with it back there?"

She was killing me and I hugged her tightly. Chuckling I said, "I could use a little help. This is kind of a funny angle."

"Amateur."

Chapter 18

An hour later we were sitting in the Rosebud Steakhouse on E. Walton Place, down the block from the Drake. It was just after nine and the restaurant was overflowing with diners. I sipped on a gin martini and Francesca enjoyed a cosmopolitan while we waited for our T-bones, medium rare with sides of creamed spinach, and steak fries. I looked at my cellphone and realized that I had put it on silent and had missed three calls from Arnie.

The waiter in a white apron placed warm bread in a basket and whipped rosemary seasoned butter down in front of us. Francesca nibbled on a piece while I returned Arnie's call.

"Hello, Arnie. Back in New York?"

"Just barely. We were delayed four hours in Vegas because of engine trouble but we finally made it in okay. How about you?"

"I'm managing. So what can you tell me?"

"Mostly good news and possibly some bad news. That girl Jenny was brought to the University Medical Center on South Rancho Drive not too far from the gentleman's club where the murder took place. It turns out the pathologist was at the conference with us and we had actually met him briefly at one of the break-out sessions. The bottom line is that he was agreeable."

"And…?" No one liked to pontificate like Arnie. I was a get-to-the-point kind of guy.

"And she was definitely raped. The kind of sexual trauma she experienced wasn't the usual kind of rough stuff you might see in a place like that. Cause of death was asphyxiation. She was placed in the tub and cut open afterward."

Not good so far. "What about the DNA?"

"That's the good news. They can't be sure. Because she was in the bath and her blood was all over the place the samples they have are all tainted. There's clearly other DNA there along with hers but they can't really make it out for certain at least not yet. Maybe not ever."

I breathed a sigh of relief. "Well, I'm sorry for her but I guess that's good for me."

"I hope so. There is one more thing you should be aware of. The cause of asphyxiation is not one hundred percent clear. There was no evidence for throat or laryngeal trauma to suggest she was strangled."

I thought about that. "Maybe she had a plastic bag placed over her head?"

"No, there would have been some signs of that too, such as conjunctival hemorrhage or at least some signs of a struggle. There was no blood or DNA under her fingernails by the way. Interesting is that she suffered multiple broken ribs and pulmonary contusions they feel definitely occurred before death. He said it was almost like a car ran over her. Basically, she was crushed."

"That is interesting. I don't know what it means though."

"Did you run her over in the parking lot and then bring her back into the room?"

"Thanks, Arnie. Besides, that's not a very subtle way of committing murder, is it?"

"Yeah well, you're not a very subtle guy, Cesari. That's all I've got for you on that subject."

"Thanks."

"One more thing, and I don't know what it means but your pal, Lancelot, asked to have a meeting with me as soon as possible. I got jet lag so I put it off until tomorrow."

"Okay, so what? Hopefully, he'll be handing in his resignation."

"I hope not. I have enough problems. Do you know what this is about, Cesari?"

"Me? I could give a rat's ass about anything that guy says or does."

The waiter served us our entrées and I said, "Got to go, Arnie."

"Was that your friend from the hospital?" Francesca asked.

I helped myself to some creamed spinach and said, "Which one? I have lots of friends. I'm a friendly guy."

She chuckled. "I'm sure, but you never told me if you have a girlfriend or wife or anything."

"Is this where we do the third degree? I don't know why women obsess so much over stuff like this."

She smiled knowing I had caught her. "Touché."

The steak sizzling on the plate was perfectly cooked and I washed a bite down with some gin, proud of myself for the way I had just handled that. She said, "So are you going to answer the question or are you going to ruin dinner?"

That was the funny thing about women. It wasn't a level playing field with any of them. They had rights and you didn't.

I said, "None of the above. Currently uninvolved and no secret wife waiting for me to hide you from. I do have a female dog but we have a strictly platonic relationship."

"What kind of dog?"

"A big one. She's an English Mastiff, weighs about two hundred and fifty pounds. Her name is Cleopatra. She looks tough but she's very friendly."

She hesitated, chewing on a steak fry. "Am I going to get to meet Cleopatra?"

I hadn't thought that far ahead. "I don't see why not."

Very quiet, uncertain if she had just stepped over a line, she looked down at her food while she ate.

I said, "An ex-girlfriend is watching her for me right now."

She looked up and took the bait. "That's a nice ex-girlfriend you got there."

"That's generally how I pick'em. Before I ask a girl out, I decide first if they'll be nice after the break-up. If I come to the conclusion that they're stable on that front then I ask them out."

Francesca broke out laughing and almost spilled her cosmo. "So, am I to assume that when you date a girl the break-up is already pre-planned?"

I grinned. "Pre-planned is too strong an expression."

"So what expression would you use?"

"I like to think of it as exploring my therapeutic options with an eye toward maximizing outcomes."

"Oh my, you are full of beans, aren't you?"

"Thanks for pulling your punch on that one." I laughed.

"And how has this system worked out for you so far?"

I smiled. "You win some you lose some. Know what I mean?"

She liked that and nodded. "Relationships are like that. So, Dr. Cesari, tell me about those scars on your chest and back? I didn't say anything at first but I think we're friends now."

"Well, as I mentioned to you the other night, I traveled a somewhat unusual path before reaching the place I'm at now, and not everyone I met was as enamored of my good looks and charming personality as you so obviously are."

Smiling she said, "Is that why you have all the muscles? You could easily pass for an athlete."

"Thanks. I learned a long time ago that a strong mind and a strong body go hand in hand."

"You're an interesting guy. I haven't met many doctors but I assume you're somewhat shall we say—different than most."

"I guess we can say that. So now that we figured me out, when can we start talking about you?"

She stiffened, finished the rest of her cosmo in one huge gulp, and said, "What is it you think I'm going to say?"

"Let's start with family: mom, dad, brothers, sisters?"

She sighed deeply and let out a deep breath. "Okay, but remember you asked for it." She paused, organizing her thoughts. "I'm an only child. My parents died in a car accident when I was two. The rescue workers had to cut me out of the back seat. I was the sole survivor of a New Year's Eve hit and run, or so the police reports say. An alcoholic uncle and his drug addicted wife took me in. The abuse started at age eight. At thirteen, I was having my own problems with alcohol and drugs and could have drunk any grown man under the table. By fifteen, I'd already had an abortion and was living on the streets. At eighteen, the courts ordered rehabilitation or jail time. I picked rehab. When I came out, I thought I'd try a change of pace and moved to Vegas. I never had any pipe dreams about becoming a movie star and don't have any real talent. I've known who I was from day one. I got lucky when I heard about an opening at *The Fall of Rome.* I only had to give Luther one blowjob to get the job. I'm HIV negative and have been clean for two years now and with counseling I actually am starting to put it all behind me. My life is not quite a Hallmark movie, now is it?"

I sat back, saddened by what I had just heard. It was obvious I was at a loss for words so she added defensively, "Is there anything else you would like to know?"

True to form, I cleared my throat and said, "Yes, are we going to have dessert? I'm still kind of hungry."

She threw a steak fry at me but laughed despite herself. "You're an asshole."

I chuckled. "Okay, this is good. We're making progress."

"What's good about it? It makes me feel bad to talk about it."

"No amount of counseling can do what we're doing here, Frankie. You need to get this off your chest with a real person, someone who wants to listen, not someone you pay to listen. You need to tell your story to someone whom you care about and who cares about you. You need to believe that whatever happened to you is not your fault in any way, shape, or form. You are as innocent as that two-year-old girl the rescue workers found so many years ago."

Her eyes watered up and she started to tremble and softly sob. I moved my chair closer to her and placed an arm around her shoulder, bringing her in close. The waiter came to clear our plates and I signaled him to give us a minute.

She shook her head. "Why are you doing this? I knew you weren't going to let go of it. I just knew it."

"I can't help being who I am any more than you can help being who you are."

"Can we skip dessert? I want to take a walk. I need some air."

I paid the bill and we bundled up for a stroll down Michigan Avenue. It was snowing lightly, but without wind it was actually a pretty nice night for a winter's walk. We meandered down the avenue with our arms wrapped around each other for warmth and comfort and did a little window shopping along the way. It was after eleven and all the retail stores were closed although the blues bars and coffee shops were still quite busy. A half hour later we reached Millennium Park and were getting pretty cold so we headed back to the hotel, arriving there at midnight. We didn't do a whole lot of talking but we didn't have to at that point. What she needed was assurance that I wasn't going to suddenly treat her like garbage because of what she told me. So I held her tightly and shut my mouth unless she said something first. She knew what I was doing and thought it was kind of funny. She hadn't met many men who put her feelings first but I guess there was a first time for everything.

In the room, we undressed and crawled under the covers. I waited patiently for her to decide what came next. After several minutes of staring at the ceiling in the dark I felt her wiggle over to my side of the bed and wrap her arms and legs around me saying, "Goodnight and thanks for dinner."

I hugged her back and kissed her lightly on the forehead.

"Good night, Francesca."

Chapter 19

"Carmine, are you a sure it was a that doctor? The one a they say killed you girl, Jenny?"

"Yes, Mama. I had seen him on TV several times just before we went to find Francesca. I know it was him. Francesca must have been in on it and that's why she helped him escape. I just can't figure what they hoped to gain. Maybe Francesca was jealous of Jenny because Jenny was the number one girl at the club. I don't know."

Carmine looked awful; two black eyes, a broken nose, and a missing front tooth, he used a cane for support. Curly stood to one side supportively, while the other guy who was shot in the leg leaned on crutches. They sat in Luther's office going through his stuff trying to figure out just what the hell was going on. Carmine's mother, Brunella, had flown out to Vegas as soon as she heard the news and arrived just as he was being released from the hospital.

She was a sharp-looking woman in great shape, maybe five feet two inches tall, approaching fifty with short business like hair and designer, red-framed glasses. She looked at Curly, "I don't understand how a this could a happen to my baby, Curly. Maybe you could explain a for me to understand a more better?"

Curly shuffled his feet and looked down. "He, um, caught us by surprise, Mrs. Buonarotti."

"Hmm, I see. Two bodyguards I pay a very well to protect a my son and they get a caught by the surprise. Is that what a you tell me?"

He cleared his throat and nodded submissively.

"Carmine, my baby boy, we need to take a care of this doctor and whoever helped him. We can't letta the people think a we are weak. They take advantage of a the situation. Capisci?"

Carmine responded, "I understand. The police are looking for him but he's gone to ground. No one knows where he is Mama."

Her temper flared suddenly. "Fucka the police. We take care ourselves. We make the example of this doctor and that puttana, Francesca. I already make a the calls to New York. His apartment, we watch. His hospital,we watch, but we need a do more to flush him out. He must a think he is safe. From a now on, we spread a the word. Luther killed you girlfriend and he admit a to everything. He try to run away, but got a hit by the car and die. I talka to the police and a the mayor. We make a the free weekenda here for everyone and they understand. Capisci? They no care anyway, one dead puttana and a one dead pimp. No one a care."

"But Mama, Luther didn't die. The doctors say he's going to make it."

She looked at Curly sternly. "You make a sure the doctors they are wrong."

Curly nodded.

Turning to Carmine she said, "Now come over here my baby boy and give you mama the hug."

Chapter 20

Leaving the Suburban parked on the street with the doors unlocked and the keys in the cup holder, we boarded a train to New York at Chicago's Union Station. It required a transfer in Pittsburgh and would arrive in Penn Station at 5:00 p.m. I paid in cash and we nestled in with fifteen minutes to spare, picking up a couple of magazines for the nine hour trip. The business class seats were roomy and comfortable and we settled in for another long day.

I toyed with the idea of calling Seymour but thought it might be better to keep him guessing as to my status and opinions. If he was innocent of any wrong doing all would be fine. If he wasn't, sooner later he would reveal himself. Somehow he was involved on a level I didn't quite understand. You don't just accidentally know mob guys who run a whorehouse out in Vegas.

The question now was where were Francesca and I going to stay for a couple of days while I sorted things out? I couldn't just go back to my loft in the Village and what about Cleopatra? Vito had a large apartment in Little Italy on Mulberry Street but it was almost always under FBI surveillance because of his nefarious activities. He was right about Brunella too. It wouldn't be smart for me to just show up there, and Cocoa was already being too nice. I couldn't drag her any further into this.

I called Vito.

“Cesari, what the fuck? Don’t you listen?” he asked annoyed.

“What are you talking about?”

“I told you not to fuck with Carmine so what do you do? You pistol whip him and shoot one of his bodyguards. Are you out of your fucking mind?”

“How did you know all of this?”

“The whole city knows. Brunella has put the word out that she wants your head on a platter and anybody caught helping you will get the same treatment.”

Damn, that was quick. I hadn’t introduced myself to Carmine but maybe he had seen my face on TV. I said, “Shit.”

“Yeah, shit, and she specifically called me to let me know in no uncertain terms how she would feel if I helped my old buddy from the Bronx.”

“What did she say?”

“That she would be very, very unhappy as in ‘cut my balls off’ unhappy.”

“Well, I’m sorry about all the fuss but it couldn’t be helped. The guy’s a real asshole.”

“Oh, great. So now we beat up every asshole we meet. You’re going to be one busy guy with a policy like that.”

“Are you through?”

“Yeah, I’m through.”

“How’s Cocoa and Cleopatra?”

“They’re both fine. She took Cleo with her to New Jersey to visit with her parents. She said she tried to call to let you know but you didn’t answer your phone. I told her about the phone change and that you’d give her a call soon.”

“All right, thanks. How’s the heat on your apartment?”

“Always there, Cesari. Always fucking there. Never lets up. I can’t even take a piss without some federal agent trying to get a urine sample. Did you get the cash?”

"Yeah, thanks. I'm all set for now. I'll let you know if and when I need more."

"So, who's the whore?"

That jolted me. "What?"

"Brunella told me that in addition to killing Jenny and slapping Carmine around that you ran off with one of his girls. I was just wondering if you were becoming unhinged."

I rolled my eyes. "I'm not becoming unhinged and don't worry about who she is. She's a human being. That's all you or anybody needs to know."

"Fine Cesari, but you just stuck your dick in a hornet's nest so watch your back."

His command of English was second only to Shakespeare. "Thanks, I will."

I hung up, smiled at Francesca, and called Cocoa.

"Hi John."

"Hi Cocoa. I'm sorry for not calling sooner. Look, I just got off the phone with Vito and I understand you took Cleo to New Jersey. Thank you for all your help. I'm sorry about imposing on you like this but I'm going to have to ask you to hang on to her for a little while longer. If you can't, then put her in a kennel and I'll pick up the tab but please make sure it's the best kennel you can find."

"It's okay. I understand that you have a situation that's beyond your control right now. Just take care of yourself. Cleo and I are getting along swimmingly. That's one of the reasons I brought her out to Jersey. My parents have a large yard she can run around in. You've got to see her with her face covered in snow."

"Any more on the news about me?"

"Yes, some. It seems that you've been downgraded to simply a person of interest rather than a suspect."

"That's good."

"Yeah well, it only made the news here in the first place because you're from New York. Well, the latest wrinkle is that apparently there are rumors that the little bunny ranch you were playing at is mob owned. There's even some speculation that you may be a victim too, you know, like caught in the crossfire of some underworld dispute and maybe buried in the desert somewhere."

"Really?"

"Yeah, it's actually been kind of interesting to follow the story. People are talking about it everywhere guessing about what happened to you."

"What's the leading theory?"

"That you're a whore master and a sex addict and that whatever happened, you got what you deserved."

"Get out of here. That's harsh."

"Remember, I'm studying piano at Juilliard. There are a lot of feminists there and they don't know you like I do."

"Thank you."

"If they did then they would really hate you."

I shook my head. Everybody's a comedian. "Thanks again."

"Just joking. So, how's it going? Really?"

"Well, I heard that so far they can't confirm with DNA that I had any contact with the dead girl and there are no witnesses that can confirm my being in the room with her so I'd say that things are looking up. There's a lot of circumstantial evidence though and that could be a problem. It's not clear yet when I'll be able to resume my life. I can't just return to work and pretend I'm not wanted in a murder investigation even if I've been downgraded to a person of interest and I'm not sure I want to volunteer myself for questioning especially now that the mob is involved. They might not require as much evidence to convict me as the police."

"So what are you going to do?"

"Right now my goal is to stay out of the crosshairs of whoever is looking for me. I'll stay in touch and keep you posted. Keep it between me and you that we've been in contact. You now have my new number so add it to your contact list. If I change phones again, I'll let you know. All right and thank you again for caring for Cleo."

"No problem. Be careful all right?"

"I will. Bye."

I hung up and noticed Francesca watching me. She said, "She sounds really sweet."

"Yeah, she is very nice."

"So what happened to you two? It's okay if you don't want to say."

"No, it wasn't that big a deal. We were both very busy with our lives. She's studying piano at Juilliard in midtown and I'm practicing downtown. We just kind of grew apart. The usual, different friends, different interests, different time zones so to speak."

"I think it's really nice that you're still friends."

"Yeah well, like I said, it was mutual, no nuclear bombs went off. We just kind of woke up one day and knew it was time to move on."

"Wouldn't it be great if every relationship ended as peacefully as that?"

I thought about, Kelly, now married with kids. I nodded and sighed. "Yeah."

As we talked it suddenly occurred to me that Frankie might have met Seymour at *The Fall of Rome*. He had obviously been there on more than one occasion so I asked, "Frankie, can I ask you a question concerning a customer at the club, a friend of mine?"

"Sure."

"It's not against some sort of code?"

She chuckled. "Yeah, right."

"There's an anesthesiologist that I work with in New York. He's the one who brought me to the club that night. I was wondering if you knew him. His name is Seymour, big guy—enormous actually, four hundred pounds easy, maybe closer to four hundred and fifty, always sweating."

"Oh, the gas man. That's what we call him. Yeah, I've never met him but I've seen him. Thank God he's never requested me. He's a frequent flyer at the club. Not every week but maybe once a month or every other month. He's a freak and gives all the girls the creeps. He's into bondage and weird stuff. Several of the girls have refused to work with him but he pays extra so Luther always found someone."

I was taken aback by this. Luther had confirmed that Seymour had been to the club on several occasions, but for him to have been there often enough that the girls had actually given him a nickname surprised me.

"Anything else you can tell me about him?" I asked.

She thought about it. "Well, actually yes. There were at least one or two times when Luther asked for volunteers to go to Seymour's hotel room rather than he come to the club. Luther said the job guaranteed a thousand dollars whether Seymour came or died of a heart attack in the process. I didn't like the idea of it especially with his reputation for the funky stuff."

"Thanks, Frankie. When you say funky stuff could you be more specific? I don't know if it matters but it might."

"I'm not a hundred percent sure. It's not exactly a sorority there at the club. We don't generally compare notes but there were stories that he liked to cause pain. You know, watch people suffer. Sick stuff. I really can't be specific. I know weird stuff turned him on. One of the girls I'm friends with said that when she went to his hotel room he made her wear an old fashioned gas mask while they—you know."

Filled with morbid curiosity I asked, “A gas mask?”

“Yeah, one like you might see in an old war movie and he put one on too. That’s why we call him the gas man. Anyway, she said the mask was hot and she could barely breathe in it and when he got on top of her she felt like she was suffocating. She begged him to let her take it off but he refused. She panicked and pulled it off anyway. He slapped her around for it and she complained to Luther. She was really frightened.”

“Oh my God! He’s an even bigger asshole than I thought. So what happened?”

“Nothing happened. Luther told her to stop whining or he’d throw her out of the club.”

I shook my head. “Wow. Well, that is interesting. I thought you called him the gas man because he was an anesthesiologist. That’s what other doctors call them.”

“No, I didn’t even know that until you just mentioned it. No one liked him. I can tell you that much. Whenever he was in town, the alarm used to go out at the club. Girls would spread the word that the he was on the way. Only they would lower their voices and whisper it like they were in a horror movie. Like this.” She stood up suddenly and pantomimed what happened. She made an overly serious face and hung her arms down low, rocking back and forth in zombie-like fashion. Then very slowly in a deep voice she said, “The gas man cometh.”

I chuckled. “Seriously? The gas man cometh?”

She sat back down. “Yeah. Was that helpful?”

“Not sure yet but it certainly raises a few more questions.” Like why wasn’t Seymour more forthright about what was going on at the club and that he had been there on numerous occasions? Was he just embarrassed by it? A guy that looked like Seymour probably wasn’t getting a whole lot of secret Valentine’s Day cards so maybe brothels were his only outlet. Throw in the fact that he was a sicko and there you have it.

I needed to think it over some more. I didn't like it when people lied to me, especially when I wake up in a dead girl's room.

Chapter 21

An hour outside of New York, I called Troy while Francesca napped. "Cesari, where have you been? Half the hospital thinks you fled the country and are either in Mexico or Italy."

"Close but no cigar, Troy."

"So where are you?"

"I'm on a train coming into Penn Station and I need a huge favor."

"Sure, anything."

"Are you sure about that?"

"What do you need? I know you didn't kill anybody."

"I need a place to stay for a few days and I have a girl with me. I'll explain later about her. I can't use my credit cards at the moment and trying to pay cash sometimes raises eyebrows in your better establishments."

I heard him sigh deeply into the phone. "John, please try to understand. Anything but that. I just don't have room. I live in a two bedroom apartment with three kids. This is simple math and what if the police find you here. They could charge me and my wife with harboring a fugitive. I know you're innocent but please don't ask me to place my family in danger. I'm sorry."

He was right. I wasn't thinking straight on that one. Before I could respond he added, "Hey, wait a minute. How about I get a room for you with my credit card? In fact, I can even lend you my MasterCard and you can get your own room. If something happens I'll just say you must have stolen it while we were in Vegas and I was unaware it was missing."

I liked that idea. Simple and clean. I really couldn't see any downside. I said, "And we'll even things out when the dust settles."

"Yes, is that okay?"

"It's more than okay. It's very white of you, Troy."

He chuckled. "You're such an asshole, Cesari. I should call the police right now. So where do you want to meet me to get the card?"

I looked at my watch. We'll arrive at Penn Station at five. That's less than an hour from now. There's a coffee shop on Seventh Avenue across from the entrance to Madison Square Garden. Let's meet there."

"See you there in an hour. Is there anything else?"

"Yeah, one more thing. Do you know where Seymour lives?"

"Seymour? You're not thinking of trying to crash at his place?"

I smiled at that thought and suddenly the image of cupboards full of Twinkies and potato chips came to me. "No, I was just curious is all. I have a hunch about something. You think you could find his address for me?"

"I'll look it up. It's got to be on file somewhere at the hospital. I'll call over to the medical staff office before everyone goes home and try to have it for you when I see you."

"Thanks Troy."

I read a magazine until we pulled into the station. There was an article about the Big Bang Theory that caught my attention. This stuff always fascinated me. From nothing came everything is how the theory goes. One day there was nothing, then nothing blew up and then there was everything and you're not allowed to ask the obvious question of so what was there before the nothingness. I had asked that question many times during the course of my higher education and nothing rattled a physicist's cage more than that one. Or even better, if there was a big bang, what exactly went bang if there was nothing there to go bang? I mean nothing means nothing, right? Science was the new religion we were all supposed to bow down to and scientists were the new high priests. Yet all religions seem to have one common core: believe me because I tell you to even though I can't prove any of it.

At five, just as the train was pulling into the station, I nudged Francesca. "We're here."

She shook the sleepies from her eyes, yawned, stood up, and stretched. We grabbed our stuff from the overhead compartment and trudged to the exit. Outside, the blustery air sent a chill through us and we gasped from the cold. It was in the teens and cloudy. The biting wind nipped at our ears. Bundled up New Yorkers hustled back and forth hurriedly to their destinations as did we.

Francesca said, "God, it's colder here than in Chicago."

"Yeah, there's the coffee shop across the street."

We crossed and entered the café spotting Troy already at a small table sipping a latte. He stood up to greet us and I introduced Francesca. We ordered coffees and sat down in conference.

"Glad to see you're okay Cesari." He was very polite and didn't mention Francesca's obvious facial trauma. He'd probably ask me about it at a later time. On the other hand, he was a cautious guy and maybe felt the less he knew the better.

"Thanks, Troy."

The coffee was hot and freshly brewed served in heavy, white porcelain mugs. It felt good going down. He passed me a white envelope. "I stopped at an ATM machine. There's three hundred dollars in addition to my MasterCard and Seymour's address in there. He lives in an old brownstone on W. 11th Street."

"I appreciate this Troy. I really do."

"I know you do. You realize of course you can't go on like this forever. Arnie and I made a pact not to talk about it to anyone. As far as we know, you went to Vegas and disappeared the first night. We haven't seen or heard from you since. For all we know you could be dead, but sooner or later you're going to have to surface and face the music. Besides, things are starting to look up for you."

"They are?"

"Right before we left Vegas, the news was reporting that the murder might have been some sort of gangland slaying. The pimp at that club was beaten half to death and found in the middle of the desert the other day. Some people are speculating that maybe he killed the girl and that her gangster boyfriend may have went after him as an act of revenge. The pimp's in a coma and it's unclear whether he's going to make it. This is some unbelievable shit you stepped into, Cesari."

"Well, I have to admit, I kind of like that version better than the one where I'm a blood thirsty murderer. So what does this gangster boyfriend have to say for himself?"

"No one knows because they haven't found him yet."

This certainly was becoming interesting. I glanced at Francesca who was sipping her cappuccino listening intently. I cleared my throat.

"Say Troy, I need to ask you one more favor if you don't mind?"

He eyed me suspiciously and sighed. "What?"

"Is there any chance you could ask Seymour over to your house for dinner?"

He snorted and coffee shot out of his nose. Francesca and I ducked as he exclaimed. "Are you fucking crazy? I'm not going to expose my wife and kids to that guy."

I laughed. "Okay, maybe you could meet him for a drink somewhere then?"

"Why? What are you going to do?"

"He's up to his eyeballs in whatever happened out there Troy, and I need to find out exactly how and why."

"Seymour? I don't get it. What's he got to do with anything?"

I gave him the short version and his eyes rolled as he said, "So you think Seymour is mixed up in this?"

"I don't think it. I know it. The question is what is he up to and what does he know about that night that I don't?"

"Look, I understand you're in one hell of a mess, but that's a tall order asking me to spend an evening with Seymour. I can't even stand being in the same room with him."

"I know Troy, but he's actually not that bad one on one. I had dinner with him. It wasn't so bad. He was actually kind of funny."

"I bet he's a riot and look how that night ended up for you."

"You have a point but I need him distracted for a couple of hours."

He thought about that and covered his face with his hands. "I'd almost rather go to prison in your place than do this."

Francesca and I smiled at each other. I said, "So you'll do it?"

He groaned. "Yeah, I'll do it. Fuck, I should have my head examined."

"Troy, it won't be so bad. I'll call you as soon as I'm done and you can dump him."

"As soon as you're done doing what? You didn't say."

"And for your sake I'm not going to. That would make you an accessory."

"Oh that's great."

"Just keep him away from his apartment for as long as you can and give me a heads up if he leaves before I call."

"Fine."

We said goodbye and left Troy in the coffee shop while he buzzed Seymour on his phone to see if he wanted to grab a burger somewhere to discuss the conference and everything else that had happened. He would text me to let me know if it was a go. In the meanwhile, Francesca and I needed to find a room for the night and get dinner because I was ready to pass out from hunger. I also needed to find a place for my duffel bag. I was carrying around three handguns and a crowbar and it was starting to make me nervous. In New York City three handguns with consecutive mandatory sentencing could get you ten years in prison minimum.

A cab dropped us off in front of the Union Square Hyatt on Fourth Avenue just a few blocks from Seymour's apartment and we checked into a room using Troy's credit card. I secured the handguns in the hotel's closet safe, and after freshening up, we headed out for a bite to eat, finding a small pizzeria called Patsy's on W. 12th Street. I carried the duffel bag with the crowbar in it.

We ordered a couple of slices with pepperoni and soda, sitting down to eat at a small white laminate table. It was a classic, old style place; small, functional, and no frills. You could eat standing up at the counter or sitting at one of the few tables present. There were dispensers with red pepper flakes, garlic, and oregano nearby if you wished to enhance your dining experience. There was even an old fashioned jukebox against the wall near the entrance. I hadn't seen one of those in ages

Looking at it I said, "I wonder if it works or if it's just a decoration?"

"It looks real. These things are starting to make a comeback like turntables and vinyl records. People are very nostalgic about things like that."

I nodded and stood up to examine it. It was about four feet high, metal on the bottom with a speaker grill, glass or plastic dome with a rolodex listing of all the songs available. To one side was a coin receptacle that was labeled *One Song 50 cents.*

I turned to the pizza guy behind the counter flipping dough high in the air and asked, "Does this thing work?"

"Sure, go ahead. Quarters only, no dimes or nickels."

I looked over at Francesca who was smiling. I fished out a couple of quarters from my pocket, perused the selections, finally settling in on a Van Morrison classic, "Brown Eyed Girl."

I sat back down and as the music played, Francesca eyed me contentedly. I took a bite of pizza and said, "So, what's on your mind?"

She shook her head and shrugged. "I don't know. This is going to sound weird, but I feel like I've known you my whole life."

"Is that a compliment? Because from what I've seen and heard so far, most of the men in your life haven't been so nice. So where does that leave me?"

She laughed. "What I meant was that you're easy to get along with. I feel very comfortable around you like I can be myself. That's a nice feeling."

I thought about that. "If you weren't yourself then who would you be? And don't say Matilda."

She grinned. "In my business, you learn to be whoever it is that is standing in front of you wants you to be. So who do you want me to be; stern schoolteacher, naughty nun, lusty maid? You name it."

I smiled and thought it about it for a couple of seconds, listening to the music. I said, "I want you to be my brown-eyed-girl."

Her grin turned into broad, happy smile. "I can do that."

I liked these kinds of conversations so I took it a step further. "So who do you want to be—really? Let me rephrase that; who are you really—inside? Not who do you want to be."

She sat back and took a sip of soda. "I like to read poetry and I'm fascinated by sleight of hand and I love to laugh. My real dream is to do stand-up comedy. You know like in clubs and things like that."

"Really? That's very interesting. Have you tried it? Stand up, I mean."

"No, I haven't had the opportunity."

"Those jokes you told me in the car. Did you write them? They were great."

"No, those were just hand me downs, but I'm going to start writing my own material."

"You should. You've got great delivery and timing. That's ninety percent of comedy right there."

"Thanks."

"Well, I'm a bit of a comedian myself or so I've been told."

She smiled. "You mean when you're not beating people up."

"Exactly."

My cellphone buzzed with a text from Troy. I read it and said, "It's on. Seymour agreed to meet him for a drink at eight. That'll work out perfectly. I'll walk you back to the hotel and then head on over to his brownstone."

"Can't I come along?"

I hesitated. "I didn't think you'd want to."

"Maybe I can help?"

"There's going to be some breaking and entering."

"I kind of assumed that's why you brought the crowbar. What is it you're looking for exactly?"

"Nothing and everything. Just trying to get to know the guy better. You know, see what makes him tick."

She ate the last bit of cheese from her slice, chucked the crust into the garbage and glanced at the wall clock.

"Let's have at it."

Chapter 22

We made our way over to Seymour's brownstone which was in the middle of the block between Fifth Avenue and Avenue of the Americas. The entire block was upscale and rowed with stately homes. Seymour lived in a very nice neighborhood. Dark and cold, there were few people out, and those who were clutched their scarves and lapels minding their own business. Troy would try to occupy Seymour for as long as he could but I doubted he could keep him longer than two hours tops. That should be enough time.

We looked both ways, hastened across the empty street, and climbed the ten or so steps up to his front door. The building was three stories tall including the above ground basement, but I only saw one buzzer and mailbox. Maybe Seymour rented or owned the whole building. The wood door was painted dark green and I examined it for weaknesses. There were three locks, probably dead bolts, and the frame was metal. It would take me forever to pry this open with a crowbar, assuming I could, and we would undoubtedly be seen by someone in the process.

"Not good, I gather?" Francesca asked, noticing the frown on my face.

I shook my head. "No, this won't work at all. I would need a sledge hammer and a chisel."

"How do you know he doesn't have an alarm?"

"I don't, but figured we could just walk away if he did."

I went down the stairs to the sidewalk and looked around. There were windows to the basement but they were boarded up and had steel security bars on them. Down the block, one of the brownstones was undergoing renovation and there was scaffolding in front of the façade. The tops of the buildings were flat and I thought about the escape hatches at *The Fall of Rome* in Vegas. Of course, there wouldn't be escape hatches here but there might be ways onto the roof from inside the homes to repair or replace the roof tops. In fact, there had to be.

"Frankie, I'm going to climb up to the roof and see if there's a way in. I want you to wait across the street and keep an eye out. You know what Seymour looks like. He's pretty hard to miss."

"Aren't you going to let me in? It's freezing out here."

I thought about it. Troy would give me a heads up, but what if for some reason I didn't get the call or text? It would be nice to have someone keeping an eye out for me as a second layer of security, but she had a point. It was in the teens, windy, and getting colder by the minute.

Relenting I said, "Okay, if I get in I'll open the front door."

"Thanks."

I walked over to the scaffolding then glanced around quickly and started climbing up the side with the duffel bag hanging over my neck and shoulder. It wasn't very difficult to maneuver as it was designed for men to have easy access up and down. The metal was very cold and stung my hands. I kicked myself for not buying gloves. Otherwise, I was pretty comfortable with blue jeans, a flannel shirt, wool sweater, gortex jacket, and knit hat. I made it to the top uneventfully and clambered from there to the roof. Looking down, I spotted Francesca shivering up against a tree watching me. When she saw me looking at her, she waved.

Very subtle, Frankie. Very subtle.

I couldn't help myself and blew her a kiss which she caught. I was losing my mind and knew it. Seymour's building was five away and I quickly and easily made it over there, finding a three foot square door with a rusted metal handle in the center. It was fully covered with roofing material which overlapped the door's opening to prevent water seepage. I tugged on the handle and it didn't budge so I tugged harder. Still nothing. I took the crowbar out of the duffel bag and inserted it under the flap of protective roofing paper finding the small gap between the door and its wood frame. Once wedged snuggly in I applied firm pressure until I heard a popping sound and the door inched upward. I opened it fully and saw that that it was secured by a simple slide lock which I had just broken.

Peering down into the darkness, I was unsure of how to proceed next. The ambient light from the city that never sleeps made rooftop visibility fair but that didn't help me looking down into the building so I took out my cheap flip phone, opened it, and held it out. The faint green light did little to improve the situation and I made a mental note that the next time I would buy a smart phone with one of those flash light apps. I felt around with an outstretched arm and unfortunately, there was no ladder leading downward. I sighed. How could I not have brought a flashlight with me? I was slipping for sure.

I briefly considered what I would do if there was someone else there such as another tenant or a roommate and guessed I would just run as fast as I could. What were the odds of that? Pretty slim probably, unless it was a mail order bride. I chuckled to myself at that but then grew suddenly concerned that I might find some poor Russian girl chained to his kitchen table.

Having made up my mind, I sat on the edge of the opening with the duffel bag around my neck and slowly lowered myself in, hanging onto the ledge with my fingers. I dangled like that for a few seconds and then, bracing myself for serious injury, let go. I hit a carpeted floor not more than three feet under me. The impact stung my knees and ankles but I was otherwise fine. I let my eyes adjust to the darkness and after a minute, started exploring the room, eventually finding a wall switch and turning on the overhead light.

I found myself in a fully furnished bedroom with a queen bed, armoire and bathroom; however, the room looked unlived in. There were no hair brushes, mirrors, picture frames, books, slippers, and the like. I opened the armoire and there were no clothes. The same with the bureau drawers. It looked like a hotel room waiting for a guest.

Exploring the rest of the floor revealed the same thing; a fully furnished apartment without signs of an occupant. Quietly, I went down the stairs and again found the same thing; another lovely spacious apartment without signs of life. One of the rooms was locked and I decided not to break in. I presumed it was a bedroom. I went to the front door, opened it, and signaled to Francesca across the street. She came running over and I relocked the door behind her.

"Find anything?" she asked.

"Not much." Her cheeks and nose were rosy from the brisk night air. "There is one thing however. The upstairs is fully furnished but it doesn't appear that any one lives there. No clothes, towels, pictures, empty refrigerator, that kind of stuff. I was just starting to look around down here and was getting the same feeling. One of the rooms down here is locked but the kitchen and living room don't seem right. There's no sign of life. It's like the house is up for sale."

Standing in the foyer by the front door, I opened the hall closet and saw nothing; no coats, scarves, hats—nothing. I said, "See what I mean?"

"Yes. What about the locked room? Are we going to break in?"

"Good question and I'm tempted but then he'll know for sure someone was here. There's still one more floor to check. Let's do that before we leave a calling card."

The door to the basement was toward the rear of this floor and was unlocked. We flipped the light switch on at the top of the stairs and descended uneventfully, happy to finally discover Seymour's living space.

"It's kind of nice down here," I commented as we looked around. There were two nice-sized bedrooms, a large, central living area with a TV, and a small kitchen. Nothing unusual. I opened one of the cupboards and found multiple boxes of Hostess cupcakes stacked neatly on top of each other. I smiled. They weren't Twinkies but I was close.

"Should I be looking for anything in particular?" she asked, scanning around the apartment.

"Can't say. I guess I'm looking for anything unusual or anything that might tie him to Luther or Carmine in a more substantial way than I already know."

We didn't find anything suspicious in the kitchen or living room. Both bedrooms were fully furnished with king beds and at least one of the rooms looked lived in. There were towels, a robe, shaving equipment in the bathroom with other paraphernalia. There was a book on the night table that he was reading called *Devil in the White City* by Erik Larson. I searched through all the drawers, closets, and cabinets but found nothing incriminating and was starting to think I was barking up the wrong tree. The second bedroom was equally disappointing. Large, inviting, nicely decorated with its own full bath but there was something slightly different about this room. The floor was tiled for one thing as opposed to the soft plush rug in the other and there was a slightly pungent odor coming out of the bathroom. It was a vaguely familiar scent but I couldn't quite place it.

Francesca saw me furrowing my brow in concentration and asked, "What is it?"

"I don't know. Do you smell that?"

"Yeah," she agreed. "Kind of acidy."

That was it—acidity. Hydrochloric acid or maybe sulphuric acid. I remembered that smell from chemistry class. You never forgot things like that.

I walked over to the bathroom and opened the closet doors and cabinets underneath the sink but found nothing but a mop, a cleaning bucket and a sponge. The odor was much stronger here but still only faint at best. I pulled the shower curtain and found a stainless steel bathtub. That was odd. I don't think I had ever seen one before. It looked almost like a very large sink. Sticking my face in to take a big whiff, I noticed the acrid scent was strongest yet here. He had used some type of industrial strength acid in his bathtub but why? My mind raced trying to think of everyday uses of acid but could not come up with any that made sense.

"John, come look at this," Francesca had been in the bedroom and came to find me.

"What's up? You find a gas mask?" I asked half in jest as I followed her back to the bedroom.

"No, but I've been looking trust me."

She pointed to a night table drawer she had opened revealing plyers, screwdrivers, duct tape and a hammer.

I said, "So?"

"You don't think this is odd to find in a night table?"

"Maybe a little, but not that much."

"Well I think it's very odd, and sit on the bed."

"Sit on the bed?"

"Yes, sit on the bed."

I sat on the side of the bed and noticed that it moved just a tiny bit. She said, "See what I mean?"

We pulled up the bed skirt and discovered the bed was on wheels. Now that was interesting. Who has a king bed on wheels? Someone who wants to move it back and forth a lot, that's who. So we pushed the bed away from its resting spot and discovered a four foot square trap door in the center of the space underneath. I pulled on the latch handle opening the metal door and revealing a series of winding stone steps leading into darkness. Cool damp malodorous air rushed into the room and we held our breath. The door was heavy and apparently self-locking with a sturdy metal rod to prop it open very similar to that found on the hoods of cars. I thought that was peculiar. Was he afraid of someone entering his home from below? I'd be more afraid of locking myself down there accidentally. Which begged the question of what exactly was down there?

Francesca looked at me concerned and asked, "What do you think?"

"I don't know, but I don't like the feeling I'm getting. Stay here, I'm going down. I hope there's a light somewhere."

Frankie grew anxious. "Be careful, John. I don't like this at all."

I descended slowly as far as I could, probing the walls on either side for a light switch but found none. After fifteen methodical steps, I found myself in utter darkness and realized that without a flashlight, it would be useless to try to investigate any further so I returned to Francesca.

"Anything?" she asked.

"It's too dark down there but I could swear I heard water."

We had just finished pushing the bed back into position when my phone buzzed with a text message from Troy. Seymour left the bar earlier than anticipated.

"Let's rock." We turned off all the lights and ran up the stairs. We hadn't really searched the entire main floor but we didn't have time to and it probably didn't matter at this point anyway. After quickly putting the room back in order, I let Francesca out the front door and locked it behind her. I then ran up the stairs to leave through the roof because I didn't want Seymour to find the door open. Even though nothing was missing that would still place him on high alert and I had every intention of returning. In the bedroom I found that I couldn't jump high enough to reach the ledge of the open roof door no matter how hard I tried. There was chair next to a desk and I positioned it under the opening.

Once on the roof, I closed the door tightly. Unfortunately, I had to leave the chair out of position. He would find that peculiar but not necessarily alarming. I ran toward the scaffolding quickly descending down to street level. Francesca helped me down the last few feet and we took off at a fast walk, holding each other and out of breath from the excitement.

Safely away, we stopped under a streetlight and she threw her arms around me, smiling. "Damn, you're a lot of fun."

I laughed. "I hope you still think that when you're sitting in a prison cell."

She glanced up at me and the look in her eyes changed. She whispered, "I think we should go back to the hotel room. I am really, really turned on right now."

All women were a little nuts I thought but said, "That's a great idea."

Chapter 23

Seymour entered his brownstone and immediately sensed something was wrong. Somebody had been here. He could smell it; perfume or cologne or after shave. There was a lingering trace of something in the air. He looked around carefully but nothing was out of place. Calling out to his mother, he didn't expect an answer at this late hour. There was no response. She was undoubtedly sound asleep. Still, it couldn't hurt to check.

He took out his keys and unlocked the door to the bedroom, flipping the light switch he saw that she lay on the bed sleeping comfortably. His entry hadn't awoken her. He didn't think it would. She had been agitated earlier and he had given her a hefty dose of Xanax to quiet her down before going out to see Troy. He turned off the light and relocked the door.

In his apartment downstairs, he saw that everything was in place so why did he have this nagging feeling in the back of his head? He wasn't an alarmist by any means. Maybe this whole let's be best buds thing with Troy had rattled him more than he realized.

Let's have a drink and hang out? What was that about anyway? Troy had never wanted to be friends before. He was second only to Cesari on the list of people he would like to see drop off a cliff and maybe he really *would* drop him off a cliff one day. His wife was kind of cute though. Maybe after he dropped Troy off a cliff he would invite her over. Hmm. Brown sugar. Yum.

Relaxing somewhat, he took his coat off and placed it in a closet. Sitting on the sofa he tried to sort out the unusual social request from Troy. Married, black, three kids, always making smart-ass comments. The whole time we were in Vegas, he never once asked to have a drink or hit the casinos or anything. Granted, the Cesari situation had thrown a damper on things for everybody but still… Now, all of a sudden, barely back in New York, he gives me the let's hang out call and all he wanted to do was talk about Cesari.

Well, he surmised, that last part made sense. Everyone wanted to know what was going on with Cesari. Thanks to him, Seymour, Cesari was now famous. He made a mental note to send Cesari his bill. That made him chuckle.

He sighed deeply. Vegas had been an utter catastrophe from start to finish and now no one knew where Cesari was. Luther was in a coma and he personally had barely escaped Carmine's wrath. He was sure that there was no way he could be tied to anything that had happened but still there were too many loose ends for comfort. He wasn't particularly worried about Cesari though. He had no idea what was going on and if the Vegas police didn't get him, Carmine would. Seymour took solace in that but he wasn't happy that someone as nasty and dangerous as Carmine knew who he was, and where to find him. He could only hope that somebody caught Cesari and he was determined to make that happen as quickly as possible.

He looked at his watch. Almost 11:00 p.m. Tomorrow was bath time for mother, something he didn't necessarily enjoy but had to be done.

Chapter 24

"Are you kidding me Arnie?" It was 9:00 a.m. and Frankie and I were having breakfast in a diner not too far from the hotel. Nothing fancy, just your basic New York diner, when Goldstein called to give me more bad news.

"I kid you not, Cesari. Lance filed a formal complaint against you with the board late last night and is threatening to go to the police. He says you punched and slapped him around right before we went to Vegas."

"He's such an asshole."

"Did you or didn't you?"

"Does he have a witness?"

"No, but you are wanted for questioning in a heinous murder and are now a fugitive from the law so people might take his accusation a little more seriously than they might ordinarily. And you didn't answer the question by the way which in itself settles that."

"He tried to kill my patient, Arnie."

"And you believe that gave you the right to administer corporal punishment to him?"

When I didn't respond he added, "Well, he's a little smarter than you gave him credit for. He knows you're in a position of weakness and now he's going for the jugular. The board is insisting I take some sort of action."

"Like what?"

"At a very minimum, I have to suspend your privileges at St. Matt's pending an investigation and ultimately, if you aren't exonerated of the Vegas thing, I may have to recommend your termination."

"You've got to be kidding?"

"John, I don't know what happened with you and Lance but this Vegas thing is serious. We have to do what's right for the hospital and the community. I can't have him escalating things in the newspapers by accusing you of aggravated assault inside the hospital. Fuck, at the very least you should have taken him outside. We can't have all of New York thinking we have Wild Bill Hickok on staff. Did you really pull his hair and bitch-slap him?"

"I can't even remember what happened in a Vegas motel room, Arnie." I said lamely.

"Be that as it may, you are hereby suspended. Do not come onto hospital property, attempt to access your medical records or contact your patients until the suspension is lifted. I'll do what I can behind the scenes to assuage the board, but in the meantime, since we are now officially short one very busy gastroenterologist, I'm going to have to let Lance see your patients."

I was seething. "Arnie, when this is over I'm going to dissect that frog."

"I'm going to pretend that I didn't hear you just threaten another physician on staff. Look, I'll keep you up to date as things progress and if there is anything I can do within reason let me know."

Forcing myself to calm down I said, "Thanks."

I hung up and pushed my plate away, sitting back in the booth. Frankie looked at me sympathetically. You didn't have to be a genius to figure out that was not a good phone call.

"Whatever it is, I'm sorry." Frankie said softly and added. "I'm sure it can't be much worse than being wanted for a murder you didn't commit."

I smiled. She had a point. "You're right about that. I just hate it when people kick you when you're down. Know what I mean?"

She nodded. "Oh boy, do I ever. So who's this frog you're going to dissect and should I warn him that a freight train is heading his way?"

I gave her the short version and she rolled her eyes. "Apparently, this guy Lancelot doesn't know you very well."

"No, he doesn't but he will—and real soon, but first things first. What are we going to do about you?"

"I thought we were doing just fine."

"Maybe you don't get it but not only are the police looking for me but most of the New York underworld as well. The icing on the cake is that possibly I really am a murdering son-of-a-bitch who might turn on you one night."

She chuckled, adjusted herself in her seat and said, "One, I don't believe for a minute you murdered Jenny. I know a set up when I see it and this one smells to high heaven. Two, I'm used to the police and tough guys. They don't bother me in the slightest. The only thing that even marginally concerns me is that I might lose contact with the only real man I've met in a long time." I started to speak and she put her hands up. "Let me finish. I don't have any illusions about what's going on here. I'm an ex-drug addict whore and you're a doctor. I get it. This is not going to be one of those ride off into the sunset romances where we have little brats running around inside a white picket fence." She paused taking a breath. "In my world when you find happiness, even a tiny bit, you grab it because you know it's precious, rare, and transient. I like being with you. You're different. You're nice and…"

She hesitated so I prompted her. "And what?"

"And you care. You helped me even though you didn't have to. Who am I? I'm nobody. I'm garbage waiting for a body bag." She sniffled and her eyes watered up.

"Frankie, no you're not. You're still a kid. You made some poor choices. Your life is still beginning. You can turn it around. You need to believe in yourself."

Overwhelmed with her emotions, she couldn't speak and turned her head to avoid eye contact. "Are you going to throw me away, John?"

I let out a deep breath and thought it over. It never hurt to have someone watching your back and she was streetwise after all. She had nowhere to go and I'd have to drop her off at a shelter if I wanted to be rid of her and how long would she stay there? Not long, I mused. I scratched my head, torn. She was tough. I'd grant her that, but if Brunella caught her with me she was going to get a lot more than a beating.

I started to strum my fingers on the table and she asked, "Well?"

"I'm thinking."

She folded her arms and pouted. "I just laid my soul bare to you and that's what you say?"

I took my wallet out and paid the bill. "C'mon let's go for walk."

It was thirty degrees outside and lightly snowing. Frankie put her arm through mine and asked, "Do you mind?"

"No, not at all."

"So, what are you thinking about?"

"Mostly about how we're going to do this."

"We?"

I made my decision for better or for worse. I liked her. "Yeah, we."

"Thanks." That made her happy and she slipped her arm around my waist and pulled mine around her as we walked along the avenue.

"You know Frankie, there's a slight chance that I may not figure this out."

She nodded. "Maybe. Then what?"

"I don't know."

"Well, don't give up yet. Besides, you seem pretty resourceful."

"Thanks."

We went shopping for a few essential items I needed for my return trip to Seymour's apartment such as a rope, a couple of flashlights, and a second throw away phone for Frankie. I called Troy at the hospital, brought him up to speed and asked him to find out Seymour's OR schedule. He told me Seymour would be tied up all day, finishing with a gallbladder scheduled to start at four. I thanked him and hung up.

"C'mon Frankie. We have work to do." I looked at my watch. It was 11 a.m. That should be plenty of time. Unless there was a last minute cancellation, Seymour shouldn't even be leaving the OR until well after six.

We hoofed it back to his brownstone and by noon I was scrambling onto the roof five buildings down. It was broad daylight and a few people watched with curiosity and then simply moved along. It was cold and snowing lightly and if some idiot wanted to play games with his life then so be it. I pulled the roof door open and discovered a second metal handle centered on the inside. Last night, I hadn't noticed it, but now I looped my rope through it and lowered myself gently rather than jumping. It was a miracle that I didn't sprain or break my ankle last evening. My weight closed the door snugly as I descended which was also good. No point in Seymour coming home and finding a pile of snow in his upstairs bedroom. The chair hadn't been moved and I returned it to its original position.

Gathering up the rope, I went downstairs, opened the front door, and let Frankie in. We quickly scanned the main floor and satisfied ourselves that there was not much there of interest and descended into Seymour's main living space. We went directly to the bedroom in question, moved the bed, and pulled open the door, propping it open with the accompanying metal bar. We paused for a minute, looking at each other.

I said, "Are you sure you want to do this? I have no idea where or what this is going to lead to."

"I'm in," she replied with confidence.

"Okay, I'll lead. It's pretty dark down there and the steps are quite steep and irregular so I'll tie one end of the rope to the bedframe and we'll use it as a guide and support."

We turned on the flashlights and began our slow, winding descent, gradually unravelling the 100 foot long rope as we proceeded. The walls were coarse, made of stone as if they had been hacked roughly and unprofessionally from the underlying bedrock. The steps were lopsided, made of stone and in some cases supplemented with cement now crumbling with age. After fifteen minutes, we reached the end of the rope but not the steps. At this point we could clearly hear and smell water so we dropped the rope and proceeded approximately another fifty feet before we leveled off into a cement lined tunnel with a pool of foul smelling stagnant water. Droplets from cracks in the ceiling pinged off the surface.

"This is disgusting." Frankie said, holding her nose. "What is it?"

I shone my flashlight around the perimeter trying to assess its size and significance. "I can't say for sure but I think we've just entered the bowels of New York City's ancient sewer system. I thought about the location of Seymour's apartment. He wasn't too far from the West Side of Manhattan and I wondered if we followed the tunnel would we eventually wind up at the Hudson River? Probably. Raw sewage wasn't supposed to dump directly into the waters surrounding the island anymore but two hundred years' worth of winding subterranean tunnels still existed. Who knew if anybody even knew of this one? Maybe this tunnel was just an artifact, a relic from a bygone era, a historical footnote in a city with a million historical footnotes.

I said, "I think we're in the city's original sewer system. Most of the flow from these old sewer lines have been diverted to modern tunnels which flow through water treatment plants before heading out. There's not nearly as much water in here as the size of this tunnel suggests it could accommodate and probably once did."

"So what do you want to do?"

"I'm sure if we follow the water westward it will take us to the Hudson River. Are you up to it? I'm curious. I'm sure it can't be more than a half mile."

She took a deep breath. I was pushing her too far. "I don't know if I like this. It's dark and creepy down here. What if we get lost? How do you even know which way is west?"

"You have a point. Maybe you should stay here by the steps. I'll go in further to explore. I won't go far or for long I promise and with your flashlight on I won't get lost." I had purchased us two powerful LED flashlights which in this utter darkness could be seen for a mile or more.

Alarmed she said, "You're going to leave me alone?"

"No more than ten minutes Frankie, I promise. I just want to get a feel for why someone might have a trap door leading down to the sewers. If you came with me I suppose we could leave one of the flashlights on the floor or on the step but what if for some reason it moved or if a rat came along and decided to play with it?"

"A rat?!"

"Actually, I'm surprised we haven't seen any yet."

"Gross."

"Frankie, we're in a sewer, remember?"

She sighed deeply as she thought it over. The possibility of running into vermin obviously grossed her out and she said, "Fine, I'll stay here but please don't be long."

"I won't."

I turned, took a wild guess at which way was west and, cold and damp, trudged along the side of the putrid water as it meandered down the tunnel. The body of water was about five feet wide and I estimated no more than a foot deep. The tunnel was easily ten maybe twelve feet wide and I had plenty of room to walk without stepping into the foul liquid.

A hundred yards in, the tunnel curved sharply to the right. Looking back I saw the light moving up and down and to the side as Frankie explored her surroundings. I continued on and followed the tunnel with Frankie now out of direct line of sight. I didn't like doing that but I had no choice. Another fifty yards and I heard a faint high-pitched chattering sound in the distance. I couldn't see anything to explain the sound but noticed that the pool of water was shrinking as I advanced and eventually dried up.

With each step it seemed the sound grew louder and barely twenty five yards further it sounded more like muffled screeching. Suddenly, I noticed two things simultaneously. The tunnel dead-ended in a brick wall and at the base was a horde of hundreds, maybe thousands of rats swarming over something I couldn't yet make out. At first they didn't notice me but as I came closer the alarm went out amongst them and they fled squealing in all directions; through my legs, over my feet but mainly through crevices and holes in the old tunnel. The rats gone, I saw skeletal remains of a human being with nothing left on its bones but a few sinews, tendons and strands of hair. They had actually bit a hole through the skull itself to get at the brains. There were no clothes or articles of identification. Had they eaten that too? I felt a wave of nausea sweep over me but managed to control it.

I leaned against the brick wall to regain my composure and heard water. Pressing my ear against the bricks, the sound of the Hudson River could be made out fomenting on the other side.

I looked down at the bones and wondered who it was. Did he or she get lost down here and simply collapse? It was a small skeleton and I suspected it was a female.

I scanned in every direction and on the other side of the tunnel my light reflected off something. I moved closer to inspect it and discovered another skeleton completely stripped of its flesh and a hole in its head.

Jesus!

A thorough search of the area produced a total of ten skeletons. My mind raced with the possibilities, none of them good and then I heard a woman scream.

Frankie!

I turned with a start suddenly overwhelmed with dread and took off at a dead run. About halfway back, I tripped on a broken piece of concrete and fell face forward in the muck, striking my head and losing my flashlight in the water. I was only dazed momentarily but alarmed that I was alone in the dark. The flashlight had either shorted or the lens had cracked. The filthy water burned my eyes and it took a minute before I could see clearly again. I searched quickly for the flashlight but realized it was hopeless and decided to make my way back by feeling along the wall. The question was, which way was back? Disoriented by the fall and the darkness, I wasn't sure, so again, I just picked a direction and went with it.

My heart sank after five minutes when I stepped on a skeleton and realized I had chosen poorly. I turned and walked as fast as I could, tracing my way back to the steps. Ten minutes later, by feel, I found the opening in the tunnel that lead up to Seymour's brownstone. I called out in vain for Frankie and clung to the hope that she had been frightened by a rat, causing her to flee back into the house, but I had a sinking feeling in the pit of my stomach. Breathless I reached the top of the steps and found the door shut tight and remembered that it was self-locking. The rope was gone as well.

Shit, what was I going to do? Then I heard it. Faintly through the door sifted the sound of Frankie crying and pleading for mercy. I screamed and banged on the door as hard as I could, stopping only from fatigue. Panting, I leaned back against the cold wall frantic and out of ideas. I had never felt so helpless. And just as suddenly the sound stopped. I beat on the door even harder until my hands were bloody. Exhausted, I began to sob. I pulled out my cellphone to call 911 but it was waterlogged and nonfunctional. I flung it down the stairs in frustration.

Without any choices left, I went back down to see if there was another way out of the tunnel. Since there was nothing but a brick wall in one direction I headed off in the other using the wall to guide me in the darkness. Progress was slow like this and after an hour I was starting to become discouraged. Would I soon be covered in rats? A macabre thought for sure but not necessarily an unrealistic one given the circumstances. I thought about Frankie and that bolstered my resolve to find a way out. I redoubled my effort but would I be too late to stop whatever it was that was happening? I was too stressed at the moment to even guess at what that might be.

I lost all track of time and for all I knew, in the dark, I could easily have been walking in circles. Eventually however, my hand tracking along the tunnel wall came into contact with metal. This was different and I groped it eagerly trying to figure out what it was. At the same time I heard a rumbling sound overhead. Looking up, I perceived a faint light. The object in front of me was a ladder and it occurred to me that I might be standing beneath a manhole cover. The rumbling sound was traffic, maybe a city bus had just passed. My heart leapt with hope as I grasped the sides and quickly clambered up. At the top, the cover was about three feet in diameter, round, and made of metal with several one inch holes in it. Through the holes, street sounds and light filtered in. It was night already which meant it was after five. I pushed the cover upward and nothing happened.

Who knows when the last time was that anybody had tried to move it? Years of dirt and grime might have cemented the cover to its seating. I tried harder and even harder and eventually felt it give with a grinding sound.

I paused taking a deep breath and started over. With a mighty heave the cover dislodged and rose a few inches upward allowing the brisk night air in, filling my lungs. I peered outward and saw that I was in the middle of a quiet street in a mostly residential neighborhood. Where in Manhattan exactly I had no idea. I had been walking for hours, albeit slowly. I pushed the cover up more and slid it off to one side to rest on the street. Hoisting myself out, I sat on the side with my legs dangling down the hole as I caught my breath.

A car rolled to a stop behind me and honked for me to get out of the way. He had enough room to pass but it was a relatively narrow street and he was being cautious. I got to my feet, left the manhole cover where it was and walked to the sidewalk allowing him to travel by in his comfort zone. It was thirty five degrees with a slight breeze. I was soaking wet, exhausted, and now starting to shiver. The first thing I noticed was that I was now on the east side of Manhattan, E. 13th Street by First Avenue. That was quite a hike I had taken and was now feeling the effects of exhaustion, hunger and exposure but I couldn't stop now. I tried hailing a cab twice unsuccessfully. I must have looked awful: wet, dirty, emotionally stressed. They probably thought I was a mentally ill street person. I was simply too fatigued and cold to try to jog the two miles crosstown back to Seymour's apartment.

I didn't have a phone but I had money so I walked into a small coffee shop, ordered a cup of hot black coffee. The waitress tried to be polite but I must have smelled awful and she recoiled from me as she filled my cup. I apologized to her, acknowledging her distress. "I'm sorry for my appearance. I've had a rough day."

She was young and sympathetic plus she liked my approach. She smiled. “I understand. We’ve all had days like that.”

“Thank you but I’m afraid my day has been a little worse than most. I have an emergency to take care of and I need a phone. I lost mine. Do you think I could make a call with yours? I would of course pay you for the privilege. Would fifty dollars for two phone calls be enough?” I took out my wallet and offered her a wet fifty dollar bill.

She stood there holding the pot of coffee deciding what to do. Letting an obvious piece of trash like me hold her cellphone was a big decision. Who knew what kind of diseases I had. I could read her mind. Kindness won out in the end. She declined the fifty and fished her cell phone out of her back pocket, handing it to me.

“Thanks but no thanks on the fifty. I can see you’re in trouble. Go ahead and make your calls. I’ll be right back.”

I thanked her and she walked back to the counter. I immediately called 911 and anonymously reported a kidnapping at Seymour’s address. I told them I saw a young woman being dragged kicking and screaming into his brownstone. I was in no position to help so I called the police. I hung up quickly. They would call back but I would be long gone and the waitress would only say what she knew, that some unkempt, smelly guy borrowed her phone to make a call.

I next called Vito. One ring, two rings. “Cesari, what’s going on?” His raspy, two packs of Camels a day voice was somewhat short of breath.

“I’m in trouble and I need help.”

Sensing the desperation in my voice he said, “How could things have gotten worse than they already are?”

“Not over the phone, okay? Pick me up now and bring me some clothes. I’m soaking wet and freezing.”

"Now? Jesus Christ, Cesari, you got some bad timing. I'm in the middle of contract negotiations with one of the restaurant owners in Hell's Kitchen."

"Is that why you're short of breath?"

"Yeah, he wasn't being reasonable."

"This is a real emergency Vito. I mean real."

"Fine."

He must have turned to someone he was with because I heard him say, "Okay boys, let him down and untie him. I got to go somewhere, asshole, but I'll be back and I expect you to have a better attitude when I do. Okay, Cesari, where are you?"

"There's a coffee shop on the corner of E.13th and First Avenue and bring me a phone." In Vito's business he required an arsenal of spare phones to avoid the FBI.

When the waitress came back, I ordered a croissant and threw a twenty down on the table to thank her. "Do you mind if I hang onto to your phone another minute or so. I'm expecting a call."

She looked at the twenty and decided that was more acceptable to her conscious than fifty so she picked it up. "Sure, you didn't have to but thanks anyway."

I smiled at her and waited for Vito. I hoped the cops took my call seriously. You never knew in a city like this. The police received quite a few prank calls every day. Thirty minutes later, Vito's black town car pulled to the curb with a screech. I signaled the waitress, threw another ten on the table to cover the bill and showed her that I was leaving her phone. I waved goodbye and thanked her.

Entering the town car, Vito was overwhelmed by my stench. "Jesus, Cesari, did you spend the day sleeping in a dumpster or something?"

"It's a long story. I'll explain while you're driving." I gave him Seymour's address and leaned forward to turn the heaters on high. "Where are the clothes and phone?"

"They're in a bag in the back seat."

I retrieved the bag and examined the contents; a white dress shirt two sizes too big with bloodstains on it, a pair of black dress pants also too large with a hole in one knee, black socks and a pair of Allan Edmond shoes."

"What the fuck is this, Vito?"

"You said it was an emergency. Did you expect me to go to Macy's?"

I made a grumbling sound. "The restaurant guy?"

"Yeah, there's also a nice sweater on the back seat that one of my guys donated."

I looked back again and spotted a nice dark green Irish wool sweater. I elected to keep my jeans on wet as they were, changed into the bloodied but dry dress shirt and donned the Irish sweater. In minutes, I was feeling like a new man. I looked over at Vito as he concentrated on the road. I hadn't seen him in a while and he seemed bigger than I remembered. He was in his late thirties, about six feet three inches and usually about 250 pounds of solid muscle. Today he was looking closer to 280 or 290 pounds, not fat mind you, just not as lean as usual. Maybe it was the winter clothes. Subtle streaks of white interrupted his thick, jet black, wavy hair but his most prominent features were his large Roman nose and hawk-like, predatory gray eyes.

He asked, "So, what's going on Cesari?"

I filled him in as we drove to Chelsea. He let out a deep breath. "Geez, so what do you think? The fat man came home early and snatched the girl? Would he do that?"

"Your guess is as good as mine but I can't imagine Seymour snatching anyone and carrying them a hundred and fifty feet straight up a steep staircase. You've never seen him. Sloths move faster than he does."

"Cesari, you don't think too straight some times. Snatching her doesn't mean he necessarily carried her up the stairs. He could have got the drop on her with a gun or knife and she walked up on her own."

I sighed. "Of course. He was supposed to be at work until at least 6:00 p.m. but he might have gotten out early."

Vito thought it over and lit a Camel.

I said, "Could you please keep both hands on the wheel, Vito, and open your window. I'd rather not die of lung cancer while I'm on the way to rescue someone."

Ignoring me he said, "I thought doctors were all nerds. Besides, let's say he came home early and found someone had entered his apartment. Wouldn't he just call the police?"

"Sure, unless he was responsible for the all you can eat rat buffet I found in the tunnel."

"Yeah, I guess this ain't looking too good for your girl, Frankie. Do you think he knows you were down there too?"

"She might have told him so I have to assume yes, but that's the least of my worries at the moment."

"All right, Cesari, let's not panic just yet. What about the big picture with this guy Seymour? Like what's his relationship to Carmine and that mob run whore house in Vegas?"

I let out a deep sigh. "I don't even want to think about that right now but obviously there's a lot more to him than meets the eye."

"Okay, let's hope for the best. If not, I'll help you take care of Seymour."

We pulled onto Seymour's block in Chelsea and saw multiple police vehicles with flashing lights and an ambulance in front of his brownstone. A small crowd of people had gathered on the other side of the street to watch.

"Pull the car over somewhere and let me out."

"Pull the car over where?"

There were no parking spaces and the street was too narrow to linger. He had slowed to a stop because of the congestion.

The police had effectively blockaded the lane and were letting cars through one at a time. We were four cars back and I got out.

"Drive around the block a few times. I'll call you when I'm ready."

"Fine."

I joined the crowd and slipped my way through to the front, casually asking no one in particular what was happening.

A middle aged guy twenty years my senior in an expensive overcoat and fedora said, "Whatever it is, it can't be good. I saw the EMT's bring a stretcher in there twenty minutes ago and they were wearing Hazmat suits."

Hazmat suits? Specially designed clothing to protect the individual from hazardous material. What did that mean?

I said, "Thanks," and propped myself up against a tree while I watched. I didn't have long to wait. In less than ten minutes, two guys wearing Hazmat suits came out carrying a stretcher with a black body bag. The crowd murmured at the sight and my heart sank. I prayed silently for it not to be Frankie but I knew otherwise. God damn it! I walked down to the corner and called Vito to pick me up.

I told Vito, and we drove in silence to his apartment in Little Italy. As we approached he said, "Keep a low profile and don't talk to any of my guys, all right? It's better if no one knows who you are. Brunella's offered a cash reward and has got feelers out all over the city looking for you and I wouldn't want to tempt anyone. There's a baseball hat and sunglasses in the glove compartment. Put them on and keep low."

He double parked in front of his apartment by the Café Napoli on Mulberry Street and got out of the car, tossing his keys to one of his men. He told two others to stay outside the apartment and give us some space.

I kept my head down and the brim of the hat low, trying as much as possible to stand in Vito's shadow. Once inside, I took a hot shower and put on fresh clothes. Vito was bigger than me but his jeans and shirt fit well enough. I bundled up my dirty clothes and threw them into a kitchen trash bag.

"Thanks for letting me come here Vito. I know you're taking a big risk if Brunella should find out."

"Forget about it. We've been friends too long. Besides, I don't think any of my guys got a good look at you just now. It's pretty dark out there. I think we're okay." He paused mulling his words. "Look, I know you're feeling down about the girl but it's entirely within the realm of possibility that it wasn't her in the body bag."

I looked up perplexed. "Then who was it?"

"Seymour maybe?"

I laughed despite my foul mood. "Seymour? It would have taken at least six to eight guys to carry him and he would never fit into any ordinary body bag."

He nodded. "I'm just trying to be positive."

"Thanks. Look, I'm going to make a few phone calls while I watch the news to see what the official statement is about what happened."

Sitting on the sofa in his living room, I clicked on the local news channel and pulled out my cell phone, dialing the St. Matt's OR. Vito disappeared into another part of the apartment to conduct his own business.

It was 8:00 p.m. but big city hospitals operate into the wee hours pretty much every day of the week and this one was no different. One of the recovery room nurses answered in a high-pitched voice and thick Jamaican accent. "Hi, tis Desiree. How may I help you?"

Good, she was a friend. "Hi Desiree. This is Dr. Cesari. How are you?"

She got all excited. Divorced, forty-five with two mostly grown children she had Cesari fever for quite some time. "Dr. Cesari? Oh my goodness. I'm fine, dear, but how are you? No one even sure if you be alive."

"I'm alive Matilda, but have a lot going on. Can I please ask you not to tell anyone I called."

"I won't tell a soul, dear. No, sir. Not me. I promise. I know you long time and I don't believe any of it. None of us do."

"Thanks. I appreciate that, Desiree." Doctors and nurses were a close knit group of people especially in the OR where we spent long hours together piecing together other peoples broken lives.

"So, what really happened out there, Dr. Cesari? Did you really go to that bawdy house? Half the girls tink so. The other half say no. I know you lusty man, Dr. Cesari. I see it in your eyes." She laughed after she said that.

"It's complicated, Desiree. Can I ask you for a favor?"

Ignoring me she continued. "The next time you need a girlfriend you call me first. All right? Desiree take care of you real good."

I couldn't help but smile. She had been throwing me not so subtle invitations like this for months. Once she even tried to drag me into an unoccupied patient room. "Once again, thanks. Now, how about that favor?"

"Sure ting. What is it you need, dear?"

"Check Seymour's OR schedule. I want to know when he left the hospital today."

"Seymour? He bad news that boy. I check right now. Hold on."

I heard her rustle a few papers on the desk in front of her and mumble to herself. She returned to me after about a minute and said, "Seymour got lucky today. He had a big vascular case at noon which got canceled so they moved his five o'clock gallbladder up. Look like he finished that at one and then he done. That boy got lucky for sure. Is that all you need?"

"Yes, Desiree. Thank you and remember mums the word on this phone call. Okay?"

"Sure ting, Dr. Cesari, and you remember I am a woman and sometimes a woman need more than a phone call to satisfy her."

I cleared my throat. "I'll keep that in mind. I promise."

I disconnected and shook my head. There's a real chance she was flirting with a murderer and couldn't care less. I shook my head. Women were funny like that. I leaned back and thought about the day's events, trying to piece it together. Things were moving way too fast for me. Twenty minutes later, Vito returned with two scotch glasses and a bottle of eighteen year old Macallan. He poured us two fingers neat and took a seat on the leather sofa next to me.

He said, "Sorry I was gone so long. I had to take care of a few things. Any news?"

"Seymour did get out early today."

"Hmm, so it was him?"

"Yeah, seems like it. The timing's right but where did he go?"

Vito sipped his scotch and crossed his legs as he thought it over. "Well, if I was some sort of serial killer or whatever and I just found out my cover was blown, I'd probably hightail it out of there as fast as I could too. You know what I mean?"

"Fair enough but where? A guy that looks like him can't hide for long. It's not as if he can blend into the background."

"Anything about it on the news yet?"

"Not yet. It should be soon though. There's no way of burying a story like this. Too many witnesses in the street who saw the body bag and had cellphone cameras."

"They must be fact checking first before they go live with it."

"Yup, that's the way I see it so we might as well relax." Two scotches and an hour later the news channel flashed to the scene several hours earlier outside Seymour's apartment.

It was a little after eleven. I said, "Here we go."

We both turned our attention to the television and I raised the volume a little. The talking head on cable news reported that not all the facts were in yet but apparently an unidentified white female was found dead in the basement apartment of an expensive brownstone in Chelsea. She was found submerged face down in a bathtub filled with sulfuric acid and her identity is as yet unknown. The whereabouts of the owner of the home, Dr. Seymour Kraken, a staff anesthesiologist at St. Matt's, are also unknown. He is being sought as a person of interest.

They flashed a picture of Seymour on the screen and Vito almost spit his scotch out of his mouth. "Shit! Is that him? Oh my God. That is one heck of a heifer you got on staff with you, Cesari. You were right. He ain't going to be able to hide for long."

"I told you."

"Sulfuric acid. Man, this Seymour guy really is an asshole."

"I told you that too." I forced myself to believe that Frankie may not have suffered much before she died but I was seething internally and wanted to tear the head off of anything. Seymour was going to suffer plenty when I caught up with him.

It dawned on me that Arnie must be having a heart attack by now so I called him.

"Cesari, where have you been? I've been trying to reach you."

"I had to change phones, Arnie. Sorry. I assume you've been watching the news?"

"Worse. I've been on the phone with the police and reporters for the last hour and a half. The minute they realized they had another doctor from St. Matt's involved in a potential homicide they came after me like a Great White off the coast of Florida. What the fuck is going on?"

"I don't know. I'm still trying to figure out what happened in Vegas. Have you heard from Seymour?"

"Nothing. I know he worked until about one today and left. I spoke to some of the OR nurses who worked with him and they said he seemed fine. The hospital is going to be in absolute pandemonium tomorrow and Seymour's not answering his cellphone."

"There's no helping the hospital being in an uproar, Arnie, and Seymour will surface with or without the benefit of his cellphone. I just don't see how a guy like that could possibly keep a low profile."

I listened as Arnie sighed loudly into the phone. "Shit. This has got to be one of the worst weeks in my life."

I chuckled. "Thanks, Arnie. Me and Seymour are wanted for murder and you think you're having a bad week because of the political repercussions."

"You know what I mean. So what's your status?"

"I'm safe and actively engaged in the pursuit of the truth."

"What on earth is that supposed to mean?"

I smiled. "It means I'll keep you posted and try not to call me unless it's absolutely necessary. Okay?"

"I guess Seymour probably won't show up for work tomorrow. That means we'll be down an anesthesiologist. That means there will be anywhere from eight to ten OR cases that will have to be cancelled."

"Arnie, get some sleep. You're overwrought."

I disconnected the call and thought that hitting the sack would probably be a good idea for me as well. I said goodnight to Vito and headed off to one of his spare bedrooms. Sleeping fitfully, I dreamt about Frankie.

Chapter 25

I woke to the irresistible aroma of freshly brewed espresso wafting down the hallway from Vito's kitchen and the sound of Sinatra singing "Summer Breeze." The alarm clock on the nearby night stand told me it was almost ten so I roused myself, cleaned up, and found Vito sitting at his kitchen table sipping coffee and eating a cannoli.

"It's about time you woke up, Cesari," he said gruffly.

I nodded. "I was pretty beat last night. Any coffee left?"

"Yeah, help yourself."

There was a bright red metal moka pot for making espresso on the stovetop and I poured myself a cup. On the table was a small pastry box from the Café Napoli downstairs with several more cannolis so I helped myself to one and took a seat.

"So what's your agenda for today?" he asked.

The coffee was wonderful. "Not sure. This whole thing is a fucking mess right now, but I can guarantee you that I'm going to find Seymour if it's the last thing I do."

"And then what?"

"I am going to ask him politely why he felt the need to kill my friend."

"Friend? Cesari, you're not being rational. She was just a hooker you picked up in Vegas. You hardly knew her. I know you hit it off and all that but you got much bigger problems on your hands right now like Brunella and Carmine. You can't just simply run around looking for that guy with half the city looking for you."

I took a bite of my cannoli and savored the sweet flavor. This one had little bits of chocolate and candied fruit in the filling. I didn't answer him for a while as I thought it over.

Finally I said, "You don't understand, Vito. Seymour is the key to everything. He's connected to what happened in Vegas and that's the reason I have a Brunella and Carmine problem."

"Maybe and maybe not. I've been thinking it over and we really don't know anything about Seymour yet including whether he killed anybody or not. So far, all we have is what law enforcement likes to call circumstantial evidence. How do we know that Seymour is even alive?"

I soaked that in and shook my head. "C'mon. You've got to be kidding. Haven't you heard a word I've been saying? There's a graveyard underneath his apartment and they found Frankie in a tub of acid. That's enough circumstantial evidence to get him eleven consecutive life sentences."

"Maybe but what are you going to say if he turns up dead?"

"I'll cross that unlikely bridge when I come to it. In the meanwhile, can I count on you for support or are you too afraid of Brunella?"

He snorted, "That'll be the day. Yeah, I'll help you within reason. I don't want to provoke a blood bath down here so we do this quietly, all right? None of my guys can be in on it. It's strictly between you and me. I got a good thing going here and you'd better not fuck it up for me."

When he finished talking he pulled out an unfiltered Camel and lit it, blowing the first drag in my direction.

I said, "Really?"

"It's my apartment, right?"

"Yes."

"Just checking."

I shook my head disgusted. There was an ash tray on my side of the table so I slid it over to him. "All right, so how do you want to do this?"

"Do what?"

"How do I get out of your apartment without being seen? I have to get clothes that fit and I want to go down to the morgue and pay my last respects to Frankie."

He coughed when I said that. "Are you fucking crazy? She was a whore for God's sake. Leave it alone."

"Leave it alone? Are you kidding? It's not in my DNA to leave things alone. You should know that. Besides, she was a nice person and I'd appreciate it if you'd stop calling her names. I liked her."

"Jesus Christ, Cesari. Do whatever you want. I don't know why I care, but don't call me to bail you out when you get picked up. As for the apartment, I'll go out first and take my guys out somewhere. I needed to check on a construction site in the flat iron district anyway. There's a couple of hoodies in the bureau in my bedroom. Find one and cover up. Between that and the baseball hat you should be okay. I haven't seen anybody casing my place and I check every day because of the feds but you never know so move fast."

"Thanks."

He reached into his pocket and came out with a rolled up ball of cash and tossed it across the table at me. "It's two thousand dollars. Don't get mugged. Need a gun?"

"No, I've got three in the safe at my hotel."

"Three?"

"Yeah, one from that pimp Luther and two more from Carmine's guys."

"Man, you keep busy. And you've got a phone. Keep it on and I'll call you when I can break free. I should have my head examined. You know, Cesari, this 'I owe you because we grew up in the Bronx together' bullshit is beginning to wear thin."

I never used that card but as long as he brought it up I said, "Just think of it as payback for all those times I saved your ass from getting beat up in the school yard at P.S. 97."

"If I recall correctly, I was the one who saved your ass over and over."

"Oh yeah, I guess I misremembered, but you wouldn't have passed a single math test from first grade to senior year of high school if I didn't let you cheat off me."

He shook his head. "Like I said it's starting to wear thin."

"If it's any consolation, I'll pay you back with free colonoscopies the rest of your life."

He cracked a smile. "You'd like that wouldn't you?"

"I dream of it every day."

"You really are an asshole. C'mon let's go."

Chapter 26

As far as I could tell no one took any unusual interest in me and I made my way out of the apartment undetected, heading over to Bloomingdales on Broadway. I picked up some new clothes including a winter jacket and knit hat, changed in the dressing room, and put Vito's stuff in a plastic shopping bag which I handed to a homeless guy on the street outside.

The news reported that they had brought Frankie's body to the St. Matt's morgue for autopsy. I had friends down there and the pathologist, Harry, was a nice guy. I spent a lot of time with him reviewing slides and shooting the bull. He wouldn't judge me. I looked at Vito's Rolex that I had borrowed from his night table. It was almost noon and I wanted to get there before they cut her up. It was going to be bad enough without having to see her internal organs being weighed on scales next to her. Sulfuric acid was one of the most corrosive substances in existence and depending on how long she had been submerged she may be unrecognizable as a human being.

Harry read slides uptown at New York Presbyterian in the morning. They were short staffed in the pathology department and he was temporarily helping out. He would be back in the afternoon to do his work at St. Matt's, including Frankie's autopsy. I wasn't supposed to step foot on the hospital grounds because of my suspension, but I had much bigger things to worry about than losing my job.

The hospital wasn't that far and I arrived at 12:15. Walking through the main lobby I blended in with the crush of people coming and going. At the main elevators, I separated from the crowd and went down a nearby stairwell to the basement, making a beeline for the pathology department. It was lunch time and everyone had cleared out to eat, but Harry, who was sitting at his desk, his eyes glued to a binocular microscope.

I gently tapped on his open door and he turned to see me. He got all excited. "Cesari, for God's sake. How are you?"

He stood up extending his hand to me. I took it and shook it warmly. "I'm okay Harry."

"Have a seat. We got a lot to catch up on. Rumors are flying fast and furious as I am sure you are aware and now this business with Seymour. I'm not sure my heart can stand too much more excitement."

He was sixty, overweight, and diabetic. He had coronary artery disease and had two cardiac stents placed last fall. According to Harry, he was living on borrowed time and maybe he was. Maybe we all were. He closed the door behind us and we sat opposite each other at his desk.

Staring at me as if I were a ghost he asked, "So what the hell is going on and why on earth would you come to the pathology department in broad daylight with everyone on the planet looking for you?"

"It's a long story, Harry, but I didn't kill anybody. You've got to believe me."

"Of course I believe you. So what do you think happened?"

"I think I was drugged and passed out. When I woke, I was in a room with a dead hooker. I have no idea what happened in between. I'm not sure why anyone would want to frame me but there it is. That's about all I know."

"So, a classic Vegas vacation."

I chuckled, “Yeah.”

“And why am I so honored by this visit?”

“The dead girl that was brought here from Seymour’s apartment last night. I was hoping you would let me see her. She was a friend of mine.”

“Jesus Christ, Cesari. You know another dead girl?”

“I didn’t know the first one. I had never met her. I just woke up in her room.”

“You say potato…”

“In any event, we were friends and I’d like to see her one last time before you go to work on her. Do you think you can allow me to pay my last respects while she still retains some semblance of humanity?”

He was silent as he thought it over. “Yeah, I guess so. Am I going to get in trouble for talking to you?”

“It’s not against the law to talk, is it?”

He snorted. “Please. The law can do whatever it wants to whomever it wants, even in a democracy. C’mon, I’ll show you the body but it’s not a pleasant sight. They called me in when they brought her here last night. So what the hell do you think Seymour is up to?”

“I haven’t the foggiest idea, Harry.”

As we walked into the morgue together he said, “It’s unbelievable. You know? One minute you think you know someone and then something like this happens and…”

He turned on the light and there in the middle of the room laid her body on a metal table covered with an opaque plastic sheet. I responded, “So you think he did it too?”

“His house, right? He’s missing right? Who else? Besides, they found all sorts of other incriminating shit there. The cops told me. He did it all right. One sick son-of-a-bitch.”

This was news to me and I guessed the police didn’t release the full details of what they found. “What else did they find in his house?”

"Oh lord. A bed with chains and manacles, containers of sulfuric acid hidden behind a false wall in his basement, a trap door leading down into the old sewers, closets full of porn, and a variety of instruments that can only be described as devices of torture."

I whispered, "Jesus…"

"Oh yeah, Seymour is one seriously ill guy. They even found a vintage gas mask in his apartment. Probably used it to protect himself from the acid's fumes. Quite noxious in general and a bathtub full would have been pretty caustic even with good ventilation which he had. Okay, are you ready, Cesari? Don't throw up on me. All right?"

"I'll be fine."

He pulled the plastic drop cloth off of her slowly beginning from her head and rested it on her abdomen. It was horrible. More horrific than anything I had ever seen in my life and I shuddered. Her face and hair were mostly gone and parts had been bleached down to bone. The same for her neck and chest. Her breasts were almost gone as well and exposed, burnt flesh and vessels were all that were left.

Harry said, "Apparently, he was in a hurry to dispose of her. He placed her face down in the tub of acid but didn't bother submerging her fully. He only used one container of acid even though he had several more. They think something may have interrupted him."

"Like police banging on his door?"

"Possibly. Anyway, they think he made his getaway through the subterranean tunnel. Do you want to see anymore?"

"No, but I would like a moment alone if that's okay?"

"Sure, I'll give you a few minutes."

He left the room to go back to his office and I stepped closer to the table. I wanted to remember this scene for when I caught up with Seymour. Still, there were a lot of missing pieces to this puzzle. He starts to get rid of the body with acid but gets interrupted and flees. What was he going to do with it afterward? Bring it down to the rats to finish off? Why not bring her down and let the rats do all the dirty work? Because that's unreliable. What if they didn't finish the job and left some bits and pieces that could be identified? And then there's his DNA that needed to be disposed of. If he raped and tortured these women he would want to make sure his DNA was completely gone. But would he have had time to rape Frankie? I thought about that. It was a little after one when I heard her scream and close to six when I saw her in the body bag. Plenty of time.

"I'm so sorry Frankie," I whispered hoarsely. I looked at her shoulder, burnt on the front half. You could see the line clearly demarcating where the acid bath reached and the normal skin and flesh. I bent down to look at her more closely. Something bothered me. Her hair color didn't seem right. It was a slightly different tone from what I remembered. Off by maybe a smidgeon. There was a box of latex gloves on a nearby table so I put on a pair and gently raised her right shoulder peeking underneath. Frankie had a tattoo of a pretty yellow butterfly. This person didn't.

My heart skipped a beat and I tried to stay calm. I was surprised, confused, and relieved. I thought about that, but if this wasn't Frankie then who was it? I walked over to Harry's office just as he hung up his phone. "Harry, do you know the identity of this girl?"

"Sure, they found her personal effects in a plastic bag on the floor in the bathroom. Her name was Tanya Ellison but I thought you said you were a friend of hers? That was security on the phone, Cesari. Someone thought they spotted you in the lobby and they're calling around for everyone to keep a head's up."

I was too stunned to react and sidestepping the question about being her friend I asked. "Isn't sulfuric acid extremely corrosive? Wouldn't it have destroyed his plumbing?"

"He's a clever bastard that's for sure. The police told me that all the plumbing including the bath tub had been replaced with high-grade corrosion resistant stainless steel which the acid shouldn't react with depending on its concentration but as an added measure he kept a supply of sodium hydroxide around to neutralize any residual acid once he was done. You can't just pour a strong alkali onto a strong acid. The reaction would be too volatile so we're guessing that he would drain the tub, rinse her off well with copious amounts of water and then flush the base down the drain to neutralize any residual acid in the plumbing. He'd have to be careful though. Sodium hydroxide itself is fairly caustic and reacts with water to give off large amounts of heat. You don't want to accidentally splash that stuff around either. These are dangerous chemicals he was playing with. He probably kept his fingers crossed that if there was a reaction it would take place in the sewer and not his pipes." He looked at his watch. "I think you'd better go now. People will be returning from lunch in a few minutes."

"Thanks, Harry."

"There's a door down here that leads out toward the rear of the hospital. It's next to the ambulance port where they drop off the bodies."

I stood up to leave and he added, "Take care of yourself, Cesari. There's a lot of buzz going around the hospital."

"I'm sure there is."

"Most of it's bad. A lot of people with axes to grind are starting to grind them. You're like a wounded lion and the hyenas are starting to gather up their courage."

I smiled and nodded in comprehension. It was always like that. "Thanks for the heads up. Anyone in particular?" I knew about Lancelot and could almost forgive him. After all, I did smack him around pretty good.

"Mostly, the other guys in the GI department. They've been jealous of your success for quite some time and now they're sensing the opportunity to take you down a notch if you get my drift."

"I get it. Thanks again, Harry. I appreciate your help and remember, for your own sake, you never saw me."

He smiled, "Saw who?"

I stepped out the back of the hospital and walked back to the hotel where Frankie and I had been staying to retrieve my weapons. I would stay there one or two more nights and then check out. I didn't want to stay in any one place too long but changing hotels every night was a royal pain in the ass. It was overcast and blustery out. Spring was still a few weeks away and winter was getting its last licks in on the city dwellers.

In the hotel room, I placed one of the handguns I had confiscated from Carmine's men in Vegas in my waistband. It was a Glock 9 mm with an eight round magazine. I left the other two guns in the safe and shoved the crowbar in the duffel bag. I was soon back on the street in search of food and a plan.

Chapter 27

What the hell was going on? Seymour sat on a cinder block in the basement of an abandoned building on the west side, sharing his space with four pathetic homeless men. He had narrowly escaped capture but the close call had unnerved him to say the least as well as the fact that he had no idea what had happened.

He got out of work early, went to the supermarket to buy dinner and arrived home just before three, finding his worst nightmare unfolding before his eyes. Someone had discovered his secret entrance to the sewers built there years ago by the bootleggers during prohibition to smuggle illegal booze in from Canada via the Hudson and as quick egress during police raids. The brownstone he lived in had been an infamous local speak-easy during the 1920's and a favorite hang-out for dangerous gangsters. It was rumored that the most notorious mobster of all, Lucky Luciano, used to frequent the place.

He found that the bed had been pushed to one side and there appeared to have been a struggle resulting in an overturned lamp. Plus there were muddy foot prints all over his carpet and the front door had been pried open forcefully, splintering the wood. Not good but who was responsible and what had happened remained a mystery.

The jig was up and it was time to clear out. That was the only thing that was certain. He had considered briefly leaving the girl shackled to the bed in the main floor bedroom but decided that an unidentifiable corpse was better than a live witness who could attest to his villainy. He was disappointed. They were just starting to get to know each other. He had barely returned from Vegas when he saw the response to his ad in Craigslist. With all that was going on he shouldn't have but he couldn't help himself. All the excitement and danger had jumpstarted his libido the way gasoline did a fire.

Oh well.

Normally, he would have let the body sit in the acid bath for a couple of days to ensure rendering it and his DNA unidentifiable before feeding the remains to the rats but he had run out of time. When he heard the approaching sirens, there was no doubt in his mind who they were coming for so he dropped everything and took off down the tunnel with the job half done. He knew the sewer inside and out and eventually found his way to this abandoned warehouse. He had practiced his emergency escape many times.

The five of them now sat around a small campfire built inside an old metal trash can and tried to stay warm. The others had foraged through the dumpsters of nearby restaurants for food which they shared with him. He closed his eyes and held his breath as he ate someone else's garbage. He had plenty of money on him and credit cards but he couldn't risk being seen at least not in broad daylight. He was perfectly aware of how easily recognizable he was.

Then there was the Carmine problem. Carmine had called him four times already between last night and this morning but he had declined to answer. What did he want any way? Cesari was his problem not *our* problem. Seymour sighed loudly. Sooner or later he was going to have to call him back. He knew that. What a mess this had become.

He looked around at the four disasters that had once been men and shuddered at how low humanity could sink. Unkempt, unbathed, clothes in tatters, missing teeth, and constantly mumbling, these were his new friends. These guys didn't look like they had seen a television in decades and would care even less had they seen him splashed across the news. He sighed deeply. It didn't matter because they would all be dead in a short while.

Chapter 28

Vito and I stood across the street from Seymour's apartment sipping hot coffee from Styrofoam cups. It was just after seven on a moonless night and the street lights glowed ominously almost as if they knew something we didn't. I carried the duffel bag with crowbar, and two new flashlights I purchased at a small hardware store.

"So, let me get this straight, Cesari. We're going back in the sewers because you think Seymour is hiding down there?"

"He has to be. Think about it. He's in the middle of giving some girl an acid bath when he suddenly gets interrupted. By what? It had to be the police I called, right? If he had come blowing out the front the door he would have been nabbed in a minute. He must have gone down the tunnel. That's what the cops think and I agree. If I were him I would have had a whole escape route planned out in advance, and if that's the case then there's a chance he might even still be there. At the very least we might get some clue as to where he is."

"If everyone thinks he went down there then why couldn't they find him?"

"Who knows? There are hundreds of miles of interconnected tunnels down there and Seymour may have been exploring them for months, maybe years. If we assume that, then he would have known exactly where to go and would have taken the fastest route to get there. The police would have been hampered by confusion and uncertainty. Think about it. Miles of subterranean tunnels, dark and putrid, not even sure if he's down there in the first place. Try to imagine the lack of enthusiasm on their part after they failed to find him in the first few hours."

He nodded. "Fine, Cesari, but I'm not climbing up to the roof. We'll wait for a good time when the street is clear and just go in the front door."

We walked up and down the block a few times until we were certain that no one was watching the apartment. Then we climbed the steps to the front door casually and with confidence as if we lived there or were close friends. Vito looked around as I jiggled the handle testing it. The original dead bolt had been replaced with a cheap substitute. The wood had been severely damaged by forced entry which I presumed was the work of a police battering ram.

I took out the crowbar, looked around and wedged it between the door jamb and lock. With a forceful heave the damaged wood splintered even further, the lock disengaged and the door swung inward. Once inside we closed the door behind us and headed straight for the stairs but I hesitated, looking at the bedroom door that was locked when I had come here the first time.

"Give me a second, Vito. I want to see this room. This is where he kept the girl."

We entered it finding a fairly large bedroom with a king bed which had been stripped down to the mattress. Everything had been taken out of the room as evidence. There was a spacious walk in closet also bare. The wood at the corners of the bed were scuffed from the handcuffs or chains or whatever he used to restrain his victims. I tried to picture the poor girl chained there in terror and it pissed me off that she was probably there both times when I came and I had missed the opportunity to save her. But what did that have to with Frankie? Did Seymour take her with him? The other thing that irritated me was the realization that had I just waited down in the tunnel with Frankie he would have come running right into my loving arms and fists. There was a small bathroom in the room with a shower but no tub so he had to bring them downstairs for their bath, but if he had two bedrooms downstairs why would he keep them up here? Another mystery.

Vito interrupted my thoughts as I seethed, "Hey Cesari, are you okay? You look like you're about to start world war three."

"I am Vito. I am. C'mon let's get down to business."

As we walked down the stairs he asked, "You would think that a guy that had this much to hide would have invested in a security system."

I thought about that. "I think he thought it through perfectly. Home alarms go off accidentally all the time and in an upscale neighborhood like this the cops are sure to respond promptly. Not something you would want with girls tied up inside."

"Good point. So better to look ordinary and hide in plain sight so to speak."

"Makes sense."

"Yes, it does."

The bedroom in question had also been stripped down to nothing. The bed was off to one side and the trap door exposed. "This is it, Vito. Ready?"

"Yeah, I guess."

We propped it open and descended with the flashlights on. At the bottom, we turned toward the city and explored the same route I had taken to the coffee shop. I asked, "You sure you don't want to see the graveyard in the other direction?"

"I'm good, thanks. You think the cops found them yet? I haven't heard anything about it on the news."

"Maybe, maybe not. The bones are a solid half mile down a pitch black tunnel. If they did then they're holding on to it for now. Maybe they want to sort it out in their minds. You know?

They might want to come up with a cohesive theory and maybe see if they can identify who they are before making a public announcement."

He agreed, and with flashlights drawn, the walk along the tunnel was not nearly as arduous as I remembered. I also realized that I had passed at least two sets of steel ladders on the other side, which were not visible to me in the dark yesterday. Eventually, we came to a branch in the tunnel and had to make an educated guess as to which direction he might have taken. If we stayed straight we would continue in the same direction I had taken previously. The branch was much smaller by half of the main tunnel and we decided that it seemed more interesting so we headed into the darkness. This tunnel wound slowly northward for a quarter of a mile before curving slowly back to the west. We discovered several more ladders and manhole covers so we were not very concerned about being trapped down there. The thought occurred to us that Seymour might have escaped through one of the manhole covers. That made me smile. I couldn't even imagine the sight of him trying to squeeze his way through one.

After close to two hours of wandering through the tunnel, passing occasional rats, and avoiding stepping in filthy water, we finally came to the end of the line—literally a brick wall. There was a ladder close by but no manhole cover above. We searched the ceiling with our flashlights and found no obvious exit. We did however find a hole in the cement wall that could accommodate a large man, perhaps one as large as Seymour.

Vito asked, "What do you think?"

"I think Seymour could have fit in here. Sure. Not easily but maybe. Let's do it."

We stepped into the crevice and now found ourselves in an earthen passageway four feet wide by six feet high. This went on for only about twenty feet eventually leading to a broken cinder block wall of an old building. The cinder blocks appeared to have been knocked out of place deliberately to create an opening and we stepped through finding ourselves in the basement of a very large and deserted building. A light glimmered dimly at the other end. I looked at my watch. It was almost ten.

Signaling Vito to follow, we advanced through the room cautiously, scanning from side to side gradually making our way over to the flickering light which appeared to be the dying embers of a small campfire in a rusted metal can. In a neat row on their backs and side by side were four older, disheveled men who appeared quite dead.

"What do you think happened here, Cesari?" Vito whispered.

I looked at him surprised at the question. They had obviously been executed. Each had a small bullet hole in his forehead. "You mean, beside the obvious?"

"Why, is the question. These guys didn't have anything worth killing them for."

I thought that one over. "Sure they did. They had memories. Maybe whoever shot them didn't want to take a chance on them remembering him."

"Seymour?"

I let that one float around a while before responding. "We'd better be careful. He may be more dangerous than we thought. I wasn't counting on him packing heat. Do you have a weapon?"

"Of course, my 9 mm and you?"

"Yeah." I withdrew the handgun from my waistband just in case Seymour was still lurking somewhere in the shadows. I doubted it but you never knew. Vito took out his pistol as well.

"This is a big place, Cesari. He could be anywhere."

"You're right but I bet he took off and that's why he killed these guys. He's on the move. He was probably waiting for nightfall."

"Where do you think he's going?"

"With any luck there's a gateway to hell around here and he fell through it."

There were several exits out of the warehouse but no sign of which direction he might have gone. Once on the street, we found ourselves on Twelfth Avenue not too far from the Jacob Javits Convention Center.

I was pissed off. We were so close and now so far. After another hour, I turned to Vito in frustration. “He’s gone.”

“Yeah, I agree. Let’s get something to eat and regroup.”

I looked at my watch. It wasn’t quite eleven and we weren’t that far from midtown so we cabbed it over to Pergola, a small, very old French restaurant on W.47th Street. The place was jammed with the after theater crowd but we managed a small table for two in the rear. Vito ordered us a bottle of Merlot and I sat there morose, sipping wine as Vito ordered dinner for both of us.

“I hope you like steak au poivre, Cesari.”

“I don’t give a damn one way or the other.”

“Okay, Cesari, enough with the long face. We’ll find the guy. We still got to eat.”

“I want him now and I want to know what happened to Frankie.”

“Well, the good news is that she may still be alive?”

“Yes, and that asshole is the only link we have to her.”

He nodded and buttered a piece of baguette the waiter had brought for us. I casually glanced around the room looking at the mostly well-dressed diners chatting about the shows they had just seen. I noticed that quite a few people were speaking French and thought this place must be the real deal.

Our steaks came with fries and a side of asparagus and we soon busied ourselves with stuffing our faces. In the middle of the second bottle of Merlot, a tall blonde guy with a striking brunette in tow entered and were seated toward the front of the restaurant, the guy with his back to me. It was that prick, Lancelot.

I almost choked on a piece of steak. Vito said, "What's the matter?"

"Nothing." I hadn't told Vito about my Lancelot problem.

"Well, drink some wine to wash it down. I don't want to have to do the Himmler maneuver on you."

"The what maneuver?"

"The Himmler maneuver."

"You mean Heimlich maneuver."

"That's what I said."

I let it go. Some things were just hopeless with him. Besides, I now had something else on my mind to distract me. Fate had just given me the opportunity to redress a situation that needed redressing. Lance had just fallen into my lap as a gift-wrapped present from heaven but how to take advantage of the opportunity was the question.

"Vito, there's a guy from work sitting over there by the front of the restaurant with blonde hair. His back is towards us."

He turned to look and then turned back. "Yeah, I see him. So what?"

"I need to talk to him privately."

"So, go over there and ask him to step outside or something."

I dabbed my lips with my napkin and made my decision. "I can't just do that. So this is what we're going to do. We pay the bill, and you fill up your glass to the top with the rest of the wine. You make like your drunk as you walk past him and spill your glass on him on the way out the door. I'll wait for him in the men's room and you wait for me outside."

He rolled his eyes. "But I'm not finished eating and I want dessert."

"Get an éclair to go." I signaled the waiter for the check and handed him cash.

Vito glared at me. "You're serious?"

"Either finish in one bite or box it up, and don't forget my duffel bag with the crowbar under the table."

Grumbling, he shoveled a handful of fries into his mouth and topped off his glass, muttering at me under his breath. I headed to the small restroom at the back of the restaurant and waited. There was one stall and one urinal. The door had an optional lock if you didn't like company while you did your business.

I waited in the stall as Vito did his thing. I could see outward through the slit between the stall door and its support wall. There was always a chance someone else could walk in ahead of Lance in which case I would have to abort but I got lucky. After maybe a minute, the door swung open forcefully and Lance came in looking upset with red wine all over his fresh white shirt, face, and hair. He was pissed and paid no attention to me as I flushed the toilet and came out of the stall facing away from him as he leaned over the sink trying to clean up. I went straight to the door and quietly locked it before turning around. I was directly behind him now as he splashed water on his face and hair to rinse off. Sensing something amiss, he looked in the mirror and saw me standing behind him. Surprise and fear flooded his features and his eyes grew wide as he suddenly realized this was not a pleasant coincidence.

He turned around saying, "Johneee…"

Before he could finish, I punched him hard in the solar plexus causing him to gasp in pain. I grabbed him by the hair and slapped him hard until both his cheeks were nice and rosy just like I remembered them from the last time. Letting go of him, he slunk to the floor, stunned and coughing.

"You've been a bad boy, Lance. You shouldn't have reported me to Dr. Goldstein and the board."

He replied hoarsely, "Johneee, I am sorry. You frightened me. I thought maybe you were how do you say—unbalanced."

"That's interesting. What do you think of me now?"

He didn't say anything, so I continued. "Well, Lance, it's like this. Last week you didn't need to be scared of me but this week you do. I pulled the pistol out from the back of my pants and let him look down the barrel.

He whimpered, "Mon Dieu! Johneee, I am so sorry."

"Are you really sorry, Lance?"

He nodded vigorously. I said, "Then I want you go into Dr. Goldstein's office first thing in the morning and tell him you were lying about me. Can you do that for a friend, Lance?"

He nodded again, tears streaming down his face. "Now give me your wallet, Lance."

He looked puzzled but handed it over. "You are going to rob me, Johneee?"

I pulled out his driver's license and studied it. "You live in a nice neighborhood, Lance. I'm going to call Dr. Goldstein at exactly 9:00 a.m. If he doesn't tell me that my suspension has been lifted and that you recanted the whole story I'm going to come to your apartment and use this to slap you around the next time." I waved the gun in his face for effect and put his license in my pocket. He could always get another one.

He cringed back. "I will do it. I promise."

"Are you certain you understand me, Lance?" I growled.

"Oui, oui."

I looked down at his beige pants and saw that he wet himself. I turned to leave, hesitated, and turned back. "One more thing and then I'll be on my way. Why did you quit your job at Cabrini?"

Suddenly, looking like a sad puppy he whispered, "Love."

"What's that supposed to mean?"

"The boss's wife, Johnneee…"

I snorted. "Oh, that kind of love." Not being in a very sympathetic mood, I left the bathroom without saying goodbye and caught up with Vito outside the restaurant.

I said, "Let's move."

"Did you clear up everything you needed to clear up with your friend?"

"Yeah, we're all good now. There was a slight language barrier but we got past it. You see, Vito, I believe that reasonable men should try to understand each other's point of view and that if we accept each other's flaws and differences then there would be less conflict and the world would be a better place."

He snorted. "You're so full of it."

Chapter 29

"The next time I call, you had better answer your phone."

Seymour winced as Carmine barked at him. He had finally worked up the courage to call him back and now Carmine was pissed. "I'm sorry, Carmine. My phone went dead and I hadn't had a chance to charge it. I called you back as soon as I could. There's been a lot going on in my life."

"So I've been seeing on the news. I didn't know you were such a sick fuck but that don't change a thing. Until we find your friend, Cesari, I own your fat ass. Capisci?"

Seymour didn't speak Italian but he didn't have to. Carmine's tone was clear enough. "Yes," he replied.

"So aren't you in the least bit curious?" Carmine asked, his voice dripping with menace.

Caught off guard, Seymour was quiet as he walked down Grand Avenue searching for a particular building in a crummy neighborhood on the lower east side. "About what, Carmine?"

"About who was in your apartment before you got home yesterday? You must have noticed something was wrong."

Stunned and becoming increasingly alarmed by Carmine's tone he stammered, "Who was in my apartment?"

"I was, asshole. Me and my men and I don't like being lied to."

"I didn't lie to you, Carmine. What are you talking about?"

"You said you didn't know the whore that ran off with Cesari after he broke my nose and shot one of my guys."

"I don't know her, Carmine. I didn't lie."

"Don't fuck with me Seymour. If you didn't know her then why did I see her go into your apartment? I decided to pay you a visit yesterday and boy was I surprised when I spotted her. And how did she know to go hide in that little tunnel beneath your brownstone? You lying piece of garbage. You were protecting her for him weren't you? And if you were protecting her then how can I be sure you're not protecting him too?"

Seymour was flummoxed, his brain racing at this new information. "I have no idea what you're talking about. I would never lie to you, Carmine, and I would never help Cesari. I hate him even more than you do."

"Yeah, you keep saying that, but I found the girl down there at the bottom of that staircase leading into the sewers and you don't seem to have an explanation. Now I have her and you have a lot of explaining to do. I expect you to swing by my hotel room tonight at eight sharp and your lies better match up with her lies or you're going to be in a shit load of trouble. I'm staying at the Four Seasons on E. 57th Street, room 514, and you'd better not be late."

Carmine hung up abruptly and Seymour shuddered. This new development shook him to the core. Carmine had been in his apartment and the police were after him. Things were spiraling out of control. One thing for sure was that he needed to find a more permanent and secure hiding place. There was absolutely no chance he was going to any meeting with Carmine, but he needed some way of keeping that maniac at bay. This news about that Vegas whore was more than just a little disturbing but what did it mean? What on earth was she doing in his apartment let alone in the sewer below? Was Cesari there as well? And if so why didn't Carmine find him?

Damn!

Looking up at the address on the front of the old building, Seymour realized that he had finally reached his destination. He stepped over a guy sleeping in the doorway and entered the vestibule. There was a corpulent man in a heavy wool sweater sitting at a small table who smiled at him. Overhead was a large sign which read *Welcome Brother.* Seymour took a deep breath and approached.

The man was large, maybe 300 pounds, forty years old with a graying beard. He greeted Seymour warmly, "Welcome brother."

Seymour said, "Hi, is this the right place?" It undoubtedly was but better to disarm the guy.

"If you're looking for truth, help, and support it is. My name is Josh." He extended his hand.

Seymour took it and smiling broadly said, "I'm Kermit. Kermit Larana."

"I got Kermit. Could you spell that last part for me?"

"Sure."

As he spelled it out, brother Josh wrote his name on a sticker with a magic marker and gave it to him to place on his clothing.

"Welcome, brother Kermit. Is this your first time here?"

"Yes, it is."

"Would you like to fill out a brief registration form for our records and statistics?"

"Do I have to?"

"Absolutely not, brother, but may I at least ask how you heard of us?"

"I did an internet search and it seemed like the perfect place for me."

Brother Josh beamed. "Thank you. I helped set up the webpage. You can go right in. The meeting is about to start. There's hot coffee and donuts on a table so help yourself. If you plan on staying the night just let me know and I'll assign you a cot and get you some blankets."

Seymour walked into a large gymnasium. To the right were a series of extra wide army cots lined up in rows and to the left was a stage with a microphone and rows of chairs. There were about a hundred attendees taking seats, talking and sipping coffee from Styrofoam cups. Seymour grabbed six glazed donuts and a hot cup of coffee and sat toward the back. This ought to be interesting he mused. In every direction he looked, he could not find even one person who wasn't as massively overweight as he was. There was nothing like hiding in plain sight. This was New York's only shelter for the morbidly obese, sponsored by the Food-Aholics Twelve Step Organization.

FATSO

Chapter 30

At exactly 9:00 a.m., I phoned Arnie to catch up and to find out if Lance needed more corrective action.

"Cesari, I'm glad you called. You're never going to believe this."

"Believe what, Arnie?"

"Lancelot came into my office at 8:00 a.m. sharp and told me that he flat out lied about you assaulting him and begged me to release you from your suspension. And I mean literally begged me, on his knees and everything. He was crying like a little girl."

"He cried? Really?"

"Yes, he did."

"Well, you know the French, Arnie. Very emotional people. What else did he say?"

"He said he's been under a lot of stress and acted out of pure professional jealousy and now deeply regrets the whole thing. I told him that if he was now telling the truth I would have to consider placing him under suspension for professional misconduct and since he was still in the probationary period of his contract he was running the risk of being fired."

"And what did he say to that?"

"He didn't care. He says he lied and deserved any punishment coming his way. I'd rather not have to suspend or fire him, Cesari. We're very short-staffed right now."

"Maybe he's not such a bad guy after all. I think you should give him the benefit of the doubt, Arnie. He really has been under a lot of stress lately especially after the way you came down on him."

"Me?! That was all your doing about the remedial training."

"Still, you're the chief of staff. I just made a suggestion."

He let out a deep breath in frustration and decided to let it go. "Well anyway, I was hoping you'd agree with giving him a second chance. Since you were the victim here I thought you should have some say in it. I know his clinical skills are lacking but as long as he's got a pulse we could still use him."

I loved Arnie. He was so practical. "Yeah, I agree. Let's start over. So does this mean I am officially un-suspended?"

"Yes, it does."

"Good. Any word on Seymour?"

He lowered his voice. "Nothing yet although I'm being hounded day and night by reporters and detectives. They're all over the place interviewing the staff trying to get a profile on him. People are getting very jumpy about it because he always seemed a little creepy. Nurses are afraid that he might be waiting for them outside the hospital. Paranoia's running high around here. Someone even thought they saw you in the main lobby yesterday."

"Really? Me?"

"Yeah, I'm telling you. People are starting to see ghosts."

I smiled. "Well, I hope you're not, Arnie."

"No, I'm not. Besides, I know you're not stupid enough to walk right into the main lobby of the hospital with the police and FBI looking for you."

"FBI?"

"Oh yeah. They were here too about that girl in Vegas and then there's the mob connection."

Of course.

"Well, you're right about me not being that stupid. So what did the Feds have to say?"

"Well, their thinking now is that the girl's pimp killed her for whatever reason. He was a guy named Luther but he's dead now too. They think the girl may have been a mob guy's girlfriend and when he found out what happened he killed the pimp."

"I've heard this theory a couple of times now and I like it, but if that's the case, why are they still looking for me?"

"They said you were the last person to see the girl alive and they would like to know if you knew anything that could shed some light on what happened that night. Like did the pimp threaten her in any way while you were there, or did the girl tell you that she was afraid for her life? Stuff like that. Remember, they're not one hundred percent sure what happened. The bottom line is that it sounds like you're off the hook. I don't know where you are or what you're up to but you can probably plan on coming back to work soon."

"Did they actually say that I'm off the hook? In those words?"

"No, not exactly. Just that their level of interest in you has diminished considerably now that the mob is involved. Plus this business with Seymour has them all doing cartwheels. They were real nice."

Real nice my ass. Arnie was so gullible. This was the oldest trick in the book when you were trying to flush someone out of hiding. Make them think they're not looking for you and tell all your friends the coast is clear. Unfortunately, even if law enforcement had lost interest in me, Carmine and Brunella, hadn't so I just couldn't show up for work on Monday.

"Well, that's good to hear Arnie but I think I'll just take a few more days off to clear the cobwebs. It's been a really long week."

"I understand perfectly. You've been under a lot of stress too. Take as much time as you need."

"Thanks, Arnie. You said the pimp died. What happened?"

"Well, the theory is the mob boyfriend took him out in the desert and beat him into a coma. He was hospitalized in bad shape but it looked like he was going to come through. Then one morning the nurse came in and he was blue and cold."

"That's interesting. So he had an arrhythmia or a pulmonary embolus or something?"

"More likely the mob came back to finish the job. He was found blue and cold and absolutely nothing amiss."

"What are you getting at, Arnie?"

"They found him blue and cold in a hospital bed, Cesari. They *found* him that way. None of his alarms or monitors went off. None of them. In this day and age that's almost impossible. The cardiac monitors, blood pressure and oxygen sensors are so sensitive they go off almost continuously even when nothing is wrong. Somebody turned them off while they did whatever it is they did, like put a pillow over his face."

"Did the FBI tell you that?"

"Not in so many words, but I read in between the lines."

"Okay, Arnie, thanks for the update."

"Are you going to turn yourself in to the FBI?"

"I doubt it."

He thought that over for a moment. "You either don't believe the FBI isn't as interested in you as they told me or you're worried the mob is also looking for you for whatever reason."

"Very good, Matlock."

"So, you think that if her mob boyfriend went through the trouble of killing her pimp in his hospital bed that he may want to have a chat with the last guy who had sex with her."

"I didn't have sex with her, Columbo, but yeah, that sums it up."

"That's not what the FBI said. Apparently, they were finally able to confirm your DNA on her and I mean everywhere."

I was silent as I thought it over. That would place me right smack at the crime scene. I let out a deep noisy breath. "Damn. I don't remember any of it, Arnie."

"I believe you but that's what they said. So you were definitely there and you definitely had sex with her. On the other hand, the federal agents really did seem sincere when they said they don't believe you killed her. Their working theory is that you had sex with her, but that you left while she was still alive. For some reason the pimp comes in, suffocates her and then slices her up. He may have been high on meth. They said he was a user. The one wrinkle that might work in your favor is that they found someone else's DNA on her in addition to yours but they haven't identified whose it is yet. Hopefully, it will be that guy Luther's."

Irritated I said, "How does that work in my favor? She was a prostitute. Of course, I wasn't the only guy who might have been with her. The point is that now I can't argue that I *wasn't* with her."

"I'm just trying to help, Cesari."

I sighed. "Thanks for saving that for last."

"I was trying to soften the news. I know that you didn't want to hear that, but there it is."

"All right, fine. So I was there and we were intimate."

"Multiple times and positions."

"Shut up, Arnie. I got it."

"Maybe you should just go talk to them. It sounds like they're on your side."

"Who, the FBI? That'll be the day when I voluntarily walk into their office."

Arnie knew that I had a sketchy background and a police record from before I became a physician not to mention continuing relationships with known gangsters under ongoing federal investigations. They would probably try to use me to go after Vito. That was standard operating procedure. Threaten and intimidate the little fish so he'll turn on the big fish. And if I didn't cooperate I might well wind up in prison on some trumped up charge. It happened all the time. You never wanted to get caught in the cross hairs of the criminal justice system.

"Take it easy, Cesari. I'm just throwing out ideas."

"Well, that one you can really throw out. Look, I got to go. I'll stay in touch, okay?"

I hung up and finished my coffee. I was sitting in a McDonalds on the corner of W. 14th Street and Sixth Avenue not too far from the Rubin Museum of Himalayan Art. Looking out the window at the snow covered sidewalk, I wondered, like everyone else, if winter would ever end. It was almost March and New York was being dumped on by hopefully the last storm of the season. There was already two inches on the ground and at least six to eight more anticipated. I pictured Seymour lying in the middle of Fifth Avenue making snow angels.

What was the deal with Seymour anyway? How did he go from maladjusted anesthesiologist to mob connected, psychopathic murderer? I had to admit I never saw that coming. Carmine and Seymour, Seymour and Carmine, that was just too hard to fathom on one cup of coffee. Plus, I was still hungry so I ordered a second cup of coffee and a second sausage, egg, and cheese McMuffin.

As I walked back to my seat, Vito entered the restaurant covered in snow, shook himself off and sat across from me at the plastic table. "Jesus, it's cold out there." He reached across the table, took my coffee, pried the lid off, and sipped it. Then he eyed my breakfast sandwich hungrily so I pushed it over to him and went back to the counter to get another one.

When I returned he said, "Thanks for breakfast, Cesari."

"Yeah. Can we talk now?"

"Shoot."

"First, any word from Brunella or Carmine?"

"Yes, my sources tell me that Carmine and a couple of his guys are holed up here in the city somewhere. I don't know where. He thinks he's been clever putting out feelers and paying guys off to keep tabs on me just in case you show up. What he doesn't know is that even though my guys might be susceptible to coughing up a little information for cash, they generally don't like him so they're not going to blow me in unless; one, the price is right; and two, they're absolutely sure I won't find out. The chump change Carmine's offering is almost insulting to my boys. So as long as you keep a low profile and I'm discrete about where and when I meet you we should be okay."

"What about Brunella?"

"She's staying in Brooklyn. There's no point in her coming down here. If and when they catch up to you is when she'll take a more hands on approach. I will tell you one thing though. Word is that they know for a fact you're in Manhattan. I don't know how they can be that certain but they are."

I thought about that sipping my coffee and savoring it. McDonalds coffee was pretty good, and that was saying something because I was sort of a coffee snob. "How can they be so sure?"

He shrugged. "I don't know but they are."

"All right. Let's say they know in a general way but not exactly where I am so as long as I keep on the move I should be fine."

"You'd better check out of that hotel. I wouldn't even stay there tonight. Just get your stuff and move."

I nodded in agreement but in the middle of a snow storm it might not be so easy to find a vacancy and I didn't want to go back to Vito's apartment. I shelved that thought for a moment and filled him in on the conversation Arnie had with the FBI.

"Well, that sucks they got your DNA. So you really did fornicate with that girl."

I shook my head. I loved when he used big words. I said, "Apparently, and yes, it sucks. To make matters worse, I think their wheels are beginning to spin on how they're going to use that to get to you. It seems they're disproportionately interested in talking to me considering that they have other more likely suspects."

"You mean they don't really believe you had anything to do with that girl's death, but since they got you by the balls why not squeeze and see what happens?"

I nodded and he added. "So what are you going to do? Blow me in?" He grinned as he said that knowing full well that would never happen. We'd been through too much together and at this point he was the closest thing I had to family.

"I should, just to wipe that grin off your face, but no, my plan is to stay as far away from them as possible until this whole thing blows over. If they don't find me they can't threaten me. They'll soon get tired and go barking up somebody else's tree. Hopefully they will have closed the case before I'm old enough to go on Medicare. It's a pain in the ass looking over my shoulder everywhere I go."

"Tell me about it. Just stick to the shadows and you'll be fine." He adjusted himself in his seat and his foot hit something hard causing him to look down under the table. "What's in the duffel bag? It felt like I hit a brick."

"It's my crowbar and the Glock."

He chuckled. "You brought a crowbar and a gun to McDonalds? Getting a little paranoid, aren't you?"

"Maybe, maybe not. You have a gun, right?"

"Of course."

"So be quiet. Okay, let's talk about Seymour. Where would a guy that large try to hide with his picture being splashed all over the news?"

Vito strummed his fingers on the table as he finished his sandwich and shook his head. "I don't know. Does he have family?"

"No, he doesn't, at least not in the New York area. He was an only child and both his parents are deceased. I had asked around about him before all this happened when I thought I might try to be his friend. I was hoping to find common interests."

"And did you?"

"Yeah, we both like pizza."

Vito chuckled softly. "I'll bet he does. Okay, Cesari, what's on the agenda today or do we just sit here and wait until the plows dig us out."

"No, we're going to scour all the shelters in the city looking for him. He's got to be somewhere that's warm and has food."

"You got to be kidding? There has to be dozens of shelters. In the middle of a snow storm we're going to hoof it all over the city?"

"That's the point, Vito, it's twenty degrees outside and dropping. He can't possibly survive without shelter in this weather. He'd have to go somewhere where they don't ask questions. That rules out hotels, so unless he's sleeping on the subway waiting for a transit officer to find him he'd have to go to one."

"What about the girl? He can't just check into a shelter with a kidnap victim in tow."

That thought made me upset. If he was a murderous sociopath and she suddenly became an impediment to his plans he wouldn't hesitate to dispatch her in some horrible way like the bones in the tunnel, the girl in the acid bath, and the four homeless men. I shuddered.

"I think we have to assume the worst at this point. I don't know what his reasoning was for taking her along in the first place but he'd have to eventually dump her if he wanted to get away."

Vito nodded solemnly. "I'm sorry, Cesari."

"Let's get started."

Chapter 31

Seymour lay on his cot in the shelter staring at the ceiling and contemplating his next move. If he had to listen to another freaking lecture about how he should eat to live and not live to eat he was going to scream. Stuck in a smelly gymnasium with ninety other morbidly obese people who hadn't showered or changed their clothes in days was taking its toll on him. Free donuts and pizza kept him from completely losing his mind but he needed a better plan. He was used to a certain lifestyle and could only slum it for so long before he lost his mind, but where could he go? The city was caught in the middle a blizzard and the forecast had just been upgraded to possibly fourteen inches by morning. He was afraid to use mass transit or a car service for fear of recognition. He hadn't seen television in two days but he knew it was just a matter of time before they found the bones of his other victims down in the sewer. Then, the hunt would really be on and he still had this gnat Carmine nipping at his heels.

Hmm, Troy had mentioned that he had a nice apartment not too far from here, but he also had a wife and three children. If they suddenly didn't show up at school people would ask questions. No, five people would be too complicated anyway. Plus, Troy was the head of radiology. He would be missed right away.

He needed someone who no one really knew well and didn't have many friends. Then it hit him. That new guy, Lancelot. He would be perfect. He just started and people barely knew his name and, from what Seymour had heard, wasn't well-liked. Where did he live?

Shit.

The subject had come up during an ERCP. Boy, talk about a guy who was clumsy. Maybe he was new but it certainly seemed like he had chosen the wrong profession. The guy had absolutely no dexterity, but where, where, where? Think, Seymour think.

Then it came to him. Yes, that was it. 18 E. 20th Street across from Gramercy Park. The French poodle had a ground floor two bedroom condominium there. He had bragged about it endlessly to the nurses and him during that case. Apparently apartments in that neighborhood were difficult to come by and he felt privileged. Seymour chuckled with glee as he remembered and hauled himself into a sitting position. It was almost five and getting dark. It was at least a thirty minute walk to get there from where he was and in this weather he knew he was going to be miserable. He felt the gun in his pocket and started to glow with confidence as he looked around at his companions.

Pathetic losers, the whole lot. Listening to them whine into the microphone all afternoon made him want to puke. It's my mommies fault, kids picked on me, girls don't like me. Jesus, get over it. So you're fat. Deal with it and move on. Being obese never stopped Seymour from enjoying life. He had plenty of women too. Granted, they were usually bound, gagged, and sometimes drugged but so what? He was living the life. At least he was until Cesari had come along. He never should have let that guy get under his skin.

He stood up to leave just as four pizza delivery guys appeared at the doorway each carrying five large pies. A fifth delivery guy followed them in with large shopping bags filled with two liter bottles of soda. As they placed the pizzas and soda on the long tables off to the side of the gymnasium, the masses on the cots began to rouse themselves, wobbling slowly upright. As Seymour watched in disgust, their laborious movement reminded him of walruses heading out to sea. Soon they would be stampeding toward the feeding trough, but already standing when the pizzas arrived, Seymour had the edge and got there ahead of the mob. He grabbed a whole pie in its cardboard box and lumbered quickly toward the door listening to their vitriol as he did.

Chapter 32

By five, Vito and I were exhausted and freezing. We'd been to a dozen or so shelters all over the lower half of the island and been disappointed each time. We realized we'd never get to all of them in one day. The snow was coming down heavy now, the sidewalks hadn't been shoveled, the plows were behind schedule and traffic was grinding to a halt.

"I'm hungry," Vito complained for the tenth time.

"C'mon Vito one more and we'll call it a day and go grab a bite to eat. Besides, what are you complaining about? I'm the one who's been lugging this crowbar around all day." We had skipped lunch and his mood was starting to turn sour.

He grumbled something and wrapped his scarf over his face as we entered the Bowery Mission in lower Manhattan. Established in the late eighteen hundreds, the Bowery Mission was an icon in lower Manhattan and could accommodate up to one hundred and fifty persons per night. I found the guy in charge and told him we were looking for a friend and he allowed us to search the building. After an hour and frustrated we thanked and bid him good bye.

"Are you sure your friend is in one of the shelters?" he asked, noting the glum look on our faces.

I answered, "No, we're just taking a guess. Given the weather and his condition he'd have nowhere else to go or at least that's what we figured."

"Well, if you give me your phone number and a brief description of your friend I'd be happy to call you if he shows up. I'm sure he would rather be in the companionship of good friends who really care about him than here. As hard as we try to provide support and a nurturing environment for people to retain their human dignity, I'm afraid we fall far short of what's necessary. It's simply the nature of the circumstances."

I nodded in understanding. He was a nice guy. "In fact, you could help us. Thank you." I gave him Seymour's description and he raised his eye brows.

"Have you gentleman tried looking for him at the HMO?"

Vito and I glanced at each other. I said, "The what?"

"The HMO. Home for the Morbidly Obese. It's New York's only shelter specifically designed for the needs of the morbidly overweight. In the company of people with similar needs they feel less threatened and intimidated to seek counselling services and rehabilitation. The shelter even provides free consultation for gastric bypass surgery, which is performed pro bono at St. Luke's Hospital."

I was fascinated. "I had no idea. Where is the HMO?"

It was just a few blocks away in the same neighborhood and after he gave us directions I asked him if he accepted donations. He asked me if the Pope was catholic. I gave him a thousand dollars and his eyes grew wide as he thanked me profusely. My spirits buoyed, I trudged through the snow barely noticing the cold.

Vito said wryly, "Very generous with my money, Cesari."

"I still have seven hundred left and besides, that information was worth it. That Seymour is one clever bastard. Home for the Morbidly Obese. Of course. No one would notice anything unusual about him there."

Ten minutes later, we shook snow off our clothes and faces and entered the shelter. There was a big guy at a small desk named Josh who introduced himself and asked if he could help us. When we told him we were looking for a friend to take home with us he merrily waved us in.

Vito smirked at the sight and I had to hold back a chuckle as well. About eighty to ninety men and a handful of women chowing down on pizza and diet soda. Not one of them an ounce under 400 pounds. Not one looked as if they had ever even considered stepping inside a gym.

"Man, will you look at that sight, Cesari."

"There but for the grace of God go I, Vito," I admonished him.

"Bullshit, this is as much a choice as doing crack."

"I'm not so sure about that."

We wandered through the crowd and were for the most part, ignored. Every so often we would get a sideways glance or a polite nod. Satisfied that he wasn't here I scratched my head and asked one of the guys there if he had met someone named Seymour recently. He shook his head and kept on eating.

Vito walked up to an empty pizza box and scraped some of the cheese off the cardboard and put it into his mouth. Two people on the other side of the table shouted their disapproval. "Hey, pal, that's for the residents."

Vito looked up shocked at the rebuke and replied. "Hey, dude, it was just a scrap of cheese."

A different guy said angrily, "That's the best part, bro. The leftover cheese."

"Jesus Christ. Fine." Vito withdrew from the table with his tail between his legs.

Josh had come up behind us. "Don't mind them. They're a little out of sorts. One of the residents ran off with a whole pepperoni pizza for himself not more than fifteen minutes ago. It was very rude of him."

I thought about that. "The guy who ran off. What was his name?"

"Kermit. He was new here and just arrived yesterday. I don't know if he's coming back. He may be too embarrassed after what he did. I hope he wasn't the friend you're looking for. It would be a shame because you literally just missed him."

"Could you describe him?"

He did the best he could but except for short brown hair and one day's growth of beard he wasn't very helpful but then I had an idea.

"Do you have a computer?" I asked.

"I have a laptop in the main office."

"May I use it?"

"Sure."

He ushered us to the shelter's office and booted up the laptop. After it connected to the internet, I pulled up the St. Matt's directory of physicians and found Seymour's profile. I pointed at the screen and asked, "Is that him?"

He turned the laptop and studied the image. Seymour was all cleaned up, hair combed, smiling, wearing a suit and tie. The guy hesitated. He didn't want to make a mistake. Gradually, he started to nod and looked up from the screen.

"No doubt about it. That's him, but he told me his name was Kermit."

Vito said, "Shit, we just missed him."

I added, "Do you remember which direction he went in?"

Josh scratched his head. "Not a hundred percent sure but I seem to remember him mumbling something about Gramercy Park when he left. So Kermit is Seymour and he's a doctor?"

"Yes, and he's very dangerous. So if he returns, call the police immediately. Don't confront him."

The guys eyes grew wide. "He's dangerous?"

"Very."

"Are you the police?"

"No, we're not."

"Are you dangerous?"

"Very."

We ran out into the brisk night air, turned right, and walked rapidly uptown along the Bowery. It was dark, snowing hard and windy. Visibility was poor and the sidewalks were a mess. We wound up walking in the middle of the street following the trail of a plow. Traffic was non-existent otherwise. We made slow progress, but in my estimation, moved twice as quickly as Seymour possibly could.

The Bowery eventually merged into Third Avenue and we walked past St. Matt's Hospital, eventually reaching Irving Place. From there, it was a straight run to Gramercy Park. Snow drifts in front of the wrought iron fence of the park's entrance approached two feet in height. We stood there looking around realizing we had reached a dead end. I was frustrated, cold, and pissed off. How could someone like Seymour keep giving me the slip like this? I had been tracking down guys smarter than him my whole life.

Vito called out to me. "Hey, Cesari, look at the garbage can."

There was a metal trash can by the curb and I went to it, finding an empty extra-large pizza box on top, freshly covered with snow. I brushed the powder off and saw that it was from the same pizzeria as the others we saw at the shelter.

"It's him," I said.

Vito opened the box and said with disgust. "I can't believe it. He ate the whole freakin' thing."

"You can't be serious. You would have eaten something out of the trash can?"

"I'm starving, Cesari. I haven't eaten anything since breakfast."

"Can we put your hunger pains on hold for a minute while I think?"

I scanned up and down E. 20th Street trying to decide in which direction Seymour might have gone. I still couldn't believe that we didn't catch up to him. As I studied the row of apartment buildings facing the park, something felt vaguely familiar.

Vito saw me furrowing my brow. "What is it?"

"I don't know. This place is familiar to me and I don't know why."

I walked up and down searching in all directions and then suddenly it came to me. I reached into my back pocket for my wallet and pulled out Lance's driver's license. "Well, I'll be."

"What?" Vito asked, shivering.

"This is Lance's apartment building. 18 E. 20th Street. He's the doctor friend I needed to speak to in the restaurant last night."

"You're kidding?"

"No, this is the place all right. I took his driver's license so I wouldn't forget, in case I needed to talk to him again."

He chuckled at that. "So what do you think? Coincidence?"

"I don't know. If it was, it would have to be the biggest coincidence in the history of the universe."

"You think he's inside with your pal?"

"It's a possibility that's worth looking into."

"Cesari, I don't mean to burst your bubble but your friend Seymour is armed, right? If we just knock on the door we're going to be greeted by hot lead."

He was right. Even worse, we couldn't just knock on the door. We had to be buzzed in. I needed to think this through and I couldn't do that standing ankle deep in snow and starving.

"Vito, let's sit down for a bite and get warm while we talk over our options. The Gramercy Tavern is just down the block. Even with the weather, I'm sure they'll still be open."

Teeth chattering, he nodded in agreement and we trudged to the restaurant. Inside, we stamped our feet, brushed snow off, and immediately felt refreshed by the warmth. The place was not that busy for a Saturday night because of the storm and we seated ourselves at the bar, looking around. The décor was classic with lots of wood, low lighting, and plush, comfortable leather chairs. The bartender, dressed formally in white shirt, black bowtie, and mutton chops greeted us warmly.

"What'll it be gentlemen?"

We ordered a couple of bourbons neat and asked if we could dine right there at the bar. He nodded and brought us a couple of menus with our drinks. After looking at it for thirty seconds, Vito put his down, slipped it back across the bar and took a slug of his Maker's Mark.

"You know what you want already?" I asked.

"Yeah, I know. You think I can smoke in here?"

"I don't know. Why don't you light up and find out."

He liked my sarcasm and smiled. "Are you ready to order, Cesari? I'm starving."

I closed the menu. "Sure."

The waiter came over and I ordered the smoked trout with green onions, pickled ramps, and kohlrabi. He turned to Vito and asked, "And you, sir?"

"I'll have rigatoni with vodka sauce and sausage, and we'll have a bottle of Chianti with dinner."

That wasn't on the menu and the waiter stared blankly at him to see if he was joking. When he was sure he wasn't, he replied as if talking to a child. "I'm afraid that this isn't one of those type of restaurants but I'm sure you would be delighted with one of the other choices."

I cringed inwardly because this could only end badly and I really didn't want to draw unnecessary attention to myself. I felt the need to intervene before we reached the point of no return so I leaned over and whispered into Vito's ear, "Listen up, douchebag. We have work to do so don't start trouble. Order something off the God damn menu and say thank you."

He pushed me away. "Relax, Cesari." Then he turned back to the bartender. "Is your manager, Mr. Garrison, here and may I speak to him?"

Polite but sarcastic the bartender replied, "Yes, of course. I'll get him but I assure you he won't be able pull rigatoni and sausage out of thin air. I'll be right back," he turned to me, "and I'll place your order in for you, sir."

I said, "Thank you."

He left and I said, "What kind of an asshole are you?"

"Is that a trick question? How many kinds are there?"

"Shut up."

The bartender and manager came up from behind Vito and the latter cleared his throat to announce his presence.

Vito stood up and turned around to meet him and the guy turned white as he stammered, "Mr. Giannelli, I had no idea it was you. Please excuse Raoul's impertinence. I hope all is well."

"If I can get something to eat soon I'll be fine," he replied gruffly and unsympathetically.

"I will take your order personally. What is it you would like?"

Vito growled, "I have to repeat myself?"

Now Raoul started to freak, picking up on his manager's anxiety. "I remember. It was rigatoni with vodka sauce and sausage with a bottle of Chianti."

The manager said, "I'll call it in to Paul & Jimmy's. They're just around the corner. Raoul put your coat on and get over there now! I'll make sure they put a rush on it and don't forget the Chianti and maybe a loaf of garlic bread."

Vito added, "And a wedge of parmigiano reggiano for grating."

Raoul's eyes were wide now. His manager said, "What are you waiting for? Get going."

Before leaving us to go back to his day job, the manager placed the bottle of Maker's Mark on the counter in front of us.

"It's on the house, Mr. Giannelli. Is there anything else I can do for you?"

"Do you mind if I smoke?"

The guy hesitated. It was clearly against the law to smoke in a restaurant. I could see his wheels spinning from the stress. Vito reached slowly into his breast pocket and came out with his usual, a pack of unfiltered Camels. The manager's eyes darted in every direction as Vito shook out a cigarette and placed it in his mouth. Coming to a very difficult decision and choosing his good health over a possible Department of Health citation, he picked up one of the candles that dotted the bar counter and held it up to light Vito's cigarette.

The manager said, "Of course not."

The man left and I shook my head. "Why do you always have to bother people?" He just smiled and I continued. "Can we get down to business now?"

He held his whiskey glass up and looked at the amber liquid in the light. "Sure, go ahead."

"Okay, the way I see it, Seymour decides for some reason the shelter is not a great place to hide. At first, he thinks he'll blend in but after a while it dawns on him that someone who's looking for him might have the same idea so he takes off. He knows Lance from the hospital and maybe is counting on him being sympathetic to him or maybe even hoping Lance hasn't been paying attention to the news. At any rate, he concocts some story to gain entrance. His priority right now, besides not getting caught, is to not freeze to death."

"So Lance wouldn't help him out of friendship?"

"No, not a chance. They barely know each other. This guy Lance just started at the hospital. On the other hand, he might help the guy out of compassion. You know bring him in and try to coax him into surrendering to the authorities. There are a lot of factors that might go through his mind."

"Okay, then what happens?"

"They eat, drink, talk about what happened. I can see Seymour studying him, trying to decide how to play the thing out."

"And how *does* it play out in your mind?"

"That's just it Vito. It doesn't play out well for Lance at all. It can't. If Seymour's the cold blooded killer we think he is, he's not going to spare Lance even if he shows him a modicum of kindness."

"Then we'd better think of a plan quick."

Raoul returned with Vito's rigatoni and Chianti at about the same time my smoked trout came. The manager placed wine glasses in front of us and uncorked the bottle, filling our glasses. The food was great and I noticed Raoul keeping a close tab on our glasses to make sure they stay filled.

I looked at my meal and as delicious as it was I suddenly lost my appetite. Talking it out like that had crystalized in my mind the severity of Lance's situation. How to gain entrance into the apartment was the big question, made even worse now by the realization that Seymour might be in control there. On the other hand, maybe I could use that to my advantage. I looked at my watch. It was after seven. Time was wasting. Think, Cesari. Think.

I smiled suddenly as Vito rhythmically shoveled forkfuls of rigatoni and sausage into his mouth. I said, "Hurry up. I have an idea"

Chapter 33

I had the manger call Paul & Jimmy's again and they sent a box of a dozen cannoli's to us in the bar which arrived as we finished eating. We said goodbye to Raoul who seemed quite relieved at our departure. As we walked down the block back to Lance's apartment building, I reviewed the plan with Vito. "Ring the buzzer and show him the box of cannolis. Tell him Paul & Jimmy's had randomly selected several people in the neighborhood for a promotion and that it was a gift from them to him."

Vito looked skeptical. "You seriously think he'll go for that?"

"He ate a whole pepperoni pizza didn't he? It's been an hour. He's got to be starving by now."

"I guess it can't hurt to try."

"Once he buzzes you in we have to be careful so that Lance doesn't get caught in the crossfire. Assuming he's still alive, that is. I'll stay in the shadows. If Seymour answers the door make sure you can see both hands before making a move. If you can't see both hands assume he's got his gun in the other."

"All right, Cesari, relax. This isn't my first rodeo. So what happens if Lance answers the door?"

"That's a good question. I've been working on the assumption that Seymour is in control in there but he may not be. Not yet anyway. To answer your question, I guess it would depend on whether you can tell if there is anyone else in there. Just be cautious all right. I don't like coming to someone's rescue and then watching them get murdered. The bottom line is if you're not sure what's going on just hand over the cannolis and walk away. At least we'll be in the apartment building and can regroup."

I stepped away from the door and Vito pressed the buzzer. He waited a few moments and pressed it again. When nothing happened, he turned to look at me, and as he did the intercom blared, beckoning him for his identity.

He went through the spiel as planned and held up the box of cannoli's to the camera for the occupant to see clearly the name Paul & Jimmy's on top. A few uneasy seconds passed, the door buzzed and we heard it unlock. Vito opened it and we both slipped in. The apartment was on the first floor toward the rear of the building and I ran quickly past the door before it opened, taking up position in the shadows behind it. Placing the duffel bag with the crowbar on the floor beside me, I withdrew my Glock from the small of my back and braced myself for the worst.

Vito sauntered up after me and politely knocked three times and someone answered. From where I crouched, I couldn't see who was in the doorway but from the shocked expression on Vito's face it had to be Seymour. Then I heard Seymour's familiar voice, "Thank your boss for the cannolis. Are you sure I don't owe you anything?"

Recovering his composure Vito said, "Nah, Paulie said they're on the house but a tip is always welcome if you know what I mean." He hesitated and added, "Are you sure you want all of these? They're not dietetic you know?"

I rolled my eyes. Don't provoke him, Vito.

Too late. Seymour bristled, "What's that supposed to mean?"

"It means it wouldn't kill you to say no once in a while."

Seymour faltered for a moment and I guessed he was unsure of himself. I assumed this was something new for him, a delivery guy insulting him. All that mattered was how badly he had worked himself up over the cannolis.

He finally blinked and chuckled, "Hey, maybe you got a point. Here's a five for your trouble. Thanks for coming out in the snow."

I let out a slow breath, relieved that the confrontation was defusing but I was wrong about that. As Vito went to hand Seymour the box, he had in mind to pull his pistol out with the other but Seymour had other plans. The door swung open quickly and the next thing I saw was a pudgy hand sticking out with the barrel inches from Vito's face.

Seymour said, "Okay, funny guy. Why don't you come in here and entertain me some more." His tone had changed considerably and ominously. The real Seymour was declaring himself. It was time to act.

Vito said calmly, "Easy pal. I was just joking."

I sprung out of my hiding place and using my Glock smashed it upward into Seymour's exposed wrist. The pistol flew out of his hand and he howled in pain. Vito bull rushed him back into the apartment and Seymour fell backward onto the carpeted floor with Vito on top. I picked up Seymour's gun and quickly closed and locked the door behind us as they wrestled. I turned around just as Vito launched a hard right into one of Seymour's triple chins.

I said, "Okay, enough. Get up Seymour, sit on the sofa and shut up."

"Cesari?! Fuck."

"Fuck is right, Seymour, and Vito what was the idea with the insults?"

"Angry guys make bad decisions. That's all."

He was right. "Well, your little plan almost got you a bullet in your brain."

Seymour sat on the couch rubbing his wrist and chin. "What do you want, Cesari?"

"Where's Lance?"

"He's all right."

"Vito, go check the other rooms. I need to explain a few ground rules to Seymour." Vito left and I stood over Seymour with my Glock pointed at him. "Empty your pockets on the coffee table."

He tossed his cellphone, wallet, and an asthma inhaler onto the table.

"Is that all? You better not be holding out on me."

"That's all."

"I didn't know you were asthmatic."

"Cold weather brings it out."

"Okay, I'm going to ask you a few questions and you're going to answer truthfully."

"And if I don't?"

This guy was a riot and I guessed that he didn't understand just how pissed off I was. Suddenly and with unexpected violence I swung the barrel across the side of his face. His head snapped away and he groaned in pain. Glaring, I waited for him to regain focus. He looked at me for the first time grasping that just as no one knew who he was deep inside, he didn't know who I was either.

Angrily I said, "Ready to start?"

He nodded.

"What did you do to Francesca?"

"Who?"

I smacked him hard with the gun again and he spit blood. His lip started to swell and my head was starting to explode from anger. I forced myself not to lose it.

He put his hands up. "I don't know who you're talking about. I really don't. I don't know anyone by that name."

I believed him. "The girl you found in the tunnel, asshole. Her name was Francesca."

"If you mean that whore from Vegas, Carmine found her there, not me."

"If you call her a whore again I'm going to knock your two front teeth out. Understood?"

He nodded.

"Back to Carmine. What do you mean he found her?"

"He was coming to see me about you when he spotted her entering my brownstone, and don't ask me about that because I don't know how or why she was there. When I came home they were already gone."

"And how do you know all this?"

"Because Carmine called me and told me. He thinks I was hiding her for you and that maybe I was helping you too."

Vito called me from one of the bedrooms. "Hey Cesari, come here. You're gonna want to see this."

I waved the gun at Seymour. "Let's go and don't be stupid."

Entering the bedroom, we found Lance, naked and face down, tied spread eagled to his bed with neckties and belts. He had a wash cloth shoved in his mouth. I looked at Seymour and shook my head.

He just shrugged.

"Let him loose, Vito. Seymour and I still have a lot to talk about."

We went back into the living room and I asked Seymour about Vegas, the bodies in the tunnel, and Carmine. Realizing defiance wasn't the right approach, he answered my questions to the best of his ability—mostly. I could tell he was holding back but I let him talk, interjecting from time to time for clarification.

I asked, "So Luther killed that girl, Jenny, and left her there figuring I would take the fall?"

"That's what everyone thinks and then Carmine unloaded on him. At least that's the word on the street. Carmine doesn't exactly confide in me."

"Why would Luther do that? Kill one of his own girls?"

"You're asking me why an asshole pimp on meth would kill a girl? C'mon, that's not a reasonable question."

He had a point. "Fine, but why is Carmine still looking for me then?"

"I don't know. Maybe he's not convinced Luther acted alone. Maybe it's because you beat the crap out of him in front of the who—girl. Maybe it's because you were the last guy to screw his girlfriend and he's pissed it wasn't him. For crying out loud Cesari, how many reasons does a guy like that need?"

"Yeah, I guess that makes sense." He was lying about something. I just couldn't tell what.

Vito and Lance came in the room and sat down.

"Are you okay, Lance?" I asked.

He nodded. "I am fine. Had you and your big friend come fifteen minutes later I cannot be so sure. He was looking for Vaseline when the doorbell rang. That is the last time I feel sorry for a fellow physician in need. He told me that he was cold and hungry and wanted to turn himself in to the authorities but that he was afraid to do so by himself. He is asshole."

"Don't beat yourself up, Lance. Guys like him are masters of manipulation and deception."

"Johneee, I cannot thank you enough."

"Don't worry about it, but I hope you don't mind if we stick around a while."

"Anything. Anything at all for you and your friend. Are you hungry? I can make omelets."

"I'm fine, thanks."

Vito perked up. "I wouldn't mind an omelet and there's a box of cannolis over there on the floor by the door. I might have one if you have coffee. Thanks."

"Of course, I have coffeee." Lance sprang into action and rushed off to his kitchen.

I looked at Vito in disbelief. "You just ate."

"I'm not a shrimp like you, Cesari."

Seymour added, "I wouldn't mind a cannoli."

My eyes went wide as I scowled at him. "Shut up unless I tell you to speak," I growled and then paused for a second to let it sink in. "Now tell me some more about that girl, Jenny. So you didn't know her?"

"Never saw her before that night."

I nodded my head slowly in thought. "And Carmine as well?"

"Yup. He tracked me down because I'd been there before and some of the girls remembered I had dinner with you."

His answers seemed reasonable but there was something I didn't like that I couldn't put my finger on. His responses were too picture perfect. Too cute. As if they'd been rehearsed in his head for just such a moment.

"So Carmine's got Frankie and is expecting you uptown in his hotel room in about fifteen minutes. What was your plan?"

"Didn't really have one. I was just buying time. I was going to call him and tell him that I couldn't make it because of the weather. He would be pissed of course but he'd accept it. So what's *your* plan? You going to call the police or not?"

He surmised that I had more on my mind than turning him over to the authorities. I was distracted and becoming growingly alarmed by the news that Carmine had Frankie. At the same time, I was relieved that she was still alive. I said, "Maybe."

Sensing an opening Seymour said, "I can help you, Cesari."

I chuckled. He had a fat lip and a small cut under one eye. "You have a great sense of humor, Seymour. Are you now planning on using your serial murderer skills for the benefit of mankind? You got us all into this mess, you slug, but go ahead. Pray tell, how can you help me?"

"You want the girl and I want a way out."

"I hope you're not trying to make a deal with me, Seymour. Because if you are, I have to warn you that I didn't slap you nearly as hard as I could have."

Lance heard that and called from the kitchen, "He is telling the truth, Monsieur Seymour."

"Don't be stupid, Cesari. I understand I'm not going free but it would be nice to have Carmine off my back. I'd rather spend consecutive life sentences in a federal prison learning carpentry than strung up in a meat locker in Brooklyn."

He was making all kinds of sense and I would kind of like to have Carmine off my back too. "What did you have in mind?"

"Let's flush him out. I'll call him and tell him I can't make it because of the weather and that there are no taxis available. He'll be pissed and then as a matter of good faith I'll suggest some of his guys come and pick me up. If he goes for the bait, that'll reduce his force by at least one, probably two. He'll doubtless have at least one more goon with him when you go to collect the girl but I think you and your ape-man friend can handle them. With any luck you might find him all alone."

Vito stiffened at the ape-man comment. "Fuck-off, chubby."

I said, "Take it easy, Vito, and what about you, Seymour? I'm supposed to just leave you here having espresso with Lance waiting for Carmine?"

"Hell no. First off, we don't give them this address. We send them on a goose chase down to that shelter in the Bowery I was staying at and I come with you. All I want is first dibs on Carmine. I'm already wanted for murder, so what's one more? Once you got the girl and he's out of the way, you turn me in."

I rubbed my chin thinking about it. He was so full of shit. That much was obvious. He just wanted to get out of the apartment figuring he'd have a better chance of escape. Like he said before, he was just buying time, but his plan made sense and if there was a chance I could save Frankie I had to take it. There was a part of me that just wanted to strip him naked and dump him in a snow drift somewhere on Fifth Avenue.

I said, "Go ahead. Call Carmine."

Vito interrupted. "Hold on Cesari. I don't mean to burst your bubble but how are we supposed to get to his hotel?"

I thought it over. "We could hijack a snow plow."

Vito laughed at that.

Lance offered, "I have a vehicle you can borrow. I keep it garaged nearby on Third Avenue."

Vito said, "No offense Lance, but we'll need a tank to get through this weather."

"No worries, my friend. I drive all the way to Quebec and back all the time, rain or shine, snow or no snow. It is a Honda Pilot, three hundred horse power, all-wheel drive, with new snow tires; the best money can buy. You will be fine. Monsieur Vito, your omelet, she is ready. I apologize but I have no parsley for garnish."

Vito went into the kitchen to eat and Seymour asked, "Can I put my wallet and inhaler away?"

"Sure, why not?"

As he picked up his cellphone to call Carmine he added, "If we're going to do this I should have your number."

I was a little suspicious. "Why? You going to call me from prison?"

He smirked. "Possibly, but I was thinking that in any operation of this sort there's always the chance of unexpected complications. It's always a good idea to have clear lines of communication."

"What are you, a Green Beret?" I wasn't planning on him hanging on to his cell phone after he made the call, but once again, he made sense so we exchanged numbers.

Chapter 34

Carmine took the bait and told Seymour to sit tight in the shelter and wait for his men to come for him in a black Suburban. Apparently, he had a fleet of them. Meanwhile, we fought our way through the snow to the garage on Third Avenue where we picked up Lance's Honda. The parking garage attendant looked at us as if we were nuts to try to drive in this mess, and maybe we were. The plows were doing their best but we still slipped, slid, and ground our way uptown toward the hotel.

Vito drove and I kept my Glock trained on Seymour in the back seat. The gloves were off with him and I wanted it to be perfectly clear what was going to happen if he did anything I disapproved of. It was the longest two mile trip I had ever been on and took us close to forty five minutes to pull up to the main entrance of the hotel.

I said, "Okay, Vito, you go to the corner and stay in the car with the engine running. Seymour and I will go up to the room. I'll text you when we're in position. By my calculation, we have plenty of time before Carmine's goons get back."

"Okay, I'll stay in one spot for as long as I can. With the roads like this I can't just block traffic forever. If I'm forced to move, I'll circle around the block. Keep that in mind."

"I will. Seymour you got it straight what we're going to do?"

"Yes, I do."

"And you better do exactly as I say—no matter what, and remember, there are a lot of people looking for you so try to keep a low profile and don't go off the reservation."

"Got it, chief."

"Don't fuck with me, Seymour. I'm not in the mood."

He didn't say anything.

Vito chimed in, "I don't know if going up to Carmine's room with this puke as your backup is such a good idea, Cesari."

"Do you have a better plan? I suppose we could always leave him down here with the car running."

Seymour chuckled. "I'm for that one."

Vito gave him a dirty look and reached into his pocket for a cigarette. "Go on and hurry up, and you better not fuck up, Seymour."

We got out of the car and a doorman greeted us as we walked through the main entrance. The lobby was bustling, noisy, and congested. Hotels must love sudden winter storms like this; thousands of stranded people willing to pay almost any price for a warm bed. Walking past the bar to the main elevators we noted two high end restaurants. No one gave us a second look. Everyone was preoccupied with missed flights, cancelled appointments and what they were going to do come morning. We barely fit on the elevator with all the other passengers and I was starting to wonder whether my plan would work with this many people around. It didn't matter. One way or the other I was going to find out if Frankie was here or not.

Arriving at the fifth floor, we walked to Carmine's room. I glared at Seymour and said, "You better pray they're in there Seymour."

He replied calmly, "They're in there."

"Okay, it's time."

I pulled out my cell phone and sent Vito a message to go ahead and call in the bomb threat. Five minutes later an alarm went off throughout the entire building signaling an emergency evacuation. Seymour stood on one side of the door, and I, the other. Lights flashed along the corridor and stressed hotel guests poured into the hallway creating a cacophony of sights and sounds. I pulled the Glock out of my pocket and gripped it tightly at my side as I braced myself for action.

Carmine's door opened and out came—a well-dressed couple in their mid-thirties with two small children. They looked very anxious. Surprised, I glanced at Seymour and he shrugged, giving me a blank look. With all the confusion and worry the family didn't even notice us and walked quickly past to the emergency exits. Before their door could fully close, I propped it open with my free hand and stared in, confused, my brain racing with the possibilities.

I turned back to Seymour puzzled and saw the glint of a small metal canister in his hand next to my left eye. He squirted the contents of his inhaler and I howled in pain, clutching my eye.

"What the hell!"

He gave me a second squirt in my right eye leaving me totally blinded and in terrible burning pain. Not quite done, he viciously kicked me in the groin and I dropped the Glock falling to the floor, helpless.

That fat bastard!

I tried to roll away from him while he kicked and stomped on me. After a minute, the kicking suddenly stopped and I lay there stunned and sightless. With difficulty, I rose to my feet and staggered into the hotel room by feel and found the bathroom. I rinsed my eyes out thoroughly in the sink with cold water and waited impatiently as my vision gradually returned.

Back in the hallway, I found a herd of people pushing and shoving their way to the emergency stairwell but no Seymour.

I let out a deep breath and looked around. The Glock! It was still on the floor not too far from where I had fallen. He hadn't seen it or maybe I had fallen on it. Either way, I still had it. A small victory perhaps but better than none. Now to find that prick before he got away.

Going down the stairwell was not an option at the moment. It was jammed with frightened people and moving quite slowly. The Plaza was a very big hotel and there were thousands of guests trying to evacuate at the same time.

I looked behind me and decided I'd be better off trying to take the elevators than the stairs so I pushed, kicked and shoved my way backward and when the crowd thinned, ran to the elevators. When one arrived, I found it packed to capacity so I pulled the gun out and yelled, "Police emergency! Everybody out!"

No one moved so I held the door open and repeated myself. Their nerves frayed, most just looked at me like deer in the headlights but finally one toward the front blinked and slowly stepped out. One, two, three more followed and soon the car emptied. I thanked them, stepped in and let the doors close, proceeding to the lobby. I didn't need the car empty but I didn't want to take the chance of having somebody standing behind me try to be a hero.

The lobby was total chaos and outside police sirens wailed announcing their approach. My mind raced but I was too busy reacting to circumstances to understand what had just happened. Seymour had betrayed me, that much was obvious. I ran back and forth through the lobby and eventually spotted him waddling post haste out the front door, making tracks in the opposite direction to where Vito was waiting in the Honda.

By the time I reached the door a fire truck and bomb squad were arriving and police were trying to restore order. As part of that plan, they were funneling desperate patrons to one side of the street to allow free access to emergency medical technicians and ambulances. A burly New York City cop directing human traffic blocked my pursuit of Seymour. Frustrated, I tried to go around him and was greeted by an even gruffer, more hostile officer. A potential terrorist attack, blinding blizzard conditions and a civilian refusing to take directions was a recipe for trouble so I backed down and went in the other direction. By the time I made it through the throngs of people on the street back to where I thought he might be, Seymour was long gone.

I found Vito in the Honda sucking on what was undoubtedly his third Camel.

"Where's Seymour and the girl?" he asked.

"Turn the car around and drive. Seymour got away. I last saw him heading the other way." I filled him in on what happened as he made an illegal U-turn in full view of the N.Y.P.D., who were otherwise preoccupied.

"You have got to be kidding me, Cesari. He slammed you in your giggle berries? Man, this guy Seymour has a pair on him, doesn't he? Brings us to the wrong hotel, escapes, and disappears in the middle of a blizzard with nowhere to go. With that kind of resourcefulness, I almost feel like I should job-offer the guy."

"Shut up."

My eyes still stung and my "giggle berries" throbbed as we drove slowly down Fifth Avenue, scanning for Seymour. My phone rang and I answered it as I stared out the window.

"Cesari?"

"Seymour? You fuck."

"Sorry about that, Cesari, but there's no way I'm ever going face to face with Carmine again. I hope you understand."

"The only thing I understand is that I'm going to pummel you beyond all recognition when I catch up with you and twice as hard if anything happens to Frankie."

"Relax, you're such a hot head. Stop being Sicilian for a minute. What would you have done if you were in my position?

Besides, be thankful I couldn't find the gun or we wouldn't even be having this discussion."

Damn, he was making sense again. "What do you want Seymour?" I demanded angrily.

"Actually, I was calling about your whore friend…"

"I told you not to call her that."

"Yeah, yeah, yeah. Well, I thought I should tell you that Carmine's got her wrapped up in room 514 at the Four Seasons on E. 57th Street. If you hurry you might even get there before his guys return."

"Why should I believe you?"

"Think about it. What reason would I have to lie at this point?"

I heard the subway in the background. "So why are you telling me this?"

"Personally, it's not in my best interest to keep you and Carmine apart. The way I see it, before tonight's over I'll only have one of you guys to worry about. Best case scenario for me is that you two wops kill each other. Win-win for the good guys. Get it."

"Yeah, I got it."

"Ta, Cesari. See you in the movies—dickhead."

He hung up.

Chapter 35

"What do you think, Cesari?" Vito asked, noticing I was in an unusually foul mood as we pulled into the underground parking garage of the Four Seasons.

I was pissed. Seymour was much more clever than I had given him credit for. "It can't hurt to try. I mean, what's the worst that could happen? Either she's here or she's not here. Either we get her or we get killed, right? I'm just irritated that Seymour got the best of me."

He found a space and we sat in the car exploring our options. He asked, "Want to try the same trick with the bomb scare?"

I thought about that. I didn't really want to send thousands more people screaming out into the snow again. Not to mention to continue diverting much needed city resources on a hoax, albeit a well-intentioned one, just didn't seem right. Moreover, there had to be some way of turning events in my favor.

I said, "Carmine's expecting Seymour with his men, right?"

"Yeah…?"

"And Seymour's supposed to be helping him find me, right?"

"Where are you going with this Cesari?"

"Well, Seymour said that Carmine found Francesca hiding in that tunnel and now was suspicious that he was helping me and that's why he wanted Seymour to come here tonight—to interrogate him. He probably thinks that because we're doctors and work together that must mean we're friends or at least loyal to each other."

Vito nodded. "That makes sense. It's what I would think."

"So let's use that suspicion to our advantage."

"How do we do that?"

"I'll tell you on the way up."

I reached into the duffel bag and retrieved the crowbar, sliding it up the sleeve of my jacket. We took the stairs to the main lobby, and just as at the Plaza, the place was a zoo. Different faces, same haggard, anxious looks.

"Have you ever met Carmine?" I asked as we rode the elevators up to the fifth floor, I looked at my watch. It was after 9:00 p.m.

"No, never and I'd rather not have the pleasure."

The doors opened and we found Carmine's room. Holding his 9 mm at his side Vito stood in front of the peep hole and I, off to one side, crowbar at the ready. Vito knocked three times on the door. In a few seconds, a gruff voice asked, "Who is it?"

Politely, Vito responded. "Hotel security. Someone complained they smelled marijuana coming out of this room. It's no big deal but we have to check out all complaints of that nature. I'm sorry for the inconvenience and I don't need to come in but I do need to at least visualize the room from the doorway if you don't mind. Please don't rush off to use a room freshener."

"One moment, please," responded a deep baritone voice.

A few seconds later, the door opened a crack and Vito slammed it all the way back with a gigantic foot kick, smashing it into whoever was behind. Caught off guard, the guy fell backward into the room with a loud thud and we rushed in. The room was a two bedroom suite and Carmine sat on the sofa in the living room nonchalantly watching television. Surprised, he froze at the sight of Vito's gun and my crowbar. Vito quickly cracked the already dazed guy in the head with the butt of his gun and he went flaccid and unconscious.

I ran to Carmine who sat slack-jawed and motionless as Vito locked and dead-bolted the door. "Where is she, asshole?" I demanded raising the crowbar menacingly in the air. He sported a metal nose splint, two black eyes and was missing a tooth as a result of our last encounter. Eyes growing wide in recognition and fear, he made no pretense of ignorance and nodded at one of bedrooms in response.

"Stand up, put your hands in the air and spin around. You carrying?" Vito had disarmed the other guy and now stood close by aiming both weapons at Carmine.

"I never carry. That's what bodyguards are for. How did you find us?" he asked, his courage gradually returning.

I punched him hard right smack in the middle of his nose, re-breaking it. He groaned then clutched his face and fell backward onto the sofa, blood oozing down from under the now flattened splint. I said, "Shut up and don't move."

Walking over to the bedroom, I cautiously entered, half expecting to see Frankie tied to the bed. Instead, she was in a dark room, half-naked sitting in a chair facing away, staring out the window. There was minimal light from a floor lamp next to her. She turned around slowly, hearing me enter and said, "I'm sorry, honey."

What the hell. It wasn't Frankie. She looked past me and suddenly I saw the reflection of a guy in the window. He too was half-naked and coming at me fast from his hiding place behind me. I turned just enough to deflect the full force of his blow aimed at the back of my skull but his weight and speed caused us both to tumble onto the floor with him on top. He gripped my right wrist to keep the crowbar at bay and clutched my throat tightly with his other hand. He stank of alcohol, cigarettes, and hooker.

I heard Vito call from the other room. "Cesari, you okay?" He must have heard us fall onto the floor but I couldn't respond with my larynx being slowly crushed. With my free hand, I tried to dislodge his death grip but he was too strong. Saliva oozed from his clenched lips and dripped onto my face. I was desperate for a solution and let go of his wrist. Reaching up, I grabbed his ear and twisted it as hard as I could, tearing it partially off. He screamed in pain, and relaxed his grip on me. I jerked my right hand free and gave him a round house to the side of the head with the crowbar. Dazed, he slipped off me. I shoved him away and struck him again with the cold steel making sure he was unconscious.

Vito appeared at the doorway and said, "What the fuck's going on in here?"

I stood up breathless and heaving. The girl had returned back to staring out the window. I said hoarsely my voice dripping with sarcasm, "It's under control, Vito. Thanks for your help. Go back and keep an eye on Carmine."

"You're welcome and I can see him from here. He ain't going anywhere."

I sat on the edge of the bed feeling my throat. Damn. I reached out and turned the girls chair fully toward me. Brunette, pretty, probably in her early twenties, she was in another time zone mentally. "What's your name?" I asked.

"Ginger—Ginger Snaps." Her voice revealed fear and drugs. "Look mister, I don't know what's going on here and I didn't have anything to do with this. Are you the police?"

"Relax, Ginger Snaps. I'm not a cop and you're not in trouble—not with me anyway. Ginger, it might be a good idea for you to get dressed and go home."

"They didn't pay me. I can't go back without money." She looked at me, smiling seductively. "Do you think I'm pretty?"

Ignoring that I said, "Ginger, it's time to go home."

I searched the guy on the floor for his wallet. He had six hundred in cash and I gave it all to her. "I hope this will make whoever it is happy."

"Thank you. You're nice."

"Thanks, now I want you to get dressed—now. All right?"

"All right."

She stood up and went into the bathroom. I returned to Carmine and noted that his other bodyguard still lay motionless on the floor. Carmine sat with his hands clasped behind his head as Vito stood guard. Positioning myself in front of Carmine I said, "Very funny. Now where is she for real?"

"Who?"

Unbelievable. Why did guys always do this to me? My whole life assholes like this underestimated me. Why, I didn't know. Maybe I looked weak. Sighing deeply and extremely frustrated, I sat on the edge of the coffee table and looked him deeply in the eyes. "Carmine, I'm wet, cold, and tired and one of your men just attacked me. I'd rather not have to hurt you even more seriously, but if you have any doubt that I will, please allow me to reassure you on that point. So which one?"

"Which one what?"

I lifted the crowbar in the air like a hammer and gently tapped him on each knee with the curved end. "Which knee cap do you want me to break first?"

He blinked. "She's in Brooklyn at Mom's house."

"You told Seymour she was here."

"No, I told him that I had her. I didn't say where. For Christ's sake, do I look stupid? This is the Four Seasons. You can't just hold a hostage here. After I snatched her, I brought her to Mom's for safe-keeping."

Ginger came out of the bedroom and said, "My ride's on the way."

I said, "That's great, Ginger."

"You sure you guys don't want to party some more?" she asked. The question seemed so surreal given the circumstances but her world was like an alternate reality compared to most.

"We're sure, Ginger, thanks. Vito, walk her to the door and make sure you deadbolt it."

She pouted and turned to leave but as she did I said, "Hold it, Ginger."

Turning to Carmine, I said, "Give me your wallet."

He had another five hundred bucks which I handed to her. She smiled, and thanked me. I had absolutely no concern that she might call the police after she left. I said, "So, Carmine, back to your original question."

"What question was that?"

"How did I find you?"

"Yeah, so how did you find me?"

"You really are a schmuck, aren't you?"

He looked confused so I filled him in. "Think about it."

"Seymour?"

"He played you, Carmine. Right now your guys are on a wild goose chase downtown in the middle of a blizzard. He sent me here to knock you off for him."

"He'd have to be crazy to double cross me like this."

"In case you haven't been reading the papers or watching television, he is crazy. Besides, he's assuming that you would be dead after tonight and then he'd only have to worry about me."

Carmine nodded, slowly connecting dots in his head. "So you and the walrus aren't working together?"

I shook my head. "How on earth did a genius like you ever survive this long? No, we're not working together, and he wasn't protecting me or hiding the girl for me. We were searching his place trying to figure out what he was up to when we accidentally found the tunnel. That's when you came along. He had no idea we were there just like you had no idea I was down there also."

"What is it with you and that whore anyway?"

I raised the crowbar to hit him and he stammered, "I'm sorry. I'm sorry. I didn't mean that. I meant why? Why all this risk?"

"That's my business. Your business is to start thinking about her like she's a human being not a commodity. Got it?"

He nodded. "Now what?"

"Now we talk unless you want me to just kill you as Seymour is hoping?" He shook his head. I continued. "I didn't think so. So what is it exactly that you want from me and Frankie anyway? We didn't do anything."

He smirked. "The hell you didn't. You killed Jenny."

"I didn't kill Jenny. I thought it was agreed Luther killed Jenny."

"Luther would never kill Jenny."

"And why is that?"

"Because he owed her everything, that's why. He was nothing, a two-bit meth addict until she came along and took pity on him. She took him in and cleaned him up. She got him that job at the Fall of Rome. Practically begged me to give him a chance. He worshipped her. No way on earth he would have hurt her. Besides, with her gone he'd be gone. He knew that, so therefore you killed her and Francesca helped you escape. Why she would help you, I don't know."

I thought about that. "So you didn't kill Luther?"

"I didn't say that. I said I don't believe he killed Jenny."

Now, I was really curious. "So you killed him while he lay helpless in the hospital even though you didn't believe he killed Jenny."

"We were trying to flush you out. Make you think you were safe. That we had our guy. It was mom's idea."

"Your mother's quite the role model."

"Fuck off about my mother."

Something didn't fit. If Luther didn't kill Jenny then who did? Maybe Carmine was wrong about Luther.

"How much time do I have?" I asked.

"For what?"

"Before the men you have looking for Seymour return?"

"All night. They called right before you got here. There was an accident on Third Avenue and they're stuck waiting for ambulances and tow trucks. They can't back up or turn around. They're in for the long haul."

"Vito, drag that guy into the bedroom and tie them both up as best you can with whatever's available. We're going to take Carmine for a ride."

When he returned, we walked Carmine down to the parking garage arm in arm. He knew better than to make trouble. He was a 'live to fight another day' kind of guy. In the Pilot, I pressed the Glock into his side and told him to call his mother.

"What am I supposed to tell her?"

Vito turned around exasperated. "That you miss her and want to come home. What do you think, asshole?"

I said, "Carmine, tell her that if she ever wants to see her baby boy again she'd better return Francesca in one piece—and put her on speaker phone so I can hear every word."

I handed him his cellphone and he began to dial but I grabbed his hand. "Wait a minute. I just had an idea. Has your mother ever met or spoken with Seymour?"

"No, she only knows what I told her about him. When she came to Vegas to see me, he had already left."

He looked at me expectantly and I explained. "Good. Tell her that Seymour turned the tables on you and is now holding you hostage for Francesca."

"And what exactly is that supposed to accomplish?"

"Ask another question and I'm going to hit you with the crowbar. Just do it and make it sound good. Remember, speaker phone." I dug the pistol deeply into his ribcage and he got the message.

He dialed Brunella and she picked up after two rings. "Ciao, Carmine."

"Ciao, Mama—Mama, I have a little problem?"

"What is a you problem, Carmine?"

"That Seymour guy. The fat doctor from Vegas. The one who was supposed to be helping me find Cesari. He came to the hotel where I was staying and…"

"And a what?"

"He got me."

"What a you mean—he got a me?"

Carmine cleared his throat and I dug the barrel in just a little harder. "It means he got me and he's going to hurt me unless you give him the girl. We are on speaker phone with him right now."

There was silence now as she digested that. I grabbed the phone from him as we waited for her response. Finally, she said, "Where are a you, Carmine?"

I answered for him. "He's in the back seat of a car with a pistol sticking in his ribs. Hi, Brunella, this is Seymour."

She lowered her voice and in as a menacing a tone as I had ever heard said, "You hurt a my boy and I send a the girl back to Las Vegas one limb at a time. I hope you understand a me."

Two could play at that game. I repositioned the pistol and pressed the muzzle hard into Carmine's groin causing him to wince in pain. "I hope you weren't planning on having grandchildren because if you don't start talking nice to me I'm going to use your baby boy's testicles for target practice."

"What you really want?" I could tell I was getting to her. She sounded just a wee bit more alarmed and less confident.

"Just the girl, unharmed."

She chuckled lightly into the phone. "You risk a you life for a whore? I no believe this. Men always a thinking with the wrong a brain."

"Don't call her that." It was starting to roil me that somehow or other her life didn't matter because of what she did to put food on the table.

Now she laughed loudly and coarsely. "And a why not? That's all a she is. A cheap whore for men to play with." She had found my button and was pushing it hard. I had to force myself not to let her take control of the conversation.

"Do you want your son back alive or should we just exchange corpses?"

Game over. "How you suggest we do a this thing?"

"In a very public location, and remember, I have guns too. And the girl better be unharmed."

"Is a too late for that but she will live. You take a doctor right away."

I held my breath, bit my lip, and almost pulled the trigger. When I didn't say anything she continued.

"You come up a to Brooklyn. Peter Luger's Steakhouse, you know? Very public, very busy. We meet at a the bar by the entrance. We come with a the girl. If I no see a my boy I cut a the girl's head off and leave on a the sidewalk. Capisci?"

I looked at my watch. It was almost 10:00 p.m. "You mean tomorrow night?"

"I mean a now. Peter Luger's no close because of a the weather. She stay open and a seat a the people until 1:00 a.m. You be there with my Carmine one hour. Now put my boy on."

I gave the phone to Carmine. "Yes Mama."

"I love you so much a Carmine. Mama fix everything." Her voice was very emotional now and I suspected she might be a little teary.

"I love you too, Mama."

I grabbed the phone back and hung up. He looked at me and shuddered, wondering what was coming next. He knew I was seething about Francesca and what possible condition she might be in. I was tempted to break a few of his bones but resisted the urge. Might as well wait and see. Besides, he'd be easier to manage if we didn't have to carry him.

Vito was watching me as my wheels spun. I said, "You heard her. Peter Luger's in one hour. You know where it is, right?"

"Of course. It's just over the Williamsburg Bridge."

Chapter 36

The storm had lightened up considerably, and it appeared that at most, we were going to get ten inches. The plows kept things moving and the excitement was starting to wear off. We had pulled to within a city block of the restaurant and double parked on Broadway in Brooklyn. We were ten minutes ahead of schedule.

Vito asked, "What now? We just walk in there and wait like she said? By the way, what was all that about with making her think Seymour has Carmine?"

Carmine added, "Yeah, I'd kind of like to know too."

I said, "First of all, there is no way on earth we are going into the restaurant. We'd be like sitting ducks in there. Our only chance is to make them come to us. By the way, thanks for sticking your neck out like this for me, Vito. I know this is going to cause a world of problems for you if it gets out."

Carmine snickered, "Yeah, I wonder how that might happen."

"Carmine, shut up. Secondly, the key to my future and yours, Vito, is to convince this schmuck's mother that Seymour is the one they want and not me."

Carmine chuckled. "There's no doubt that fat boy is going to get his comeuppance but that doesn't exactly let you or your boyfriend here off the hook."

Vito said, "He's got a point, Cesari. I just hope this girl, Francesca, is worth it."

I thought about that. Was she worth it? I barely knew her myself. I turned to Carmine. This was the most dangerous time for any hostage. The moment before the exchange was when most of them got killed. All it took was for some slight thing to go wrong or for someone to get a little jumpy. It was certainly no time for false bravado. If Carmine wanted to get out of this unscathed, it would be best to be as cooperative as possible.

"Carmine, you want to live through this thing, right?"

"Of course."

"Well, it's kind of spiraling out of control. Don't you think?"

He nodded. "Yeah, a little."

"I know that you had feelings for her but nothing's going to bring Jenny back. I didn't kill her. I don't know who did but it wasn't me. I was drugged and set up. Why and by whom I don't know. Seymour, we know, is a total asshole and a probable serial killer. For all I know, he may have had something to do with what happened in Vegas. The bottom line is this; he set you up for me to kill tonight and I chose not to. That must mean something to you. I'm not your enemy, not really. That girl Francesca didn't know anything about Jenny's death when she helped me escape. She just saw a guy in trouble with the law and didn't think it was that big a deal. She certainly meant no disrespect to you or Jenny."

Carmine was listening intently. "What are you suggesting?"

"Look, I know I roughed you up pretty good out there but you were beating on a friend of mine, after all."

"That's supposed to make it better?"

"No, but I could just kill you now and drive to the nearest airport for a long vacation."

He didn't respond to that so I continued. "You live and you let me live. Quid pro quo. A life for a life. Your mother wants blood. I get it. She already thinks Seymour is involved so let's give her Seymour. You convince her that he is responsible for everything that has happened and that I got dragged into it because of him and even though I roughed you up a bit it's not worth anymore aggravation. Everybody's sense of honor is appeased."

He smirked, "Sure, and just like that you two go about business as usual?"

Vito had been absorbing my logic and liked it. It was better than a street war. He looked hard at Carmine, "Listen up, moron. Do you want bodies piling up waist deep all the way from Mulberry Street to Atlantic Avenue? And remember one thing: you're going to be the first one to go down when the shooting starts, so be reasonable."

Carmine didn't say anything but the look on his face said he was coming around to our way of thinking. I said in a softer tone, "What do you say, Carmine? Do you think we can work this out like adults? Nobody wants a war."

Slowly he said, "Well, except for my wounded pride it does kind of make sense." He could feel a way out and didn't want to blow it. Of course, I didn't trust him but it was the best I could come up with on short notice. He had a point about his wounded pride.

I said, "How much would it take to make your pride feel better?"

Carmine smiled broadly as he suddenly felt in control for the first time. He thought it over and I said, "C'mon Carmine? We don't have all day."

"Hmm, a broken nose, a missing tooth. You made me look weak in front of my guys. How about a cool million?"

Vito got agitated, "Fuck that you little weasel. I'd rather…"

I put my hand on his shoulder to calm him down. "A million it is. Anything else?"

"Yeah, I've always wanted a piece of the action down on Mulberry Street."

Vito said, "You're crazy. That's my turf."

Now I got angry. "Will you shut up? We're trying to negotiate."

"Trying to negotiate, by giving away my business? Why don't you give away some of your colonoscopies?"

Carmine chuckled at that and said, "I'll tell you what? You let me have everything south of Canal Street, from the Bowery up until Broadway including all the Mahjong and massage parlors and I promise you won't ever see me."

Vito was stunned. "You want all of lower Manhattan including Chinatown? Is that all? Why don't I cut off my hand and give it to you as well?"

I said, "Oh c'mon Vito. You know Chinatown's a pain in the ass. He'd be doing you a favor." The gang situation there was a constant disruption to business. The language and cultural divide also represented a daunting challenge and after years of trying he had only made a slight dent in the restaurant businesses there. He had complained often to me that it was barely worth the effort to him. The massage and mahjong parlors were a different story.

He said, "You can have from the Bowery up until Centre Street, and I get the rest up until Broadway. Since I'm giving up territory and future earnings, Cesari, you're responsible for coming up with the million."

What an asshole. A million was nothing for him. I said, "Fine."

We all shook on it.

I asked, "What kind of car does your mother travel in?"

"She has an Audi Q7, black with tinted windows."

"How many guys does she usually have around?"

He thought it over and said, "Two at all times and sometimes three. Joey, her driver is always there and Simon the Jew, her bodyguard. It's plus minus after that depending on what's going on."

"Simon the Jew?" I asked.

"Yeah, Simon Lefkowitz. He grew up a few doors down from us in the neighborhood. Always wanted to be a wiseguy. In some people it's in their blood. You know? Anyway, we call him Tannenbaum for short."

"Tannenbaum for short? I don't get it."

"Tannenbaum, like in the Christmas carol, O Tannenbaum. Because he's as big as a Christmas tree."

I shook my head in disbelief. "All right, so two for sure, maybe three, but this is a special night so there may be even more depending on who she could muster up on such short notice."

"Hey, you really are smart."

I eyed him curiously wondering if maybe secretly he really did want me to kill him. I said, "Shut up."

Vito chuckled. "You know, Cesari, this is really a great plan except for one thing."

"What's going to prevent Carmine from blowing the whole thing up once he's free?"

Carmine responded wisely, "I would never do that and don't forget to bring the million in cash. I don't accept personal checks."

I said, "You'd better not double-cross me Carmine. Okay, let's move on. In this weather your mother will probably double park outside the restaurant and wait a few minutes. They'll want to be sure that we are inside first, and they'll leave at least one guy in the Q7 with the engine running when they do come in." I paused for a moment thinking it through. "The question is, will Brunella come into the restaurant or wait in the car?"

Carmine said, "She'll come in. She'll want to see me."

Vito and I nodded in agreement. Brunella was too much of a hands-on person in general and this was her baby boy. She'd be eager to see what kind of shape he was in. I also had no doubt that once she felt Carmine was safe, Vito, Frankie and I were as good as dead. Which was why I had no intention of going into the restaurant. There would doubtless be guys waiting in there as we speak. Luger's was a notorious hangout for Brunella and her men and her apartment was only blocks away. She could've had guys there in minutes after our phone call. We had to get to them by surprise and while they were still outside.

I called Brunella on Carmine's phone. She answered, "Carmine?"

"No, Brunella. It's Seymour."

"What you want? Where's a my boy?"

"We're running a few minutes late because of the snow but we'll be there soon so keep your girdle on."

She hesitated, clearly pissed off by my tone. "Anything else?"

"No."

She hung up.

I said, "I'll get out and walk the rest of the way. You two stay here."

"Mind telling me what the plan is, Cesari?"

"I've got to convince her that her only option is to turn Frankie over to me or Carmine is a goner. For that, I need him removed from the transaction but accessible. I'll text you Brunella's phone number. When the time is right you call her and put Carmine on as a sign of good faith. Once they're on the way you clock him good and we'll meet up somewhere."

Carmine jumped in. "Is that really necessary? The clocking part? Aren't we on the same side now?"

"Shut up or I'll do it now," Vito growled.

I said, "Sorry, Carmine, but Vito's going to need a head start and can't take a chance on you changing your mind. Besides, we'll never be on the same side, and until I get Francesca back safely all we have is a bunch of very dangerous people facing off with different agendas. So until we make the exchange, consider yourself on the endangered species list. If all goes well, then we move forward as planned. I'll deliver your money within a week and you can start moving your men into Chinatown. Now smile."

"What?"

"I said smile."

He made a goofy half-hearted attempt and I snapped a photo with his cell phone. Outside the car, I took several photos of its license plate and the street sign overlooking where we were parked.

I went up to Vito and said, "Okay, keep an eye on him and wait for my call."

He turned toward Carmine and lit a cigarette, his pistol resting in his lap. "Hurry up."

The restaurant was a block away and I walked slowly toward it until I spotted the Q7 double parked directly out front with the engine running. I crossed the street and ducked into the shadows between two old buildings. There was a small apartment building on one side of me and I watched several workers shoveling snow so the residents could get out in the morning. Hiding behind a dumpster, I had a clear view of the driver's side of the car but they couldn't see me.

I texted the picture of Carmine smiling to Brunella and then called. "What is this a mean?" she asked.

"It means Carmine's alive."

"And?"

"And I'm not going into the restaurant. He'll be safe as long as you do what you're told."

She was silent as she thought it over. "You are clever man, but I have a the girl."

"Yes, you do, but do you want to risk the life of your precious son for that of a cheap whore—a play thing for men?"

She chuckled as I used her own words against her. "So what I do?"

"Roll down all the windows so I can see who is in the car."

"Where is Carmine?" she asked as all the windows came down simultaneously.

"Not far from here." I saw Frankie clearly. She was on my side of the car in the second row. I couldn't tell what kind of shape she was in other than exhausted. She looked out the window and took a deep breath. Everyone in the car scanned around searching for me but I was adequately concealed.

"Okay, now I want all four doors to open and everybody to get out of the car except for the girl. Keep the engine running and leave the keys in the car."

Two big guys got out of the front and Brunella came out of the back. "What about a my boy?"

I sent her a picture of the Honda and its license plate.

She looked at her phone. "Yes, but where is a the car and how do I know he still alive?"

"He's alive. Now close all the doors and start walking down Broadway in the direction of the bridge and you'll find him. If you don't start walking at once or if there are any surprises waiting for me, like a guy hiding in the back seat I didn't know about I will detonate the Honda immediately and Carmine will suddenly be singing in the choir again only this time with the real St. Michael. Understood?"

She sighed. "Yes." She said something I couldn't hear to someone in the Q7 and another guy suddenly appeared on the side walk.

"Now start walking."

I called Vito. "They're coming. Call Brunella now and let Carmine say hello so they know he's alive and then get out of there as fast as you can. I'll meet you around the block."

After Brunella's group passed out of sight I came flying from across the street and hopped into the driver's seat without saying hi to Frankie. The important thing was to get the hell out of here as quickly as possible. Two blocks away I pulled to a stop and texted Brunella the street sign where the Honda was located which was in the opposite direction I had just sent them.

I looped around the block and found Vito trudging in the snow in my direction. He shook snow off his shoes and pant legs and jumped in out of breath. Francesca had slumped down sideways onto the back seat and I suspected she was drugged to keep her quiet and passive. Vito shook her a few times and she could be roused easily so I wasn't too worried. I would check her over more carefully once we were safely out of there.

Halfway to my hotel, Carmine's phone rang. "Yes, Brunella."

Yelling into the phone, "You son of the bitch. You are going to pay. That whore is going to pay. Your whole family is going to pay."

"Whoa. Slow down. What happened?"

She was almost hysterical. "My Carmine, my poor baby. He's a no breathe. I skin a you alive, Seymour. I cut a you balls off and a feed a them to my dog."

"Take it easy, Brunella."

What the hell was she talking about?

"You bastardo! I come for you. I come for you. If it takes a me the rest of my life I will have a my revenge."

She hung up.

I looked at Vito who said, "Just drive."

"What happened?"

I pulled the big SUV onto South 9th Street and away from Luger's, intending to put as much distance as I could between us and Brunella before circling around to find a different route back to Manhattan.

"So…?"

"C'mon, Cesari. Don't ask questions like that. I just saved us both a lot of aggravation. You didn't think I was going to give up my hard-earned business to that low-life, did you? Besides, I just saved you a million bucks. The best part is she thinks

Seymour is the one responsible. I made sure he reinforced that part with Brunella right before he hung up."

Stunned, I let out a deep, frustrated breath. "I can't believe you."

"Relax. There was no way he was going to live up to his end of the bargain anyway. The minute he got free, Brunella would have been all over us and you know it. The guy was a born rat and I did him a favor too."

"Oh really? And what was that?"

"This whole thing started because he was in love with that girl, right? Now he's with her in heaven or wherever."

I glanced in his direction and shook my head. There was no point in responding to that one. "Where's my crowbar?"

"I left it in the Honda."

"With all my finger prints on it. Thanks."

"You should've said something."

"I didn't think I had to."

"You're pretty ungrateful considering I just did all the work."

"Grateful for what? Upgrading my status from being wanted in one state for a murder I didn't commit to being wanted in two states for two murders I didn't commit."

"You need a drink. I just told you this is perfect. No one even knows you or I were here. Brunella thinks Seymour kidnapped Carmine and by extension, snuffed him. We'll have Lance report the car stolen. I'm telling you. It's the perfect crime."

He was making some sense. I'll grant him that. The trouble was every time in history someone thought they committed the perfect crime they usually wound up getting hanged. I said, "I guess you never heard of Leopold and Loeb?"

"No, I haven't. Who are they?"

"Geniuses like you. They thought they committed the perfect crime and spent the rest of their lives in prison wondering what went wrong."

"Just drive, will you? You're negativity is dragging me down."

By the time I crossed the Manhattan Bridge back into the city it was close to midnight and Frankie was starting to come around from her deep slumber. She was relieved to see me and curious about Vito. She hadn't met him yet. At the hotel, she could walk but needed help and I mostly carried her up to the room. Vito took Brunella's Q7 and headed back to Little Italy. He would probably abandon it somewhere tomorrow or chop it up. It wouldn't be good if somebody found it outside his apartment.

In the room, Frankie was still pretty groggy so I laid her on the bed and undressed her. I wasn't happy by what I saw. Multiple fresh bruises on her torso, her black eye which had looked like it was starting to heal the last time I saw her was all puffy again, and it looked like she had been burned with a lit cigarette in several places including her breasts. There was dried blood on her panties and genitals and rope burns on her ankles. Almost afraid to find out what had happened, I pulled the cover up over her and watched her breathe.

I felt my internal thermostat about to blow and willed myself down from the ledge. Stay calm Cesari. This girl needs calm now. Not more insanity. My high priority was to get her out of the combat zone. I didn't share Vito's confidence that all would be well. Letting her stick around me was a mistake I never should have made, but where could I take her?

I nudged her gently and whispered, "Frankie." Her eyes fluttered a little but she didn't respond so I shook her shoulder a little more briskly and said, "Hey there." This roused her and she rubbed her eyes, yawned, and tried to muster a smile. I had to give her credit. She was a whole lot tougher than half the guys I knew. She'd been to hell and back. "How do you feel, Frankie?"

I sat on the edge of the bed next to her and she reached out to hold my hand. "Like a million bucks compared to the look on your face. Tell me what happened."

So I did. When I finished, she said, "Thanks. Now take the frown off your face. I'm okay and we're together."

"Frankie, I need to get you away from here to some place safe so you can heal up."

She nodded in agreement. "I know. I'm very sore."

"And unfortunately, this isn't over yet. The heat's going to be on worse than ever."

"I figured from the way she was cursing in the car. I was goofy but not completely out of it. She was really pissed, but before I passed out for good I also thought I heard your friend say that everything was going to be all right?"

"He did say that but he also likes to read comic books."

She chuckled. "I get it. He needs to curb his enthusiasm?"

"Exactly. I mean I hope he's right but I'm not going to bet our lives on it. I know I've asked you this before but is there anybody you can stay with in the metro area I can take you to? You know, friends, family, anybody?"

She thought it over. "No, not really. There's only that abusive aunt and uncle I told you about and I'd rather die than ask them for anything."

I thought about Cocoa but she was in New Jersey with Cleopatra. Still, she had an apartment in the West Village not too far from mine but that was a problem since either Brunella or the FBI were undoubtedly keeping an eye on my place. I doubted I could walk into that neighborhood without someone spotting me. Besides, I hated to drag Cocoa into this. She was already doing enough by taking care of Cleo. No, I needed something further uptown away from the hostilities. Leaving the city using public transportation would be difficult, especially in Frankie's battered condition. On the other hand, I could always use Brunella's Q7, but what if she reported it stolen? A hot Audi

SUV would stick out like a sore thumb. No. Then it hit me. I'd bring her to Kelly's. She wouldn't be happy about it but might agree. It was worth a shot. She had a heart of gold.

I called Vito.

"Yeah."

"Vito, don't lose the car just yet."

"I wasn't going to. I changed my mind."

"Really?"

"I decided to give it to Lance as a replacement for his. He's going to have to report the Honda stolen anyway or Brunella might think he had something to do with Carmine. Besides, he's not going to want it back with bullet holes and blood all over the back seat."

I loved the way he thought. Lance does us a favor by lending us his car so Vito does Lance a good turn by murdering somebody in it and then replacing it with a stolen vehicle.

"You know, Vito, why don't we just buy him a new car rather than give him one that could potentially land him in a lot of hot water like if Brunella tracks it to him."

"You think?"

"Yeah, I think."

"Okay, it seems like such a waste. I mean it's a great car, but all right, I'll get rid of it."

"Great decision and we'll make it up to Lance."

"You mean you'll make it up to Lance."

"Fine, I'll tell him to report the car stolen. Now will you be quiet and listen. I need you to drive me and Frankie uptown in the morning."

Chapter 37

The next morning, Frankie and I had Belgian waffles drowned in Vermont maple syrup for breakfast. She ate like she hadn't seen food in weeks. There was nothing like being on the receiving end of a little torture to work up one's appetite.

"Okay, Frankie, I can't help it. I have to ask. What are those marks on your ankles?"

She sipped her coffee and said, "The wicked witch of the west tied my ankles with rope and hung me naked upside down in her basement from one of the rafters next to rows of prosciutto. She'd poke me with a stick over and over and spin me around in circles. Eventually, I'd pass out and wake up on the cement floor. Then repeat. She blamed me for getting Carmine beat up and causing all the trouble out in Vegas."

"You caused all the trouble? How so?"

"If I hadn't helped you escape, you'd already be rotting in a prison cell or even better, you'd be buried out in the desert somewhere. She even suggested that maybe I plotted with you to kill Jenny out of pure jealousy because of her relationship with Carmine."

I thought it over. We were dealing with some very sick and vengeful people. This was my world as far back as I could remember. I sighed. "I'm sorry about that."

She shrugged. "It's water under the bridge now."

I studied her as I ate. God, she was tough. Most people, men and women, would be in a state of emotional shock after that. I must have grimaced because she said,

"Relax, I'll be fine. When you've lived on the streets like I have all sorts of shit happens. I've woken up in dumpsters after a bender with rats picking at pizza crusts on my chest and trust me, there's nothing I hate more than rats. Look, don't get me wrong, I'd love to kill the bitch but what's done is done. I'm just glad to be alive."

Jesus. That was a hell of a long view on things.

"Well, I'm glad that you're so well grounded, but I'm angry—very angry, to say the least, by what happened to you and—I'm sorry. I feel like it's all my fault and that I never should have let you come with me."

She smiled. "Don't be getting all chivalrous on me now. I'm a big girl and I made up my own mind. You only think you made the decision. That's the art of being feminine."

"Well, nonetheless, I'm going to be honest with you and there's something you should know about me. I don't like it when girls get hurt. It actually stirs something deep inside of me. It's a very primitive rage that I sometimes can't control."

She looked at me warmly as if we had been friends forever and said softly, "Take it easy cowboy. Like I said, I knew what I was getting into but thanks for caring. Besides, the important thing is that we're together again."

I thought about that. Were we *together*? In what sense did she mean that?

Suddenly she chuckled. I said, "What?"

"I knew I had you pegged right from the beginning. In Vegas when you risked getting caught to return my car. I thought to myself this guy is either bat shit crazy or an irreconcilable do-gooder and now I know. You're Mr. Smith Goes to Washington." She laughed at her reference to that old Jimmy Stewart movie.

"It was a great movie but I think I'm more the bat shit crazy type."

"I don't think so. If I wasn't in so much pain right now I'd come over there and jump on you or—maybe you could come over here and jump on me." She grinned seductively.

Black eye, swollen lip, and hotel robe, did nothing to tamp down her raw sexuality. I was tempted but chuckled and sidestepped the offer. "How about we finish breakfast? We have a lot to do and Vito will be here in an hour to pick us up."

She made a pouty face. "So what's the agenda for today?"

"First I call a friend who lives on the Upper West Side to see if she'll put you up for a few days. I haven't seen her in a while but she's very nice and I think she'll understand. I also want you to see a doctor, maybe a couple of them, a gynecologist at least." She nodded but didn't say anything. She knew what I was getting at. There was no need for anyone to get graphic.

I continued, "We both need new clothes so a shopping trip is in order too."

"This friend of yours. That would be very nice of her to allow a total stranger to stay with her."

"Well, she's a nurse and she is very nice. Besides, I'll vouch for you." I smiled after I said that.

"By your tone I'd guess you were very good friends…?"

"We dated for a while and we're still friends and by *your* tone the answer is yes I still care for her a little—a lot."

She grinned. "This is fun."

"Really now. Is it?"

"Yeah, so what happened? Is she the one watching the dog for you?"

"No, this is a different friend. That one's in New Jersey right now and what happened is she got married."

"You have a lot of friends."

"This one is a little different."

She nodded clearly enjoying this. "Special?"

"Yeah—very."

Desperately trying to keep a straight face she said, "So she got married. Without your permission I gather?"

"Sort of." She chuckled quietly and I said, "Well, I'm glad that my pain has brought a modicum of joy into your life."

The dam broke and she started laughing out loud. Then she stood up and came over to me, sitting on my lap. Putting her arms around my neck she pulled my head down for a gentle kiss. She said, "You really are too funny for words."

"Am I?"

"Oh yeah. So you're going to ask this ex-girlfriend of yours, who's married and who you're obviously still in love with, if she'll take in a hooker for a few days? Is that the plan?"

"We can leave the hooker part out."

"Okay, that might be smart. So what else should I know about the situation so I don't accidentally step on a landmine?"

"Her name is Kelly. She's a nurse at St. Lukes Hospital on the west side, has twin girls, a little over a year old and her husband is an accountant."

She got serious now realizing how difficult this had to be for me to talk about. "I'm sorry."

I hesitated for a moment. "You don't know the half of it."

"Am I supposed to guess?"

"No, forget I said anything. Let me make the call."

She cupped my face in her hands. "Oh no you don't. We've come this far. C'mon, I want to hear."

I hesitated and then said, "It's the kids…"

She shook her head, puzzled. "What about them?" Then, little by little comprehension dawned in her eyes. "Oh my God. You've got to be kidding me? They're your kids?"

I didn't say anything and stared downward.

"I'm so sorry, John. This has got to be horribly painful for you."

"It was, it is, and it may always be."

"Do you get to see them?"

I shook my head. "No, not much at all. She declined a paternity test and I couldn't force her. She married just before they were born so technically and legally they are his kids."

"But you're sure they are yours?"

"Wait until you see them."

"Now, I'm dying to. Your life is better than any soap opera I've ever seen."

I had enough. "C'mon, you need to get dressed."

She had barely disappeared into the bathroom when my cellphone buzzed. It was Arnie.

"I thought you were only going to call for emergencies, Arnie?"

"Good morning to you too and this is an emergency—sort of."

"I'm listening."

"First off, St. Matt's is crawling with mobsters and some of them apparently know you."

Now I was interested. "What do you mean by that?"

"I'm glad I got your attention. What I mean is that some mob guy named Carmine Buonarotti got himself shot in the chest three times at close range last night and was brought here for emergency surgery. His crazy mother is hysterical and has decided to camp out in the waiting room with several guys the size of small mountains. She's acting like we all work for her and on more than one occasion asked several nurses and doctors when they had last seen you and Seymour—especially Seymour. And when I say, asked, I mean more like interrogated."

I was shocked and alarmed. I blurted out. "He's alive?"

"Who?"

"Carmine?"

"For the moment. Last I heard he was completely unresponsive but stable. He was in surgery all night and was just transferred to the ICU. The bullets just barely missed his vital organs. He lost a ton of blood and was in deep shock when he arrived. I wouldn't bet on his chances but he's young and healthy so you never know. Why do you ask? Do you know anything about this?"

Ignoring him I asked, "How did he wind up in St. Matt's? Aren't they from Brooklyn?"

"It's funny how you know stuff like that, Cesari. Yes, they are from Brooklyn. When the ambulance came to pick him up they were going to take him to Maimonides since it was the nearest hospital but his mother ordered the driver to bring him here."

Great.

I said, "Okay, this qualifies as an emergency."

"Cesari, don't you get it? These guys are looking for you and Seymour as in *dead Vegas hooker* looking for you."

"I got it, Arnie. Thanks for the heads up. Just remember, you haven't seen or heard from me since the plane ride out there."

"I'll try. My secretary already told me that the mother made an appointment to speak with me in an hour and that's not all…"

"What else?"

"The FBI heard about what happened to Carmine and they are on the way as well. They called to find out what's going on, but they said they needed to talk to me in person anyway. This brings us to emergency number two."

"Arnie, please…" The guy was so dramatic.

"They identified the other DNA found in and on the girl in Vegas." He paused for effect. "It was Seymour's and it was all over her just like yours."

I was shocked by that revelation. "Seymour's DNA? How was he even in the database? He wasn't a suspect."

"Apparently, a few years back he submitted a sample voluntarily to determine his ancestry and genetic makeup. Unbeknownst to him, they incidentally passed it along to the national database for record keeping and statistics."

I was silent as I tried to absorb this news. We had arrived together in Vegas, checked in to the hotel together, and almost immediately went out together for dinner. We were never apart until I woke up in her room later that night. He swore to me that he didn't know her but obviously that was another lie.

"Are you still there, Cesari?"

"Yeah, I'm still here. I'm just thinking. Arnie, can you be more specific about his DNA samples. What kind of samples and where did they find them?"

"It was semen and they found it in all the usual places. What did you two do out there? Have a party together with this girl?"

"No, don't even say that. I need to think this over."

"Okay, but do yourself a favor and stay away from St. Matt's."

"Thanks for the call."

Chapter 38

"Well, that's too bad about Carmine," Vito mused as he drove up Central Park West to Kelly's apartment building. "I don't get it, though. Three slugs in the chest at point blank range and the son-of-a-bitch survives? I pressed the gun right over his heart. For crying out loud, how could I have missed? What more does a guy have to do? Unbelievable."

After he picked Frankie and me up, we stopped at Macy's for an hour to buy new clothes. Frankie picked up a snazzy Michael Kors leather purse which perked up her mood considerably. I nodded at Vito. "Worst case scenario for sure. If and when he wakes up there's going to be hell to pay."

"He's undoubtedly going to be pissed and there's no way of getting to him now."

"Let's keep our fingers crossed that he doesn't make it."

Vito let out a deep breath. "Damn, I knew I should have done a head shot. Last time I make that mistake. Anyway, back to you. Don't you think you should have called ahead first? I mean isn't there some sort of code about not bringing new girlfriends to your old girlfriend's apartment?"

Frankie who was sitting in the back seat said, "That's sweet. He thinks I'm your girlfriend."

Great.

"Thanks for the advice, but we're not going there to socialize. Besides, if you hadn't come so early I might have had time to call her."

"Fine, it's my fault, but what if she's not home or doesn't want to take Frankie in?"

I grunted. "Then we go to plan B."

"Which is?"

"I don't know yet so if you'd be quiet, I'll call her now."

"You're going to call her now? We're already here." We were approaching the upper end of the park where her apartment building was.

"Fine, go around the circle and let us off in front of the building. Might as well just go in. It's Sunday, so she's probably not working unless she's on call. If she's not in, we'll go hang out for a while. There are a couple of cafés and coffee shops not too far from here on W. 110th Street."

"One more thing Cesari."

He pulled the car to a stop in front of Kelly's building.

"Omar, remember him?"

Frankie said, "Who's Omar?"

Vito explained, "He's Kelly's husband and doesn't appreciate my good friend Cesari's peculiar sense of humor like I do."

I said, "Shut up, Vito. We'll be fine. Besides, it's been months since I've seen either one of them. Everybody should have calmed down by now."

"What happened?" Frankie asked.

"The last time Cesari made a house call to Kelly like this, Omar came home unexpectedly and found them playing doctor in the bedroom."

Frankie thought that was hysterical and started giggling. "This just gets better and better."

I said, "Thanks, Vito"

"Well, I just want you to be sensitive to the fact that he might be a little edgy if you show up out of the blue like you are about to do right now."

"Fine, I'll be sensitive. I'll call later if I need anything but let's plan on catching up for dinner. How about Lupa's on Thompson Street, say about seven? The food's always great there. By the way do you have any cash on you?"

"What do I look like, a bank?" He fished inside his coat and came out with a roll of money. "Here. There's six or seven hundred."

I took it and handed it to Frankie. "Be friendly but try to keep a low profile. The less they know about what's really going on the less risk for them."

She nodded and we got out of the car, said goodbye to Vito and entered the apartment building. I found Kelly's buzzer and pushed it. Looking around, I noticed it was a pretty nice building. She and Omar had upgraded from their previous apartment down on 62nd Street and Columbus Avenue. I couldn't help myself and kept tabs on her. Creepy, but not against the law. Letting go wasn't my strong suit. I buzzed twice more and she finally answered.

Sounding harried she said, "Hello. Who is it?"

"Hi, Kel, it's John."

"John, who?"

Frankie muffled a laugh and I made a face at her.

"C'mon Kel. It hasn't been that long."

"Cesari? Is that you? You sound different."

"It's me."

She was silent for a few seconds as she thought it over.

"How'd you find me?"

"Please, Kel. It's sort of an emergency."

"John, you should have called."

"I know, but like I said, I have a bit of a crisis and need your help. Can you let me in and I'll explain? I promise I won't be long." After a few seconds, the door unlocked and we took the stairs up to her third floor apartment.

She was waiting with the door open and was surprised to see I had a companion. Looking at Frankie's face she became concerned, "Oh my goodness. What happened to you?"

I said, "It's a long story and it's the reason why we're here. This is Francesca. Francesca, this is Kelly." They politely shook hands and I waited with arms outstretched for a hug. Kelly and Frankie both looked at me as if I were the most pathetic human being they had ever seen, but finally and out of pure pity Kelly embraced me gently and just as quickly pulled away.

She said, "Come on in and tell me what's going on."

We entered a beautiful, spacious apartment and took a seat on a large comfortable sofa.

"Nice place, Kel," I commented scanning around at the high ceiling and upscale décor. LeRoy Neiman art work decorated the walls.

"Thank you. It costs an arm and a leg. Can I get you some coffee or tea? I was just about to have some myself."

Frankie and I nodded and agreed on coffee. After she disappeared into the kitchen Frankie poked me and whispered, "She's beautiful."

"Yeah, I know."

"You could have mentioned that she was black."

"What difference does that make?"

"None, I guess."

Kelly returned holding a serving tray with three cups and a pot of coffee. She sat opposite us and we helped ourselves.

I said, "Thanks, Kel. By the way you look great." And she did. Five feet four inches tall, long wavy hair, and luscious green eyes, I always thought she could have been a model. She filled out her jeans with absolute perfection.

"Thank you, Cesari. Ever the smooth talker."

I smiled, blushed a little, and cleared my throat. "So, is anybody—home?" I asked looking around wondering if Omar was nearby. I was a little apprehensive about his reaction to seeing me.

She sipped her coffee studying me. "Why don't you get to the point of the visit?"

"Sure. Well, Frankie here is a friend, and as you can plainly see, she has had some trouble recently. She was living with an abusive boyfriend and obviously can no longer stay with him. He's going crazy looking for her to finish the job and I was hoping you could put her up for a few days until he calms down and she can collect her thoughts. In the meanwhile, I will be looking for a more permanent solution for her."

The coffee was hazelnut flavored. Not my favorite, but I sipped it politely waiting for her response. Kelly was not thrilled by my request. "Cesari, can I speak to you for a moment in private?" She put her cup down, stood up, and signaled for me to follow. I put my cup down on the tray and trailed her into her bedroom, half expecting to see the girls but they weren't there.

Once alone, she closed the door behind her. Her eyes flashed with anger. "Does this look like a homeless shelter to you? There are places for battered women. What if her crazy boyfriend tracks her down here? I have kids."

Instinctively, I took a step back and raised my hands defensively. "I understand what you're saying and I would never place you or the girls in danger, but the shelters are sometimes even worse for defenseless women, Kel. I assure you that her boyfriend will never find her here. He's just not that smart."

"Great." The look on her face told me she was too soft-hearted to refuse someone in need. She couldn't even pass street people without emptying her wallet. As we talked, I looked around the room and noticed something amiss but what?

"Kelly, I promise you she won't be any trouble. Look, it's Sunday. Just let her stay for a day or two and I'll pick her up during the week. Where is Omar, by the way?" It suddenly dawned on me that the last time I saw him I was in his bedroom just like now. I started to grow a little nervous and definitely did not want to be found in a compromising position like that again.

Kelly looked uncomfortable and hesitated and that's when I realized what was wrong with the bedroom. There were no pictures of Omar, no wedding pictures, no family portraits, only framed photos of Kelly and the girls.

Softly she said, "He, um—moved out a few months ago." She sighed and bit her lip trying to hold back her emotions. Suddenly she sniffled and went to the night table to grab a tissue.

As sympathetically as I could I said, "I'm sorry, Kel. What happened?"

She sat on the edge of the bed. "I asked him to leave."

I sat next to her and held her hand. "Do you want to talk about it?"

She murmured almost as if talking to herself. "I found stuff-—pictures on his laptop…" She just let it hang out there. There was no need to expand. In this day and age, it was all too common.

"I'm sorry, Kel. Please tell me it wasn't the kind of porn that might land him in jail?"

She looked up at me. "It wasn't porn at all."

I was puzzled. "Then what?"

"There were pictures of him. Lots of pictures. Whole albums full of them. Apparently, he has been leading a secret life. He—he likes to dress up."

Omar was a transvestite?! I was speechless and unsure of what to say. This kind of thing had to be devastating for any woman. Finally I said, "Kel, I'm so sorry but you know something? A guy cross-dressing as a woman in the privacy of his own home isn't the end of the world."

She smirked. "It was nothing as tame as that and it wasn't in the privacy of his own home. He likes to dress up as—get this—

the lead singer from that 70's rock band, KISS. He confessed he's been doing it for some time now. Keeps his costumes at work and has been making up lies about going to conferences and late night meetings but there's a club downtown that caters to this kind of creepy stuff."

A black guy who liked to dress up as Gene Simmons from KISS. I was having trouble wrapping my head around this. If I didn't feel so bad for Kelly I might have laughed out loud.

"Kelly, I feel for you. I really do, but like I said it's not the worst thing a guy could ever do."

"First of all, lying to your wife over and over is the worst thing a guy could do but it does get worse. After I confronted him with it and it was out in the open he told me that he wanted to go on a KISS cruise."

"A KISS cruise?"

"It's a ten day bender with the band that leaves out of Bayonne makes a few stops like at Miami and San Juan and eventually winds up at some resort in the Bahamas for a three day orgy before returning. Apparently, at least the way he explained it, everybody dresses up as band members, gets drunk, and sings those awful songs from the seventies until they pass out every night."

"Every night? You've got to be kidding? Grown people do stuff like that?"

"Can you imagine being trapped on a ship or an island out in the middle of nowhere with people who can't let go of the past and think it's cool to play dress-up? I told him no way. First of all the kids are too young and I wasn't ready to leave them yet. Secondly, I told him that he needs help."

"And what did he say to that?"

"He didn't agree and said that as long as we were being honest it was always his fantasy to make love to me while he was in costume."

"Get out."

"Oh yeah, he's got a real fetish. Even worse, I'm supposed to dress up too. Get this, I'm the drummer, you know, the cat guy. Can you believe that?"

"Oh man. That is sick—and weird."

"Then he said he was sorry I didn't share his passion but that he had no intention of giving up going out clubbing with his friends and that he was glad it was out in the open and that I would just have to accept it. I told him it was either Gene Simmons or me and you know the rest."

"Yeah, he made a really bad choice."

"That's my life. Pretty pathetic, isn't it?" She buried her head into my chest, sniffling.

I held her close. "I don't know what to say, Kel. I almost can't believe my ears. I'm so sorry."

She looked at me. "You really didn't know? I thought maybe you came up here to gloat and give me the *I told you so* routine. I know you never liked him."

"I never said I didn't like him and how could I have known?"

"The same way you knew that I had moved to a new apartment. I never told you that."

"Oh. Well I didn't know about Omar and I am truly sorry."

"Are you?" she asked studying my face for sincerity.

"I really am, Kel. I would never want you to be unhappy for any reason."

"I know but I didn't exactly treat you very well. I mean that restraining order I put on you last year. I felt bad about that. I shouldn't have told the judge that you're a racist."

"Racist *and* a pedophile, but now we're splitting hairs. It doesn't matter. It's water under the bridge, Kel."

"I know but I should have invited you to the girl's first birthday party. That was wrong."

"Like I said, water under the bridge."

"Yeah, but reporting you to the police on Christmas morning just because you wanted to give the girls a present was absolutely horrid of me."

I cleared my throat. "Okay, there's no point in rehashing ancient history. What's past is past. Where are the kids anyway? I'd like to see them."

"They're at my aunt's in Yonkers. I had to take call this weekend, and well you know—the unpredictability of not knowing when you might suddenly have to go in to the hospital makes it difficult to care for small children. I just dropped them off last night." She hesitated and added, "I'm sorry you missed them."

I nodded. "That's okay, but it looks like you might be open to me visiting them more often. Am I right?"

She nodded. "We could talk about that if you don't hate me."

"Kelly, I could never hate you."

"Do you really mean that?"

I nodded, "Never."

"By the way, the answer is yes, your friend can stay here for a few days. I'll be in and out if she doesn't mind."

"Right now all she wants to do is curl up with a good book somewhere."

"She can use the sofa and I have a whole book case full of novels she can choose from. The other room unfortunately just has cribs in it, no bed."

"The sofa should be fine. She's not very needy." I hesitated, looking around the bedroom. "Hey, Kel."

"What?"

"Do you still have that camisole I gave you way back when?"

She laughed and punched me playfully, "You're incorrigible. C'mon, let's go back to the living room. She's waiting."

We found Frankie sipping her coffee comfortably curled up on the couch, and Kelly welcomed her to stay for as long as she felt necessary. Over the next hour, we all got acquainted as my mind spun with the news about Omar. Incredibly, Kelly had been so wrapped up in her own personal crisis and caring for the twins that she hadn't heard about my exploits in Vegas so I decided to let sleeping dogs lie.

"So, Kelly, are you still working in the endoscopy department at St. Lukes?" I asked.

"Yes, and we've been insanely busy thanks to the new center for bariatric surgery that opened six months ago."

This made me curious. My hospital didn't offer bariatric surgery. "How does that affect the endoscopy department?"

"Oh my God. Are you kidding? Bariatric surgery is all the rage like tummy tucks and liposuction used to be. Nobody wants to just go on a diet and exercise anymore. Well, all those patients need to have upper endoscopies and screening colonoscopies prior to their surgery to assess their anatomy and make sure they don't have cancer. We're so busy right now that we have at least two full days and sometimes three full days of those cases per week. I've been assigned to assist with all of them. Apparently, I'm the surgeons' favorite assistant." She smiled and made a pretend curtsey.

Frankie asked, "What's bariatric surgery?"

Kelly answered her, "It's the medical term for surgical procedures performed on the stomach to help people lose weight. There are several types of surgical options available, but they all basically do the same thing. They reduce the size of the stomach so that the person gets full fast and physically can't get as much food in. Anyway, that's what I do all day long several times a week."

She seemed frustrated so I asked, "Is that bad?"

"Well, not bad but stressful. First of all, there are new surgeons crawling all over the place. Each one likes to do things differently and that can be difficult. Secondly, these patients are generally very complicated and their extreme weight places them at high risk for cardiopulmonary complications. They all have sleep apnea and bad things happen all the time. Also, a lot of them are referred from the shelters and their hygiene isn't all that great."

I remembered the guy at the Bowery Mission telling me about this. "What is that all about Kel? I heard that cases referred from the shelters are being done on a charitable basis."

"Well, yes and no. The patients aren't charged anything, but the hospital gets reimbursed a hefty fee from Medicare and Medicaid. They in turn float nice bonuses to the surgeons depending on how many patients from the shelters they perform surgery on. Technically, it's not fee splitting, which is against the law, but in reality it is. The government thinks that if they take everybody with a weight problem and fix it through surgery then they win in the long run because those patients will have fewer medical and surgical problems down the road such as diabetes, hypertension, coronary artery disease, hip and knee replacements, etc. that they will have to pay for. Anyway St. Lukes was chosen as a pilot program to test this theory of benevolent government intervention."

I nodded. That was interesting, especially the part about not being fee splitting. I wondered how they pulled that off and guessed somewhere somebody kept an unofficial count of how many surgeries each surgeon performed and then based on that, end of year bonuses were calculated. Maybe it wasn't that hard to do after all. I hoped nobody was saving the records. That would be a great way for everyone to go to jail. Fee splitting and self-referrals were severely frowned upon by the government unless of course the politicians got their cut.

Still curious, I asked, "What's the onus on the patient if any?"

"None, all they have to do is show up, receive minimal pre-surgical counseling, blood work, and agree to stay for short-term rehab before they are released. They don't even have to submit identification if they don't want to. Our government is tired of paying for healthcare for people who won't take care of themselves."

"So, they'd rather pay for pre-emptive surgery and cut their losses."

"You got it."

"Wow."

Chapter 39

Lupa's was dark, crowded, and noisy when I arrived at ten after seven. Vito was already seated in the rear, sipping from a wine glass and munching on bread dipped in extra virgin olive oil. He wore a fedora cocked at an angle partially obscuring his face. I sat and poured myself a glass from the already half empty bottle of Chianti.

"How long have you been waiting?" I asked.

"Fifteen minutes."

I raised my eyebrows, looking at the bottle. "You must be thirsty."

"I needed it. It's been a long day. Brunella is on the war path. She wants blood more than ever, Cesari, and there ain't any way of stopping her now. I've been on the phone all afternoon trying to calm people down but with Carmine in the ICU all bets are off. The only thing slowing her down is; one, she's so worried about him she won't leave his bedside; and two, the FBI is all over the place. They can feel something big is going down over this."

"So, what's with the spy hat?" I asked, grinning.

"You're the last guy who should be laughing right now."

"Relax. Carmine's in a coma, right? So until he wakes up, Seymour's going to take the full brunt of her anger, and who knows, he may never wake up. Did you go see him?"

"Of course I did. Me and everyone else in the city went down to St. Matt's this afternoon to express our regrets about what happened. We also promised we would do whatever it took to bring in the guy who did it."

I nodded. "All right, so now what?"

"So now we eat. I'm starving."

We both ordered the rabbit arrabiata with buttermilk potatoes which the waiter assured us was out of this world. While we waited we finished off the first bottle of Chianti and ordered a second. I filled Vito in on what I had learned about Seymour's DNA.

He furrowed his brow in thought. "I don't get it. So he was with her too—the same night? How?"

"I don't know, but it's a fact. I don't get it either. He said he never met her."

"Yeah, I remember him saying that but obviously he lied, but why? So did that pimp Luther kill her or not?"

"You heard Carmine. He said no way because Luther worshipped her, and he knew them both better than you and me."

The waiter served our meals and we ate for a while thinking things over. Vito broke the ice, "Maybe we're thinking about this all wrong. This guy Seymour. He's everywhere involved in everything, and we know now he's a sociopathic killer, right? Maybe he killed the girl in Vegas. I mean why not? He's totally nuts."

"Well, it's possible, but most serial killers follow some sort of pattern unless a crisis intervenes disrupting their activities. For instance, clearly Seymour would lure people to his apartment on some pretext and then either drug or overpower them. Based on how we found Lance tied up, I'm assuming he used them for sexual gratification and when he was done, dumped them in the sewer system, probably with an acid bath first. The girl in Vegas was totally out of line with that pattern, and then there's the lack of motive."

Vito thought about that for a minute, dipping bread in olive oil. "I'm not sure a serial murderer needs a motive, but I think you're missing the point about what happened in Vegas, Cesari."

"Enlighten me."

"That was no accidental death scene. It was an intentional set up to frame you for murder. So if he did do it, he was deviating deliberately from his usual MO. He had sex with her the night she was murdered, that's for sure. He must have been right there in the room with you."

"Why would he do that? He must have known they might find his DNA."

"Maybe he couldn't help himself? Maybe that's part of his compulsion. Maybe that's why he put her in the bathtub. Because it was as close to his ritual as he could get under the circumstances. Maybe he wasn't worried about his DNA being found on her because she was a hooker and he figured he could always explain it away. Let's just pretend for a moment that we know for a fact he killed the girl in Vegas to set you up for murder. The real question is why would he do that? You mentioned the lack of motive."

"And you said he didn't need one."

"Unless this murder was personal for him and had nothing to do with his psychotic side. So why would he want you to go to prison? Did you not get along with him?"

I thought about that as I finished my meal. "I don't know. I mean we weren't pals or anything, but murder? To be honest, I did kind of pick on him a little about his weight but I hardly think that required that kind of extreme response. Besides, if he drugged me and I was unconscious, why not just kill me instead framing me?"

"Because maybe he wanted to humiliate you the way you've been humiliating him. And a life sentence in the Nevada state prison is as close to hell on earth as there is. Now that I think about it, it makes perfect sense. Look at the reaction I got when

I picked on him at Lance's apartment. He was ready to blow me away over nothing. He's obviously extremely thin-skinned when it comes to his appearance. It probably goes back to some childhood issues."

I was getting a sinking feeling in my stomach. Was this really all about a few fat jokes I made to an overly sensitive sociopath? I took a deep breath and let it out. Then I remembered talking to Arnie about the autopsy report on the girl. He said she died from asphyxiation with multiple broken ribs as if a car had slowly run her over or—a 450 pound guy was lying on her for an extended period of time.

Shit!

"Okay, it's a possibility that would explain a few things. He drugs me, I sleep with the girl and pass out. He comes in later and either rapes her or pays her. Either way, it ends up with him crushing her to death. Then he puts her in the tub and makes me look like Jack the Ripper. I wake up prematurely and everything goes sideways. Sounds good so far?"

"I'm telling you. That's what happened."

"Except for one thing I don't understand."

"Which is?"

"When I questioned him in Lance's apartment, he freely admitted to killing those girls in the sewer and the girl in his brownstone. So why would he insist that he had nothing to do with the girl in Vegas?"

"He told us why. He knew the game was over and he was going to prison no matter what. He said he'd rather take his chances there, than in one of Carmine's meat lockers. He also knew that as long as Carmine believed it was you he'd have a chance of getting away with that one. If he had told you the truth, it's possible you might have somehow convinced Carmine."

Vito's analysis was very convincing. "One more thing, Sherlock. I don't believe that I would go to Vegas, get high or whatever and have sex with a hooker every which way. That's not me."

"Save it for the jury, Cesari. You did and that's a fact. So whoever you think you are, you weren't that night."

For some reason this really bothered me. Self-control and being particular about who I slept with was something I prided myself on. I wasn't Mr. Clean by a long shot. That much I knew. I was what you might call, a serial monogamist with occasional day trips off the reservation, but hookers and random encounters—never. Even drugged, I had trouble accepting that.

Vito finished his meal then wiped his face with his napkin and signaled the waiter for the bill. He reached into his pocket and withdrew a tightly rolled up wad of twenties, placing it on the table next to me.

"It's a thousand. Let me know when you need more. Now I have to go. Lay low, all right? I'll let you know when things cool off. In the meanwhile, I'll do my best to misdirect as many people as possible. So do me a favor and don't make a fool out of me by walking down Mulberry Street in broad daylight. Even though your pal Seymour is Brunella's high priority it still wouldn't be smart. She might think that nabbing you might help her catch him."

I nodded and thanked him for the cash. He left first and I followed ten minutes later. The sidewalks had been cleared and the snow was already starting to melt so I decided to walk a bit to organize my thoughts as I drifted in the direction of Washington Square Park. It was very hard for me to believe that Seymour had orchestrated this whole thing as an act of revenge. On the other hand, he clearly was a sociopath of the first order and therefore I shouldn't underestimate him or make any assumptions about his motivations. I was quite certain that all those girls and maybe some guys he killed said the same thing right before they died—why?

I was convinced of one thing though. One way or the other he was going to pay. No mercy—none. I clutched the duffel bag with the crowbar and pistol tightly as I walked. I looked at my watch. It was getting late and I needed to find someplace to stay. My apartment was on Sixth Avenue on the other side of the park but I dared not go there. As I pondered this, my cell phone buzzed in my pocket.

"Kelly, what's up?"

"John, Frankie and I were just talking…"

"About what, Kel?"

"I have a king bed and—well, Frankie and I are both kind of petite. We can easily fit in the bed and never even know there was someone on the other side."

I chucked. "Well, go ahead. You didn't need to ask my permission."

"I'm calling because if Frankie and I share the bed that means the couch is available for you. I know you don't have anywhere to go right now and Frankie told me you gave her all your cash."

Hmm.

I was amused. "Well, if the bed is really that big maybe all three of us can fit in it?"

She chuckled. "I see you haven't lost any of your charm, Cesari. So should I get out an extra blanket and pillow?"

I thought it over. It was Sunday night and the weather had eased up. I was bound to find a hotel room but it was almost ten and I was exhausted. I'd been pushing it hard the last few days and it was catching up to me. I really didn't feel up to hotel hunting right now.

"I'll be there as soon as I can catch a cab."

When I arrived at the apartment Frankie was already asleep in the bedroom with the door closed. Kelly had made up the couch with a sheet, blanket, and pillow.

I sat down on it and said, "Thanks, Kel."

She sat next to me and curled her legs under her the way girls do. "You're welcome. We felt bad for you wandering around the city with no place to go."

Just then it hit me. "Hey, wait a minute. How did you know I had no place to go?"

She smiled, "Frankie told me. She told me everything including the fact that she's—a working girl."

I rolled my eyes. Great, just when we were starting to establish trust. Now she knows I lied to her. "Kel, I didn't want to involve you any deeper than necessary."

"Relax, Cesari, I understand. She's very nice. Poor thing. What a life."

I nodded. "Yeah."

She shook her head at me. "Boy, you really do know how to get in trouble, don't you? Having dinner at a brothel? What next? Lunch at a massage parlor?"

"Kelly, it wasn't like that. I didn't even know it was a brothel."

"So she said. She also told me that she—um—how do I say this delicately—has enjoyed the full Cesari experience."

I threw my head back and covered my face in embarrassment. "She didn't."

"Well, I asked her point blank since we were in full disclosure mode."

I groaned inwardly. "Kel, I can explain."

She chuckled. "Explain what? That you're a man? I already knew that, and you don't owe me an explanation. I shut you out, remember?"

I nodded. She was right and yet I still felt like I betrayed her. Why did my heart pound whenever I was near this woman? My whole body surged when she was around.

"I do have a bone to pick with you about something else, however."

"What's that?"

"Frankie told me how you saved her life in Vegas and how you've continued to risk life and limb to protect her here in New York as well."

"And…?"

"And you may want to knock off the super hero stuff a little because there are more important things you have to start thinking about."

"Such as…?"

"Two little girls who would like see their daddy one day." As she said that, tears formed and her eyes welled up.

I was speechless and all choked up myself. "Thank you for saying that, Kel." It was the first time she had ever admitted to me or anyone else that they were my kids. This was a huge step for her.

She nodded. "I think I'll go to bed now. We'll talk more tomorrow. If you're sleeping when I go to work I won't wake you. I already showed Frankie where the basics are in the kitchen."

"Thanks."

She disappeared into the bedroom and I turned off the lights, stripped down to my shorts and got under the cover. I had a lot to think about for sure, and though I closed my eyes and tried to will it, sleep just wouldn't come to me. After about an hour, I heard the sound of the bedroom door opening and closing softly followed by muffled feet on carpet heading in my direction.

A hushed voice called out, "John…?"

I could barely make out her outline. "Kelly? Is everything all right?"

"I can't sleep."

"Neither can I."

"Move over."

I scrunched to the inside of the sofa as much as I could and she picked up the cover and slid in next to me, wrapping her arms around me. I held her tightly, found her lips and kissed her like it was my last day on earth. I stared at her in the darkness as excitement overwhelmed me. I was afraid to speak for fear of ruining the moment. My breaths came in short rapid bursts and my heart pounded as my hands ran up and down her feeling the silk negligee she wore.

I whispered. “Is this…?”

“It’s the camisole you gave me. I saved it.”

Chapter 40

Groggy and confused, I woke from a very deep and happy slumber. Sunlight pouring in from the eastward facing windows made me squint, and out of one eye, I saw Frankie sitting in a chair across from me, legs crossed, reading a book. She wore one of Kelly's robes and her hair was wet. There was a large mug of coffee sitting on the glass coffee table in front of her, steam gently floating upward from it.

"Good morning, sleepy head."

I grunted. "Maybe. What time is it and what are you reading?"

"It's eight thirty and it's called, *Tripwire*. It's one of the Jack Reacher novels. Ever heard of them?"

"Yeah, I tried reading one once. They were too violent for me."

She thought that was funny. "Want some coffee?"

"Does a piranha like the taste of exposed, raw human flesh?"

She chuckled again. "You should do stand up. Black, right?" She stood up to walk into the kitchen.

"Yes, thank you, and you're the one who's going into comedy, remember? Maybe I could help you write your material." I sat up, rubbed my eyes and yawned.

She returned and handed me a mug of coffee. I sniffed it and gently took my first sip, feeling it race throughout my body.

Good stuff. I was feeling great and was still glowing from last night.

"How was your night?" Frankie asked, smiling.

"It was good, thanks, and yours?"

"I slept real well. That bed is so big. I couldn't even tell if there was another person in it. In fact, she might have spent the entire night out here for all I know." She wore a canary eating grin on her face.

"What are you getting at Frankie?"

"Nothing really. It's just that when I showered this morning I found naughty lingerie on the bathroom floor and since it wasn't mine…"

"I am quite certain I have no idea what you're talking about, and furthermore, if our host decides she wants to try on her own clothes in the middle of the night then I'm pretty sure it's none of our business."

"Relax, I don't care. I think it's great. I like her. Too bad about Omar. She told me all about it. How weird is that?"

I shook my head. How two women who were total strangers could feel comfortable sharing the most intimate details of their lives was beyond me. "Well, I'm glad you and Kelly are getting along, and yes, it's very weird."

"So want to bring me up to speed or is that top secret?"

"No, it's fine. Besides, you already know most of it. You might as well know the rest. I'm convinced Seymour murdered Jenny and tried to frame me for it. Not a hundred percent sure why but I plan on asking him when I find him. Downtown is hotter than ever because of what happened to Carmine. Vito and I hope he dies quickly because then Brunella will be preoccupied with finding Seymour and leave us alone. If he lives and remembers what happened then Vito and I are in a lot of trouble. The FBI and NYPD are swarming over that part of the city trying to figure things out."

"And you're super pissed at Seymour, and have no intention of dropping it and trying to resume your life?"

I chuckled. She was cute in a she has no idea who I am sort of way. "Not a chance. I want to find him for a variety of reasons not the least of which is to explain to him that kicking another physician in the family jewels when he's not expecting it is very impolite. Look, you sit tight here today, all right? Please don't leave the apartment."

"What about food? Her refrigerator is pretty bare. All she has is a dozen eggs, bottled water, diet Pepsi, and baby food. I'll need to do a little grocery shopping."

I didn't like that. "No, please don't. I'll go to the store later. If you have any requests you can think of just text me."

"Fine. I can live on eggs for a while."

"Thanks, I'll feel better."

She nodded but her expression changed. It appeared to me that something was bothering her so I asked, "Is everything all right?"

"Yeah, I guess. So Kelly's available—that's kind of perfect for you. Isn't it?"

Hmm. I saw what she was getting at. I said, "Well, I must admit that it's a very welcome surprise."

She nodded and spoke very softly. "So two's company and three's a crowd. Maybe I should find another place to stay. You two have a lot of history and children. I don't want to be in the way."

"No, definitely not. I want you to stay here and so does Kelly. Your safety right now means a lot to me. Kelly and I will figure it out once things settle down. And Frankie, I know that we've…"

She turned her head and I heard her sigh. She murmured softly, "I knew you were going to throw me away. Guys always throw me away, but we had some fun, right? Kelly's the queen bee. I get it."

I stood, walked over to her, and pulled her up, wrapping my arms around her. "I'm not throwing you away. I do care about you—very much and I'm sorry if you're feeling hurt."

She pressed her head into my chest. "Don't be. You're both very nice and I'm happy for you."

"Thank you."

I finished my coffee and went off to shower and shave, using Kelly's razor and antiperspirant. Thankfully, she had a couple of new toothbrushes in a drawer and soon I felt like a new man. I put on my jeans and the nice thick wool sweater I bought at Macy's. It was the first day of March and I looked out the window at Central Park. Despite the recent severe storm, it was clear winter would soon beat a hasty retreat. The sun was shining, the snow melting, and people walked briskly. The temperature was supposed to be in the mid to upper forties today, practically a heat wave.

I said goodbye to Frankie and let myself out, very distracted now by Kelly and having trouble getting last night out of my head. Being close to the point where I couldn't focus on what I had to do, I decided to get it out of my system and go see her at the hospital. No one knew me at St. Lukes which worked in my favor; however, she'd be busy and might not have time for me. Plus, she may already be regretting coming to me last night. Women were like that. They were as unpredictable as the wind and they tended to think things through too much. Geez.

I stopped at a florist a block from the main entrance and picked up a dozen red roses. That should do the trick, and in five minutes, I sauntered through the main lobby toward the elevators. The endoscopy department was a short ride to the fifth floor and I entered the patient registration area.

At the counter a young receptionist in her mid to late twenties greeted me warmly. "Good morning. How may I help you?"

"I'm a friend of Kelly Kingston. She's one of the endoscopy nurses. I was wondering if I might speak to her."

The receptionist saw the roses and smiled broadly. "Why don't you have a seat and I'll see if she's available."

"Thanks."

I took a seat and looked around the crowded waiting room. This was a busy department for sure. Most people sat casually reading magazines and newspapers or playing on their cellphones, an almost constant sight now everywhere. There was an occasional anxious face. One particularly nervous woman reading a newspaper kept looking in every direction. She seemed very jumpy. People handled stress very differently; but mostly not well, especially when it came to their own health-related problems or that of a loved one. Maybe she was afraid that she or whoever she was with had cancer.

Moments later, the receptionist returned looking for me. "Kelly's tied up right now but said that you should come in and wait in the nurse's break room for her unless you had to go somewhere."

"No, I'll wait for her."

"Just follow me then Mr…?"

"Just John. Everybody calls me John."

"I'm Tara, Mr. John," she said jokingly. "So I see Kelly has been a good girl."

"Isn't she always?"

"Yes, she is, but she's been having a rough time lately. This is just what the doctor ordered."

She led me to an unoccupied small twelve foot square break room with a small round table in its center. There was a sink, refrigerator and coffee machine. I sat down and thought things through while I waited. I couldn't go back to work until things settled down. This thing with Carmine had distracted everyone's attention, including the FBI and Brunella's. That was good. Brunella's psychological obsession with her son eliminated the possibility of forgiveness on her part so it would be best for everyone if she could find someone appropriate to vent her vengeful spleen on and Seymour was the perfect choice. Nothing would satisfy her more at this point other than his head on a platter and I intended on hand delivering it. But where was he? I strummed my fingers on the table deep in thought. There was a copy of the New York Post lying face down in front of me and I turned it over to see the front page.

Holy shit!

Photos of Seymour and I were plastered front and center, side by side. My heart skipped a beat and I gulped as I quickly read the lead story. They had finally found the bodies in the sewer system and realized that they had a serial killer on their hands. They were starting to connect the dots. They had found my fingerprints in the apartment and on a flashlight they found near the skeletons linking me to the criminal investigation. Law enforcement was now working on the theory that Seymour and I may have collaborated to commit these sensational murders. As a result, there was now renewed interest in the murder in Vegas as possibly being connected with the "sewer rat slayings" as they were calling them.

I let out a deep breath and decided to get out of there quickly. Throwing the newspaper back onto the table, I left the roses and hustled out of the break room. To my right was the waiting room from where I had come. I could see the receptionist talking to hospital security. How? The lady in the waiting room, of course. That's why she was so edgy. She recognized me. To my left, were the endoscopy rooms, main OR, and recovery room. I couldn't go there dressed like this. Directly ahead of me were the male and female locker rooms.

I ran to the male locker room and looked around eventually finding a pair of green surgical scrubs my size. Quickly changing into them, I donned a hat and mask as well. The mask hung loosely halfway down my face in a relaxed position. I tossed my clothes into an empty locker but kept my cellphone and wallet. But now what? I was still a stranger in a strange place. I went through as many open lockers as I could, looking for something useful. Eventually on a wall rack I discovered several white lab coats that people had hung while they performed their surgical procedures. I found one with a stethoscope folded in its pocket and an ID badge clipped to the front. The lab coat was way too small for me so I slung the stethoscope around my neck and attached the ID badge facing backward to my breast pocket. I worked hurriedly trying to stay one step ahead of the alarm that was sure to come.

Leaving the locker room behind, I walked through the bustling central OR corridor into the recovery room deliberately slowing my pace to be casual. The place was filled with patients recovering from their recent surgeries and endoscopies. There was a big electronic monitor on the wall listing the patients' names, what bed they were in, who the doctor was and their status; pre-op, in surgery, recovering.

Something caught my eye on the patient board. I saw the name Kermit—Kermit Larana. He was in bed 8 in recovery from gastric bypass surgery. Kermit was the name Seymour had used as an alias at the shelter. I hadn't thought to ask if he had given them a last name, but Kermit was such an unusual name that I couldn't help thinking it odd to see it again so soon. I studied the board carefully and something else bothered me about the name. Larana was vaguely familiar. Then it came to me. Larana—La rana. My high school Spanish was slowly returning to me. La rana meant "the frog" in Spanish. Kermit the frog. What an asshole.

Deep in thought I hadn't noticed one of the nurses come up to me. "Can I help you, Doctor?" she asked trying unsuccessfully to see my ID. She smiled, too polite to challenge me any further. It was a big hospital and not every nurse knew every physician especially in the rapidly growing surgical department that Kelly had told me about.

With an air of confidence, looking at her ID, I asked, "Good morning, Marilynn. Could you tell me what room Mr. Larana will be going to? I assisted in his surgery and I would like to check in on him later."

"Sure thing. I'll check for you." She went behind the nursing station, ruffled through a few papers and came back to me. "It seems that he won't be going to the inpatient wards. We're waiting on transportation to bring him back to the shelter from where he came."

I was surprised. "I thought all the shelter patients had to stay for a few days for dietary counseling and rehab."

She seemed surprised too. "Yes, usually all the shelter patients do but he underwent the lap band procedure as you know. It's the least invasive of the bariatric procedures and has the quickest recovery time. According to his paper work, he insisted on being discharged immediately back to the shelter and we legally can't keep him here against his will. He'll be fine. We'll send a visiting nurse to the shelter to check on him later today and again tomorrow."

"Fair enough. When are you expecting the transport vehicle to arrive?"

"Any minute. He's been out of surgery nearly an hour and a half. He's a little groggy, but mostly awake and doing well. You can see him before he leaves if you want. He's in bed 8."

"Thank you for your help. I'll check in on him in a minute."

She smiled and walked away. I took the stairwell down to the emergency room to find the ambulette coming for Seymour. Thinking rapidly, I assessed the situation. He was post-op and even though he was coming out of anesthesia well, he would be strapped securely into a stretcher for transportation to the shelter. For liability reasons, they couldn't allow him to simply roam freely in the back of the vehicle. There would be two transport technicians trained with basic life support skills in case something happened.

My brain raced. What to do? Two of them and they didn't know me. A slew of other people around, and perhaps security. My cellphone buzzed.

"Kelly?"

"John, did you see the newspaper today?"

"Yes, I did, unfortunately. Did you get the roses?"

"Yes, thank you. They are beautiful. Is that why you took off without saying hello? I saw the paper lying on the table next to the bouquet."

"Yes, I saw a security guard talking to the receptionist and I assumed he was looking for me."

She laughed. "I don't blame you for being paranoid. I read the story. If I didn't know you, I'd be suspicious too, but the security guard was Javier. He's in love with Tara, the receptionist. He comes up here every day to talk to her. If you're still in the building I'd like to thank you in person for the flowers and—last night."

I let out a sigh of relief and the thought crossed my mind to go back up to see her in person but I didn't want to let Seymour out of my sight. The situation was extremely time sensitive. Besides, there was no point in pushing my luck about being recognized. "Well, that does take a load off my mind. I am still here, but unfortunately, something just came up and I got to run. I'll do my best to come to the apartment tonight."

"You'd better, Cesari. It wouldn't be fair to just waltz back into my life, drop a hooker off and disappear again."

She was joking—mostly. "I know and I promise to do my best."

"All right then. See you later."

"See you later. Oh, before I forget, Kel, could you go to the men's locker room and pick up my clothes? I left them in locker 37."

"You left your clothes in the men's locker room? What are you wearing?"

"Scrubs."

"Why?"

"Kel…"

"Forget it. I don't want to know."

"Thanks."

I hung up as I walked through the ER and found the ambulance port where patients were dropped off or in this case picked up. There was one full-sized ambulance parked off to one side and a smaller van-sized ambulette that had backed up to the entrance. This was for Seymour. I was sure of it. The transport guys were probably upstairs loading him on a stretcher.

It crossed my mind to call the police but Seymour was such a rat that I decided he needed proper tending. He framed me for murder and now forensics had me linked to all of those other atrocities he committed in his brownstone. He'd confess but would probably drag me down with him just for the fun of it. The kind of justice he needed wasn't on the menu in our system. No—no police for Seymour.

As I stood outside the ER, I bummed a cigarette off of a nurse enjoying her break and chit chatted with her about her day to appear casual. Nurses smoking outside of emergency room entrances was as normal a sight as heart attacks inside. In a few minutes, she was joined by several friends and wandered off. Left alone, I thought through the Seymour situation. He had volunteered for a lap band procedure obviously to radically alter his appearance as quickly as possible. In a few weeks, he would barely be recognizable and Kelly had said that no questions were asked of volunteers from the shelter. Clever Seymour, but not clever enough.

What did he think was going to happen when he returned to the shelter? Even if Josh, the guy in charge, didn't blow him in when he returned, sooner or later the police would think to search for him there. Then it hit me and a chill ran up my spine. He wasn't going back to the shelter. The nurse said he was almost wide awake. He'll figure out some way of suckering these poor transport guys into stopping the ambulette and let him free. Then, I'd bet everything, he'll kill them and leave the city with the van.

Could he do that just two hours after surgery? Just then I remembered a famous quote from history, "Desperation is great motivation." I finished my cigarette and tossed the butt away just as the stretcher with Seymour on it rolled into view with the transport guys at either end and my plan crystalized.

I took a few steps away so no one could hear me and called Vito. "What?" he asked.

"Vito, I need you in a hurry. Meet me at the shelter where we found Seymour staying. You got wheels?"

"What's going on?"

"I got Seymour. They're bringing him to the shelter in a medical transport van. You have at least thirty, maybe forty minutes to get there. It's important you get there before they start unloading him."

"Shit. I'll have to use Brunella's Q7 then. My town car got buried in by the plows on Third Avenue. Everything's melting but not that fast."

"So use the Q7."

He let out a deep breath. "I already took a big enough chance driving you to Kelly's in that thing. I'd rather not push my luck."

"Well, put on your big boy pants and let's go."

"Fine."

As I hung up, I heard the transport guys pushing and pulling Seymour's stretcher up the ramp into the back of the van. They grunted from their labor. I couldn't offer to help in case Seymour was awake enough to recognize me. When they finished, they closed the back doors and walked to the front of the van to let themselves in.

It was time to act. I walked quickly to the passenger side just as they were buckling up and introduced myself. "Hey guys. I'm Dr. Cesari, one of the new surgeons on staff."

The closest to me replied affably, "Hi, Doc. What can we do for you?"

The driver started the ignition.

"I was in surgery and missed my ride down to the homeless shelter. I was supposed to do pre-op physicals for tomorrow's cases. Is there any chance I could bum a ride with you? Once I'm done I'll take a cab back."

They looked at each other and the driver leaned over. "I don't see why not but you'll have to sit in the back, if that's all right? I have to warn you though. It can get a bit bumpy back there so buckle up."

The guy closest to me started to unbuckle. "I'll let you in."

I put my hand up. "Thanks, but you don't have to. I worked as an EMT and transport driver in medical school. I know my way pretty well around these vans." Looking past him, I could see that the front of the van was separated from the back by a reinforced metal panel so that in case of an accident the patient's stretcher and other equipment didn't go crashing through the windshield. There was a small six inch square door in the middle of the panel which they could slide open and check on things. I said, "I'll knock when I'm settled in."

I went around back and climbed in keeping my face away from Seymour who appeared to be sleeping. I still had the surgical mask dangling on my neck and now put it fully on my face. Sitting down, I gently rapped on the panel and felt the van lurch forward. The guy in the passenger seat opened the small door looked in and gave me a thumbs up. Although he seemed puzzled by the sight of my mask, he didn't say anything. He probably thought I was afraid of catching something from

Seymour. He closed the small door and we settled in for our drive. Soon, loud, heavy metal rock seeped through from the front of the vehicle.

I turned toward Seymour and realized that I didn't have anything to be concerned about. He was snoring comfortably still experiencing the effects of his recent anesthesia. There was a blanket draped over him to keep him warm. I couldn't see, but presumed he was strapped in snugly on his stretcher so that he didn't accidentally roll off. The stretcher in turn was securely braced to the floor of the van. I looked around the vehicle and saw several familiar sights; an EKG monitor, CPR equipment, IV tubing and oxygen tank, stacks of gauze, bandages, and strong nylon surgical tape not the paper kind.

Excellent.

I waited a few minutes into the trip and unbuckled my seatbelt, standing unsteadily to reach for the surgical tape. I planned on placing a couple of strips over Seymour's mouth in case he woke up and recognized me. In addition I would have to restrain him better. The straps holding him in the stretcher were meant to protect him, not imprison him, and he could easily wiggle himself out if he so chose. As I rocked and swayed, I pressed one hand up against the ceiling to steady myself.

Suddenly and with great force, Seymour, who had only been feigning sleep swung a pudgy fist at me landing a direct blow once again in my love plums. I gasped and doubled over in pain, falling to my knees.

Son of a bitch!

He snarled, grabbed my head, and rolled off the stretcher on top of me, his great weight crushing me to the floor of the van. He hadn't had time to remove the restraints from the lower half of his body, and was still strapped down when he had seen his opportunity to overpower me. Because of this, only part of his massive body had me pinned as he desperately tried to wiggle the lower half free.

I was in agonizing pain and already seeing stars when he head butted me. Confused and dazed, but not out, I willed myself back into the fight. In the small confines of the back of the van I didn't have much room to maneuver. The bulk of his weight now on my chest, my lungs screaming in pain, I suddenly realized his intention. He was going to try to crush me to death like he did to Jenny and the others.

But I wasn't a 110 pound girl. I was a 220 pound male who had spent many years of his life lifting and lowering heavy metal objects off the ground monotonously for hours on a daily basis. As a result, I had overly developed chest and back muscles and could resist him as long as I remained conscious. He realized that and tried to head butt me again into submission. I saw it coming and reached up with my right hand before he could launch his attack, and clamped it hard on his larynx.

He wheezed loudly, let go of my head and frantically clawed at my hand. As he struggled, I plunged my left thumb into his right eye and gouged him deeply until blood trickled out. He would have screamed but couldn't with my vise-like grip on his throat. He pulled away to escape but I followed him, yanking his hands off of my wrists allowing me to choke him harder. His eyes were turning red and his face purple as I felt his strength waning. I pulled my surgical mask off as he was starting to lose consciousness and his eyes registered the shock of recognition just as he passed out. I immediately let go of him and hoped I didn't crush his larynx. I really wanted to deliver him alive to Brunella who I knew would have much more fun things planned for him.

I waited a few seconds and his breathing returned. Shallow and with difficulty at first but soon normalized. He would be all right. I squirmed my way out from under him and sucked wind from the exertion. There was no way I could lift him by myself back onto the stretcher so I unbuckled his feet and let him lie face down in the center of the van. I bound his wrists tightly behind his back and then his ankles with multiple layers of surgical tape. I worked up a sweat rolling him face up and covered his mouth with several strips of tape in case he woke up. I listened carefully for sounds of good airflow when I was done. A guy as large as Seymour was undoubtedly a mouth breather and probably had some degree of obstructive sleep apnea but I assessed that he would be okay. Just then my phone buzzed with a text message from Frankie.

"How about pizza for dinner?"

I smiled and texted her back okay and returned my attention to Seymour. If the guys up front were to open the port hole now, I'd have a lot of explaining to do so I decided to pre-empt them. I shoved my face into the small opening blocking their view behind me and knocked. The door opened and the guy on the passenger side asked, "Everything okay, Doc? You really shouldn't be out of your seat."

"Yeah, I know. I had to stretch my legs a little. I'll go back now. It's pretty boring back here and this guy snores like crazy. How much longer do you think?"

The driver chimed in at this. "At least ten to fifteen minutes, Doc. The shelter is way down town. Is he okay?"

"Okay, thanks. He's fine. You go back to driving and I'll keep an eye on him."

"Thanks, Doc."

After he closed the door I moved as far away as I could and dialed Vito.

"I'm almost there, Cesari, relax."

I whispered into the receiver, "Okay, make sure you act quickly. When the drivers get out, hustle them into the van and then follow me in the Audi."

"We're going to kidnap city employees?"

"Only for a short while. We can't let them raise the alarm until we're well on our way and bring me a jacket or sweater or something. I've been wearing hospital scrubs all day and I'm getting cold."

"Where are your clothes?"

"I'll explain when we get there."

"Where are we going?"

"The Bronx."

Chapter 41

I drove the medical van with Vito riding shotgun. One of his men followed us in the Audi. Vito looked through the open porthole at the two transport guys and Seymour to make sure they hadn't moved. One of the transport guys lay strapped on Seymour's stretcher, the other sat quietly on the chair I had used and Seymour lay still on the floor. He had come to but, between today's sedation and my throttling, was quite weak. We restrained the transport guys with a combination of nylon surgical tape and plastic IV tubing. We took away their phones and wallets. They were young and too scared to do anything rash but it never hurt to take simple precautions.

Overpowering them was easy. When they went to the back of the van to open it, Vito closed in on them fast with his 9 mm. As the rear doors opened I grabbed one by the hair and dragged him inside throwing him on top of Seymour. Vito shoved the other one in at gunpoint. The whole thing took less than ten seconds. We closed the van doors and politely explained the new arrangement. Shock, fear, and confusion made them docile and we promised not to hurt them if they cooperated. Vito's menacing face and pistol convinced them that teamwork was the best course of action.

"Where exactly in the Bronx are we going, Cesari?" Vito asked.

"Cardinal Spellman High School. Remember it?"

"Of course I remember it. It was the best six years of my life."

I chuckled. "Me too. Well, on Baychester Avenue across from the football field way in the back is the old school bus garage. It was abandoned five years ago when they built a new one. We'll hide there and plan strategy. I thought about staying downtown somewhere, like in one of your garages, but there are way too many federal agents sniffing around, not to mention Brunella's men."

"How do you know all that about the Spellman bus garage?" he asked as I swung onto to the FDR Drive northbound. Traffic was light and I cruised along.

"Maybe if you went to a reunion once in a while, you'd know what was going on with your alma mater," I answered wryly.

"Excuse me, but I don't have the same fond memories of high school as you do. I wasn't the social butterfly you were."

I chuckled. "It's not my fault that girls liked me."

"Girls liked you? Now that's an understatement."

"It's your own fault, Vito. You acted like an asshole all the time."

"Shut up. I was shy. That's how I overcame it."

"By beating the crap out of anyone who went near a girl you liked? You were an asshole."

He finally let out a soft laugh. "Yeah, maybe—a little."

"Call your guy and tell him that we're going to make a slight detour and drop the transport guys off in the parking lot of the Bronx Zoo."

He made the call and I followed traffic on the Bronx River Parkway getting off at the Bronx Zoo exit. Five minutes later I pulled into the massive deserted parking lot and parked as far away from the entrance as I could. There was no one around. The zoo was open but early March following a recent snow storm wasn't exactly peak time for families to visit. I went to the rear with Vito and opened the doors. All eyes were on me, wondering what was going to happen. I released the two transport guys and helped them out of the van which they nervously exited. I would've been anxious too.

I said, "Wait for us to leave and then go. You never saw us, okay? I'm going to keep your wallets and cellphones in case you forget what I just said and I have to come find you."

They glanced at each other with apprehension and the senior one said, "We won't forget. Where are we?" Several hundred yards from the main entrance he couldn't quite make out the sign.

Vito said, "You're in heaven."

Without another word, we returned to our seats and sped off with the Q7 close behind. In fifteen minutes, we reached the abandoned bus garage behind our former high school. It was a large, old wooden structure that had fallen into decay across from the snow covered football field. The new, shiny garage was about a half mile away and was twice as large to house twice as many shiny modern buses. The old garage had no neighbors as it butted on the periphery of the Edenwald low income housing projects. Perfect. No one asked questions in places like this.

"How are we going to get into it, Cesari?"

"How hard can it be? It's made mostly of wood. We'll park out front and take a look. C'mon."

There were three oversized but ordinary looking garage doors with rusted metal handles at the bottom like you might see attached to any suburban home. Bending down, I grabbed the handle and pulled upward and much to my surprise the door groaned, creaked and slowly opened. It was very heavy and difficult to move so I redoubled my effort.

Straining and out of breath I said, "Vito, help me."

He crouched like a weight lifter, grabbed the bottom of the door with both hands and heaved. His lieutenant saw us toiling, got out of the Audi and joined us. Soon the door was over our heads and we went inside. We found an old rope attached to the track mechanism and used it to pull the door the rest of the way open. I guessed that was the backup system in case the electric motor failed. There was a normal door to the side of the garage's entrance. It was dead bolted from the inside and I unlocked it. Once the medical van was safely out of sight we cut its engine and reclosed the garage door. Vito and I went back out to the Audi to confer in private while his guy politely took a cigarette break. It was 3:00 p.m. and the high school was letting out. In the distance, we could see uniformed teenagers pouring out of the school and heading for their respective bus stops.

"Remember those days, Cesari?"

I nodded. "Like it was yesterday. Don't you wish sometimes you could go back and do it all over knowing what you know now?"

Vito was way too practical for these kinds of conversations. "Only if I could have the money I have now or else what's the point?"

"Yeah, I guess. Okay, we'll call Brunella when it's dark. In the meanwhile, send your guy out for some sandwiches and hot coffee."

"We got to stay here? Why don't we just go to a diner and eat like human beings?"

"I'd rather not leave him unguarded. I guess you can go if you want. Bring me back a chicken parm sandwich if you can find one."

"And if I can't?"

"Anything that's hot, all right? Tuna melt, eggplant parm, sausage and peppers, anything. I'm cold and haven't eaten anything since breakfast. Oh, and leave me a gun if you don't mind?"

He reached into his coat pocket and handed me a .45 caliber Kimber and then left. I went back into the garage and sat in the van. I thought about starting the engine for warmth but I had read too many stories about carbon monoxide poisonings from people doing stuff like that. As a compromise, I turned the key in the ignition enough so I could use the interior lights.

My phone buzzed again with another message from Frankie. *"Low fat milk, please."*

She was killing me. I texted her back okay again and then called Arnie.

"Cesari, I'm glad you called. This is some unbelievable stuff going on. Before I begin with that, I spoke with the surgeons who operated on that guy Carmine. I guess I didn't get the full story when I spoke to you about him. You'll never guess why he's still alive after receiving three gun shots over his heart at close range?"

"Arnie please. No guessing games. I have a lot going on."

"Because his heart wasn't there. He has situs inversus."

"You're kidding?" Situs inversus was an uncommon genetic variant whereby all the major organs were on the opposite side of the body where you might ordinarily expect to find them. His heart was on the right, not left side.

"Isn't that incredible? I mean his lung on that side is a mess and he's got chest tubes sticking out of him and who knows if he'll make it out of here alive but still pretty damn amazing. Lucky for him, but maybe not so lucky for the guy who shot him."

"Fascinating. What else?"

"Don't be cranky."

"I'm not but I'm busy."

"The FBI talked to me again this morning. They wanted more information about Seymour only this time they came with a police psychologist. They're trying to profile him as best they can, and you too, by the way, but he's the main guy for sure. What a nut case. I can't believe we worked with that guy for so long and didn't pick up on anything."

"Arnie…?"

"Well, when they went through his apartment in addition to finding the girl in the acid bath and the trap door and all those other skeletons in the sewer, they found a bizarre room on the main floor of the house where he kept the girls hostage before disposing of them."

"Girls? All the skeletons were female?" I remembered the compromising scene we found Lance in.

"Yes, why?"

"Just curious."

"Anyway, when they entered the room it was fully furnished but with ancient curtains, bed spread, radio, an old TV, furniture etc. On the dresser were pictures of his mother, alone and with him as a child. The closets were filled with his mother's old clothing. The only modern things in the room were the steel handcuffs they found attached to the bed posts and the rocking chair."

"Rocking chair?"

"Yeah, there was an old rocking chair by the window probably made in the 1940's by the look of it they said. Apparently, he would sit the victims up for a while every now and then. They could tell from the scratch marks and blood they found on the arm rests."

I sighed. "Terrible."

"It gets worse. Several of the skeletons had broken femurs."

"Femurs? What do you mean?"

"The forensics people think he may have tried to sit on their laps while they were cuffed to the chair."

"Jesus Christ."

"Yeah. By the way, most of the skeletons found in the sewer had multiple broken ribs and they suspect they were crushed to death like the girl in Vegas. And now that they found Seymour's DNA on that girl out there the FBI are convinced that he murdered her too."

"Where does that leave me?"

"They're not sure yet whether you're an innocent victim or some type of enabler. As far as they're concerned it's a toss-up. One scenario is that you seduced the girls with your good looks and greaseball charm, and then turned them over to Seymour to do his thing. Maybe he paid you off or gave you a piece of the action. Kind of far-fetched I know, but they brought it up."

"Please tell me you're kidding."

"Unfortunately, I'm not. I told them there is no way you had anything to do with this."

"And what did they say to that?"

"They said you'd better come in to talk to them before some of these theories become firmly entrenched in their minds."

I sighed. "Thanks Arnie. So what's the deal with Seymour? Got some sort of mommy complex?"

"They're still putting it together but it's definitely a possibility. You know, big fat kid, gets picked on all the time. Has trouble getting girls. The only woman in his life that treats him well and overlooks his physical shortcomings is his mother. She died several years ago of natural causes and he apparently snapped. His need to be with a woman who accepts him for who he is overwhelms him. He can't find one through normal means and somehow lures substitutes to his brownstone. Once there, God only knows what he did to them but certainly putting them in his mother's bedroom and trying to relive happier times was part of the scenario until he tired of that or his sexual desire for them overwhelmed him."

Then he brought them downstairs for fun and games followed by an acid bath. He clearly tortured them before he killed them. The shrinks think the reason for that may be his severe disappointment when he realizes that they really aren't his mother, or his anger at himself for his inability to control his physical need for them. They found traces of blood on his bed sheets and in the grooves of a pair of plyers that he kept in his night table. I don't even want to think about that. The only thing that's not clear is whether he is so delusional he really believes his mother is alive or whether this is just some complicated role playing game that turns him on. We may never know for sure."

I took a deep breath and let it out slowly. "Damn."

"Yeah, it's pretty bad."

"Well, I was just calling to let you know I was still alive and was curious how Carmine was doing."

"He's hanging in there. It's still too early to know for sure what the long-term prognosis will be but he's definitely improving."

"Okay, thanks Arnie."

"Are you doing okay? I guess this news is a mixed bag."

"Yeah, kind of depressing. I mean we knew he was bad but this kind of news really puts a face on it. I'll stay in touch."

"Okay. Talk soon, all right?"

"Yeah."

I clicked off and sat there thinking about it. Carmine had situs inversus or else he'd be dead. What a stroke of bad luck for Vito and me. And then there's Seymour… Those poor girls. What a way to go.

I called Vito.

"Keep your shirt on Cesari. I'm having trouble finding a place that makes decent Italian food."

"Fine, do me a favor."

"What?"

"Find a hardware store or Walmart and pick me up a crowbar."

I opened the porthole and looked in on Seymour. He was awake and turned his head in my direction. He made an unintelligible muffled sound through his taped mouth and I saw dried blood caked on his face around the bloodshot and swollen eye I had thumbed.

"Don't worry Seymour. It'll be all over soon."

Chapter 42

By the time Vito returned with a hot meatball sandwich and a crowbar, it was after 5:00 p.m. and I filled him in on things as I ate.

"Unbelievable," he said after learning about Carmine's situs inversus anatomy. "But I'm not surprised about Seymour though. It was obvious that he was half-baked. And I wouldn't worry too much about the Feds. They're just blowing smoke. They've done that to me dozens of times. You just have to look them in the eye and say prove it or shove it. Never back down or show fear with those guys."

"Yeah." I looked at my watch. "It'll be dark soon. It's time to call Brunella."

She answered right away. "Who is a this?"

I had spoken to her previously pretending to be Seymour so I masked my voice speaking in a low guttural tone. "It doesn't matter. You're looking for the fat man, right?"

She was silent for a few seconds. "Yes."

"Well, I have him. He's up in the Bronx gift-wrapped for you in the back of a medical ambulette. Go to Cardinal Spellman High School on Needham Avenue. You can't miss it. In the back just past the football field is an old bus garage that should've been torn down. He's in there."

"How I know this not a trap?"

"A trap? Why? Besides, you don't have to come yourself. Send some guys but with a big car or a massive trunk."

"Who are you and why you do this a for me?"

"Let's just say I'm a concerned citizen and would like to see the hostilities come to an end before any more unnecessary blood is shed."

She thought about that. "I send men up there. One hour." She hung up without saying goodbye.

"Okay Vito, it's a time to say a the goodbye to Seymour." I said mocking Brunella's accent which made him chuckle.

He said, "I'll meet you outside in the Audi."

Holding the crowbar, I went to the back of the van, opened the doors and climbed in. Seymour looked at me nervously. He had no idea what was coming but just like one of his victims, he knew that it was inevitable. He lay on his back with his large bulk sandwiched between the stretcher and other equipment. I checked to make sure his restraints were still fastened tightly and they were. Leaning over him and without warning, I ripped the tape off his mouth. He grimaced and sucked in air like it was his first day out of the womb.

"Hey Seymour. I just wanted to let you know that Brunella is on the way. She's very excited to meet you."

"Brunella? Carmine's mother. Why does she want me?"

I smiled. "You'll find out."

"Cesari, let's talk about this. C'mon we can work it out. I got money."

I wanted to laugh but couldn't. "I don't think so Seymour. The world will be a better place without you, and besides, there are too many dead girls and their families that need closure. By the way, are you going to tell me what happened in Vegas? I know you killed the girl out there so don't bother lying to me again, and I kind of got a handle on some of it. You were pissed off at me for the way I treated you. I got that much. So you set me up for some sort of fake sexual assault charge. I assume you paid Luther and the girl to drug me, but why did you decide to kill her? Some sort of last minute change of plans?"

He sneered as if he thought I was mentally challenged, but as he thought it over I could tell that he came to the conclusion that it might be better to keep me engaged. He said, "I guess it doesn't matter who knows what at this point."

He was right about that. "Not really."

"Well, you got the gist of it. You were drugged and she was going to cry rape, but in reality, she was dead the minute she accepted the job. She just didn't know it. How she could have been so stupid as to think that I would leave a loose end like her floating around is beyond my comprehension. The fact that you went ape-shit on her with the knife was just icing on the cake. Where did you get the knife from anyway?"

I bristled at him. "What?! I didn't do that to her. I thought you did. Are you lying to me again?"

My temperature was rising and I raised the crowbar causing him to shrink away. "I'm not lying. I admit I killed her but cutting people up isn't my thing. I crushed her and left her on the floor. I just assumed you woke up in a drug fueled haze and went berserk. Why would I lie?"

"Because it's what you do."

"Look, whatever helps you sleep at night, all right? But if you didn't do it then I don't know who did."

He was such an asshole. I wasn't even sure why I was wasting my time on him. "Was Luther in on the murder?"

"No, not at all. He helped set everything up but after we brought you to the room, I paid him and he went back to the restaurant. He didn't want to be anywhere in the vicinity when the police came."

"And you?"

"I told Jenny to call me when she was done with you and before she called the police. I offered her a bonus for an encore performance with me."

I shook my head with disgust. "With me unconscious on the bed?"

"*Because* of you being unconscious on the bed."

I thought about that and guessed that somehow, in his warped mind, that act made him feel superior to me. I said, "And then you called the police using her phone?"

"No, I never called the police. It wouldn't have made sense. She was dead and you were unconscious. I know how the place works. Sooner or later somebody would've found you. It would have seemed more natural that way."

"The police received a distress call from Jenny. Who made it if not you?"

This news seemed to surprise him and he contemplated it for a moment. "I don't know. She wouldn't have made it before I got to the room because if the police came while I was there she never would have gotten paid. Besides, I was with her a solid half hour, maybe longer. That would have been more than enough time for the police to respond to an emergency call on the strip and she certainly wasn't calling anyone after I left."

I thought about that. Something didn't add up but I was running out of time. "You know, Seymour, a guy like you really might have benefitted from some serious psychiatric intervention."

"Oh please, Cesari. I don't need lectures."

I considered smacking him with the crowbar but my cellphone buzzed loudly in my pocket. "Hi Kelly."

"Cesari, you're coming to the apartment later, right?"

"Yes, Kel, I was planning on it. I'm almost done."

"Good, because Frankie and I did a little grocery shopping so you don't have to stop."

"I thought she wanted pizza."

"She did. We'll do that tomorrow."

"Okay, fine. Well look, I'm a little tied up right now, but I'll see you later."

"Bye."

I hung up and turned back to Seymour who looked at me in disbelief. I said, "All right, Seymour, I don't have any more time to waste. Dinner's waiting."

"Who's Kelly?"

I chuckled. This guy never stopped. "None of your business. Now open your mouth."

"What?"

"Seymour, there are two ways we can do this. One is you open your mouth or the other is I beat you with the crowbar until you're unconscious and then I open your mouth for you."

He took a deep breath and opened his mouth. I said, "Wider."

He opened it as wide as possible and I quickly placed the crowbar in crosswise as far as I could, wedging it tightly between his back molars. He instinctively struggled as fear and panic entered his eyes.

I said, "Take it easy big guy. You're not going anywhere and I can't afford to have you try to talk your way out of this with Brunella."

He grunted and squirmed as terror took hold but he was helpless. I took out the .45 Vito had given me and using the butt end as a hammer slammed it as hard as I could upward into his chin using the crowbar as a fulcrum. His lower mandible cracked as did several of his teeth. He jerked, groaned, and then passed out from the pain. I removed the crowbar along with three teeth. The force of the blow must have caught his tongue because it was already turning purple and starting to swell. I closed the van doors and went outside.

Climbing into the passenger side of the Audi I said to Vito, "Let's go."

"Did you and Seymour have a tearful goodbye?" he asked smiling sarcastically.

"Yeah, he was all broken up."

Chapter 43

He dropped me off in front of Kelly's apartment. I had to make a decision where I was heading with Kelly and Frankie. I was thrilled that Kelly had warmed up to me but she was feeling bad about Omar and probably just needed a pick-me-up. I hated the idea of just being the rebound guy. Part of me wanted to accept that role if that's all she was offering but part of me still felt very strongly about her and knew I would eventually be devastated by it. Then there was Frankie. She was starting to have feelings for me but had accepted that Kelly was my alpha female. I didn't want them to be rivals. That would be bad for everyone.

There was only one solution. I needed to disappear and not stay at the apartment. Kelly could use some companionship and Frankie needed a safe place to heal. If I was out of the picture it just might work out. I would pick up my clothes and make up some excuse why I had to leave. I could check in by phone to make sure everything was all right.

When I knocked on the door Kelly answered. "Hi."

"Nice apron, Kel."

Wearing a pretty, floral patterned apron she smiled and hesitated before letting me in. I got the impression she might have kissed me if Frankie wasn't standing behind her watching.

I walked in and took off the jacket Vito had brought me. "Hi Frankie."

"Hi John. Why are you wearing hospital scrubs?"

"It's a long story. Everyone have a good day?" I asked.

They both said yes and Kelly said, "C'mon in. Dinner is almost ready. You can open the bottle of wine. Frankie, would you mind setting the table? There are dishes in the overhead cabinets and utensils in the drawers just below."

"I'd be happy to," answered Frankie.

I said, "Thanks, but you don't have to set a place for me, Frankie. Kelly, I was a little tied up when you called earlier but I had a sandwich with Vito about an hour and a half ago. I'm not that hungry right now."

Frankie said cheerfully, "I'll set one anyway. You never know. You might want to try it."

She had a point. "Fine."

I uncorked a bottle of Pinot Grigio and poured three glasses as she set the table. Kelly served the stir-fry and we sat to eat. I sipped my wine and studied the two women in front of me, detecting a subtle yet undeniable tension in the air. I had slept with both of them and even though they were being friendly, I doubted it would last long. This was one of those situations that catholic school never prepared me for. I looked at Kelly and then at Frankie. Kelly looked at me and then at Frankie. Frankie looked at her plate. She was the odd man out and obviously was acutely aware of that. Fortunately, I was a man with a plan.

I cleared my throat. "I have to meet Vito later. It'll be late so I probably will just stay over at his place tonight. There won't be any need to make the couch up for me, Kel."

Frankie was instantly alarmed and said, "But you told me it wasn't safe for you to go down there right now!"

Kelly asked, "Because of the police?"

Frankie added, "Yes, that, and there's some crazy mob woman, Brunella, who wants his butt in a sling because he beat up her son trying to help me."

"Thanks for the update Frankie." I said drolly.

"Well, it's not safe for you to go there and you know it."

Kelly said, "Not to mention you made the headlines in today's news, remember?"

"He did?" Frankie asked almost gagging on her stir-fry.

Kelly answered. "Front page of The New York Post no less." She filled Frankie in on the details as I felt myself losing control of the conversation.

This wasn't going quite as I had hoped. I said firmly, "Nonetheless, I have to go but I do promise to be careful and stay in touch. Now if you both don't mind, I'd like to clean up and change. Kel, did you remember to get my clothes from the locker?"

"They're in the bedroom. I don't like this Cesari. It doesn't make sense. Call Vito and tell him to come up here."

"Yeah, that's a better idea," added Frankie.

Jesus.

"He can't come up here. He's got too much to do and I already told him I'd meet him. I promise I'll be careful. Look, if it will make everyone feel better I'll go late, after ten. Whoever is looking for me will have to take a break some time. I'll let Vito know. That should be fine."

They glanced at each other and rolled their eyes in frustration.

I finished my wine, stood and said, "Okay, I'll see you guys in a couple of minutes."

As I walked away I could hear them tsk, tsking me. I didn't mean to make them worry. Turning Seymour over to Brunella had greatly reduced my risk but I had no intention of telling them about that. There was no point in making them accessories after the fact.

I went to the bedroom and spotted my clothes in a neat pile on a chair. Before changing, I decided to shower quickly to cleanse myself of Seymour's stench. When I was done, it was almost 8:00 p.m. and there was a bottle of Johnnie Walker Black on the coffee table with three glasses already poured. I was a little surprised.

"I don't remember you being a scotch drinker, Kel."

"I never was until Omar got me started and Frankie wanted some so why not? C'mon, have some with us before you go. We have a lot to be thankful for. Besides, I'm off the next two days." She was in a decidedly better mood now and Frankie too.

"Really? So what do you have planned tomorrow?" I asked.

"Going to pick up the kids in the morning for starters."

Frankie said, "Can I come with you? I'm dying to meet the kids."

"Sure, I'd like that."

I said, "Frankie, don't you have to make a doctor's appointment?"

Kelly answered for her. "Already taken care of, Cesari. Tomorrow afternoon at 3:00 p.m. with my gynecologist. We'll be back in plenty of time. All right, is everybody ready for a toast?" They hoisted their glasses up so I picked mine up as well. We clinked and sipped to each other's health.

Kelly suggested we watch a movie before I went to see Vito. Frankie concurred and I nodded. I didn't care what we did as long as I wasn't here when the lights went out.

"So what's playing?" I asked watching her scroll through her channel selections on the flat screen TV opposite the sofa.

Kelly said, "How about *Gladiator*? It's starting now and I've always wanted to see it."

Frankie nodded vigorously in agreement. "I've never seen it either. I heard it's really good."

I was surprised. Not that they hadn't seen such a widely acclaimed movie but because I didn't think women went for that kind of manly *cut your head off* stuff. I said, "It is really good; which is why I've seen it four times. Isn't there something else we can watch? I really don't think it's your kind of genre."

Frankie laughed. "You don't think we can handle it? Don't be a wet noodle. We want to see it."

Kelly said, "Yeah, don't try to keep us down."

I smiled. "Okay, suit yourself, I don't care. I never get tired of watching guys in skirts kill each other."

Kelly got up. "Have a seat, Cesari. I'm going to get a bowl with ice so we don't have to keep getting up."

I sat toward one end of the sofa and Frankie toward the other with a space in between for Kelly. When she returned, she turned the lights down and nudged me with her knee to move in toward the center so she could sit at the end with me in between them. I made a face but scooched over. I hated being in the middle and I didn't know why. Maybe it was because I liked to lean on the arm rest or maybe it made me feel trapped. Now I couldn't cross my legs. Plus, I felt kind of silly trying to keep up with conversations on either side. I sighed deeply.

The movie started and we settled in. Fifteen minutes into it Frankie picked up the scotch bottle and refreshed her glass. Kelly leaned across me with her glass and Frankie obliged. As a matter of courtesy, she refreshed my glass as well.

Thirty minutes into it the glasses filled themselves again, despite me shaking my head no. I said to Kelly, "Hey, take it easy."

"Relax, Cesari."

Frankie said, "Hey, this is fun."

Kelly agreed.

I said, "If you like watching people get slaughtered and their homes burned I would have to agree."

"That's not what I meant silly. I meant this—us."

"Yes, it is," Kelly concurred. "I haven't laughed in a while."

I said, "If you wanted to laugh you picked the wrong movie."

Kelly answered that with, “Don’t be grouchy.”

They both started giggling. Then Frankie said, “Hey, I want to make another toast.”

“Go for it, sister,” Kelly said egging her on.

She stood slightly unsteady, raised her glass and said, “Here’s to gladiators.”

Oh brother. A glass of wine, maybe two, and two scotches and she was already gone.

Kelly raised her glass too. “I’ll drink to that.”

Hesitantly, I raised my glass wondering if I was going to get to see the rest of the movie in peace. We clinked again and I watched as Kelly and Frankie downed their glasses in big gulps insisting I do the same. What the hell were they thinking? Is this what girls did when guys weren’t watching? Am I one of the girls now?

Frankie plopped back down on the sofa next to me and Kelly refilled the glasses. They were more or less quiet for the next ten minutes when Frankie said, “That Russell Crowe is quite a hunk.”

I looked at her noticing that she had slid closer to me. I could smell the scotch on her breath. Before I could say anything in response Kelly chimed in. “I bet he’s got a big one.”

They both started laughing uncontrollably. Frankie raised her glass. “Here’s to big ones.”

Kelly also raised her glass. “Someone had to say it.”

Jesus Christ! I looked on shocked and Kelly nudged me, smiling a big Kelly smile. “C’mon, don’t you agree?”

I didn’t know what to say and suddenly saw myself sitting on the couch next to Oprah while an audience full of women hissed me. I raised my eyebrows and said, “I guess.”

They chugged their scotch and I took a small sip of mine. Frankie said, “He didn’t drink his all the way.”

Kelly pouted. “You have to drink. That’s the way it works.”

“Really?”

Frankie also was upset. "Don't ruin the fun. C'mon."

Letting out a deep breath, I downed the rest of my scotch. Thankfully, the bottle was almost empty. I was feeling the effects of the alcohol. My toes were a little numb and I was definitely getting fuzzy. In fact, I had lost my place in the movie. Even worse, I'm not sure that I cared.

Kelly stood and wobbled into the kitchen and returned with a huge smile, holding a bottle of vodka in one hand high in the air and shot glasses in the other. She danced and twirled her way back to the sofa and landed in my lap, laughing. She was flat out drunk.

She said, "Frankie, pour us a shot, will you girl? I want to make a toast."

"Got your back, girlfriend," Frankie said in response as she took the bottle and filled three shot glasses.

I looked at my watch. We had just finished a bottle of scotch in little over an hour. That was pretty good by any standards. I said "Um, Kel. Am I missing something? Maybe we've had enough?"

She put her arm around my neck, looked at me and raised one eyebrow. "Frankie, he thinks we've had enough. What do you think?"

Frankie slurred, "It's never enough."

Laughter again as Frankie passed around the shot glasses. I had one arm around Kelly and Frankie was sitting next to me way too close for comfort. She said, "Bottoms up big boy."

What the hell was going on? We downed the shots and after five more I had no idea what my objection was in the first place. In fact, I could barely recall what I was going to do when the movie ended. Wait a minute, it just came to me. Were they trying to stop me from going downtown by getting me drunk? Of course they were. Asking a guy to watch *Gladiator* was like putting a piece of cheese in front of a mouse.

Kelly staggered to her feet and exclaimed merrily, "I have an idea. Let's play truth or dare."

"Great idea," shouted Frankie slapping my thigh with her hand.

Ouch.

The movie was almost over and I was seeing double. There was no way I was going to play truth or dare. This whole night had degenerated into a teenage girl's pajama party.

I said, "I don't think so."

Deciding it was time to leave, I started to stand and Kelly pushed me back down and Frankie latched onto my arm. "Where do you think you're going?" Kelly demanded, smiling.

I looked at the four of them, two Kellys and two Frankies, saying, "I can't remember." They both guffawed.

"C'mon, play with us. It'll be fun," Kelly pleaded and then using the remote, turned the TV off. She knelt on the floor in front of me leaning on the coffee table.

Frankie scrunched next to me on the sofa. "Pretty please."

For crying out loud. This was so stupid—and unnecessary. I felt like saying *I know what you two are up to*. Exasperated I said, "Fine."

They started cheering.

Kelly said, "I'll start." She turned to Frankie. "Truth or dare?"

"Truth."

"Have you ever worn men's underwear and whose if you have?"

Oh brother.

"Ewww. Never. My turn. John, truth or dare?"

"Dare."

"Pull your pants down and do a shot of vodka."

Kelly cackled loudly.

"I'm not doing that."

"You have to," she admonished.

"No, I don't."

"Kelly, tell him."

"John, you have to."

Chuckling I stood up, unbuttoned my jeans and pulled them down a few inches while Frankie poured me a shot. When she saw she said, "Hey, that's cheating. All the way down."

I took the shot glass from her and chugged it. "Sorry but you didn't specify how far down."

Kelly smiled. "He's got a point."

Frankie pouted. "Cheater. Okay, it's your turn."

"Okay, Kelly. Truth or dare?"

"Truth."

I hesitated. We were all very drunk by now and it would be easy to say or do something stupid. I suddenly didn't care. "Kelly?"

She smiled and her face glowed from alcohol. "Yes, John."

Holding her hands, I gazed into her beautiful green eyes which were opened wide and beckoning. Soft and large with long lashes, they were angelic and brought me to my knees every time I looked at them. I said, "Do you still love me? Because I never stopped loving you." I paused for a moment feeling my heart race and added, "I love you Kelly—with all my heart. I always have and I always will."

Her smile slowly faded from her face as her lips started to quiver and her eyes welled up. Slowly she stood and careened off to the bedroom, crying.

Damn! I buried my head in my hands and took a deep breath. What's wrong with you, Cesari? Just because she slept with you doesn't mean she loves you. This was the twenty-first century. It didn't even mean she necessarily liked you.

The room was suddenly very quiet. Frankie asked, "Are you okay?"

"I just laid it all on the line, Frankie, and got burned so I guess the answer is not really."

When she didn't say anything, I turned toward her regretting my peevish tone. She had a serious look on her face which I couldn't read. "What are you thinking?"

She replied softly, "I think that if you ever told me you loved me in just the way you told Kelly that I would gladly give you my life."

She inched close and placed her hand on my thigh.

Chapter 44

My head throbbed and my mouth felt like it was stuffed with cotton balls when Kelly's door buzzed loudly at 2:00 a.m. I had fallen asleep fully clothed on top of her bed and she lay next to me under the covers. I was pretty disoriented and couldn't quite remember exactly what happened after vodka shot number four. I had made a fool out of myself with Kelly and had followed her into the bedroom but she was in the bathroom crying. So I laid down on her bed intending to wait until she came out so we could clear the air or at least so I could apologize for ruining the night. The buzzer screeched impatiently again.

I slid off the bed and went to see who it was, passing Frankie sprawled out on the sofa with her mouth wide open. I remembered something else now. Frankie had made a pass at me which I politely declined. I chalked it up to alcohol and hoped everyone would wake up with amnesia.

I pressed the intercom button. "Who is it?"

"It's Vito. Let me in."

I buzzed him in and waited with the door open. A minute later he appeared at the top of the stairwell looking agitated.

He said, "Cesari, pack your bags."

"Take it easy. Come in and keep it down. Everybody's sleeping." I went over to the sink, poured myself a tall glass of cold water, drank it down and tried to focus. "So what happened?"

He looked at Frankie and the liquor bottles and rolled his eyes. "I should be asking you that same question."

"Am I going to have to repeat myself?"

"I paid one of the ICU nurses at St. Matt's to let me know if there were any changes in Carmine's condition. I told her to call me day or night and she just called. Less than an hour ago he opened his eyes and started talking."

Shit.

"You're kidding?"

"Start packing."

The news jolted me and my hangover suddenly took second place. "Can we tone down the drama? You said he's talking but what is he saying?"

"You think I want to find out?"

"Look Vito. The guy was severely traumatized. He may not remember things too well if at all. Let's not panic."

"That's not something I want to count on, Cesari. We either need to finish the job or start running. If word gets out that I shot him I won't have any support from anybody. Needless to say your head's on the chopping block too."

I let out a deep breath. My head's been on the chopping block for a while but this would definitely shut down any possibility of reconciliation with Brunella. Could we get to Carmine in the ICU? Maybe. My brain raced with options.

"Let me go splash some water on my face and let Kelly know I'm leaving."

"Where are we going?"

"I don't know yet but I need coffee and we need to let them sleep."

In the bathroom, I freshened up and brushed my teeth. Rousing Kelly, I told her I was taking off. Whether or not she would remember was a different story. Back in the living room, I nodded at Vito and we left the apartment, grabbed a couple of black coffees at an all-night diner down the block and caught a cab to St. Matt's. The Vietnamese driver didn't speak a word of English but seemed to understand where St. Matt's was.

"This sucks, Cesari, and it's all your fault."

I raised my eyebrows at him. "My fault? You're the one who shot him."

"Yeah, but you dragged me into this in the first place. You took advantage of our friendship."

"Oh please, spare me. What about me? I had a great medical career. I helped people."

Vito was indignant. "And I don't? Is that the way you see it?"

"How on earth do you help people?" I asked, astounded by his logic.

"Look, I provide services and entertainment to people who for a variety of reasons can't go through normal channels. They in turn respect what I do and in their gratitude compensate me well."

"Jesus Christ. Is everybody on this planet delusional? I'm a doctor, Vito. I don't go around killing people."

He laughed. "Now who's deluding himself? Doctors kill more people every year than any other single profession and I include the military on that one."

"Are you quite done yet?" Talking with him for a few minutes like this was exacerbating my hangover.

"So what are we going to do when we get there?" he asked.

I sipped my hot coffee and felt it reach the back of my eyeballs propping them open. "I don't know. Right now I just want to see how alert he is before I buy a plane ticket out of here. Is your nurse contact still there? She might be able to help us."

"No, she was just leaving when she called. She wasn't feeling well so they let her go home early. You think Brunella is there?"

"That's a tough call. I'm sure she's discussing Seymour's personality flaws with him as we speak but when she hears Carmine's waking up she'll probably head over to see him as soon as she can break away. So I don't know."

"Do you think there's a chance we could take Carmine out tonight?"

"That's a different question entirely. It's two in the morning. Whoever is guarding him will be a little sleepy and now that they have Seymour, everybody will probably be lightening up a little. So, maybe, but I just don't see how we could pull that off without getting caught. Every nurse there knows me."

I thought that one over for a minute. Even if I had unrestricted access to Carmine what would be the best way to do it without leaving evidence? Smother him with a pillow? Inject him with potassium? They acted too quickly. I would still be in the room when his monitors would start ringing. Guns and knives were out of the question for the same reason. It had to be some delayed action that ended his life after we had left the room and something no one would suspect. It had to appear more or less natural. The guy was recovering from massive trauma and internal bleeding. He was still in critical condition so that his physicians wouldn't be totally shocked if he took a sudden turn for the worse. It happened all the time at this stage of the recovery period.

I suddenly snapped my fingers. "I got it."

"What?"

I looked out the window. We had reached Union Square Park and were just a few blocks from the hospital. I leaned forward. "Driver, stop the car. Vito pay the guy."

Vito paid him and followed me into the center of the park as I searched around looking for what I needed. "Hey, Cesari, mind telling me what's going on?"

"Shh, I have an idea. Look, over there." He followed my gaze to a group of three men sitting on a bench talking. They were in their late twenties, unkempt, smoking marijuana. One had a blanket wrapped around his shoulders. The temperature was in the low fifties without a breeze. Not exactly summer but not particularly cold either.

"Cesari, you have got to be kidding me. They're crack heads."

"Exactly."

We approached them nonchalantly and they stopped talking, taking notice of us. I said, "Hey guys."

The one with the blanket nodded but didn't speak. He was white with long hair in dreads and a scruffy beard. I assumed he was in charge. The other two were just dirty. Denizens of the street, addicted to whatever, living from day to day. I was sure they were trying to determine if we were the law so I decided to break the ice quickly. "My friend and I are not cops."

They liked that and seemed to relax a little. The guy under the blanket said, "How can I help you?"

"I need to score a hit—a big hit, preferably Smack, and I need a needle too."

"You sure you're not a cop?" My approach was too direct and too white bread for him, like I had seen it on television or read about it in a book, and he was still suspicious.

"I'm not a cop and neither is he. Vito tell them."

Vito said, "I'm not a cop."

The guy thought it over. "How much of a hit?"

"How much you got?"

The guy smiled. "I got ten bags left. It's been a slow night. You got money?"

"I'll need a needle and a spoon."

I took out the roll of money Vito had given me and asked, "How much?"

The guys eyes went wide when he saw the cash and I noticed the two other guys gradually move to either side hoping to outflank us. I didn't like the look in their eyes. Vito noticed as well and quickly pulled out his Glock. Everybody froze in place.

"Don't be stupid." I admonished. "Everybody stay calm."

The leader raised his hands and said, "Be cool, man. Here's your stuff. No need for violence." He handed me the small plastic bags along, with a couple of needles and a tablespoon. "Peace."

I threw three hundred in cash on the ground in front of them and we backed away in silence. No one said anything. A single hit bag ran about ten bucks so they were making out. Hopefully, they would be so filled with joy they would forget they saw us. Safely away, we quickly exited the park heading for St. Matts.

Vito was irritated. "What the hell was that all about? We going to get high before seeing Carmine?"

"No, but I have an idea and I'll need your help. Now shut up and listen."

Chapter 45

Once in the hospital, we made a beeline for the ICU stopping in the public restrooms outside the entrance. We emptied as much of the heroin into the spoon as possible added a few drops of water, cooked it with Vito's lighter and sucked it up. By repeating the process we were able to use all ten bags and fill both syringes.

Proud of my work, I looked at Vito. "Okay, cap off the needles and put them in your pocket and let me do all the talking."

"You sure this is going to work or just make things worse?"

"I'm not sure of anything but that his condition is extremely fragile right now. The last thing he needs is a heroin overdose and since his body is filled with narcotics from post op pain meds and his recent surgery, no one will be able to pick it up in a lab test. The best part is the reaction won't be instantaneous and will give us a chance to get out of here. Regardless, I'm not going in the room with you. I'll keep the nurses occupied just in case things go sideways and I need plausible deniability. I still plan on working here when this is all over. Remember, inject both syringes into the little plastic nipple in the IV tubing and then get out the hell out of there. And don't forget to take the needles with you."

We left the bathroom and walked up to the ICU entrance. The double doors were closed and locked so I pressed the button and stood in front of the overhead camera.

A voice crackled over the intercom. “Dr. Cesari, is that you?”

“None other.”

The door swung open and we proceeded directly to the nursing station where I waved hello to several sleepy nurses sitting at a dark quiet desk. They looked at me as if I was a ghost.

The senior nurse Barbara smiled and stood to greet me. “My, oh my. I thought I’d never see you again let alone in the middle of the night.” She was a battle-hardened forty year old, thrice divorced, man-eater. Rumor had it she had a tramp stamp that said: If you’re reading this then you ain’t pushing hard enough.

“Good to see you as well, Barb. How are things?”

“Things are fine but the real question is, how are you? And who’s your cute friend?”

“Vito say hello to Barb.”

“Hi Barb. It’s a pleasure to meet you.”

“Hmm.” She was quite attractive in a large breasted, wide hipped, I’ll take you down whenever I feel like it sort of way. She was always on the prowl, like a tiger. “So tell me, Cesari, what on earth has been going on and are you guilty of half the things they say you are?”

“Barb, we’ve known each other for years. You know I’m not. I didn’t do anything you might have heard, seen, or read about.”

“You didn’t have sex with that hooker out in Vegas? The one they say you might have killed.”

I stammered. “I didn’t kill her.”

“But you did have sex with her right before she was murdered?”

Damn. Why did women care about stupid details like that?

I sighed. “It appears that way.”

“Why are you guys here, Cesari?”

“That guy, Carmine, the one who was shot. He’s a friend of ours. We went to school together. We heard he’s coming around and just wanted to make sure he’s okay. You think we could see him?”

She looked at me like I was crazy and then chuckled. “Are you serious? It’s three in the morning and you’re wanted for homicide or whatever. I can’t let you into that guy’s room even if your cute friend is undressing me with his eyes.”

I looked at Vito who had the most neutral of looks on his face. She either had a wild imagination or more likely was offering a trade. I said, “I understand. How about you let Vito in to see him and you and I can catch up over coffee? He was mostly Vito’s friend anyway.”

She said, “Well, I like coffee. How about you, Vito? Maybe you can join us after you say hi to your friend?”

“Yeah, I like coffee and did I mention that Vito’s unattached.”

Vito blinked and she smiled. I liked modern women. It was so nice to lay everything out in the open. She said, “He’s in bed 9. Come along, Cesari, and tell me why I shouldn’t call the police on you.”

“Is there anybody in there with him?” Vito asked.

She replied, “His bodyguard of course, and don’t wake him. He’s like an octopus with my girls. He’s sleeping in a reclining chair.”

We went into the nurses break room where there was a pot of bad coffee and small Styrofoam cups. She filled one for me and I sipped it, wincing. It tasted like it had been made several hours ago, possibly several days ago.

She sat opposite me at a small table. “So what really happened and what’s going on with Seymour? Is he really a serial killer like the papers are saying?”

I sighed and nodded. “I’m afraid so. I think he killed the girl out in Vegas too.”

She rolled her eyes. “Wow.”

“Yeah.”

“And what about you? No one believes you did anything but it sure looks bad, like maybe you helped him.”

“I had nothing to do with any of it, Barb, but I know it looks awful. I’m still trying to figure out what I should do, but I definitely appreciate your support. My morale has been kind of low lately.”

She nodded, thought it over, and relented. “If you want to see your friend, go ahead. I never saw you.”

But I didn’t want to see my friend. I wanted to keep her talking so that she would remember I was with her the whole time if it ever came to that. “Thanks, but this is kind of nice talking to you. We haven’t chatted in a while.”

She looked at the wall clock. “Aww, that’s sweet but I really have to make rounds.”

“I understand. I’m sorry to see you’re on the night shift again. That must be a royal pain.”

“You’re telling me? I’ve been trying to move to days for months now. I even threatened to quit.”

“You did?”

“Yeah, so they offered me a nickel more an hour to stay.”

I snorted. “And you accepted that? It’s insulting.”

She laughed. “Well, it’s better than a nickel less an hour which is what they said was going to happen if I kept complaining.”

As I chuckled, Vito appeared in the doorway. “Carmine’s sleeping and I don’t want to wake him up. He looks pretty bad.”

Barb said, "What did you think he was going to look like?"

I said, "I think we'll go now."

She looked disappointed. "No coffee, Vito?"

"He smiled, "Can I take a rain check?"

"Sure can. Well, I have to get back to work. Good night guys."

"Good night, Barb—and Barb…?"

"Yes?"

"You never saw us, right?"

She grinned. "Saw who?"

Hastily exiting the hospital, we breathed a sigh of relief and hailed a cab. I turned to Vito. "So how'd it go?"

"Like a charm, except you didn't tell me there was a camera in the room."

"Shit, sorry."

"No problem. I just repositioned it before I did anything. The bodyguard was snoring. He's going to catch hell if they ever find out what happened."

"You remembered to take the needles, right?"

"Yeah, I got them in my pocket."

"Good. Now let's keep our fingers crossed. Not everyone dies of a heroin overdose but in his frail state and the fact that they will have low suspicion as to what's going on, it just might work. Besides, we gave him enough to kill a horse. So Carmine looked pretty bad, huh?"

"He was awake, actually, but very weak. He could barely talk. Didn't even open his eyes. I told him I was the night nurse."

I chuckled. "Really?"

"Yeah, he was so drowsy he barely knew where he was, but I'll tell you this. We did the right thing tonight."

"How so?"

"He was really out of it, right? So I leaned down and whispered Hey Carmine, who did this to you? And you know what he said?"

"What?"

"Two assholes from the Bronx."

Chapter 46

I crashed at Vito's, exhausted, and when I woke at 11:00 a.m. I noticed three missed calls from Kelly so I dialed her.

"Hi Kel."

"John, where'd you go? We were worried."

"I'm sorry. Something came up. Vito needed me in a hurry and it was late so I slept at his apartment. I tried to tell you but you were really out cold. So was Frankie." She sounded fine and I was optimistic that she was so drunk last night she didn't recall much.

"You did? I don't remember that. I guess we really did overdo it, didn't we? John, why did you have to go there?" she asked with concern in her voice. I had forgotten about the ruse they had tried to keep me uptown.

"It's okay, Kel. I'm fine."

She sighed. "Will you be coming back to the apartment?"

"I can be there in an hour. I just need to shave and shower."

"Frankie and I are on the road right now. We're on our way to Yonkers to pick up the girls from my aunt's. In fact, we're almost there. We'll probably stay for lunch and then come back. Frankie has a doctor's appointment at three."

I smiled. "Okay, I'll see you then."

After showering, I found Vito in his living room sipping espresso while talking animatedly on the phone. I went into the kitchen, poured myself a cup from the pot on the stove and rejoined him, taking a seat on his sofa. After a minute or two he hung up, looked at me and broke out into a broad smile.

"He's gone."

Assuming he meant Carmine, I breathed a sigh of relief. "Any fall out?"

"Not yet. Word is that about a half hour after we left, he quietly lapsed into a coma and stopped breathing."

I knew there had to be much more than that, but so far so good. "Brunella must be hysterical."

"I'll say. I heard that she showed up in the ICU while they were trying to resuscitate him and that she fainted and wound up in the emergency room herself.

"Geez."

He rubbed his hands together clearly contented with his work. "All right Cesari. Things are looking up for us. Carmine's finally dead like he was supposed to be and Brunella's got Seymour. Case closed."

I had to admit it. Everything seemed to be falling into place nicely. "I agree. Things should start to settle down from here. I might even go have a chat with the FBI to clear the air. They got nothing on me but pure speculation and they have way more on their plate now anyway."

"I'm not sure I like that idea, Cesari. Why don't you just wait to see if they come looking for you."

"I could do that. The only real question is whether Brunella will still hold a grudge against me for what I did to Carmine in Vegas."

He contemplated that for a moment and said, "After Carmine's funeral and the dust settles we'll know better but at least then I'll be able to put a word in for you. You know, that maybe you were a victim of circumstances etc. etc. I'll play up the Seymour angle hard with her and that he caused all the trouble. She's smart. She knows it wouldn't be good for business at this point to continue the bloodshed. Nonetheless, it wouldn't hurt for you to go on a little vacation if you know what I mean. Let's give Brunella some space to grieve."

I thought about that. I should talk to Arnie. "You're probably right."

"Okay, Cesari, I got work to do."

"Are you dismissing me?"

"That's exactly what I'm doing."

I chuckled. "I can take a hint. I'll talk to you later."

I let myself out and walked over to my apartment on Sixth Avenue near Washington Square Park, figuring it was probably safe. The entire city was preoccupied with Seymour's disappearance and now, Carmine's death. I hadn't been there in over a week and scanned around carefully before crossing the street to enter the building, just in case. Once in the apartment, I immediately noticed that the place had been ransacked by the police looking for evidence. It was water under the bridge now so I locked the door behind me and started tidying up. Holding my nose, I dumped everything out of the refrigerator into a large heavy duty garbage bag and then swept up broken glass softly muttering under my breath.

The bedroom was a disaster. The mattress had been turned upside down and every item of clothing in the closets and the drawers had been tossed onto the floor. After a couple of hours the place was starting to look normal again so I took a break and called Arnie.

"Cesari, have you heard?"

"Tell me."

"That mobster, Carmine, died last night."

"Really, I thought he was doing better?"

"Well, better is just a relative term when you're in the condition he was in."

"What happened?"

"It's not clear. He appeared stable and at about three in the morning suddenly went into respiratory distress and had to be re-intubated. It's possible he was getting too much narcotics for pain or that he just wasn't ready to be extubated. Who knows? He might have had pneumonia. Anyway, he started having grand-mal seizures which they couldn't break and eventually went into cardiac arrest. While all this is going on the mother shows up and starts having fits; screaming and tearing her clothes. She passes out and has to be brought to the ER. Even worse…" He lowered his voice as if someone might be listening. "We may have committed the worst case of malpractice I ever heard of."

He got my interest with that. "How so?"

"Remember, I told you he had situs inversus?"

"Yeah…?"

"Well despite the fact that it was written all over his chart, in the middle of all the pandemonium, everyone forgot. During CPR they placed the paddles on the wrong side of the chest and injected epinephrine directly into his lung not his heart."

"Oh boy."

"You're telling me? When the mother finds out about this we are talking major lawsuit at a minimum."

"Does she have to find out?"

"You know she does, Cesari, and I'm the one who has to tell her. The only thing that could possibly make this worse is if we tried to hide the facts from her."

He was right. "Sorry about that, Arnie. I don't envy you. By the way, how's Lance doing?"

"He's fine. Really seems to have calmed down and accepted his role here. I'm keeping my fingers crossed. He starts his remedial training in ERCP at Sinai next week. Hey, I found out why he left Cabrini in the middle of the night. Get this, he was having an affair with the chief of GI's wife. When the guy found out, he fired Lance on the spot."

I already knew this, but that was Arnie for you, a day late and a dollar short. "Well, how about that. I knew there had to be a good reason. Say, Arnie, I don't mean to change the subject but how would you feel if I took a couple of weeks off?"

"Sure, if you want but you don't have to by the way. I don't know if you've heard but it's pretty clear Seymour acted alone in the sewer murders. They scoured his hard drives and found the ads he placed on Craigslist to lure the girls to his brownstone. So the theory that you were helping him seems to be out the window as far as I can tell. In Vegas they also found a connection between him and the dead pimp including multiple phone calls, text messages and emails. He's been going out there on a regular basis for at least two years. When they interviewed the girls at the ranch out there they all knew him. They even had a nickname for him, the gas man. The New York police have turned the case over to the Feds and the Feds told me that at this point they would like you to come in and give a statement but that they're really not after you. I think you should, Cesari. I have the name of a good lawyer if you want. You might as well bring this thing to a close and get on with your life."

I thought about that. I knew Vito would disapprove but I really did want to get on with my life. "I think I will talk to them Arnie, but I already have a lawyer. Thanks."

"That's my boy. You're starting to be reasonable. I feel like I should look out the window to see if pigs are flying by."

"Arnie…"

"Sorry."

"Okay, it's settled. I'll take a couple of weeks off, and by the time I return, I'll have everything straightened out with the Feds."

"Great."

After I clicked off, I cleaned up and caught a cab up to Kelly's apartment arriving just before 6:00 p.m. She and Frankie were busy preparing dinner and I suspected some type of salad with chicken. I greeted them and got right to the point. "Hi guys. So where are the girls?"

Kelly said, "They had a long day and just passed out. Sorry, I couldn't keep them awake. Come with me and we'll take a peek."

We walked together into the twin's bedroom. They each lay peacefully sleeping in their own crib. The room was decorated in playful pastel colors with a dominant yellow theme highlighted by pink accents and stuffed animals.

Kelly put her arm through mine and beamed. I said, "They're beautiful, Kel, like their mother."

"Thank you, but I see so much of you in their faces. I did from day one."

I smiled. "For their sake, I hope not."

Kelly chuckled. "You know, John. I spent a lot of time talking to Frankie today. I kind of like her. She's very sweet."

"That's good. Can I assume the doctor's appointment went well?"

"She's fine. Well, I've been thinking—I need the company and she needs a place to stay so I was considering asking her to be a nanny for the girls at least for a short time until she gets back on her feet. It would be a great help if she agrees. What do you think?"

I hesitated just a fraction, thinking about last night but discarded my concerns. She was drunk, I was drunk, we were all drunk. Besides, no harm, no foul, right? I said, "I think she's really nice. I approve of the idea and I think she will too."

"I knew you would but I'm glad to hear it anyway. I'll ask her after dinner. It will be such a relief not to have to truck the kids back and forth to Yonkers every time I'm on call." She then became silent as if thinking something over. She looked at me in earnest. “John—I didn’t answer your question last night. That was inconsiderate of me.”

Uh oh.

I really didn’t want to review the litany of reasons why it could never work out between us. Been there and done that. Well, if she didn’t have amnesia then I would have to be the one so I feigned ignorance and said, “Which question? I was pretty plastered last night.” That was easy. Now we could both move on without any awkwardness.

She didn’t buy it and forged ahead. “You asked me if I still loved you.”

Our eyes met but I didn’t say anything.

She hesitated, started sniffling and glanced at our sleeping angels. “John, I never—I never stopped loving you. Not even for one second of one minute of one hour of one day.” By the time she finished, she was so choked up she could barely speak and tears streamed down her face. I wrapped my arms around her and she did the same to me as she continued. “With every beat of my heart I could feel your soul next to mine. I always have. We were meant to be together.”

“But I thought…?”

“I was wrong for pushing you away. I was trying to fight something I shouldn’t have. When you love someone you have to accept them for who they are not who you want them to be.”

I was overwhelmed with surprise and joy. The kind of joy that if you’re real lucky you may experience once in your entire life. After a few moments of poignant silence I whispered, “Kelly, I have loved you with all of my heart ever since the first day I laid eyes on you. I know that I am probably the most imperfect man you will ever meet but if you let me I will work hard every day for the rest of my life to be worthy of your trust and of your love. I promise to be the best father your children could ever wish for and—the best husband any woman could ever want."

She looked up at me confused and I brushed a tear from her eye. "John…?"

"Kelly—we've wasted way too much time. Will you…?" I choked on the words. I had never proposed to anyone before and didn't realize just how vulnerable it could make you feel. What if she said no? I mean, just because she loved me didn't necessarily mean she wanted to go any further. I was suddenly massively confused and filled with self-doubt.

"Will I what?" She asked, looking puzzled.

My heart pounded in my chest and I was having trouble breathing. Feeling as if I was in front of a crowded theater with no clothes on, I tried again, stammering. "Will you…?"

She smiled, amused. "What?"

I couldn't look at her and say it. Fear of rejection overwhelmed me. I needed an escape route. I said, "Stay here."

Leaving her in the bedroom, I walked quickly past a somewhat bewildered Frankie in the living room to the hallway outside the apartment. Pausing for a moment to take a deep breath and collect myself, I called Kelly on my cellphone.

"John, what's going on? Where'd did you go?"

I scanned around. If she said no I could run down the stairwell and hide my hurt feelings. I took a deep breath. "I'm in the hallway outside the apartment."

"Why…?"

I interrupted her. It was now or never. "Kelly, I love you. Will you—marry me?"

My heart pounded so hard I could feel it all the way to the top of my ears as I waited for the sky to fall. There was silence for a moment as she digested my offer. She said with newfound authority in her voice, "Don't move, Cesari."

I hung up and stared at a spot on the wall. I was agitated and sweating. My desire to flee was overwhelming. I needed water. Moments later, the apartment door opened and she followed me into the hallway. Throwing her arms around my neck, she pulled me down to her and kissed me tenderly.

She whispered in a breathy voice, “Yes.”

Frankie stood in the open doorway watching.

Chapter 47

Seymour swung gently to and fro in a gentle arc, barely conscious and barely caring. He had been hanging cold and naked by his ankles from a steel I-beam all night in Brunella's basement in Brooklyn next to rows of home-made prosciutto. He had killed enough people to know that the end was near. He had given up any hope that he was going to get out of this alive. His broken jaw was extremely painful but nothing in comparison to the pain Brunella and her men had been inflicting on him. The old hag had stamina that was for sure. She had participated with every lash and every blow torch application, and personally enjoyed poking him with the cattle-prod. It didn't matter, death wasn't too far away and he welcomed it. Maybe he would see his mother again. Wouldn't that be nice?

He had passed out once or twice and they threw buckets of ice water on him to revive him. He had nothing to offer them in exchange for a reprieve of his suffering. With his broken jaw, he couldn't even beg for clemency. Even worse, they didn't want anything from him. This was pure blood sport for them and he didn't even know why. Carmine had died and she blamed him, that much was clear, but he didn't even know about it until they had told him. Then it hit him.

Cesari! Of course. That peckerhead was always at the bottom of his problems. It had to have been him but how he managed to throw him under the bus was a mystery. He looked around through bloodshot swollen eyes, his arms dangling downward. With outstretched numb fingers he could almost touch the floor. The witch had taken a break and had been gone for a while. He couldn't tell how long because he had lost all track of time. Maybe she was taking a witch nap. If only he could explain to her that it was Cesari she wanted to punish.

He heard the door to the basement creak open and knew his suffering would soon begin again. Brunella came down with several of her men and took a seat at a small table she had set up to watch the festivities. The men set a plate in front of her and opened a bottle of wine. As they served her he could smell the pleasant aroma of veal parmagiana waft through the air. The bitch was going to eat dinner?

In between mouthfuls of veal she ordered one of her men. "Let him a down, Tannenbaum." A big guy, the size of a small barn, unhitched the rope that held him suspended in the air and he crashed to the floor, laying there barely able to feel his face.

"Sit him up."

Grabbing him roughly under his arms, they heaved him up to a sitting position. He leaned against a steel support post as he gradually felt his equilibrium returning.

Brunella hissed at him as she lit a cigarette. "You kill a my baby boy, Carmine. For that, you must a suffer for long time. No die quick. Long a time." The determination in her voice caused him to shudder and he made a whimpering sound as if he was trying to speak but couldn't form the words. The one called Tannenbaum kicked him in the side to shut up.

"You must a drink to stay alive," she ordered.

Another guy standing next to Brunella opened a plastic bottle of something, maybe soda, maybe a sports drink, shoved a straw into it and handed it to him. It occurred to him that with his great weight serving as a source of nutrition all he needed was fluids and he might live for weeks. He refused to allow that. He took the offered drink and threw it at the wall. He immediately felt the painful shock of the cattle-prod shoved into his side by Tannenbaum. He winced, gasped, and pissed on the floor. After two failed attempts at rebellion, he eventually took the bottle and drank the sweet liquid, sucking it down through the straw in one long draft.

Brunella finished dinner in silence, pushed her plate away and strummed her fingers on the table studying him like a cat might study a mouse. His brain raced with ways to alleviate his suffering. If only he could convince her that she had the wrong guy. After an ugly and menacing silence, she said, "You sleep. I have a big a day planned for you tomorrow."

Alarmed at this, it suddenly came to him how he could communicate and he whined at her, desperately gesturing with his hands for a pen and pad to write on. He was rewarded with another jolt from the cattle-prod and then another.

Brunella finally interceded, raising her hand. "Enough, Tannenbaum." She looked at Seymour with contempt. "You want a tell me something?"

Recovering from the latest bursts of electricity, tears streaming down his face, he nodded weakly and again signaled with his hand for a pen. She took a drag from her cigarette and blew it out in his direction as she thought it over. Finally coming to a conclusion she said, "I know already what you want a say."

His eyes went wide and he was suddenly confused. She continued, "You want a say that you no do. Somebody else a killa my boy. Am I no right?"

He nodded vigorously, his heart pounding with hope. She understood. She really understood.

Turning to her men she laughed sarcastically.

“They all a say the same thing.”

Chapter 48

"This is such bullshit, George." I was angry and hissed at my attorney. "You made me wear a suit and tie for this kangaroo court. I can't believe it." We had been arguing since 8:00 a.m. when we met for breakfast at a nearby diner to review my situation. It wasn't my clothes that bothered me. I was frustrated and needed to lash out at someone.

George was a Bronx boy too. In his early fifties, in solo practice, he had represented me several times over the years. He was an inch shorter and twenty pounds heavier than I was. A solid weightlifter type of guy, he had taken his fair share of punches back in the day. He rode a massive Harley and liked to hang out in biker bars in his free time. Right now he looked very corporate wearing a three piece, gray wool suit, crisp white shirt, and blue tie.

"Relax, Cesari. First of all, it's not court, it's a deposition, and I can only tell you what the FBI told me they could do. It doesn't mean they'll do anything and as far as the suit is concerned, it always helps to look like an upstanding citizen. Besides, I don't know what you're complaining about. You look great. You should dress like this more often." I wore a two piece navy suit, white button down shirt, and solid red tie. I looked like a politician and let out a deep sigh.

I had spent the last two nights at Kelly's apartment and when I left this morning to meet George I had tried hard not to let on to her the gravity of the situation. She thought this meeting today was simply a formality because a week ago that was what I was led to believe. But since then they had found Seymour's mutilated body floating in the East River and public angst had reached a fever pitch. Whoever had dumped Seymour in the water had tied a cinder block to his ankles but hadn't taken into account the buoyancy of fat and he had easily floated to the surface where he was discovered head bobbing up and down in the current. Now, with no one in leg irons, the Feds were giving me the full court press.

We were standing outside FBI headquarters at Federal Plaza in Manhattan. It was a beautiful day and the temperature approached sixty degrees. George had been negotiating with them all week for the terms of my voluntary testimony. They in turn had laid out a list of potential charges and options at my disposal. It appeared that they had me by the short ones should I not cooperate. Not wishing to be on the run for the rest of my life, I decided to take George's advice and play ball.

However, the bastards had slipped a last minute monkey wrench into the works. They had called George late yesterday afternoon and told him the new conditions and I was indignant. I said, "Look, George, I'll cooperate to the best of my ability, but I'm not going to wear a wire for these guys. Vito's my friend. That's just not going to happen. I'll do anything but betray him like that. If they want him in an orange jumpsuit they'll have to figure it out for themselves. Besides, I didn't do anything and they know it."

He nodded and looked quite somber. "Very admirable, Cesari. That may be your position at the moment, but consider this, there's an avalanche of circumstantial evidence that's piled up against you. One, you were with the dead girl in Vegas and freely admitted you fled the scene. Probably wasn't smart to do that if you were innocent like I know you are. Two, they found your finger prints in Seymour's apartment and on a flashlight near the skeletons in the sewer. Once again, circumstantial, I know, but it certainly appears that you might be connected."

"Oh c'mon. They know Seymour acted alone and I already explained to them what I was doing in the apartment. They should be thanking me for cracking this thing wide open for them."

"They would be more grateful if they had Seymour to interrogate, but they don't and never will. The public is on edge even more now since they found his corpse because the only thing scarier than a psychopathic serial killer is someone who isn't afraid to torture and murder a psychopathic serial killer. Understand? Right now the citizens are demanding somebody be locked up and you're all they got."

"I can't believe this. I'm innocent."

"I'm going to ask you one more time. Do you know what happened to Seymour? Because if you did, that would go a long way with these guys. They need someone to feed to the press and the public."

I thought about that and sighed. Admitting I kidnapped Seymour and turned him over for mob justice would probably not help my case. In fact, it would probably make things a lot worse for me. I said, "No, I really don't. Now, do you have any good news for me?"

"I understand how you feel, but you've been evading the law for two weeks following a felony and bodies are turning up everywhere you go. It's understandable that the feds are a little ticked off, and then there's the vehicle in which Carmine was shot. The steering wheel and doors had been wiped clean but there's the sticky matter of the crowbar they found with your finger prints all over it. Not good."

"But he was shot not bludgeoned to death," I protested. "I was helping Lance remodel his apartment and I forgot my crowbar in his car."

"Yeah, right. How could I forget? Look, you're singing to the choir, Cesari. We've been going over this for hours. To a jury of twelve New Yorkers you seem like a guy that should be put behind bars just on the principle of the matter. And you're lucky that doctor friend of yours, Lance, is sticking to his guns about his car being stolen because if he even hinted that he loaned it to you, you'd be up that proverbial creek."

"You sound like you don't believe him?"

He rolled his eyes. "Please..."

"So now what?" I asked dejectedly.

"Okay, let's go over this. Murder—not a chance. The burden of proof is too high. Accessory to murder—hmm. I don't like that one, but probably not. Multiple counts of obstruction of justice. Oh boy, we definitely don't want to go there. You'll light up like a Christmas tree on the fourth of July."

Another comedian.

"Great. So, what am I looking at potentially?"

"Depends on whether they play softball or hardball, but I'm thinking not more than one or two years—tops. Bargain it down..." He rubbed his jaw thinking it over. "You're basically a good guy—and juries do like doctors. I'd bet you wouldn't spend more than six months inside, like Martha Stewart. Enough to catch up on your reading and make friends with a few rappers."

I looked at him deadpanned. "Are you out of your freaking mind? I'm paying you five hundred bucks an hour and this is what I get?"

"For seven hundred bucks an hour I could get it down to three months."

"What?!"

"That was a joke, Cesari. Lighten up."

Great, a funny lawyer.

He continued, "Look, they may not charge you with anything but if they play rough, there's always the option of wearing the wire. So smile a lot and be cooperative. Don't say anything unless I tell you it's okay. Just follow my lead, all right? They might just be blowing smoke to intimidate you. All right, are you ready?" He glanced at his watch. "It's almost eleven."

I snorted, "Yeah. How long is this going to take anyway?"

Sarcastically he asked, "Are you in a rush?"

"A friend of mine has been dog-sitting for me in New Jersey and I was hoping to beat rush hour traffic when I go pick her up this afternoon."

George shook his head, clearly frustrated. "I'm glad you got your priorities straight, Cesari, but the answer is I don't know. I would bet at least an hour, probably two, maybe longer. There's a lot of stuff we have to go over."

Just as we reached the entrance George turned to me and said, "One more thing, I got my own federal government problems so my fees are cash only, all right?"

Nice guy.

"I got it, but how about we stay focused on me? I just got engaged to be married and really don't have time to go to prison."

George shook his head and rolled his eyes.

"The Feds are going to love you, Cesari."

Chapter 49

Four hours, four cups of coffee and three trips to the bathroom later, I was ready to pass out from fatigue. A burly, sullen faced agent named Howard Drexler had been pinning my ears back mercilessly in front of a camera. We went through my story again and again and again. He was hoping to trip me up but failed. I had been to this rodeo before with much worse characters than him. He was an experienced guy maybe forty years old and looked like he spent a lot of time in the gym. He knew I was holding back something but wasn't sure what.

George intervened, "Agent Drexler, my client has been fully cooperative and truthful. I assure you that he doesn't know any more than what he has already told you."

Drexler snorted, "Yeah, right. Your client stinks to high heaven and you know it. Sooner or later I'll figure out exactly what he's hiding. Pretty convenient that your pal, Seymour, shows up dead just days before you come in here."

The interrogation room was a standard fifteen foot square, antiseptic white with a two-way mirror and cameras on the walls. The table and chairs were metal and uncomfortable. The coffee sucked and I didn't like his attitude.

I said, "I already told you he wasn't my pal. I hardly knew him."

"Yeah, right. I remember you saying that."

Objecting vehemently George said, "Dr. Cesari is an upstanding citizen. He's an outstanding member of the medical community and in good standing at one of New York's finest hospitals. He is the victim of circumstances and his behavior during these difficult times is quite understandable."

Drexler slammed his hands down on the table. "Your client is an unmitigated asshole and I don't care how many degrees he has."

I was hungry, frustrated and losing my patience. He had just pissed on my leg and I wasn't happy about it. Abruptly I stood up and angrily said, "You got nothing on me so shove it up your..."

George quickly grabbed my arm to calm me. Drexler furrowed his brow and was silent for a while thinking it over. He said, "Let's move on to a different topic."

Looking at George, I rolled my eyes and sat back down. What more could he possibly want to talk about? George said, "Whatever we can do to help, Agent Drexler. We're all on the same side here."

He said, "How could I forget? Why don't you tell me about that hooker who helped you in Vegas?"

I was wondering when he was going to get to that. He had asked a few brief questions early on but that was it. It was almost as if he was saving something special for last.

"I already told you all I know."

He sat back in his chair and folded his arms in front of him. "So tell me again."

He was a cocky bastard for sure. "When I woke up, I panicked and ran into the hallway. She saw me, brought me into her room, and showed me the escape hatch in the bathroom. I never saw her again. I don't even know her name." I had decided to leave Frankie out of it. She was too vulnerable and with her past, I was afraid these guys would destroy her. Correction, I knew for a fact these guys would destroy her.

"You didn't find that strange? Some prostitute you don't know just decides to help you?"

"What can I say? I have a nice face. Look, I was drugged in a whorehouse with a dead girl I never met before. What's your definition of strange?"

Drexler snorted. "Fine, did you know that she used to date Carmine Buonarotti?"

Now that one took the wind out of my sails and I had to hold back my surprise. "I told you I don't even know her name. How would I know something like that?"

"Well, she used to be Carmine's main squeeze before the dead girl, Jenny, came along and took her place. According to the other girls at the Fall of Rome she didn't exactly take it too well either."

My brain raced with this news and I felt a knot forming in my stomach. "What does this have to do with anything?"

"A lot. So pay attention. Are you sure you never saw her again? Because she's missing and several of the girls at the club think she might have run off with you."

He had clearly knocked me out of my comfort zone and knew it. "Well, they're confused."

George interjected. "Agent Drexler, maybe it would help if you got to the point. One of the girls from the brothel has disappeared. We get it but what's that have to do with my client?"

"That's what I'm trying to figure out. Everywhere your client shows up somebody dies or goes missing. Only in this case, it would behoove him to think harder about whether he has seen her since that night."

I leaned forward, thoroughly engaged. "And why is that?"

"Because the knife we recovered at the scene of the murder was wiped clean—almost. We found a partial thumbprint on the handle. Not enough by itself to identify whose print it was."

I said, "So?"

"Well, for a while we thought it might have been your print but it didn't check out. Then your pal Seymour surfaced as a homicidal maniac so we naturally turned our attention toward him but it didn't match his either. Now this is where it gets interesting." He paused for effect and I listened intently not sure where he was going with it. "We decided to go over the crime scene again only this time we had someone climb up the bathroom ladder and sweep both the inside and the outside for prints and guess what?"

I couldn't help myself and blurted out. "What?!"

"They found a couple of your girlfriend's fingerprints with traces of the victim's blood on the outside metal handle. One of the prints was a thumbprint which matched up perfectly with the partial one on the knife."

I gulped and my heart skipped a beat. I suddenly felt really hot. This didn't make any sense.

"What are you getting at?" I asked my heart sinking.

"You tell me, Cesari. You're the one with the nice face."

I couldn't accept the implication. Frankie? No way. My brain raced for a benign reason that her finger prints could have been on the murder weapon but I couldn't think of one. She didn't exactly lie to me about Carmine but she wasn't forth right about her relationship with him either. Why did she help me escape?

I said, "Look, I'm not as smart as you guys. I'm sure there are lots of reasons her prints could have been on that knife. Maybe she helped Jenny chop onions one night."

Drexler cracked a smile—a very small one. "Very funny, but there's one more thing. Our forensics people have been having a tough time with this case but they finally seem to have come to a conclusion. They believe that the girl was crushed by Seymour the way he did to those other girls in New York. Only he must have been in too much of a rush because she didn't die. She was unconscious when he left the room but still alive. We now think your girlfriend found her there half-dead, dragged her into the bathroom and finished the job, escaping through the roof."

I couldn't believe my ears and suddenly remembered Seymour's adamant denial of cutting Jenny up. He insisted that he had only suffocated her. Then there was the 911 call from Jenny's cellphone. Seymour said he didn't make it and there was no way Jenny could have and if she didn't then…? Oh my God! I was rapidly becoming alarmed for Kelly and the kids. What if it was true? I wanted to call Kelly but the FBI had confiscated my phone until after the interview.

"Why would she do it? Because of Carmine?" I asked, desperation in my voice and beads of sweat forming on my brow.

"To regain her rightful place on the throne? Sure, that's certainly a possibility. Don't ever underestimate jealousy, Cesari, especially when it comes to women. There could be a number of other reasons of course, but I like that one the best."

"But why would she help me escape? That doesn't make sense." My voice almost cracked under the strain.

"Sure it does. I've given it quite a bit of thought and the answer is quite simple. You wake up ahead of schedule and run into the hallway before the police nab you. She spots you and makes a split second decision that it's far more important to her who they don't blame, rather than who they do blame. In front of a dozen witnesses she helps you and takes a very public beating for it. She had to have known what the consequences were going to be. However that suited her purpose because it permanently cemented in everyone's mind that she could not possibly have known what happened to Jenny. Only someone totally innocent or totally crazy would have helped you that night. You were the best alibi she could have hoped for and there's more—much more"

I felt like I was going to throw up.

Chapter 50

I ran out of the FBI building in a cold sweat with George in hot pursuit. I should have told them where Frankie was but I couldn't accept what they had said about her. I had to give her a chance to tell her side. Deep down, I knew there had to be some logical explanation for all of this. George grabbed my arm. He was agitated and out of breath. "Cesari, what the hell is going on?"

"I can't explain George." When I turned on my cellphone I saw three missed calls from Kelly and a series of texts asking me why I hadn't called all day and that she had dropped the kids off at her aunt's in Yonkers. She and Frankie were going to a play and dinner afterward if I wanted to join them. She didn't say which play but indicated that they might stop at Sardi's on W. 44th Street across from the Shubert Theater. I called multiple times but she didn't pick up.

"What do you mean you can't explain? Do you know where that hooker is or not?"

I broke away from him and stood in the middle of the street urgently hailing a cab. "I mean what I just said. I can't explain." A yellow cab with an Indian driver pulled up and I hopped in, giving him directions to Kelly's apartment. Rolling down the window I said, "I'll call you as soon as I can, George. Thanks for your help today. I'll send you a check."

As the car pulled away he called out, "Cash. Don't forget. Cash. Not a check."

Twenty minutes later, I threw a fifty on the front seat, jumped out of the car before it came to a full stop, and sprinted up to Kelly's apartment. It was after 7:00 p.m. and I doubted they would still be here but I had to try. I had hoped to catch them before they went out. I fiddled frantically with the key Kelly had given me and burst through the door, calling out for them.

Shit.

No one was here. I called Kelly again on the phone but no answer. I didn't like the feeling I was getting. Frantically, I searched the apartment for a clue—anything— and then I saw it and held my breath. The chef's knife was missing from its space in the wood butcher block on the counter. I checked the sink and then the dishwasher. My heart pounded and my fear grew when I couldn't find it. This couldn't be happening.

Calm the fuck down, Cesari. There has to be some logical explanation. You're letting your imagination carry you away. Frankie's been through a lot recently. Maybe a night on the town was a little nerve-wracking for her and she wanted the security of having a weapon with her. Maybe it was Kelly who took the knife. Who was I kidding?

Suddenly, I remembered what Frankie had said to me when she found out Kelly and I had slept together. "I knew you were going to throw me away. Guys always throw me away."

My head throbbed as I started to panic. The theater district was crowded but it was also quite large with many dark passageways and alleys between buildings. All Frankie had to do was lure her into one of those alleys after the play, kill her, and make it look like a robbery. Two young women, alone, late at night in a dangerous city, a violent assailant, who wouldn't believe it? I had Frankie's phone number but I hadn't wanted to alert her. Besides, what if I was wrong? Talk about looking foolish. Well, better to look foolish than to be right. I called her.

"Hello, John."

I breathed a sigh of relief. "Frankie, where are you guys?"

"We're in the theater district. Are you okay? You sound out of breath?"

"I'm fine. Is Kelly there? I've been trying to reach her but she's not answering her phone."

"We had a busy day so she might have put it on silent to catch a break. Right now she's in the bathroom. We just got to the theater. I'll have her call you as soon as she comes out. So how'd it go with the FBI?"

I bit my lip, thinking. "The deposition went fine. Which play are you seeing? I think I'll try to make it down there and join you."

"You're being silly. You'll never make it in time. Besides, can't the girls have a night out together?"

The sound in her voice made me shiver. There was something decidedly different, something icy and ominous in her tone. I started to shake. "Frankie?"

"Yes, John."

"Frankie, please…?"

"John…?"

My voice cracked and trembled as I went all in. "Please don't—hurt Kelly."

She was silent for a few seconds. "It's going to be all right, John."

Oh God!

In for a penny in for a pound. "Amelia, I can help you. Please let me."

There was more silence before she responded. "You've done your homework. I knew you were resourceful. How'd you find out?"

"The FBI figured it out. They found your fingerprints on the knife you used to kill Jenny and on the escape door in her bathroom."

"What else did they tell you?"

"I know you've been playing me ever since we met in that hallway in Vegas. I know you've been bipolar since you were ten years old and prone to fits of severe depression and anger. I know that you had a twin sister named Francesca and at the age of sixteen you stabbed her to death in a fit of jealous rage over some boy. You spent two years in a psychiatric facility and escaped. It was a minimal security place and one day you just disappeared. You've managed to keep a low profile until now. I also know that you're not an orphan. The FBI has already contacted your parents. Amelia, please, don't make this any worse than it already is."

She hesitated and might have been crying. Barely audible she murmured, "Carmine was good to me—until Jenny came along. Then everything changed. She stole him from me. She didn't even know how much I hated her for it. She needed help moving you around that night and setting things up so she called me. I was in her bathroom when Seymour showed up. I stayed in hiding while he raped her. I could have helped her but I didn't want to. She deserved it and then she didn't even have the decency to stay dead. All I did was put her out of her misery."

I exhaled. "Where'd you get the knife?"

"We all kept one in the bathroom just in case."

I nodded. "Tell me where you are Amelia. I'll come down and we can talk it over. Kelly is a mother of two small girls. Let's leave her out of this. I'll do anything you want but please—please don't hurt her."

"Kelly is a bitch just like Jenny and Francesca. They always get what they want and I get nothing." The anger in her voice was as startling as it was frightening.

"I'll do anything, Amelia. Please, just give me a chance."

"Anything?"

"Anything."

There was an ominous silence as she thought it over. Then slowly she whispered through tears, "Tell me that you love me."

I hesitated. "I love you, Amelia."

She laughed bitterly. "You really do love her, don't you? Well, I'll be sure to pass that along. Bye, John." She paused a moment and added, "We had fun, didn't we?"

"Amelia…?" She hung up and I raced to the door, bounded down the stairs to the street and caught a cab to Sardi's. I didn't know where else to go. On the way, I called Agent Drexler and admitted that I had lied to him about my relationship with Amelia and told him what I suspected she was up to. Naturally, he was pissed but agreed to meet me at Sardi's as quickly as possible as a starting point for the search. I was relieved that he shared my sense of urgency.

I reached the restaurant and frantically searched in every direction. It was dark, approaching 8:00 p.m., and I hadn't a clue. I just needed to do something. Across the street was the Shubert Theater. The scrolling marquis announced that tonight was the last night for Matilda.

Matilda?!

During our escape from Las Vegas, Amelia had mentioned that Matilda was her favorite childhood book and how much she had wanted to see the play. I went to the ticket counter and asked the woman if there were any seats available. She politely informed me that I was out of luck. Going around to the rear of the building I found the employee entrance and a couple of stage hands catching a quick smoke before the start of the show. No one challenged me as I let myself in. In fact, they seemed amused or high and I wondered what they were smoking.

Inside was a madhouse of activity, as crew and cast readied themselves for action. Everyone was too pre-occupied to care about me. I was just another guy in a suit, so I wandered through the back stage area trying to get a view of the audience. One last time, I tried to call Kelly but again she didn't respond. Just then, loud applause erupted from the audience signaling the start of the show.

In the dark, I bumped into a metal pole and realized that it was actually part of a series of ladders leading to the catwalk over the stage for the crew to access lighting, cameras, and other support equipment. This would give me the best view of the audience so I climbed up slowly until I reached the top, easily twenty feet over the stage. There were one or two other guys up there with me fiddling with wires and lighting angles. They didn't pay any attention to me. They had their job to do and presumably I had mine.

On hands and knees, I crawled as stealthily as possible. No easy feat in dress shoes. Eventually, I reached a positon where I had a reasonably good view of the audience from the curtain's edge and scanned around carefully row after row. There they were! Balcony, left-center, three rows from the front. Not bad seats. They looked happy.

Now what?

I took out my cell phone and called Drexler, quickly updating him. As I returned the phone to my pocket, I was startled by someone tugging on my pant leg, and dropped it to the stage below. I looked back and saw a stage hand who ordered me quietly to get down.

The phone hit the wood floor and clattered loudly, causing everyone in the audience and cast to suddenly stop what they were doing and look up at me. I had to act quickly and decisively. Any unusual activity might provoke Amelia into hastening her plans, but turning back now wasn't an option so I grabbed the edge of the curtain and leapt off the catwalk. The curtain tore under my weight and I floated briskly toward the center of the stage rolling to a stop. The audience gasped in horror and the cast shrank away from me. I immediately jumped to my feet unhurt and looked toward the balcony.

Kelly and Amelia saw me and rose to their feet in shock and surprise. Without hesitation I hurdled myself off the stage into the front row of patrons. Stepping on arms, legs and shoulders, I mercilessly made my way to the aisle and bolted toward the balcony as people screamed and called for security. Others rushed for the exits as mass hysteria suddenly swept through the crowd. I fought my way up the stairs through the mob and entered the balcony from the left side, spotting Drexler and one of his men coming in from the right. Amelia saw me first and then Drexler with his gun drawn.

Kelly stared at me wide-eyed in bewilderment, and with no chance of escape, Amelia reached into her Michael Kors handbag, retrieving the twelve inch chef's knife. From behind, she grabbed Kelly by the hair and arched her head backward. She held the blade up to Kelly's exposed throat and screamed, "Stop!"

Backing up slowly, she pulled Kelly with her until she reached the balcony railing. Drexler and I froze in place. I pleaded, "Amelia, put the knife down. This has gone on long enough."

She didn't respond. Her eyes darted back and forth and down behind her. Those who remained in the theater pointed and shouted their fears. Kelly was off-balance in an awkward position. Any moment could be her last.

Drexler said, "I'm special agent Drexler with the FBI, Amelia. Let's be reasonable. There's absolutely no chance of you getting away with this so let's not hurt anyone else."

Amelia looked at me. I could see the fire in her eyes but she was unusually calm. "I'm never going back there, John."

"Amelia, you need help. I will stay with you every step of the way. I promise. Just put the knife down and let Kelly go."

Our eyes met and she held her gaze there steadily and then said softly, "John, say it again. I need to hear you say it one more time—please."

I glanced at Kelly, and Amelia pressed the blade into her flesh a fraction more. Kelly winced. She was confused and frightened. I whispered hoarsely, my voice dripping with fear. "I love you, Amelia."

She paused for a few seconds, the tension thick. Finally, she said, "Thank you for that."

Suddenly, and with great force she thrust Kelly forward unharmed, pointed the knife into her own abdomen and rolled backward over the railing. The crowd below roared in horror. I rushed forward, hugging Kelly who was trembling uncontrollably. Drexler ran to the balcony railing gun extended searching for her as the other agent ran down the stairs.

"Are you all right, Kel?" I asked gently as I held her tightly in my arms.

She nodded. "What just happened?"

"It's a long story. It might take a while for you to wrap your head around it. Let's get you somewhere safe and I'll fill you in on the way."

Agent Drexler holstered his weapon and hustled down the stairs with us following close behind. Below, we found the other agent kneeling by Amelia checking her carotid pulse. She lay face down on the floor between two rows, the point of the blade projecting several inches out from her back. Blood stained her cream colored top and pooled beneath her. Her head lay at an unnatural angle, eyes staring lifelessly at nowhere in particular. The agent looked up at us and shook his head.

Kelly buried her head in my chest and started to sob. "Why, John?"

I let out a deep breath and shook my head.

"Sometimes there is no why."

The End

About the Author

John Avanzato grew up in the Bronx. After receiving a bachelor's degree in biology from Fordham University, he went on to earn his medical degree at the State University of New York at Buffalo, School of Medicine. He is currently a board-certified gastroenterologist in upstate, New York, where he lives with his wife of twenty-nine years.

Inspired by authors like Tom Clancy, John Grisham, and Lee Child, John writes about strong but flawed heroes.

His first four novels, Hostile Hospital, Prescription for Disaster, Temperature Rising and Claimed Denied have been received well.

Author's Note

Dear Reader,

I hope you enjoyed reading The Gas Man Cometh as much as I enjoyed writing it. Please do me a favor and write a review on amazon.com. The reviews are important and your support is greatly appreciated.

Thank you,

John Avanzato

Hostile Hospital

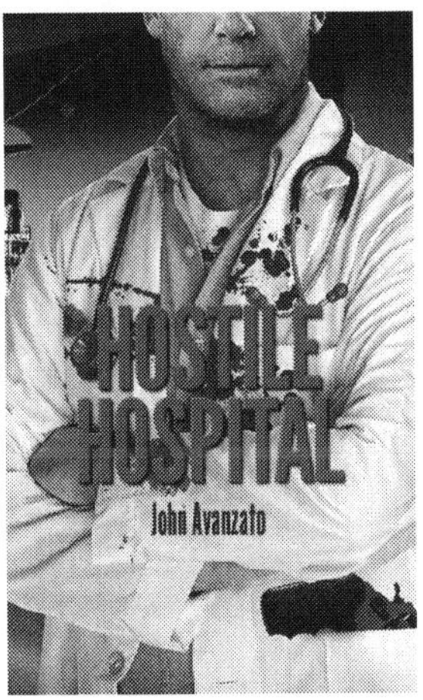

When former mob thug turned doctor, John Cesari, takes a job as a gastroenterologist at a small hospital in upstate New York, he assumes he's outrun his past and started life anew. But trouble has a way of finding the scrappy Bronx native.

Things go awry one night at a bar when he punches out an obnoxious drunk who won't leave his date alone. Unbeknownst to Dr. Cesari, that drunk is his date's stalker ex-boyfriend—and a crooked cop.

Over the course of several action packed days, Cesari uncovers the dirty little secrets of a small town hospital. As the bodies pile up, he is forced to confront his own bloody past.

Hostile Hospital is a fast paced journey that is not only entertaining but maintains an interesting view on the philosophy of healthcare. If you aren't too scared after reading, get the sequel, Prescription for Disaster.

Prescription for Disaster

Dr. John Cesari is a gastroenterologist employed at Saint Matt's Hospital in Manhattan. He tries to escape his unsavory past on the Bronx streets by settling into a Greenwich Village apartment with his girlfriend, Kelly. After his adventures in Hostile Hospital, Cesari wants to stay under the radar of his many enemies.

Through no fault of his own, Cesari winds up in the wrong place at the wrong time. A chance encounter with a mugger turns on its head when Cesari watches his assailant get murdered right before his eyes.

After being framed for the crime, he attempts to unravel the mystery, propelling himself deeply into the world of international diamond smuggling. He is surrounded by bad guys at every turn and behind it all are Russian and Italian mobsters determined to ensure Cesari has an untimely and unpleasant demise.

His prescription is to beat them at their own game, but before he can do that he must deal with a corrupt boss and an environment filled with temptation and danger from all sides. Everywhere Cesari goes, someone is watching. The dramatic climax will leave you breathless and wanting more.

Temperature Rising

John Cesari is a gangster turned doctor living in Manhattan saving lives one colonoscopy at a time. While on a well-deserved vacation, he stumbles upon a murder scene and becomes embroiled in political intrigue involving the world's oldest profession.

His hot pursuit of the truth leads him to the highest levels of government, where individuals operate above the law. As always, girl trouble hounds him along the way making his already edgy life that much more complex.

The bad guys are ruthless, powerful and nasty but they are no match for this tough, street-smart doctor from the Bronx who is as comfortable with a crowbar as he is with a stethoscope. Get ready for a wild ride in Temperature Rising. The exciting and unexpected conclusion will leave you on the edge of your seat.

Claim Denied

In Manhattan, a cancer ridden patient commits suicide rather than become a financial burden to his family. Accusations of malfeasance are leveled against his caregivers. Rogue gastroenterologist, part-time mobster, John Cesari, is tasked to look into the matter on behalf of St. Matt's hospital.

The chaos and inequities of a healthcare system run amok, driven by corporate greed and endless bureaucratic red tape, become all too apparent to him as his inquiry into this tragedy proceeds. On his way to interview the wife of the dead man, Cesari is the victim of seemingly random gun violence and finds himself on life support.

Recovering from his wounds, he finds that both he and his world are a very different place. His journey back to normalcy rouses in him a burning desire for justice, placing him in constant danger as evil forces conspire to keep him in the dark.

KCM Publishing
a division of KCM Digital Media, LLC

Made in the USA
Middletown, DE
10 April 2017